Photo: Lisa Baker

Margareta Osborn is a fifth-generation farmer who has lived and worked on the land all her life. She also writes about it in the *Gippsland Country Life* magazine. Home is the beautiful Macalister Valley of East Gippsland where, with her husband and three children, she spends many hours in the mountains in which her novels are set. She is the author of the bestselling novel *Bella's Run*, and a novella, *A Bush Christmas*.

Hope's Road

MARGARETA OSBORN

BANTAM
SYDNEY AUCKLAND TORONTO NEW YORK LONDON

A Bantam book
Published by Random House Australia Pty Ltd
Level 3, 100 Pacific Highway, North Sydney NSW 2060
www.randomhouse.com.au

First published by Bantam in 2013

Copyright © Margareta Osborn 2013

The moral right of the author has been asserted.

All rights reserved. No part of this book may be reproduced or transmitted by any person or entity, including internet search engines or retailers, in any form or by any means, electronic or mechanical, including photocopying (except under the statutory exceptions provisions of the Australian *Copyright Act 1968*), recording, scanning or by any information storage and retrieval system without the prior written permission of Random House Australia.

Addresses for companies within the Random House Group can be found at www.randomhouse.com.au/offices.

National Library of Australia
Cataloguing-in-Publication Entry

Osborn, Margareta.
Hope's road / Margareta Osborn.

ISBN 978 1 86471 316 9 (pbk.)

A823.4

Cover photographs © Getty Images
Cover design by Christabella Designs
Internal design and typesetting by Midland Typesetters, Australia
Printed in Australia by Griffin Press, an accredited ISO AS/NZS 14001:2004 Environmental Management System printer

Random House Australia uses papers that are natural, renewable and recyclable products and made from wood grown in sustainable forests. The logging and manufacturing processes are expected to conform to the environmental regulations of the country of origin.

For Hugh
with love

*'If I had my life to live over again …
next time I would find you sooner
so that I could love you longer.'*

McCauley's Hill
Gippsland, Victoria

Prologue

The girl clambered through the boundary fence. Spindly arms, matchstick legs, long brown hair flying in bits across a grubby face. Her clothes were getting caught on the razor-sharp barbed wire. He could see her little body twisting this way then that, trying to unsnag herself. She was a determined little devil. Would she be game enough to set foot on the place?

Others had come before her: sneaky little bastards trying to get the better of him. They'd come on good days and he'd only shot at the air above their heads.

Today? Well, this day was different. He was mad. Wild crazy off his head.

That morning, Mae Rouget, gliding down the main street of Narree. Immaculately dressed, beautiful as ever – every inch the princess who should've been his. The woman who had remained in his dreams for years . . .

Joe took another look in the gun scope at the boundary. The girl had made it through the wire and now was standing looking up at his hill, one hand on her dirty brow, another on a slight hip. She was dressed in buttery yellow shorts and a mud-coloured top that he guessed had once been white. The sleeves of the shirt were torn and decorated with splatters of ruby-red. The barbed wire had obviously cut a bit deep, although it hadn't stopped her from getting through. She was a McCauley: that was for sure.

Joe contemplated her a minute longer, made a decision and started to sneak down the slope through the scrub using a track barely discernable to the eye. As he snuck along the path that hugged the boundary fence, tall box and ironbark trees with their thick, crusty trunks stood sentinel in the adjoining state forest.

He swung inland, creeping past massive red gums that stretched resplendent limbs to capture air and sky. Centuries old, they had seen their fair share of hard times, just like the elderly man sidling under them. The scattered eucalypts then gave way to dense burgan and black wattle scrub, determined in its effort to claim this eastern side of the hill. The thick bushes, with their understorey of bracken fern, hid him from anyone looking up. As he rounded a blind corner he startled a grazing wallaby, sending it on an erratic escape, bounding back towards the scrub that surrounded his property on three sides – this rocky, dry hill with its miserable soil. The place he called home.

It took him a good five minutes to reach the bottom of McCauley's Hill, but there she was. She hadn't moved: still stood standing like she was contemplating what to do next. A Jack Russell ran around at her feet, nose to the ground, the scent of rabbit probably wafting from the burrows threaded through his gravelly mountain. She couldn't have been any older than five or six. It was the granddaughter.

He pulled up his gun. 'Get the hell off my farm, you land-grabbing little fucker!'

Chapter 1

The currawong's cry floated on the wisp of a breeze into the dairy. Tamara McCauley hauled down on the milking machine, urging the final milk to keep flowing into the cups attached to the cow's teats. With the new run-off property to pay for, she needed every drop she could get.

'Whoot, whoot weee-ow,' the pied currawong called again. Piercingly, this time.

It was going to rain. The bird was an infallible storm predictor. And she'd just ordered irrigation water, damn it. This would send Shon over the edge. Tammy shivered and automatically fingered her left eye. The bruise was turning a light bluish-purple colour.

The marriage was over, of that much she was sure. She was going to kick him out, however frightened she was of the confrontation.

Tammy pulled off the teat cups, let the platform of cows go

and followed them out to a nearby paddock to latch the gate. Gravel crunched on the driveway and she looked up to spy a small white car sitting beside the mail-drum at the entrance to the farm. Lucy. Just finished her night shift, no doubt. She would want a cuppa and some toast before heading home to bed. Of course that was after she'd finished rubbing the prodigious stomach of the Buddha sitting hidden in the grass beside the old gatepost. Wealth and good fortune was supposed to be the reward for such loving care and Lucy couldn't go past the old fella without stopping and giving him a tickle. Tammy wasn't sure what the forty-year-old nurse was wishing for though. To Tammy's mind her friend had it all – a lovely quaint cottage painted a delicate shade of lavender, a lazy tabby cat for company and a nice pot-belly stove to keep her warm.

Not like the homestead here, which was a cold, dark place most of the time. Heavy antique furniture guarded a century of memories and, when Shon was around, the place was filled with tension and anger. They had a cat somewhere too but it knew to stay out of the way.

Tammy started to trudge back towards the dairy, her gumboots flipping and flapping against her slim legs. She wished so hard for a life filled with love and family again. After her grandparents had died eight years earlier it had seemed like all the light and energy had disappeared. The only family she had left was her husband, a man who was currently stomping on their marriage as though it was dog shit. The only man in the family left standing.

Well – that wasn't *entirely* true. Her eyes flicked up towards the mountain partially shrouding the farm in its early-morning shadow. So deep was the cleft at the base of the mount, the sun hadn't yet penetrated that part of its eastern face. Shadows left a deep scar at the bottom of the rising bush, a black space like a roaring monster's mouth, warning all and sundry not to enter. Tammy stifled a shudder. Well, that was a pretty apt representation of old Joe McCauley, the man who owned the mountain.

A smudge of smoke wafted lazily through the crisp air, probably from Joe's chimney. Tammy squinted: if she looked hard enough there were actually two wisps of smoke up there on McCauley's Hill. The one to the south came from Travis Hunter's; he was the new wild-dog trapper, moved in six months back. The plume to the north was old Joe's, and by the size of it his fire was burning well this morning, which meant Joe himself was up and about. She really shouldn't have to tell whether her great-uncle was alive and kicking from a curl of smoke, but that was life here in the Narree Valley – life for the remaining McCauleys at least. Some disagreement between him and Tammy's grandfather had led to this point. He was her only relation but he hadn't spoken to her since she was a small kid, and that had been to swear at her for trespassing.

She was only six at the time. Had gone home repeating the word he'd used – had seemed to take such delight in. 'Fucker. Fucker.' Rolling it around her tongue until she got the inflection right. She'd sounded just like him – that crazy old man! She'd yelled it at Jack the dog, when he took off after a rabbit, and stood there, proud of herself. She hadn't known her grandfather was coming up behind her with a bowl of dog food.

The Tabasco sauce her grandparents had put on her tongue that night for saying such a word had burned like heck. They hadn't asked her where she'd heard it, which was just as well because she would have had to lie. Even back then she sensed it wasn't good to talk about the man who had a face like her grandfather's but was never mentioned by name.

As Tammy walked, she gazed out beyond her farm towards the Great Dividing Range guarding this little hamlet in Gippsland from the rest of the world. She sighed. Montmorency Downs, her family property, went back five generations. A place inexplicably linked to her by blood, dirt and, once upon a time, by love. At the moment she wished she were a long way away.

Her eyes drifted back to the gateway and the little white car. Lucy was still rubbing the old guy's tummy. Putting two fingers to the roof of her mouth, Tammy let out an ear-piercing whistle. Lucy stood up and waved, then moved towards her vehicle.

Shon had given her the concrete cast of the Buddha one Christmas a couple of years back. A backhanded slap at his wife's Catholic roots, she guessed. A wife who, he'd stated the night before, was worthless and useless.

'I feel nothing for you. Nothing, ya hear me! You're a frigid bitch of a thing; I wish I'd never laid eyes on ya.' Shon's ruddy face had pulsed with fury. Purple veins stood out on his temples as he pinned her down on the ground with his knee in her chest. 'Give me those bloody keys. I'm going.'

'You're not getting them. You can't leave for the weekend. I need you here!'

She may as well have spoken to the Buddha. Shon ignored her then just like he'd ignored everything she'd said for the last few years.

'Give me them fuckin' keys!' He was unrelenting, sitting his solid weight on her thrashing legs, pulling at her arms, ruthlessly digging the car keys out of her hand. 'Where's that big almighty God of yours now?' he taunted, with one last jab into her chest with his knee. He got up, victorious, keys dangling in his hand. 'Fuckin' pissed him off too, I'll bet.'

The disgust on his face as he looked down at her was enough.

She'd lain on the ground, trying to not show fear or how much she hurt. Trying not to give him the satisfaction. But he knew. His triumphant smile told her he had her right where he wanted her. Way down low – as low as her self-esteem could go. Oh yes, Mr Shon Murphy was all-powerful, wearing king's clothes last night. And she, Tammy McCauley Murphy, was the doormat he could wipe his boots on whenever he felt like it. Well, she'd show him. My oath she would. Enough was enough.

'Gidday!'

Tammy hadn't heard the car reach the yard.

'What's up your gander this fine morning?' asked Lucy as she emerged. 'Your face looks like it's swallowed a lemon.'

Tammy shook her head, tried to stop her hands from trembling. 'The only lemon around here is that Ford you're driving.' She dodged as her friend threw a fake punch with mittened fists.

'You better watch out, woman, or one day you'll feel the end of my glove up close and personal. I'm doing boxercise, did I tell you?'

Tammy rolled her eyes. 'Last week it was Zumba, this week it's boxing. What's next week? Pole dancing? When the hell are you going to stick to one form of exercise, Luce?'

'As soon as I get rid of this spare tyre I've been lugging around.' Lucy grabbed at her middle and pinched at a roll beneath her tasselled jumper. 'Variety is the spice of life. I can't get it from this diet I'm on or from a bloke, so I've only got exercise left. I just have to find something that suits me. That goes for both physical activity *and* men.' Lucy's smiling face suddenly turned thoughtful. She wrinkled her nose, causing the tiny stud clinging to the side of it to glint in the sun. 'Mmmm . . . pole dancing? Now why didn't I think of that?'

'Forget I said it. Boxercise sounds fine.'

'Oh, you can talk – you tiny little thing. Metabolisms like yours make me sick. I swear you could live on chips and cakes for a whole month and you wouldn't put on a kilo. Not fair, Mrs Murphy, not fair at all.'

Tammy scowled. She didn't want to hear that surname this morning. 'It's Ms McCauley to you, you insolent witch.' She tried to smile to take the sting from her words. It nearly worked. The thought of Lucy pole dancing was what did it. Those short stocky legs, entwined around a stainless-steel pole.

'C'mon, woman, you might get some toast if you're lucky. You need feeding up, with everything you've got going on in your life.'

Tammy started to turn and walk towards the house. It was right about then that Lucy noticed her limp.

Bugger.

She grabbed at Tammy's arm, spun her around. 'What happened to you?' She wasn't playing any more; the look in her eyes was serious.

'A cow kicked me this morning while I was bringing her into the cow-yard. It's nothing.'

Lucy leaned in and took a closer look at Tammy's face. 'And what about this? How'd the cow kick you up there?' A soft hand cupped Tammy's chin and turned her face into the light. 'That *fucking bastard*! He's bloody well gone and done it this time. He's hit you, hasn't he?'

'It's nothing, I said.'

'Like hell it's nothing. He can't do this to you, Tim Tam.'

The pet name her grandpa gave her when she was little.

'He can't do this,' Lucy repeated. Her fingers reached out to probe around Tammy's left eye.

Tammy quickly moved her face away. 'Let's just go and get some toast, okay?' And she turned towards the homestead, long unsteady strides covering the distance to the sprawling, mocha-coloured brick house. Moving fast. She could hear Lucy huffing and puffing behind her, and knew she should wait, or at least slow down and let her long-time friend catch up. But she also suspected that if she did – if she turned her face towards her – that would be the end. The thing that would finally break Tammy down into tiny pieces. And she couldn't afford that. Not at thirty-six. She'd already broken and repaired herself once – after her grandparents died. She was frightened she wouldn't have the energy to do it all over again.

So she put her head down and kept walking.

Chapter 2

Joe McCauley was downright pleased with himself. He'd beaten that bloody Travis Hunter this morning. It had taken a lot of cunning and more than a little bit of luck, but he'd done it. He'd got his fire going and smoke pouring from his chimney before that bastard. Finally.

Of course, it was largely thanks to a bladder that didn't seem to be able to hold its quota, sending him out for a piss long before sunrise, but he had a good fire going as the sun hit the horizon. In fact by the looks of the girly curl of smoke coming from his chimney, Hunter's wood was wet.

Joe chuckled to himself and downed another gulp of hot black tea. The man wasn't living up to his name at all. Some *Hunter* he was if he couldn't get a good piece of dry wood up here. The bush around them was jammed with yellow stringybarks, black box and red gums, all just waiting for a chainsaw to bite into their deep rich bark. (Although Joe would have been the first man to have a go at anyone who tried it on a living tree. There were plenty of fallen pickings for a man's fire.)

To be fair to the other bloke, this spell of cold nights and mornings had come on them pretty quick, and Hunter spent a lot of time trapping wild dogs to earn a crust for him and his boy. Probably hadn't had time to put in a store of wood for the winter.

Sitting in his rocking chair on the verandah of his miner's shack perched high on his mountain, Joe felt good. Which was a bit different from how he'd been feeling the night before. What he'd seen through the scope of his rifle hadn't sat well with his conscience. Oh, he hadn't thought anything much about it at the time, just sent his gun sight in another direction. But the scene had played on his mind for most of the evening, not letting him sleep. He had bloody Nellie to thank for that one. The woman was six years in her grave but he still heard her. By God he did. Rabbiting away in his ear as though she was still there at his side.

Even back then, it had been: 'Joey, you really should make it up with that poor girl. She's done nothing wrong by you and she's the only family we've got left. You're nothing but a stubborn old fool! For goodness sake, Joey, go see her. She's so sad with her family all gone!'

But he wouldn't listen. Did nothin'. And Nellie would sigh, ruffle what remained of his hair and walk away shaking her head. She'd never go against his decision though, and had gone to her grave not knowing Tammy either.

Regardless, he knew what she would have said about last night's action down on the flats.

Shon Murphy, the prick, had the girl on the ground. And he'd swung a fist. Joe had quickly shifted the rifle to the north, not wanting to see or think about what was taking place on

Montmorency Downs. The place that, by rights, should have been half his. Not this rock-laden, bush-encrusted hill.

There'd never been any good outcome from tangling with the Murphys, of whom Shon was one of the worst. Shades of his father, but with a meaner streak, hidden under all that palaver. A charmer who gave with one hand while seeing what he could flog from behind your back with the other. That bloody Tammy had got tangled up with him years back.

There was a time when he'd pondered that maybe Nellie was right. That the sins of the parents — or in this case the grandparents — shouldn't be foisted onto a child, and that he should acknowledge he *did* have family in the Narree Valley. But the installation of a *fucking Murphy* at Montmorency had sorted that one out. Be buggered if he was going down that drive, the fifth-generation homestead of the McCauley family, and have a Murphy greet him as host.

Things might have been different if he and Nellie had been able to have kids. If their children had needed cousins to play with. If he'd been able to meet his brother's eye and say, well I've got what you've got, regardless — a wife, kids, a farm. But his farm wasn't a good one and they hadn't been able to have children, much to the eternal grief of his wife. She would have made a beautiful mother. The best. Always picking up stray or injured animals in the bush, bringing them home and lavishing her nurturing side on them. It was with regret and no small amount of tears that she let them go back into the wild once they were well enough. A bit like the flood of tears that came with her two miscarriages and thereafter each month when, yet again, she would bleed.

Joe sighed. Yes, his Nellie was a good 'un. One of the best. She didn't deserve the hand God had dealt her. No kids, little money and a grumpy old bastard of a husband. But she had endured it all with the good grace and nature of a bloody saint. And now she was gone, leaving him rocking up here on his hill all alone. It had taken him a long while to get used to not having her around.

'Ahhh . . . Joey, my love, you do go on.' And she'd have that soft look in her eyes which meant he might get lucky later on when the lights were turned down and the lavender-scented bed sheets were whispering softly around them.

So now it was just down to him. Besides that do-gooding chit of a girl who married a fucking Murphy and thus reneged her right to call herself a real McCauley!

He didn't need no one. He rang in his shopping list to the Narree supermarket and that hippy nurse Lucy Granger picked it up for him and dropped it at the drum down at the gate in return for some firewood. A wary stock agent appeared every once in a while to organise the sale of his animals. Travis Hunter had taken to silently dropping a fresh hindquarter of deer off to him whenever he made a kill. It gave him a bit of variation from the odd sheep he slaughtered. And then there were the rainbow trout he sometimes caught, fresh from the Grace River, a half-day round trip on foot.

Life was grand and he didn't want no other bugger disturbing him. He got all the entertainment he required through the scope on his rifle and didn't need any prick within a bull's roar of his place. And if they came, well, he was ready. He had his gun, his dogs and his temper. That usually got rid of even the most persistent of bastards.

Chapter 3

'Yoo-hoo! Anybody home?' A sponge cake clasped in an arthritic hand appeared around the doorway. 'Ahhh . . . there you are! Just thought I'd bake a wee little sponge to welcome you as the newest member of staff.' A vision in crocheted red cardigan, cream Peter Pan collared shirt and tweed skirt stood before him.

The vision moved closer, too close, causing him to scoot his chair back towards the filing cabinet. *Clunk!* His head hit a protruding drawer. Damn.

In the small radio room of the shared offices of the Department of Conservation and Lake Grace Ambulance Station there was barely room to stand up.

'Don't go causing yourself injury now. We've lobbied those blessed politicians long and hard to get you here. Last thing we need is a WorkCover claim in your first few months! Oh, I'm forgetting my manners. Beatrice Parker is my name, and baking this cake is my game.' She chuckled, her beady little blackcurrant eyes twinkling. 'I love a good rhyme, don't you? Mmm . . . anyway, best keep tracking. Can't waste time yakking.' She chuckled again. 'Enjoy your day, Mr . . . ?'

'Hunter. Travis Hunter.' He finally found his voice, and tried to scramble to his feet, putting out a hand as he did so. 'Nice to meet you too, Mrs Parker,' and promptly tripped over the four-pronged walking stick standing to attention in front of its tiny owner.

'Goodness, boy! You're the best they had to send us? Your balance is atrocious. I'm hoping your kiss of life is better – I'd reckon you'd give a good one, eh?' Squinting black eyes swept from the tips of his size-12 workboots to the top of his brown hair.

Trav didn't know what to say, but he now knew what it must feel like to be a helpless moth tacked to a pin-board. She must have him confused with the new ambulance officer. He was a wild-dog trapper. He opened his mouth to correct the woman but took another glance at the sponge. It was a beauty and looked just like the ones his mother used to make. Sweet icing smothered the top while cream and jam spilled from its middle. And he hadn't had his breakfast. 'Ah . . . I'm not sure, Mrs Parker, but I've never had any complaints in the past.'

'I'll bet you haven't. Can't say I'd be avoiding those lips of yours if I were a generation or two younger. Anyhow, best be away and on with today!'

He could have sworn she winked before placing the sponge in his hands, grabbing the walking stick and clumping out the door. He stood there looking down at the cake, feeling guilty. He should have owned up.

He normally steered clear of town, which explained Mrs Parker's mistake – how could she know which of the strange men in the offices was him and which was the new ambo? He kept himself to himself. But he had had a backlog of reports to complete for the Department of Conservation and he didn't have or *want* to have a computer at home.

'And by the way . . .' The blackcurrants were back. 'Have you a family, Mr Hunter?'

Trav winced. 'One boy, Mrs Parker.'

'A wife?'

'No, Mrs Parker.'

'She leave you?'

'Yes.'

'Why?'

Christ, she was persistent. Best just say it, once and for all. 'Couldn't handle responsibility.' Yeah, like he could? What a farce.

'Just like my Donald. He left too.' A wrinkled hand swept along her temple in momentary agitation, lifting a tendril of elegantly styled, blue-rinsed hair.

'I'm sorry.' Wasn't much he could say. You never got over them leaving you, just learned to live with it.

'You a bush or city boy?'

'I was born here, but we moved to a property north of Yunta when I was a little kid. The old man inherited a station on the road to Arkaroola.'

'Why're you here then, not there?'

Why indeed? He often asked himself that question. Unfortunately the answer, as always, hurt like hell.

'My father left the station to my older brother when he died and my mother's family property here became vacant. She's in the little Lake Grace nursing home now. She wanted to come back to the mountains and I wanted to bring the boy up on a farm.'

'Mmm . . . figures. Show me your hands.'

Trav held out two big paws, palms up, calluses and all. Not sure why he was doing this old lady's bidding, but hell, he may as well humour her. After all, he'd got a sponge, even if it was by default.

'Looks like you know how to get them dirty.'

There was a flutter of her right eye again. Was it a wink? Surely not. Wearing those pearls she looked as straight as the Virgin Mary.

'Well, I'd best be off. Another delivery to make this morning. New little girl, a teller at the bank. Tra-la-la.' She waggled her be-ringed fingers and was gone.

Trav let out a deep breath, one he hadn't realised he'd been holding. He was guessing it would take all of . . . oh . . . ten minutes for those snippets of information to spread from one end of Lake Grace to the other. There wasn't too much distance between the newsagents, chemist, bank, bakery, stock agents and corner café, and he reckoned it would take Mrs Nosy Parker less than that to do them over.

He spared a thought for the new teller at the bank. Beatrice Parker would chew her up and spit her out for smoko. He was thirty-nine – a jaded, cynical old fart – and he'd struggled to keep his head.

An orange flag caught his eye as it whizzed past the window. He stood up and took a peek through the fake wood venetian blind. Make that five minutes. Mrs Parker, on a motor scooter, riding flat-knacker up the footpath, was heading for the chemist, the first in the Lake Grace line of shops.

He sat back down in the chair, his six-foot frame folding gracefully, and dropped his head against the backrest. He still didn't know if he'd made the right decision six months earlier to move so far from the red dirt of the South Australian and New South Wales border, where he'd been a boundary rider. The Narree Valley was a lush, green Ireland plonked in the furthermost south-eastern corner of Australia. It was like he'd come to another country. And Lake Grace was a small town which thrived on a daily fodder of gossip. He'd purposely avoided the likes of Mrs Parker until today. He should have known that in doing so he'd probably just encouraged her.

'I see you've met Mrs Parker?' Rob Sellers, the community ambulance officer, walked in from the ambulance station next door.

'How'd you guess?'

Rob pointed at the sponge. 'Legend material, those sponges. The locals nearly kill each other at the Friday Street Stall to get their hands on one. She either likes you or wanted information.'

'Information,' said Trav as a glob of cream dripped onto the plate. He still felt guilty.

'Well, it looks like she was happy with what she got,' said Rob leaning over to look out the window, where Mrs Parker's orange flag could be seen flying past the stock and station agent's en route for the corner café. 'She should make it in time for a morning latte and natter and clatter.'

'Morning latte and *what*?'

'Natter and clatter. All the old ducks meet there on a Friday to drink coffee, gossip and do craft. They teach the young mums how to knit and sew and stuff. And because there're so many kids in there, it's natter and clatter. Mind you, we blokes stay clear of the joint. Best to head out to the roadhouse if you want a sausage roll on a Friday.'

'Right.'

'And you'll be fair game today.'

'What?'

'They've been trying to find out about you for ages. New good-looking single bloke in town? They'll want all the goss.'

'Right.' Trav revisited in his head what he'd told Mrs Parker. It was enough. 'I think she was after the new ambo officer, actually, but she found me instead.'

Rob laid a hand on Trav's shoulder. 'Wouldn't be too sure about that. She's a cagey one, our Beatrice. Anyhow, don't worry, mate. Plenty of nice, nubile young women around here for the both of you, all wanting to snag a husband. You'll be fine. We'll have you married before you can say bloody Lake Grace. Mark my words.' Rob stood back and winked.

'You don't say,' commented Trav. Marriage? Again?

No way.

Chapter 4

'So what happened? Are you leaving him?' Lucy was sitting at the table watching Tammy pour boiling water into two mugs.

Tammy fiddled with the kettle, taking time to put it back on the stove. She jiggled the teabags, found some teaspoons in the sink, dragged a bag of sugar out of the pantry and refilled the sugar bowl. Anything to delay answering the question.

But Lucy was an aged care nurse and she knew all about out-waiting silence.

When Tammy could avoid it no longer, she dumped the mugs on the table and sat down. 'What happened with what?'

'Oh, for God's sake, Tammy! You know exactly what I mean.' Lucy moved forwards and pointed at Tammy's eye. 'That! What happened with that?'

'He hit me. He went nuts because I wouldn't give him the keys to the ute, all right?' Tammy's hand strayed up to touch her cheek. 'And yes, I'm leaving him. Well, I have to work out how to make *him* leave. This is my farm, after all. My grandparents left it to *me*.'

Lucy looked thoughtful. 'Yeah, I suppose they did. But why didn't you want him to have the keys?'

'Because he was going to *her*!'

Lucy sat back in the chair with an audible sigh. 'So you know?'

'Know what?' Tammy's head snapped up. 'What is it that I should know exactly? What hasn't my *best friend* been telling me?'

Lucy blushed, the redness stealing up from her uniform collar to her face. 'I didn't know for sure. What was I supposed to do? Come and tell you all the rumours and innuendo flying around the pub in Lake Grace? I don't think so, sunshine.'

'Oh God, it's gone that far, has it?' Tammy put her hands over her eyes. 'Everyone in town knows about them?' She sank down towards the table, wanting to melt into the wood.

Lucy nodded slowly. 'I so wanted to tell you but I didn't have any proof, Tammy. If I did I would have been right here blabbing. But I was hoping it was all just pub talk.'

Tammy could hear it was hurting her best friend to tell her this. But damn it all, it was hurting her more. She peered at Lucy through her fingers. 'It's not, is it? Pub talk?'

Uncomfortable silence.

Her husband was a lying, cheating, abusive bastard.

'Yes, he's having it off with Joanne.' Lucy sighed. 'You know, the new publican?'

Oh, Tammy knew her all right. Long tumbling black hair, snake-like eyes, jingling, jangling jewellery, tight skirts, strategically undone buttons and a cleavage Tammy would just about die for.

'I wasn't sure until I saw them both coming out of the pub together yesterday lunchtime,' said Lucy. 'Shon had his hand up her skirt as she leaned into the car to get something and she wasn't pushing him away. Then, as they said goodbye, well, let's just say they weren't exactly shy . . .' Lucy blushed again.

So they were flaunting it in public and in broad daylight! Tammy got up from the table, taking her mug with her. 'You know, Luce, I thought marriage was supposed to be forever.' She paced around the table. 'To have and to hold from this day forward . . . forsaking all others . . . all that kind of *shit*!' The crash of a china mug breaking against the wall rang loud in the kitchen.

Tammy stared, appalled at her sudden act of violence. She sank to her knees, scrabbling at the broken shards of china. 'That cup belonged to my mother. It was a Royal Doulton special edition. My grandparents gave it to her when she turned eighteen.' She could feel devastation starting to overwhelm her. Waves of it, curling insidiously around, ready to dump her among the detritus of her shattering life.

Tammy reached for the chair to haul herself up. Why wasn't she good enough for the man who was supposed to be her soul mate? All she'd ever wanted was a family. Her own family. What was the harm in all that?

'Oh Tammy. C'mon, mate. You should have kicked him out years ago. You know that. How long has he been abusing you?'

'He hasn't hit me before now.' No, Shon was too clever for that. He hurt her where no one could see. Who was she really trying to kid here?

'Mate, he's been abusing you for years. It's not just hitting that hurts.'

Lucy was right. The scars were there. Her self-esteem was shot to hell. Shon had always been clever, skilfully manipulating her into thinking she needed to please him and to ensure his life was good.

'Plus, why let the arsehole have his cake and eat it too? He's stringing you along because of the McCauley name, the property, the status in the community he thinks it gives him. Then he takes up with any old floozie with tits.'

Tammy winced. What did that make her?

Lucy read her expression. 'Oops, sorry. I didn't mean you. You're his wife.'

Yes and a whole lot of good that had done her. Obviously their marriage vows didn't mean a bloody thing to Shon. 'But why, Luce? It'd all started out so good. We had so much fun together, shared the same dreams. I loved him. I thought he loved me. When did it all go wrong? What did I do?'

'Honey, that's just the thing. You didn't *do* anything. That man deliberately manipulates your emotions to take away your sense of self-worth. In actual fact, men who abuse women like this feel powerless themselves.'

Tammy thought about that. Things had gotten worse over the last few years. At night when she came in from the dairy, Shon would be sitting in his chair, feet up on the pouf, beer in hand, watching the news. He wouldn't even acknowledge she'd come in the door, wouldn't say hello or pass the time of day. It was up to her to get the tea, lock up the chooks, feed the dogs and do the myriad other chores it took to shut down the homestead for the night. Shon would just sit there ignoring her until his tea landed on the table, dead on six-thirty. Always six-thirty and woe betide if it wasn't.

'Can't you do anything right?' he'd rage. 'I'm off to the pub. At least I can get some food and decent company there!'

Company all right. Joanne, the publican-cum-hooker.

She knew she wouldn't see him again now until tomorrow night; his part-time job as agronomist for a big national seed company took him all over Gippsland during the day. When they married they'd agreed he'd keep his job four days a week until they started a family. She had her workman, Jock, to help with the heavier work on the farm, and could run the rest herself. The extra money had come in handy to pay the creditors when her grandparents died, but she hadn't seen much of it since.

Shon had always resented the fact it was her farm, her life that he had become a part of. It hadn't been *really* apparent at the start, just little comments like . . . 'I'll have to ask the *boss* about that,' or 'I've given up my life to come and live yours.' He'd been a travelling grass-seed salesman living out of cheap motels and pubs when they'd met, so she wasn't sure how that one worked.

After she'd inherited the property, Shon had pressured her to sell up. He'd tried to coerce her with visions of a different life, something beyond milking twice a day, irrigating and agronomy. She'd refused. She loved farming, and there was no way she could sell Montmorency.

Lucy's voice interrupted her thoughts. 'Promise me one thing, Tammy?'

'What?'

'That from today you'll at least start living life outside of this farm.'

Tammy thought about that. Why the hell not? Bloody Shon was enjoying himself, after all. It was about time she did too. 'Okay, I promise.'

'Right. Give me two minutes.' Lucy disappeared onto the closed-in back verandah and Tammy could hear her tapping on the computer keys. Minutes ticked by, then the sound of bouncing footsteps. Lucy reappeared in the doorway, a triumphant grin on her face. What was she up to?

'I'll pick you up at seven-thirty Sunday night – no excuses.'

'Where're we going?'

'Narree.'

Tammy's senses went on high alert. 'What for?' she asked tentatively.

'Pole dancing.' Lucy tried her best to look coy. 'Hanging upside down always gives you a new perspective on things.'

Chapter 5

Joe splashed the dregs of his cup of tea over the side of the verandah. A few drops caught the dog at his feet, causing it to flinch in its sleep. 'C'mon, Boots. Move that fat lazy arse of yours. Time to get some jobs done.'

The dog opened one eye to check on his owner, assessing the urgency of the command. He shut it again when he saw no real movement from the rocking chair.

At eighty-nine years old, Joe knew exactly how his dog felt. Aged bones soaking up the warmth of the early morning sun were hard to shift. And the view laid out in front of them took some beating. Although Boots had obviously grown immune to it, Joe never tired of looking out over a kingdom he'd come to think of as his own, breathing it in, making its goings-on a part of his life, albeit from the safe distance of his hill.

The majority of the Great Dividing Range – the gently undulating Narree foothills rising to the soaring peaks of the likes of Mounts Cullen and Adelong – were all there in a steely blue: a private view of rugged, remote magnificence right at his own door. At the base of the range, shining paddocks of emerald green smothered the flats, with dots of black and white Friesian cows interposed with the occasional caramel-coloured Jersey. Shelter belts of native trees skirting around fence-lines gave the land the look of a patchwork quilt, with the Narree River and its weaving splayed across the rich fabric like elaborate silver appliqué.

An early-morning breeze flowed over the paddocks below his house, the spear grass rippling like giant ribbons in the sun. It was strangely relaxing yet disturbing at the same time, all that long, dry grass close to his old miner's shack. Time to move the cattle into the front part of the farm: he didn't need a fire hazard at his door.

Joe tipped the rocking chair back then forwards, back then forwards, gathering momentum at each rock. On the third tip he dropped his feet to the floorboards and heaved himself up, letting the momentum get him upright.

The chair tipped back and clipped Boots's long hairy tail. The dog leaped into the air, yelping, and Joe staggered slightly sideways before groping at a verandah pole to steady himself. 'Fuck it, Boots.' Joe was more pissed off than contrite. He was finding he was stumbling a bit more every day, especially if there was a change due in the weather. Any alteration in atmospheric pressure seemed to make his knees and ankles seize up, particularly in the mornings. All part of getting old, he supposed. He didn't like it, though. Not one little bit.

Joe bent over and scratched behind his old border collie's ears. The dog was still licking his tail. 'Sorry, mate. Didn't mean to hurt ya.' Boots leaned into his wrinkled and veiny hand, thumping his tail in ecstasy. It never took much to make a dog happy. Shame humans weren't the same. Joe's eyes flickered back out to the east and the rich green spread of Montmorency Downs. Nothing he could do about that, regardless of Nellie's yabbering voice in his head.

'Righto, enough dilly-dallying about. We're off. Bales of hay to feed this morning.' He dumped his mug on top of the flattened bollard beside the verandah steps and clumped his way to the rack near the front screen door. Sambar deer antlers of different shapes and sizes held coats, hats and vests, all in varying states of disrepair.

Joe shrugged himself into a ripped oilskin with a barely discernible green chequered flannel lining. A flying cap with fluffy Biggles-like muffs for his ears went onto his nearly bald head. A pair of black, heavy gumboots onto his socked feet.

And then they were off. Man and dog. Down the steps, into the bright morning, where dewdrops were still shining through spider webs on the corrugated walls of the barn.

Joe made his way to the lean-to shed that housed an ancient Fordson Major tractor, an iconic piece of machinery. He checked the oil and water then climbed aboard, cranking over the engine. After a few false starts the cold motor caught and fired. The noise was raucous, drowning out the kookaburras who'd started cackling and destroying any peace that had remained.

Joe backed the tractor out of the open side of the barn. 'C'mon, Boots!' The dog slunk around the side of the tractor, setting his sights on the hayshed behind the house. 'Shame you can't open gates,' yelled Joe. 'That'd make you worth keeping.' Boots ignored him, and climbed through a fence that was missing a top wire then pissed on a post that was leaning sideways into the breeze. Joe swore Boots could understand him better than anyone, and dogs certainly had their own ways to thumb it at their owners.

There were only a few gates on Joe's eight hundred acres. The solid, galvanised ones fronting the roads and bush tracks circumnavigating the farm, the one into the hayshed yard and the mallee gate separating the front half from the back part of the property.

Joe let his cattle roam the place. He didn't understand all this new-fangled stuff about cell grazing, wagon wheels and strip feeding. Truth be told he hadn't *wanted* to understand it. For to do that meant change, and he knew he wasn't so good at change; never had been.

He clambered down off the tractor and opened the gate to the hayshed yard. Got back on the vehicle and trundled through. Using the hay forks on the front he picked up a round bale, backed the tractor around and with the rear hay grabs picked up another one. He'd had hydraulics fitted to the old girl. It'd been worth it. One round was worth twelve or so small bales and lifting smalls had been hell on his back. Nellie had forced that change on him and, though he'd never admitted it to her, he was glad. His back had been caning him.

Joe drove the tractor out the gate, closed it and set off across the paddock. He stopped when he remembered he'd left his other dog, old Digger, chained to the side of the pigpens.

By the time he got there, Digger was yelping in a weird strangled kind of way, straining at the chain. 'Settle, boy. C'mon, pull back so I can let the clip off.' But Digger was having none of it, and he had the chain pulled so tight he was choking himself. 'For fuck's sake, you idiot, gitback!' Joe reefed on the dog's collar, which loosened the pressure enough for him to undo the clip. Digger took off towards his mate Boots, who was hanging out by the tractor, chewing on a rat's head he'd found beside the barn.

The two dogs started to fight over the tasty morsel, rolling and barking, biting and snapping at each other until the rodent's head was forgotten in the rumble. Suddenly another blur of black appeared, snatched the delicacy and made it back to the barn with blistering speed. By the time the two dogs realised what had happened, the black cat was up on top of a thick timber rafter, looking smug and chewing ravenously.

Joe chuckled to himself. He didn't need anything but his animals around this place; they were trouble enough. He climbed back aboard the tractor and took off, the dogs streaking out in front, barking and jumping around like a pair of excited hooligans. 'Git behind. Git *behind*, I'm telling ya!' Joe roared at them. Through naked gateways with latches hanging limp, beside fences lying on their side, and past posts devoid of wires, they made their way towards a mob of cattle camped in scrubby bush at the far reaches of the farm.

There had been a time in his life when Joe had cared. Really cared about himself, his life and where it was going to take him. He'd been in his twenties, bursting with youth and enthusiasm. He and his older brother, Thomas, had been set to take on the world. Sons of a well-respected man, a shire councillor, with a prosperous farm that had been in the family for generations.

But there'd been the war and life had thrown its greasy tentacles around them. Things had changed and, with no extra workers to be found, they'd had to work their arses off to keep it all afloat. Being needed on the land, he and Tom had entered the war late. And they'd been lucky, for both of them came home, a fact which at times had made his mother publicly bow her head when faced with the grief and envy of others, while in her heart she rejoiced at her good fortune.

But that good fortune hadn't lasted.

Thanks to a dark-eyed brunette called Mae.

Joe had spotted her at the Lake Grace Centenary Ball in 1946. It had been a warm summer night, laced with the scent of roses and wisteria. A stylish, toe-tapping band had been brought in from Melbourne. A supper to rival a Menzies high tea was laid on by the competing cooks of the area, and the decorations had made the Myer Christmas windows seem dowdy. All the ingredients were in place for a wonderful night to meet a beautiful lady. And at thirty years of age Joe was looking for the woman he could spend the rest of his life with.

There at the invitation of country cousins with whom she was holidaying, Mae Rouget blew into his life with all the force of a hot and howling north-westerly. Draped in a strapless tangerine ball-gown of the softest chiffon, she was a knockout. Glossy, long brunette hair fell in waves onto a slim back. Her sultry full lips and dark eyes made him want to tell the rest of the world to go hang itself and leave him completely alone with this vision. She was all he'd ever want or need and he finally understood the meaning of love at first sight.

When she opened her mouth and spoke, what little sense that remained in his head dissolved. It was a voice straight from heaven. Perfectly pitched yet with a slight lilt of huskiness curling at the finish: enough to get any man's libido up and attentive.

He hadn't let her out of his arms the whole night and he was sure she was as besotted with him as he was with her. She'd given him no reason to think otherwise, refusing all other dancing partners, gazing into his eyes.

He'd gone home walking on air, incessantly checking that

her phone number was tucked safely into his inside pocket. A promise for dinner and dancing the following weekend.

A few weeks and two dates later he was planning how to make her his – where he'd get the money to buy her the engagement ring she deserved, when to tell his parents and brother, who was away buying a new bull for the farm.

He could have just about kissed old man Parker when he'd made the offer of a job falling trees with his bush-gang. 'Just for a month, maybe a bit more, to get me outta trouble. Bloke laid up with a crushed foot and I've got a nephew comin' down from Queensland to step into his spot. Takin' him a time or two to get here though. What do ya reckon, Joey? Can ya dad spare you to help me out?'

Joe knew Tom was due back any day, so he said yes right away, thinking of that glittering diamond ring he'd now be able to afford.

He'd hitched a ride up the bush with old Parker, worked his arse off for six weeks, seven days a week, dawn till dusk, and made enough money to buy what he wanted. He waltzed home excitedly fingering the rolled-up notes and jangling the many coins now in his pockets.

To find his parents all in a tizz of excitement.

'Oh Joey, you'll never guess! Thomas is getting married. It's so exciting. After they're married they'll move here and your dad and I can now buy one of those lovely new homes I've been eyeing off in Lake Grace.' His mother's normally pallid cheeks were touched with rosy-red circles as she moved around the big farm kitchen making a special celebration tea. 'But don't worry, love, you can live with us. Oh Joey, she's just beautiful and Thomas is so happy and in love. Such a whirlwind romance! I'm dying for you to meet her.'

At that moment Tom walked through the door. 'About time you came down from those hills. Good to see you, little brother. I've brought a few good-looking bulls home. Love the look.'

Joe stroked his new beard, the result of weeks without a razor and the need to keep his face warm on the higher mountain-ash-clad peaks. 'Yeah, good to see you too. Mum says you're getting married? Congratulations.' He pumped his brother's hand. 'Where did you meet her?'

'Down in the city. She's our stock agent's wife's cousin. They went to boarding school together.'

Joe breathed a sigh of relief. It wasn't Mae then. She wouldn't have been a boarder, living in the city and all. He felt the tight band on his chest loosen. Didn't know why it'd been there in the first place.

'Anyway, she'll be here in a sec. You'll love her, Joey. It's a bit rushed, I know, but she's the one. The best thing that's happened to me.' He put his arm around his younger brother's shoulders and gave them a squeeze.

And Joe was pleased for Tom, knowing how seriously he shouldered the mantle of being the eldest McCauley. Three generations of expectations fell heavy, and Joe was happy Tom had found someone to share the load.

'Thomas?'

The world stopped, lifted up on its axis and moved slightly left.

Only one person in the world had that husky lilt to her voice. Joe spun around to see his brother moving towards the beautiful creature framed in the doorway.

Glossy, long brunette hair fell in waves onto a slim back. Sultry full lips lifted to take Tom's ardent kiss. Dark eyes swept across the room over his brother's broad shoulder, widening in startled shock at the sight of Joe.

But it was the different expressions that followed which cut him to the very core.

First, sudden comprehension.

'Mae! My darling girl, welcome to our home . . .'

Chased by measure.

'Mae! How lovely you look. Come and meet my other handsome son, Joe.'

And lastly – regret.

'I'm Mae. How do you do, Joe? It's so nice to meet you . . .'

The fingertips of her slim hand were touching his – those dark eyes looking at him like he was a stranger – while her other hand was clasped tightly by his brother. Now he understood the meaning of complete and utter devastation.

He turned and left. Grabbed his kitbag from where it had been discarded on the three-quarter-bed in his room only an hour before. And walked out of the house.

Never to make his way down the gravelled drive of Montmorency Downs again.

Not ever, in sixty years.

Chapter 6

'Want some toast?' said Travis. The kid was rustling around up in his bedroom loft like a possum loose on the roof. It was driving his father nuts.

'Billy! You want some toast?' Travis yelled this time.

'Huh?' A shock of red hair appeared over the rails of the platform above Travis's head.

'I *said*, do you want toast?' Travis drawled it out, sarcastic and slow.

His son flushed bright pink and stammered back, 'I'm sorry, Dad. I didn't hear you.'

'Any wonder with all the racket going on up there. What're you doing?'

Billy looked shamefaced then stared up at the ceiling so close to his head. 'I've lost somethin',' he whispered.

'Speak up, boy!'

'I've lost something,' the child said again.

Travis considered him for a moment. What was the kid up to? Billy snatched a quick glance down at his father then peered back up at the ceiling, but not before Travis saw momentary fear and a glint of tears in his eyes.

For fuck's sake. 'Well, hurry up and find it and get down here for your breakfast. I've got things to be doing.'

Travis slapped two pieces of bread in the toaster and rammed them down to cook. He hated it when the child looked at him like that, but Billy frustrated the heck out of him. It was hard having the kid around when he was so used to being on his own.

The child started his possum-like rustling again and Trav tried to block it out as he mulled over his plans for the day. He had traps to check over towards the boundary of freehold land and the state forest near Sunny Point. There was a bit of fencing that needed doing on his own place and he had to get into town sometime, do some grocery shopping and check on his mother, Diane, at the nursing home. There'd been a message on the answering machine from one of the nurses. Diane was out of incontinence pads or something.

Overhead, a yell of glee coincided with the toaster violently throwing its cooked bread up and out of the contraption and onto the floor.

'Shit, shit, shit,' said Travis, scrabbling for his and Billy's breakfast on the floor. He didn't have any more bread either. It would have to do.

'I found it!' called Billy as he swung his way down the ladder to land on the floor, an Akubra clutched tightly in his hand. He slapped it on his head, managing to look both delighted and contrite at the same time. 'I thought I'd lost my hat.'

'You never wear a hat inside,' growled Travis, 'it's rude. Didn't your grandmother teach you that?'

'Sorry, Dad.' Billy quickly snatched his most prized possession off his head.

Travis glared at his son then pushed a plate over to him. 'Here, eat your breakfast.'

The two of them ate in silence. A knife, butter and Vegemite were pushed back and forth across the bench. The kettle whistled on the stove, the only merry sound in an otherwise quiet house. Trav started to make himself a cup of tea. He moved towards the fridge, stuck his head inside and said to his son, 'You want some milk?'

Billy munched away at his toast, oblivious, completely lost in his own dream world.

Travis sighed, swung away from the fridge, milk in hand, and contemplated the child. What was he going to do with him? He was a dreamer just like his mother. Travis felt a kick to his gut at the thought of her. The desertion and divorce still rankled, even after eight years. 'Billy! Do you want some milk?'

'Huh? Oh, milk. Yes, please, Dad.'

Travis couldn't help but focus on the word 'Dad', because Billy used it a lot, like it was a new toy to be batted around and played with. He couldn't blame the kid: they'd hardly seen each other in the last six years.

He pushed a glass of milk towards his son.

'Thanks, Dad.'

There it was again. And all the responsibilities that came with that incongruous three-letter word. The thought of being solely accountable for ensuring Billy made it into adulthood, scared the shit out of him.

Tammy was just starting to crank the tractor over when Billy Hunter walked up wearing the new Akubra hat his father had given him for his tenth birthday.

'Gidday, Billy! Just in time, mate. Grab the motorbike, will you? You can ride on ahead and open the gates for me.'

Tammy couldn't help but smile at the boy's happy skips as he ran to do what she'd asked. He was a funny kid. No mother, and a father who worked all day every day. From what she could make out, the child pretty much dragged himself up. Such a shame, because he was a good boy, who particularly loved riding the four-wheel motorbike. She watched him haul off his felt hat and place it reverently on the shelf in the shed. Pulling a helmet down over his red hair, he jumped on the bike, pulled in the clutch to start it in gear and fired the engine, just like she'd taught him. The child had learned a lot since he'd arrived on her doorstep a few months earlier, asking if there were any odd jobs he could do.

Satisfied the boy was organised, she drove the tractor out through the double gates and headed down the cow-track. A big metal bucket filled with a load of dirt and clay bounced around in front of her. Billy whizzed past her, an intent look on his freckled face. He was going to fly right past the gateway she wanted opened, the rate he was going. Tammy stuck her fingers into her mouth, curled her tongue and whistled him up. The child should hear that. It was a ripper of a whistle. Her grandfather taught her how to do it when she was only little.

Billy stopped and looked around. Tammy pointed at the set of gates to his left and he jumped off the bike and opened them. In the paddock beyond the gates, a concrete trough sat looking lonely on an eroded mound of dirt. The boy rode the bike across to it and waited patiently for Tammy to follow him.

She gestured to Billy to help her line up where the dirt was needed. Billy ran up and guided her into where the worst of the erosion around the trough was. He used all the correct signals: a shake of his hand to lower the bucket; a thumbs up when she'd reached the right position. Then he jumped out of the way so Tammy could dump her load to fill the gaping holes.

Billy slapped his hands together, brushing off some sticky clay, and Tammy gave him a wide smile to indicate another job well done. The poor child needed every bit of encouragement he could get – from what Tammy could see, he didn't get much at home.

Recently, she'd started letting him bring up the cows on his own, wash the cow-yard down, help set up for irrigating and pull the irrigation bungs to allow water out into the paddocks. She'd even let him use her computer to do his homework as he didn't have one at home. The teachers nowadays always seemed to want projects typed up.

'Surely your dad would buy you one if you need it for school?' she'd said to him.

'Nup. He said he ain't got no use for them new fandangled things.'

Tammy couldn't believe it. 'What did your teacher say when you said you didn't have one?'

Billy had stared at the grass at his feet and mumbled, 'I didn't tell her.' When he glanced up she saw such vulnerability in his eyes. He looked like a begging puppy. 'You said I could use yours, didn't ya?'

'Didn't *you*, Billy. *You*, not ya. And yes. Yes, of course.' But Tammy was still angry about it. Didn't that bloody Hunter man know his son needed a computer in this day and age? Didn't he know his son needed his attention full stop?

'Did Miss Greenaway say anything about some of your homework being handwritten at the parent-teacher interviews you had last week?'

'Nup. She was too busy flicking her hair and giggling at me dad.'

'*My*, Billy. My dad,' reminded Tammy.

Billy rolled his eyes. '*My* dad, then.'

'You mean your father actually spoke to her?' Tammy had met Travis Hunter only once but she knew he didn't like to talk much. Billy made up for the apparent lack of conversation at home when he came to Montmorency. Around her, the child barely paused for breath.

'A few times but then he left in a hurry when Miss Greenaway started to smile all stupid, like this,' said Billy, as he stretched his mouth into a simpering grin. Tammy couldn't help laughing, which made the boy play the fool more. He started blinking like he was batting his eyelashes, which made her laugh even harder.

Finally she had to ask him to stop so she could breathe. 'She didn't do that, did she?'

'Yup. She did.' The child stopped. 'What does it mean, Tammy? A smile like that?'

Crikey. How to answer that question? She didn't know anything about Travis Hunter's love life. 'I'd say it means she likes him, that's all.'

'Mmm . . .' Billy looked pensive then. 'Sometimes, on the bus, Katie Barfield does that kind of smile to me too, when her brother Evan isn't looking.'

'Is that the Barfield kids from over the river? Didn't their dad die in some accident there a while back?'

Billy sighed. 'Yup, he did. Their granddad helps their mum look after them now.'

There was something in the boy's tone that made Tammy pause. 'And that's okay, isn't it?'

'Yeah, it's just –' The boy looked out across the paddocks up towards McCauley's Hill. 'It's just, well, the kids at school treat them different from me. My nanna brung me up a bit too but it's like I'm weird having a mum that just ran away, like she didn't want us. Katie's dad died in an accident. He didn't mean to leave them. And they've still got a granddad who helps their mum. Like they've got the whole Big Mac family still. Mum, dad and two kids.' The boy frowned before going on. 'But I've only got a cheeseburger; no mother, no brothers or sisters. Nanna's in an old people's place. I've only got Dad, you see?'

Tammy did see. All too well. With only her grandparents raising her, and Mae being so distant and standoffish, she understood exactly what the kid was saying. But she couldn't help him and the one person who could, his father, for some reason wouldn't. Damn the man to hell!

'Tammy?' said Billy. 'Are you all right?'

She looked down from her place on the tractor and was a little shocked to see that while she'd been ruminating on Billy's situation, she'd driven the tractor back to the hayshed and parked it in a spare bay.

'Yes. No worries. Sorry, Billy, in my own dream world, mate.'

'I'll be going then. That's if you got no more work for me?' His face looked earnest and not a little eager.

Tammy hated to disappoint him but there wasn't much else the child could do for her today. 'No, mate. All done.' At Billy's downcast look, she added, 'Thanks heaps for the help, though. Takes a lot longer on my own.' The child gave her a dazzling grin that turned the red-haired little urchin into a handsome boy. 'What do you think you'll do now?' she asked. It was Saturday, no school. Though she knew that, when his father wasn't home, the child just bummed around the bush up on the hill, playing imaginary games. As a kid, she'd done it herself.

'Old man McCauley killed a sheep last night. Just baled it up in a corner of the paddock, got a knife and slit its throat. Totally cool. Might go see what he's gunna do next.'

Tammy frowned. She knew only too well what Joe McCauley thought of trespassers. Especially kids. 'You be careful over there, Billy. The old man doesn't take too well to folks spying on his business.' She'd found *that* out thirty years back.

But Billy was already pulling off his helmet and donning his Akubra again. 'I will,' he called as he slung out of the drive, pedalling his old BMX like a maniac. 'See ya!' he called.

'See *you*, Billy,' Tammy muttered, smiling and shaking her head as she watched him go.

Suddenly the child did an about-face in the drive and came back.

'Hey, Tammy!' he called. 'I forgot. Can I use your computer? I've gotta do a speech for school on Monday. Need to type it up.' Billy was level with her now, flinging his bike into the grass, walking over, pulling a grotty-looking piece of paper from his back pocket. 'See. I got it all written out. I just need to type it up.'

'Sure. Go ahead. What's your talk on?'

'Three minutes on meself.'

'Three minutes on *my*-self, Billy,' Tammy said with a smile.

Billy glanced at her with a wicked grin. 'No. Not on you. That'd be too hard, with all that history and stuff you've got here at Montmorency. It'd take waaay too long.'

Tammy laughed. 'Tell me a bit of your speech,' she said, leaning against the front of the tractor. The poor kid was probably supposed to be practising it in front of someone. Maybe if he had four legs instead of two he'd garner more attention from that father of his.

Billy's face flushed. 'I ain't much good at it,' he said, swiping at his nose in agitation.

Tammy decided to ignore the *ain't*. 'Try me.'

Billy flattened out the piece of paper. Cleared his throat. 'Me name's Billy Hunter and I'm ten years old. I live on McCauley's Hill, just out of Lake Grace in the Narree Valley with me dad, Travis Hunter. He's a dog trapper with the De . . . De-part – ament of Conservation.' He looked across at Tammy, shame-faced. 'I can't say it. I can't say De-deapartment.'

Tammy smiled. "Course you can. Follow me. De. Part. Ment.'

Billy said, 'De-apart –' He shook his head. 'That's not right. What did you say again?'

Tammy pitched her voice a bit louder. 'De. Part. Ment.'

Billy looked surprised. 'There's no "a" in the middle, then?'

'Only in the "part" bit.'

'Right,' said the boy. 'So it's just De-part-ment. Department.' The child grinned as he ran the word together. 'I've got it, haven't I?'

Tammy nodded with pride. 'You've got it.'

'Department, department, department.' He started to run off towards the house (and presumably the computer) chanting at the top of his voice, 'Department, department . . . I heard it. I got it! *Yes!*'

Chapter 7

Travis threw another strip of wattle bark into the old copper. The water was just starting to boil nicely and turning an inky black. Perfect. He threw in the new Lanes dog-traps the Departmental blokes had dropped in the other day. The Conservation mob constantly kept changing the design of the traps he was to use, so it was an ongoing thing, making the traps smell as much a part of the environment as he could. A dog's sense of smell was one hundred times that of a human and they were damn smart. Some of the old blokes smoked their traps; others made a fire with gumtree leaves and dumped the traps in it. Some just rubbed the metal in dirt and found that worked. He preferred to use a mixture of methods. The wattle bark for some traps and just plain old soil for others.

It was a perfect day up here on his hill, in the bush. He didn't have anyone to annoy him and he liked it like that. He wasn't certain where Billy was but suspected he was floating around spying on someone. Old Joe or the McCauley girl down the bottom of the hill. Or maybe even watching him? Travis let out a sigh. His son, with his big eyes so like Katrina's. He was finding himself getting more and more annoyed with the kid when he wouldn't shut up. Sometimes it'd just become easier to ignore him. Trav liked his peace. Liked to be in his own head.

But now he was paying the price: an ten-year-old who sometimes glanced at him like a scared dog about to dodge a kick. The look in Billy's eyes this morning . . . Trav winced, remembering. It reminded him of how he used to look at his own father. It was obviously one thing to have a son, but another entirely to be a dad.

It was all still so new, this living with Billy again. Maybe he shouldn't have shipped the kid off to his grandmother so young? Trav threw another log onto the fire as he ruminated. But there really wasn't much else he could've done, was there? Well, except leave his job on the dog fence, and he hadn't wanted to do that. Surely it had been better for the kid to be brought up in Burra, go to school with other kids, rather than being out in the scrub? Billy had seemed happy enough with Diane Hunter and Trav had tried to visit when he could. It had all been working out fine until his mother had had her stroke. Life's a bastard, thought Trav, as he pictured his once active but now incapacitated mother.

Diane had done a good job with his son. He owed her a lot and that's why he'd brought her back to Lake Grace and why they were here at Belaren, although he had to admit the boy seemed to relish it too. The kid's bush skills were second to none and that had really surprised him. Like now, even *he* wouldn't know if Billy was watching him. He didn't know where it'd come from, this desire to be at one with the bush, especially since the boy had been living in town for the last few years. He wondered if it was a quirk of genetics, something inherently born to the males in their family? He couldn't see his own father consciously imparting such knowledge even though he'd been a dog trapper too.

His father was more likely to pit himself against the elements and see who could win. Take a swig on a bottle whenever he damned well pleased and pretend he didn't have a family to go home to. He'd been an old bastard, Jack Hunter. Trav hadn't realised how different his childhood had been until he'd met Katrina and her 'normal' parents. He winced again. Even after eight years it hurt to think of what could have been. He'd lost touch with Kat's extended family years ago. Her parents had been in their mid-forties when they'd had their daughter. They'd moved on into a nursing home not long after Kat had left and then they'd passed away within weeks of each other. Together, always together. Shame they hadn't instilled that ethos into their daughter.

The sound of a car labouring up a hill caught his attention. He loped towards the rocky outcrop which would give him a view of the whole Narree Valley. From here he could see his own driveway, and the vehicle currently traversing it. It was red, that much he could ascertain. Shiny and clean, judging by the glints coming off the duco in the late afternoon sun. Sporty looking too. Spoiler, mag wheels. A younger person's car. Either that or a mid-life crisis kind of vehicle.

The car kept coming and Trav weighed his options. He could disappear into the scrub but that would mean leaving his fire unattended and he really didn't want to do that. He could put out the fire but any dumb fool would know it was very recent. He sighed. Damn it. He'd have to hang around and talk to whoever it was. Maybe they'd leave quick?

As the car turned around the last corner to the house he strode back towards the yard, his hand automatically moving to smooth down the buzz cut which had forced his normally wavy brown hair into submission. He settled his face into an impassive expression while piercing blue eyes took in the vision exiting the vehicle, inch by inch. Something he hadn't seen up on this hill in a very long time. A female. An attractive one at that.

Ms Jacinta Greenaway slowly emerged from the snazzy car like a cat.

'Travis? How lovely to see you. Just thought I'd drop by.'

Inwardly, Trav groaned. Outwardly, he slung a half-wave in the air and moved forwards quickly, in the hopes he could head her off before she moved too far from the vehicle.

'Jacinta.'

'Call me Cin, Trav. What a beautiful . . . er . . .' She stalled as she took in the old and ugly cement-sheet cottage. ' . . . view. What a lovely view.'

He'd give it to her: she was a trier. There had been a few of them over the last few years. Always trying to coax Trav into their bed. It wasn't that he didn't appreciate the sights and sounds of a good woman. Far from it, he liked them all right – at a distance. It was just that in the early days he hadn't been able to think beyond Katrina. And now? Well, now he just couldn't be bothered. Worst thing was, women seemed to be attracted to 'couldn't be bothered'.

'Thanks. If you don't mind I'll keep it to Jacinta, you being Billy's teacher and all.'

Jacinta started flapping her hands as though she wanted to brush his words away.

'Billy might get teased by his mates if they heard me calling you by your nickname,' he said, scrambling for another reason.

'Oh yes, I see. Of course.'

Trav could tell she didn't *see* at all. Hell. This one was going to be harder to put off than he'd thought. 'So what brings you to McCauley's Hill, Jacinta? We don't often get visitors up here.'

'Well, I was just passing by –'

'On a dead-end road?' Trav raised an eyebrow.

Cin looked slightly pissed off. 'Well, actually, now you mention it, there's a little problem with Billy. Your son.'

'I'm well aware he's my son.' Trav might have been playing it cool on the surface, but his stomach muscles were clenching. 'What's he done?'

'It's what he's not doing that is the issue.'

'And that is . . . ?'

Jacinta sighed, then right before his eyes pulled on another persona. In an instant, it seemed, the flickering eyelashes and the sultry expression disappeared. 'He's been wagging school. Over the last month he's missed at least four days. And there's been no note.'

'Four days?' *Shit.* What was the little bugger up to?

'Yes. And I thought you should know about it. Much better for me to tell you in person rather than over the phone, don't you think?'

'Four days,' Trav muttered to himself. He never saw Billy off to school, relying on the kid to get ready by himself. Trav had to be gone by five-thirty so he was out in the bush early to check on or set his traps. 'Right then. I'd better find him and together we'll see what's going on.'

'Oh no, Travis. That's fine. I'll leave you to talk to him.'

'No. I'll get him now. He'll be close by somewhere. Here, you sit down on this stump.' He kicked a tree butt across the gravel and dumped it in front of the red car. 'Just plant your bum – I mean sit here and I'll be right back.'

His last view of Jacinta Greenaway was the one in the rearview mirror of his LandCruiser ute. She looked down at the ironbark log with distaste and then kicked it with her pointed high-heeled shoe.

Chapter 8

Travis found Billy on his second try. One glance at Joe's place from the T intersection at the bottom of the hill and he could see the old man pottering around his sheds. Billy wouldn't be spying on him today. By the looks of it nothing was happening there that was interesting enough.

That left Tammy McCauley, or should he say Tammy Murphy? Billy had been doing some odd jobs for the woman. Trav drove his ute a half a kilometre along Hope's Road in the direction of the Montmorency homestead and pointed his bonnet down the driveway to the house. He could see by the absence of the copper-coloured Mitsubishi Triton ute that Shon Murphy wasn't around. Thank God for that. He couldn't stand the bloke. There was nothing genuine about the man. Plus, according to the boys at the Department, he was cheating on his wife, the bastard.

He remembered the first time he'd met Ms McCauley Murphy. He'd gone with Billy for a drive into Narree. The kid had disappeared while he was getting their groceries, reappearing just as Trav was going through the checkout. He was carrying a Narree Toyshop bag in his hand.

'What's in that?' he had asked sharply.

Billy had silently opened the package for his dad to take a look. Three Matchbox cars for his dirt heap.

'Where'd you get the money from?'

'Ms McCauley's paying me to do a few jobs for her. And she's really nice. Lets me ride the motorbike.' The kid's eyes were sparkling. Guilt – the guilt Trav always felt when it came to Billy – kicked hard at his guts. 'I wear a helmet,' Billy added quickly. 'And she's shown me how to ride nice and quiet like.'

'You sure she really wants you there?'

The light in Billy's eyes died. *Pooft.* Just like that. Trav's guts churned all the more. He did that to the boy all the time and cursed himself for it while at the same time feeling incapable of doing anything else.

The kid mumbled, 'Well, I think so . . .' The remainder of the sentence hung in the air between them . . . *not like some people.*

Trav grunted, paid for their groceries and walked out the door, loaded the bags into the back and then got into the ute, waiting for the boy. He wasn't coming. Where was he? Trav looked around and spotted him.

A woman stood at the door of the supermarket investigating the paper bag Billy was holding out. Dressed in neat denim jeans that cupped her backside like a second skin, a chocolate brown shirt, dangling beads and elastic-sided boots, she looked as sexy as hell. Her heart-shaped face was animated as she pulled a racing car out of the bag. She was laughing now, and Billy was giggling along with her. Trav hadn't seen that in a long time – his son laughing. Whatever was going on was obviously very funny and Trav found himself undoing the seatbelt, exiting the ute and sauntering up to them.

'Good morning,' he said. 'I'm Billy's father, Travis.' He dipped a finger to his hat and tried a half-smile. Smiling was definitely one of his rustiest skills. That and talking. And sex.

The laughter had dried up as he joined them. They both looked at him in consternation. One pair of assessing dark brown eyes. Another smaller pair of concerned hazel. Trav sighed. So much for joining in on the joke.

'Hi. I'm Tammy McCauley,' the woman said. 'I'm just admiring Billy's new cars. Classy way to spend your pay packet, that's for sure.' She smiled at Billy. Trav wanted her to smile at him like that. All warm like you were the only person worthy of her attention at that moment. And then there was that voice. It reminded him of rich chocolate. Sinful yet sweet.

What had got into him? He never mooned over a woman. In fact having one in his life wasn't even on his to-do list, as long as that was. He loved Katrina. Correction. *Had* loved Katrina. She'd killed anything he was ever going to feel for the opposite sex.

His heart seemed to have other ideas. Eight years was a long while. Maybe it *was* time to move on? Yeah right, Hunter. Move on to a married woman. Just what he needed, more complications.

'Mr Hunter? Travis?' Tammy was talking to him again and Trav realised he must have been staring because Billy was looking at him like he'd grown two heads. He could almost see the boy's mind working. *What the heck's got into the old man?* He quickly pulled himself together. The best form of defence was attack, right? 'Billy tells me he's working for you. Sure you want him? He's pretty young and all –'

'I'm not too young, Dad!' Billy piped up, indignant. Then the boy stopped like he'd just realised who he was talking to. 'I'm the right size. Ms McCauley said so,' he squeaked.

Travis frowned at his son, pissed off at the interruption. 'How about we let Ms McCauley answer that one, Billy?'

Tammy moved to stand behind the boy, and placed two hands on his scrawny shoulders. 'He's the perfect size for a farmhand, Mr Hunter. Not too small that he can't drag a pressure hose around the cow-yard and not too big that he can't clean out the chook nesting boxes. You're built for both jobs, aren't you, mate?'

She had an almost proprietorial air around his son. He had to battle with his natural inclination to tell her to get her hands the hell off his boy. But then he noticed the way Billy leaned into her body, like a pup seeking reassurance off his mother, and he had to bite his tongue.

The woman was obviously trying to help. But she just made Trav feel all the worse. He already knew he wasn't much of a father. He didn't need some do-gooding Tammy McCauley Murphy to tell him so, that's all.

And now he'd been told his son was wagging school, and he had to admit to the kid's teacher he had no idea where the boy was.

Trav pulled his ute up in the yard large enough for a B-double milk tanker to turn around in. Two dogs came screaming around the side of the dairy, yelping their heads off but wagging their tails as they ran. They could probably smell dogs all over Trav's ute. His dog boxes on the ute's tray were empty, but that didn't mean their scent was gone.

Tammy McCauley appeared around the corner of the cowshed. He got a better look at her this time. She was slim and finely built, brown hair clasped tightly back from her face in a ponytail. In the middle of pulling on a peaked cap and donning sunglasses, she had a frown on her face. When she worked out who was in her drive, the frown deepened into a scowl.

He wondered what he'd done to deserve that. 'Just wondering if Billy was around here somewhere?'

'And why would you care, Mr Hunter?'

'What?'

'I said, why would you care?'

'I know what you said.' Trav could feel his own hackles rising. He couldn't for the life of him work out why she was so angry. 'I just want to know if my son is here as I need him to come home. Now.'

'He's here. Working on my computer. Because you won't buy one. Have you ever thought what damage you're doing to his schooling by refusing to get him one?'

'I don't see that it's any of your business, Mrs Murphy.'

'It's Ms McCauley to you. And it is my business. That poor kid has to come down here and use my computer to do his homework because his father won't buy him one of those "newfangled" things. Computers are part of the modern world whether you like it or not!'

What was it with the females in this valley today? Now he knew why he'd avoided them. 'Ms McCauley, I have no idea what's got your goat this afternoon, but I'd appreciate it if you didn't take it out on me. Give me my boy and I'll get out of your way.'

'What's got my goat? What's got my *goat*?! Listen here, Mr Hunter, if you spent a little more time looking after your son than wandering willy-nilly round the bush looking for four-legged animals, then I think you'd find he might stay where he's supposed to be. At home with you.'

That struck a raw nerve. Finding out Billy was wagging school from a lollypop on legs was one thing, having this stick of dynamite giving him curry for not looking out for the boy was another. He sucked in a breath, trying to hold onto his temper. 'Where's Billy?'

She pointed in the direction of the back verandah of the house then spun on her neat, well-proportioned legs and stormed off. Trav watched her walk away and wondered how anyone could make such a graceful exit wearing gumboots. But, man, she was a piece of work. Her snug backside sashayed as she high-tailed it in the direction of the dairy. Her ponytail swung in agitation and those boots found every puddle in their path. Splat! Splat! He suspected his face was at the bottom of every one.

Trav shook his head and walked towards the homestead. Compared to his place this joint was huge, all angles and windows. And old, and quiet.

'Billy? *Billy!*'

A tousled head appeared from behind a screen door. 'Dad? What're you doing . . . ? I mean, yes, I'm here!'

'In the ute. Now.'

'Yes, sir. I'll just shut the compu –' Billy shot his father a look before continuing, 'No, maybe I won't. Coming!'

Trav spun on his Redbacks and walked to the ute. He was revving the engine when a red-haired streak came flying across the yard and clambered up beside him. He could feel the boy's nervous sideways glances, but he wasn't going to put the kid at ease or let him know what was coming. No bloody way. His son would be punished – grounded for a week – and he'd think up as many boring jobs as he could for him to do. He'd teach the little bugger to wag school.

And he'd show that siren with the liquid brown eyes he was a *responsible* father, whatever that was supposed to be.

Chapter 9

What had got into her? Travis Hunter must think she was hell on wheels. Which, at the moment, she was.

Bloody men.

Tammy grabbed hold of a piece of poly pipe and went out into the cow-yard to bring up the first row of cows to be milked.

What was his story, being a single father and all? He looked like Mad Max meets George Clooney. There was something animal-like emanating from him, something rough, primitive and raw, yet he was good-looking, in a tough kind of way. He disturbed yet at the same time intrigued her. He wasn't overly tall but he was solid, with a close-cropped head of sandy-brown hair that looked like it might curl if left to grow. Nothing too remarkable about all that. But it was his eyes, a piercing blue, that had struck her. They seemed to see right into her soul.

Tammy absent-mindedly swung the cups onto the cow's teats. Billy's mother wasn't around so Hunter must have left her or something. He'd been here for about six months but she hadn't sighted him much. Hadn't even known they'd turned up until one day she saw Billy waiting for the bus down at the intersection of Hope's Road and the Narree–Lake Grace roads. The boy sure as heck hadn't come from Joe's place so that left only one option. The old Hunter joint. Lucy hadn't been able to shed any light on the details: Travis Hunter preferring to keep to himself, which nearly killed Lucy as she loved a good gossip. Especially about someone so enigmatic.

Crikey, what must that man think of her now? She had no right to blow up at him like that. Just all this stuff with Shon, then Billy arriving and looking like a little lost soul. Damn it! Didn't that man see what he was doing to his son? The kid was desperate for love, for a father. And where the hell was he? Up the bush playing with dogs. He left Billy alone for hours on end. No wonder the child looked feral half the time – though that appearance belied the guts of it. The boy was capable of a lot. He was intelligent, loved words, loved learning but just not in the traditional way. Billy really needed a schoolroom set in the scrub, one that was part of the environment. To learn by doing in the real world rather than by rote in a stuffy classroom.

And Tammy couldn't shake off the feeling there was something else wrong with the boy. He was so bright but sometimes couldn't get really simple stuff through his head. Something was holding him back. She just couldn't put her finger on what it was.

Whatever, she needed to apologise to Travis Hunter. She'd had no right to meddle in affairs that weren't anything to do with her. She had enough troubles of her own. She'd go later this evening, after she'd finished her jobs and had tea. Shon was staying in Cann River in far East Gippsland tonight, so she didn't have to concern herself about him coming home.

※

It was around seven-thirty when Tammy let herself out her back door, gathering up the paperwork she'd found printed beside a humming computer. She decided to walk. The night was bright with a full moon and it would do her good to trudge up that hill. She'd had a shower, slapped some concealer around her eye to blot out the bruise, donned a pair of clean Wranglers, a soft blue shirt and her Redback boots. Leaving her hair to float around her shoulders to dry, she walked down her driveway and along Hope's Road, hesitating as she got to the low level crossing. Up on the bank of the Backwater Creek and casting dark shadows in the moonlight was a decrepit bark structure. It had once been a hut for an elderly prospector named Cecil Du Pont. Such an auspicious name for a vagabond who lived in hope of finding gold.

She walked on, around the corner and then through Travis Hunter's front gateway. As she climbed the hill, she started to puff and wondered at her stupidity. She should have brought the ute. Damn. So much for feeling cool and fresh. She was sweating and cursing as she topped the rise that led to the house yard.

A smart red car sat in the drive. She hadn't pegged Travis Hunter as the owner of a girly car like that. She slid past the vehicle where it sat shining in the moonlight, let herself in through the garden gate and walked onto the old wide verandah. She spotted a beer fridge, dog kennel, and a blackened metal washing machine inner drum that had seen better days. It was stacked with firewood. Obviously the drum was all ready to be set out in the yard and lit on a clear night, so you could watch satellites, cook jaffles, drink beer and pretend you were camping up the bush. Tammy felt a stab of jealousy. She wished Shon enjoyed doing that type of thing. She used to do it as a kid with her grandfather. Cook marshmallows and draw pictures in the sky with the end of a burning stick.

She sighed and knocked on the door. The sound of crashing crockery came from inside, followed by a high-pitched squeal. What on earth was going on in there? She knocked again and a head of red hair appeared at the door. Billy slid back the glass.

'Tammy? Gee, you look pretty!'

'Thanks, Billy, you little charmer. You forgot this stuff when you left.' Tammy thrust out a handful of papers. 'I thought you might need it for your speech on Monday.'

The boy ducked his head in embarrassment as a voice came from behind him somewhere. 'Who's there, Billy?'

In for a penny in for a pound, her grandmother used to say. So when Billy moved back reluctantly, she stepped through the doorway and past the curtain, to see a sight which would have been funny if it wasn't so shocking. Jacinta Greenaway, the lower-grades schoolteacher, was on her knees in front of Travis Hunter. All Tammy could see were acres of blonde hair but she'd know that voice anywhere. Slightly breathless, almost childlike in its intonation. 'Ohhh, Trav . . .'

Hunter looked like he was in ecstasy, or was it agony? Hard to tell from this angle. If she moved a step to the right maybe she could work it out.

'Dad, it's Tam – Ms McCauley.'

Travis started, stood up straight and now Tammy could see it was agony cloaked with embarrassment. 'It's not what it looks like, Ms McCauley.'

Jacinta squealed again. 'Trav, I can't do it if you stand like that!'

Hunter immediately bent back over and the blonde hair disappeared into his groin once more, a hand coming up to wave hello – or maybe it was goodbye? – to Tammy as she went.

Tammy grinned and leaned against a post that extended above her head and supported what looked like an old wire gate on its side, holding a harvest of apples. 'And just what do you think it looks like, Mr Hunter?'

An agonised expression crossed Travis's face once again.

'Oooh . . . I think I've got it!' Jacinta put her head up for a breath before diving back into action.

Travis glanced at Tammy. She quirked an eyebrow in question. He sighed and shrugged his shoulders as he held himself up over Jacinta. 'She dropped the dish of lasagna and it shattered on the bench. I've got the stuff all over my front here, glass shards and all.'

'Well, why don't you just take off your clothes?' suggested Tammy, smirking. The next moment she wished she could snatch those words right back because Travis Hunter's piercing blue eyes fixed on her from across the room. Her face blazed with embarrassment. Where the hell had that comment come from? She was a married woman; she had no right to flirt with someone who was possibly still married as well. *And* he had yet another woman on her knees in front of him. Shit.

Tammy cleared her throat and stood up straight. 'I should be going. I just wanted to drop off this information for Billy. He's got a speech to do at school on Monday.' Her chin lifted in challenge. *There, did you know that, Mr Hunter?*

Jacinta's head appeared again and she made to stand up, bringing with her a bag of clinking glass that dripped with tomato sauce and pasta. 'We'll have to make do with salad and garlic bread, boys! Yes, we're doing public speaking – talking about where we live, our families, what we do in our spare time, all that kind of stuff. It'll be such fun, won't it, Billy?' The woman's voice lilted upwards with excitement.

Billy's head dropped and he muttered, 'I don't know about fun,' before excusing himself. 'Thanks, Tammy,' he said as he hoisted himself up a ladder to a loft-like structure next to the apples. A mezzanine floor? His bedroom perhaps?

Tammy glanced back at the couple in the kitchen. Seeing them all together – Billy, Trav and Jacinta – reminded her of what a family was supposed to look like, which gave her pangs in her gut. If only. She sighed and focused on the two adults on the other side of the kitchen bench. It made for a cosy twosome, the pair of them standing there. Jacinta came up to Hunter's nose, all fragile and feminine.

Tammy peered down at her own jeans and shirt. Always jeans and a shirt. Then back at the schoolteacher. No wonder men went for women like Jacinta Greenaway and Joanne, who really knew how to work it. Pull on a tight, shortish skirt, a shirt with buttons or a V-neck to drip cleavage that didn't need a Wonderbra to enhance the look. Spend an hour in the bathroom with a hair straightener, slather on some makeup and pull on a pair of killer high-heels and *voila*! There you had it, a dick magnet. Tammy sighed. She couldn't handle the man she had let alone attract anyone else.

'I'll be going then. I'll leave you to it . . .' she said with a mocking smile. 'Whatever *it* is. I'll let myself out.'

Tammy turned to go but as she made it through the sliding door she found Hunter right behind her. 'Not so fast, Ms McCauley.' He shut the door after him, cutting off Jacinta's voice as she called Billy down for tea. 'This really isn't what it looks like. She came to talk about Billy and then . . . well . . . didn't leave.'

Tammy stuck a hand in the air. 'Mr Hunter, you don't owe me any explanations. You can do whatever you damn well like. If you want to spend your nights with someone half your age who looks like Lady Gaga, then go right ahead.'

'Trav.'

'What?'

'My name's Trav.'

'Well, *Trav*, I'll be off. Thanks for the interesting entertainment. That was better than SBS TV.'

'Lady Gaga, huh? Never heard of her but she sounds interesting.' A half-smile crossed the man's face. It transformed him. Tammy sucked in her breath. Christ. 'It must have looked pretty funny.' There was a husky edge to his voice, as though it wasn't used to being tuned in to normal conversation for extended periods of time.

It made her remember the other reason why she was up on top of McCauley's Hill at this time of night. 'I also came to apologise.'

'What for?'

'For this afternoon. I was way out of line, yelling at you. What you do with your kid is your business. I've got enough troubles of my own without messing with yours.'

'How'd you get here?'

'On foot. Did you hear what I said?'

'On foot?'

'Yes, I used my legs,' said Tammy exasperated. 'I said I'm sorry!'

'Yeah. Yeah. No worries. You mean you walked all the way up here by yourself? In the dark?'

'It's hardly dark. The moon's out.' Tammy could feel her hackles rising again, damn the man. 'I'm not precious, you know. I can look after myself.' Her eyes flicked back towards the house and the shiny red car.

'I'll run you home.' He moved towards his ute.

'No! I'm fine.' She did not need him doing anything for her. 'Thanks all the same,' she added before setting off down the drive.

She tripped on a rock. Trav went to help her back up. 'I'm really fine,' she said as she righted herself and took off at a clipping pace, only to just miss a renegade branch sticking out from a gum tree at head height.

'Very fine,' she said again. Move, McCauley. Get the hell out of here before you make a *complete* fool of yourself.

'Thanks for bringing the stuff for the kid.' The yell came floating down the hill to settle around her shoulders as she tripped on yet another rock.

No worries, *Trav*, Tammy muttered.

She was just about at her own gateway when the shiny red car blew past, showering her with grit and gravel. A hand was in the air, blonde locks and glittering rings on show, as the vehicle roared past.

'Bye, Jacinta,' muttered Tammy. Nice enough girl but did she have to make it *so* apparent she wanted Travis Hunter? Where had subtlety disappeared to? Then again, perhaps she was getting old. Maybe it was all about just putting it out there. Come get me, big boy, I'm all yours, you don't even have to ask. Joanne and Jacinta. Two peas in a pod. God, now she *was* getting cynical. Joanne would eat the poor schoolteacher alive, any day.

She was in front of the dairy when she heard the whistle of a turbo diesel motor out near her front gate. The vehicle had passed the drive and turned into the gateway of the hayshed. She watched as the lights did a 360-degree turn, then slowly made their way back to her driveway. The ute then propped and the driver turned off the motor. The lights disappeared but just before they did she saw the shadow of a man in a hat in the driver's seat. Shon? But it wasn't a twin-cab ute. And why would he be casing the joint out?

She fled inside, slamming the screen door. Switched off the back light. Watched through the louvre windows.

A few minutes later the ute started again, the noise of the motor rumbling across the paddock in the clear air. So, whoever it was, they weren't trying to be quiet.

It was then, as the ute pulled away, that she realised it was a LandCruiser. Travis Hunter. Checking on her. Making sure she'd got home safely. She moved back outside and watched the path of the vehicle as it disappeared then reappeared through the low level crossing at the creek. Sure enough, at the T intersection it turned left and then right, and up the hill it went. The last she saw of it were the tail-lights turning the final bend, and then ute and man disappeared, swallowed by tall box and ironbark stands.

Chapter 10

Shimmering azure water beckoned to Tammy from across the street. The photos advertising discount flights to the stunning islands off the coast of Queensland were in the window of the gift shop plus travel agency. Maybe she should just book a flight here and now, take off somewhere.

Tammy pushed her trolley of groceries away from the supermarket and towards the parked ute. Beyond the main street lay the lake, the pride of Narree. The water glinted in the sun. There were some school kids rowing, their sculls skimming along the surface. Oh, to be that age again. Young and carefree.

Ten years of marriage – almost a third of her life – wasted and not even a child to show for it. Shon hadn't wanted to start a family too early. Now, that was probably a blessing. Imagine dragging a child through divorce courts and property settlements. Not that there'd be much to settle. The property was hers. Only the run-off block had Shon's name on it. Still, she needed that land to run her dairy herd on during the winter to give the farm a break.

But how exactly was she going to get that two-timing, lying, cheating bastard safely off Montmorency? She'd have to engineer a confrontation with him. When he threatened to leave, just tell him to go, rather than begging him to stay as she'd done countless times over the last two years. What an idiot she'd been.

Unloading the groceries into the ute she pondered whether to just get in and go home or find some lunch. Shon was due back that afternoon. She decided to get lunch. Put off the inevitable.

As she walked towards the bakery, she spied a new gallery setting up shop a couple of doors down. Might be worth a look. She bought a roll and bottle of mineral water and then slowly moved towards the new store.

Displayed on its own in the window was a painting. Tammy suddenly forgot about eating lunch. The picture was incredible. It was of a woman, naked but tastefully so. Sphinx-like, her body was female, but with dainty feet rather than the haunches of a lion and she was adorned with the most incredible wings of iridescent colours, open to catch the rays of the sun. She was standing on the edge of a cliff, appearing to lean into the wind, face upturned as though she was sensing something. Her eyes were closed, a slight smile touched her face. It seemed the creature was about to take flight into her future. Tammy stared at the figure some more. Then it hit her what the angel was smelling, seeing, leaning towards.

Freedom.

'She's beautiful, isn't she?' A voice came from the right.

A tidy-looking stranger stood beside her. She was kitted out like a solicitor or a banker in a suit. 'Alice Stringer. I own the gallery.' The woman caught Tammy's look of surprise. 'No, I don't normally dress like this but I've just come back from the bank. Got to walk the walk, talk the talk.'

Tammy blushed. It wasn't the first time she'd wished her thoughts weren't transmitted so plainly to her face. 'Tammy McCauley. I'm sorry. Stereotyping I guess. Arty types don't normally – '

'Dress in suits, I know. I'll go out the back and slip into my kaftan if that makes you feel any better?' Alice Stringer's green eyes glinted mischievously.

Tammy warmed to the woman immediately. 'So . . . how much?' she asked, waving her hand towards the window.

'I'm not sure I want to sell her, actually.' Alice's gaze moved greedily over the picture. 'But who am I kidding? I need the sale. This is actually a numbered print of an original painting. It's one of a series of three. I have number two in the shop but it's just arrived so I haven't unpacked it yet. I'm trying to get number three but it's taking a while.'

'Who's the painter?'

'Reyne Jennings. She's becoming big in the art world. Her original paintings are starting to sell for a *lot* of money.'

And Tammy could see why. The execution and detail of the print in front of her was exceptional.

'Would you like to see the second one?'

'Would I ever!'

'Well, you finish your lunch and I'll unpack it.'

Tammy looked down at the forgotten roll in her hand. The bite she had taken tasted awful. 'I don't want this any more. I'll just get rid of it and follow you in.'

Tammy moved up the street to deposit her rubbish, contemplating the picture. She had inherited a love of art from her grandmother. Shon had never had any time for it, so she hadn't bought anything since they'd married.

What was stopping her now though? Why should Shon dictate to her any more?

She walked into the gallery and found Alice on her knees extricating another print from its packaging. When the picture was finally revealed, both women sucked in their breaths. It was unbelievable. The angel had taken off and was flying. Slipstreams and eddies buffeted her magnificent wings, causing the iridescent colours to sparkle in the sun. Her free-flowing clothing reminded Tammy of a picture she'd once seen in a children's Bible of the Archangel Gabriel. The sheaths of cloth around the figure in front of her floated with serene grace. The expression on the woman's face was one of sheer bliss. Freedom. Happiness. Love. The print was numbered 4/100, exactly the same as the one in the window.

Tammy knew she had to have them. They contained everything she was feeling, especially the need to throw off the shackles of submission and subordination forced on her these last few years.

'I'll take them. Both of them.'

'Don't you want to know how much first?'

'No. Yes. Well, how much?'

Alice named a sum which made Tammy pause. But she swallowed and said she'd take them all the same. She might just have to dip into the principal of her inheritance from her grandmother, but she didn't care. These prints symbolised her future and she needed a talisman to hang onto, to give her the guts and determination to do what needed to be done. Get rid of Shon.

'I'll let you know when the third print comes in. You can have that for a reduced amount seeing you're taking these two. I haven't seen a picture of it yet, but if it's anything like these, you won't be disappointed.'

Tammy watched as the woman retrieved the first print from the window and packaged them together. She felt a small kernel of satisfaction uncurl in her belly. They were perfect. She could almost feel herself inside the sphinx-angel's body, riding the wind, energy suffusing her whole being.

She was doing it. Getting her life back. Baby steps, that's for sure, but still it was forward motion.

And that was what counted.

Chapter 11

The antique milkcan sat squat on its side, a thick slot cut into the lid for the day's mail currently spilling from its rusty depths. Tammy pulled the ute into her driveway, wound down the window and hauled out the letters. The old Buddha stared at her from his spot by the front gate-post. She'd never rubbed his belly; she left that kind of hocus-pocus stuff to Lucy. Her friend's fascination with the blasted thing was the only real reason she left it there. That and Shon. She paused, glanced towards the homestead. He was home. She could see his ute. She looked back at the grey effigy. Maybe it was time to take the sledgehammer to it.

Then again, maybe she *should* try rubbing the old bloke. Maybe he could help her kick Shon out.

She jumped out of the ute and stomped towards the Buddha. Squatting down she rubbed her hand over the old fella's prodigious belly. Round and round she went. Give me the strength, the guts and the determination to do this. To follow through, kick the bastard out, to survive and learn to live my life again.

A ute rumbled past on the road behind her. She automatically turned to see who it was. Two people peered through the LandCruiser windscreen: one an earnest little boy, the other a rugged-looking man with a half-smile on his face. *Caught you*, he seemed to be saying. Blushing, Tammy flung her hand in the air in acknowledgement and quickly stood up, swiping her palms against each other.

Shon's twin-cab was parked hard up against the garden fence. He always did that, as though he was clinging to something solid, claiming his right to be there. She marched up the path, taking big long strides in an effort to reinforce her determination to do what had to be done.

'Shon? Shon!' she yelled as she walked in the door. 'What're you *doing*?' She could hear him, swearing and slamming cupboard doors. The homestead looked like a team of thieves had ransacked the place. Kitchen drawers were turned inside out, the doors on the sideboard in the living room swung dejectedly while the contents lay strewn across the floor. Tammy followed the trail of destruction through the formal lounge and down the long passage towards the main bedroom of the house.

He was standing beside their antique solid oak bed.

'What's going on?'

'What the fuck does it look like? I'm leaving. Finally got my ticket out of here.'

The words took the wind clean out of her. *She'd* been going to tell *him* to get out, so why was she so shocked that he'd got in first?

'I don't love you and I hate living here.' He had turned from the cupboard to look at her. His eyes were hard and spilling with distaste, his face contorted with anger and frustration. She wondered if he'd ever really loved her.

'It's all about *you*. Your family,' he raged, his cheeks swelling with self-righteousness. 'Now it's going to be about *me*.'

'What?'

'I'll be wanting half of the farm of course. You'll be hearing from me solicitor.'

'Half the farm? No way. You can't do that! It's mine.'

'Just watch me.' And then he grinned, sly and malicious.

Why had she let things go on this long? She could feel her heart breaking into tiny pieces. Her eyes strayed to the wedding photo above the bed on the wall. He'd been so charming and loving back then. When had it all changed? When had he decided *she* wasn't what he wanted any more?

And now their marriage was over, and he didn't give a damn.

'You will be fighting me the whole way, Shon Murphy. You have no right to this property. No right at all. It was left to *me*.'

'Yeah well, what about all the work I've done on the place? I've a right to a part of it and I'll be having it. I need the money for me half-share in the pub.'

He was going into business with Joanne? 'You were planning this all along, weren't you? Living here, rooting her and just waiting for your chance.'

He refused to look at her.

Poor Joanne. Tammy was shocked that she could actually feel sympathy for the duped woman. She probably thought she was getting a god. In reality she was getting the devil's spawn.

'Well, go on,' she said, battling to keep her voice steady. He was never going to know just how much she was hurting. 'You've been threatening to leave for long enough. Just get the hell out of here.' She turned and walked back up the passage, through the kitchen, and out the back door. Kept on walking until she could see neither him, his ute nor the property.

She glanced up at McCauley's Hill. A glint of glass flashed in the sun, catching her eye. The old bastard was up there on his verandah, probably observing all this through the scope on his rifle. He'd be having a ball, watching and laughing. She wished with all her heart that she could go up there, be with family. But that was never to be.

She had no family. No one. Not any more.

※

Up on his hill Joe shifted forwards in his rocking chair. A movement in the grass made him swing his gun towards the east. A whole pocket of bloody rabbits had burrowed out the side of the hill below the house. Little shits. He envisaged blowing up their holes with dynamite. That'd do the trick. Plug up the ends of the burrows bar one, shove a few sticks in and *bang!* Bloody beautiful. Rabbit parts flying everywhere. But it wouldn't do his hill no good either. No good at all. He was having enough trouble with erosion as it was, what with the crumbling soil structure and the rabbits undermining it all.

Nope. Maybe he could gas 'em? Only problem was the last time he did that he'd nearly gassed *himself*. Somehow the stuff had come up through his shower drain hole; the greywater must've been running into a rabbit burrow. He'd had to sleep out in the shed in his swag for a week, waiting for the smell to disappear. Bugger that for a joke. He could try baiting them but he had the bloody dogs and they'd eat anything.

Joe sighed, reached down to fondle the ears of the old dog at his feet. Boots shuffled in, obviously loving the feel of his owner's hand.

So, thought Joe, I'm back to the gun.

A bit of grey fluff bobbed up and Joe was quick to bring the scope of the .22 rifle up to his eye. The barrel wobbled as the old man tried to get his balance. 'Bloody rocking chair,' he muttered. He should build himself a rail around the verandah, then he could rest the gun on it. He settled himself, concentrating on the grey smudge moving in his gun sight. He slowly breathed out, increasing the pressure on the trigger as all the air left his lungs.

Bang!

The dogs jumped. Joe jumped. And the bunny ran on, unmarked and more determined than ever to make it to his burrow and safety.

Fuck it!

The old man brought the rifle scope back to his eye to have another go but his attention was caught by a glimpse of blue, moving at a cracking pace, heading north. It was the girl. She reminded him of a good horse. She had long thoroughbred-like strides, head held high to the sun's rays. A hand coming up every now and then to wipe the eyes. Mmm . . .

At the sound of a ute he swung the scope back towards Montmorency Downs. It was that prick Murphy, coming down the drive in his twin-cab. Why he needed a twin-cab, Joe didn't know. It wasn't as if he'd produced any little buggers. Fancy mixing McCauley blood with that Irish scum's. Where the hell was the girl's brain the day she'd married that bloke? Most likely down south. That lot of Murphys always were a showy bunch, strutting here and there like bloody cockerels. The angle of their dangle was pretty huge according to local folklore.

Murphy's ute seemed to hover at the front gate. There was a buggy in the back. That'd be right. Off to have a game of golf, leaving the girl to deal with all that irrigation water he could see pooling in the channel. She was obviously about to start watering the place and it was a big job on your own. Shon Murphy was a miserable bloody bastard to leave her to it.

Funny thing was Murphy hadn't always been like that. When the girl's grandparents had been alive, Murphy had pitched in right beside Tammy. At the time Joe had been thinking maybe he was wrong about the bloke. But then had come the accident eight years ago and the fight to save the place from the creditors. Tom must've been running pretty close to the wire to keep Mae in the style to which she'd become accustomed. Joe snorted. It was that air of entitlement she carried around with her. She'd always thought she was better than anybody else, him and his brother included.

According to the stock agent her grandparents had left Tammy the place wholus bolus and that had pissed Murphy right off. Something to do with his name not being on the title when he reckoned he'd earned it. That was back in the days when Joe was still puttering around up the bush, cutting firewood and ripping a few posts, while other men his age opted for the local bowling green. Old habits died hard in a bushman. He'd camp away most of the week, coming back to the house – and Nellie – on weekends.

He hadn't wanted to know what was going on down at the bottom of the hill, but Nellie had been right onto it, drawing the stock agent out over scones and jam and cups of tea. Ah, she'd had the way of it, Nellie, to get people to talk without them even knowing they were doing it.

A bit like his own mother, Daphne.

Despite the fact he tried to push it away, Daphne's voice replayed in his head, as it had done countless times over the years, 'Oh, Joseph, you're breaking our hearts! Make up with Tom. You're *both* married now.'

His parents, and also he suspected his brother, hadn't realised Mae Rouget had been with him first. They had assumed the rift was because Tom had got married, breaking their brothers' bond, and despite his mother's heckling, Joe's pride would never let him tell otherwise.

He heaved a sigh. It was a bit late for recriminations. They were all gone now.

Joe adjusted the gun scope a bit more, focusing in on the rear seat and tub tray of the ute. Sheesh! There was more than golf clubs in the back. Suitcases, big striped plastic bags; much more than was necessary for a trip away. Fishing rods, a bar fridge, a leather chair, and was that a mattress shoved in the side, flapping around like Rolf Harris's wobble board?

'Good God, is the man *leaving*?' Joe muttered to Boots and Digger. He leaned down again and fondled the first pair of ears that came within reach.

He trained the scope back south. Sure enough the blue blur was disappearing over the other side of the hill, following the trail of power lines towards the massive irrigation weir of Lake Grace. A couple more loping, sure strides and one more swipe of a hand and the neat figure was gone. Over the horizon and out of sight.

Meanwhile the vehicle was still hovering at the Montmorency Downs gateway, and then it was moving, turning right towards town, slowly sneaking along the road past the hardwood post and wire boundary fence erected after the awful accident years before that killed young Patty O'Hara. Terrible mess that one. Joe shuddered, turned his attention back to the vehicle.

The ute was moving idly along as though its driver had all the time in the world. Then Joe saw the camera. The bastard was taking photos. What the –?

A few minutes ticked by, more photos, and then the engine noise changed as the driver cranked the ute up a gear and took off.

'Good riddance to scum,' Joe muttered to his dogs. Below him two tails thumped their agreement.

After Shon had left, all was quiet around the valley. So the old man decided to swing his scope around, towards the scrub that hunkered down on the edge of his property.

He spotted something wandering in his paddock. It moved fast, then slow. Fast then slow, running then dropping into the grass. The person – because that's what Joe decided it was – moved closer and closer, skulking around the perimeter of his sheds. Then he couldn't see the bugger, much and all as he tried. Joe didn't want to leave the verandah because up here he had the chance of a good shot. Though he didn't want to hit 'em. Just scare the bastard, whoever it was.

Why the hell couldn't people just leave an old man alone? He didn't do nothin' to nobody so why should they come botherin' him? But they had, over the years. And he could imagine why. 'Mad old Joe McCauley' they called him. He knew that and guessed it had become a bit of a dare to sneak onto the place, say you'd been there and not been shot.

A flutter of blue and red caught his attention.

There it was again. Joe leaned forwards in the chair, squinting his rheumy eyes to bring the material into focus. It was somewhere near the barn, moving fast. He scanned the ramshackle cluster of outbuildings sitting beyond the more modern machinery shed. A glimpse down near the old stable between the corrugated iron walls and the wood shed.

He shifted the rifle in his lap. Squinted down the barrel – and brought that wee scrap of colour up and into focus.

It was that dratted kid again. Surely he'd seen all there was to see in them sheds. What was the little shit doin' here? All an old man wanted was a bit of peace and privacy.

'Get outta there, you little bastard! Get outta me sheds before I come tan your measly little hide black an' blue!'

The scrap of colour didn't move, but stayed crouched down near the ground, drawing something in the dirt with his fingers.

The old man rocked forwards with the rifle and kept the kid in his sights until a flash of grey out to his right caught the attention of both man and dog. Boots took off running from the verandah, barking, eyes set on his quarry, a bobbing white tail.

'Stay behind. Stay behind!' the old man roared again. The dog halted.

'Get behind I say!' The dog took one last look then skulked back under the rickety verandah steps. Not happy.

The old man sat back into his chair. 'You're not destroying me afternoon's entertainment in one go. We'll have a bit of fun first.' He brought the rifle back to his eye, wishing he'd already put that rail up on the verandah.

The scrap had moved again, skirting around behind the decaying pig sheds. 'Comin' round to see what's set you off, I'll bet,' he muttered to the sulking dog.

He moved the gun, keeping his sight on the blue and red moving towards him. 'Whaddaya want? A fuckin' invitation ta piss off?' he yelled. The kid couldn't miss hearing that one. But the blue and red kept sliding towards him. Towards the old verandah. Darting behind any structure that was close.

Suddenly the wisp of grey fur popped back up from the grass and took off, tail bobbing. The dog moved fast, darting out from behind the steps. The kid came in low and hard from the opposite direction. The bunny sat up and assessed his diminishing options.

The gun boomed.

The bunny danced.

The scrap was more red than blue.

The gun report rolled around the valley, hitting trees and scrub, rumbling across the paddocks and hills until it was gone. Long gone.

Until it was nothing.

And the old man was falling. Down and down.

His last coherent thought: What the fuck've I done?

Chapter 12

Where was Billy? The kid should have been here helping him; instead he'd run off somewhere a couple of hours ago and Travis hadn't seen him since. He held the spirit level up against the corner post he was putting into the ground. It needed to be a bit more to the left. Shit. Would he never get the darn thing straight? He swiped at his brow with his arm. He was sweating enough from digging the hole, now he was soaked from trying to get the fence in line. He pulled his shirt from out of the waistband of his jeans and hauled it over his head. He flung it at the ute and missed. Bugger it! Where was that bloody kid?

He knew Billy wasn't at Tammy's 'cause he'd just seen her marching up and over the hill, ramrod straight, steaming along like an express train. Something obviously had her gander up again today.

Trav couldn't say when he'd learned to read people's body language so well. Maybe it came from a childhood trying to gauge the mood and temperament of his old man. Knowing when to dodge a blow, or a sideswipe of a hand. Or maybe it was all the time he'd spent on his own in the scrub, reading the trees, the tracks, the sign, the moods of animals and the bush itself.

It hadn't helped him read Katrina though. Trav's shoulders slumped. Right from the start he'd been attracted to her free spirit, the way she flitted like a beautiful butterfly to this and that, drawing people to her like a welcoming light on a dark wintry night. She'd been so different to him. What did they say? Opposites attract? That sure had been the case with him and his former wife. She'd brought out a part of his personality he hadn't known existed. Fostered a more lighthearted side that had helped him realise there was bright colour in the world, not just grey and white.

Funny how you could read people who didn't matter so much, but not the ones you loved. Could he have done something if he had known what was running through Kat's head? Oh, he could have tried, bent himself in all directions, prostrated himself even in an effort to make her stay when she realised that babies meant responsibility. But it wouldn't have worked. She would still have left. It just might have taken a little longer. More time for Billy to grow up and realise what was missing from his life when she finally did piss off.

Trav pushed at the big stringybark post. All this surmising was getting him nowhere. He'd hopefully have a load of cattle coming next week, that's if he got this bloody post and stay-set fixed up before the Lake Grace mountain cattle sales.

In reality, he could have put any new stock he bought up the back. He had five hundred acres after all, but he wanted to eat out the paddocks around the house first. Make the place a bit more firesafe. And he needed the weaners to keep things ticking over. Buying in and growing out beef cattle made his share of the funds that kept his mother in her nursing home. She was comfortable there and it also meant his wage was then free to support himself and Billy.

Belaren was formally his mother Diane's property. A place she and his father had tried to farm when Trav was little. They'd eked out a living but his old man had worked up the bush as a dog trapper to make ends meet. Then his dad had inherited his own family's property, north of Yunta. So they'd all upped and moved to South Australia, putting Belaren in the hands of a caretaker. All he could remember of that time was his mother crying, forever crying, as she moved from her beloved mountains of blue and grey bush to an outback flatland of red dirt. From lush green improved pastures to silver bindi-eye saltbush. From purple chocolate orchids to pink onion weed. From a twenty-six inch average annual rainfall to just eight reluctant inches. From pure and fresh underground water thirty feet below the surface to seventy feet and saline.

He and his older brother, on the other hand, had loved it. An old square functional house built of local stone, outbuildings to match, devoid of all mod cons like mains power and a washing machine, plonked in the middle of eighty-two thousand acres. Sheer bliss for two bush boys and, in appreciation, they went feral, fleeing at the slightest excuse from their School of the Air lessons.

And his father? Well, after the euphoria of being back where he belonged wore off, he slowly drank himself into a stupor. Wasn't much else to do, except make sure the livestock had enough water and feed, which the two boys did for him, and then muster a couple of times a year. Oh, and slaughter the odd sheep. He could still picture the old man on one particular occasion, bottle in one hand, knife in the other, a wether hung from the back of the ute, blood pouring from a slit throat. He and his brother had thought it hilarious, watching their father trying to drunkenly butcher the carcass. His mother, silently observing from the desolate and bare verandah, had just turned and walked back inside.

His old man wasn't interested in newfangled ways of farming, of improving the land and its capacity to run stock. He wasn't interested in anything beyond the bottom of the bottle. And his mother had worn the whole job like a martyr, until he, Travis, was twelve. Danny, his brother, six years older, had finished with school early and was bumming around the station, trying to keep the place ticking over and showing a liking for alcohol too.

Then his mother walked. Towing Travis along, she piled luggage into the old Holden Kingswood and drove out the front gate. Before leaving she'd given Danny an ultimatum: stay or go, his choice. He chose to remain with their father.

Diane never returned to a mangy life of marital abuse. She'd moved to Burra, rented a house and put Trav into school. Worked her butt off to provide a living for the two of them. And later on she'd taken in Billy for him . . .

Thank goodness he'd finally been able to bring her back to where she belonged, the place she had always called home. The sanctity of Lake Grace.

He lined up the level against the side of the post again. The bubble centred dead true to the middle. Gotcha, ya bastard. Trav smiled in grim satisfaction. Now for the stay-set.

He was just straining up some wires when a small pair of hands appeared out of thin air to pass him a pair of pliers.

'Thought you might need some help,' said a female voice.

He was so shocked he didn't even say thanks, struck dumb to see her standing there, all liquid brown eyes, looking so fragile and small but holding the pliers with a hand that was tanned, muscled and used to work.

Tamara McCauley used the pliers to pull the wire he'd been straining through and tie it off. 'Next one?' she asked, her head quirked to one side.

'Umm . . . yeah. Right.' He mentally kicked himself up the bum. Move it, Hunter. Stop acting like a gawky teenager. She's a woman. The lower half of his body responded, I'm well aware of that! It was that goddamned voice. It was low and sweet, and then husky when you least expected it. Seductive and inviting. He could listen to it forever.

'How about I run the wire and you can strain and tie it off?'

Yes, that sounded good. Get her away and stop him making a fool of himself.

'No worries.' His voice sounded false and he knew his half-grin probably wasn't much better. She walked off down the slope out of his personal space, which Trav was well aware was a great deal bigger than most people's – he spent so much time alone.

She ran the wire, reeling it off the wire spinner as she went, making his job one hell of a lot easier. He should just thank his lucky stars she came along when she did. Forget that she was a female who made his long dormant male bits perk up. Just get on with the job at hand.

But he couldn't stop his eyes following her, checking out the neat butt that gently swayed from side to side as it went.

'Pull yourself together,' he muttered.

'You say something?' she called.

'No, umm, yes. Just wondering if you've got better things to be doing?'

'Well . . .' A shadow crossed her face but she chased it away with a determined smile. 'Can't say I have. You going to lounge around all day and yak or are we going to finish what you've started?'

'Right.' You've just been told, Hunter.

They worked silently and well together, like a neatly rehearsed concerto comprising wire, hands and pliers. It took a little while to get the fence looking like a real one that would do a decent job and Trav was surprised by how he could work with this woman without feeling he had to say anything at all.

Then she was beside him again and he was back having trouble keeping his mind on the job. Her perfume was wafting around his nostrils. He could hear the small gasps she made as she tied off a particularly tricky knot.

They were just finishing when the gun went off.

Bang!

'Bloody old Joe.'

'Bloody old Joe.'

Their voices competed. 'Jinx,' said Tammy automatically. She grinned up at him and then slightly ducked her head.

Trav got the feeling that grin was in spite of herself. She lapsed back into silence as she worked to tie off the final wire. 'There. Done. Nice working with you, Trav.' She handed over the pliers and went to walk away.

'Hang on,' he spluttered, annoyed for some reason by her abruptness. 'Can I offer you a drink? Or at least some thanks for helping me out here. You can't just walk off!'

'Can't I?' she said, swinging back around to face him.

'No, you can't.' He wondered why he was now being so short with *her*. 'But then again, I suppose you can. It's your life.' He reached a hand up in agitation to ruffle his buzz cut. And caught her checking out his belly, his chest, his body.

Aha. So calm and collected on the surface. But what was underneath that smooth exterior? Perversely, he had a mind to find out. 'Look. Let me start over.' His brain started screaming a siren-like warning: She's *married*, you *bloody idiot*!

Then again maybe that was actually a *real* siren he was hearing.

An ambulance siren. Coming up *their* road.

Both Trav and Tammy swung and took in the white van with its flashing blue and red lights belting along Hope's Road. It flew past the gateway of Montmorency Downs, still coming towards McCauley's Hill, barely buttoning off the throttle as it swung right at the T intersection, at the base of the mountain. There was one property down the end of that road. And unless there'd been a car accident on the dozy little lane lying peacefully in the afternoon sun, it was the only place the ambo could be headed to.

Old Joe's.

Chapter 13

'Jump in the ute!' Trav took off at a run, Tammy hard on his heels. He had the LandCruiser in reverse and was already backing up as she made it to the passenger-side door. She swung aboard and he floored the accelerator. 'We'll take the shortcut across the paddocks,' he yelled. Swinging wide around the new corner post he hit the top of the driveway sideways and Tammy couldn't help but wonder if *they* were the ones who were going to need the ambulance.

'Settle, Trav,' she said, instinctively reaching out to place her hand on the big one which was working the gearstick. He pulled away like she'd jabbed him with a needle. The ute, in mid gearshift, clunked into neutral, sending the vehicle running full pelt down the hill.

'*Travis!*' yelled Tammy as she flung herself forwards and rammed the gearstick into third. The engine speed kicked in, rapidly slowing the vehicle down. The motor roared its disapproval as both Tammy and Trav were thrown against their seatbelts. The motor was screaming its injectors out. Trav jabbed the clutch and moved up a gear while flexing the fingers of his left hand.

Tammy couldn't help herself. 'For land's sake, I don't bite. Crikey, you could have killed us!'

Trav threw her a look which was somewhere between agitation and fury. And here she was thinking she was doing the neighbourly thing. She'd spotted him trying to push that damned post into position and eye up the fence-line all by himself. Realised she could pound out her frustration and anger over Shon by walking towards Lake Grace, or use all that negative energy on something productive. Plus, if the truth be known, she just didn't want to be by herself. She was sick of spending so much time alone.

Enter Travis Hunter and his blasted fence. So she'd offered to help. What an idiot. Although, and the thought was grudging, the eye-candy factor hadn't been a bad side benefit. All those muscles, pecs and decs. Sheesh! Cords of them travelling down a tanned chest and disappearing into a pair of jeans that screamed *everything in here is male*! The sheer animal attractiveness of the man was breathtaking.

Shame his demeanour didn't match.

He could do his own bloody fencing next time. She folded her arms and willed herself to stay calm. As the ute flew across the rough shortcut towards Joe's place she wondered what the hell the old man had done.

⚜

The vision that greeted them wasn't good.

Just below his verandah, the old man was face down in

the dirt. Totally still. Wild, grey-white hair lay tangled over his head like a dish mop that had seen better days. A leg was cocked at a crazy angle. His arms were spread wide to embrace the earth he was kissing.

Perfectly placed across Joe, a child lay prostrate. A boy with a shock of red hair.

And the blood was everywhere. Spilling from the bodies to pool like beads of water refusing to soak into sodic soil. Mean soil which didn't encourage life meeting unforgiving human blood. The red claret was terrifying in its quantity. Macabre in its presence. Sinister in its intent.

'*Billy!*' Hunter yelled as he flung himself from the ute, running towards the figures on the ground.

'*Billy! Joe!*' Tammy's voice caught in her throat. Oh. My. *God*. What had the old man done? Who had he shot? Billy? Himself? It was a bloodbath. She ran towards them.

The ambulance siren screamed, coming up from behind.

Two dogs danced around the bodies. Confused, they darted forwards then back, barking and yelping. The place was bedlam.

Except for the two silent bodies.

Just lying there.

Hunter came to a halt, sliding the last few metres across the ground on his knees.

'Billy!'

Suddenly the boy's head lifted. 'Dad?'

'Bloody hell! Are you all right?' Trav could feel his heart pounding so loudly he felt like it was about to explode from his chest.

'Yeah, I think so.' The boy started to move, a little dazed, slightly wobbly. First one arm, then the other. His earnest face propped to the side, looking up at his father.

'Are you hit?'

'Shot, do ya mean? Nah, it's the rabbit. I've got it here in me hand. Mr McCauley's not good though. I can't hear his heart.'

'Mate, you won't hear it properly in his back. Can you move? Can you get off him?'

'Yeah, I was just trying to see if he was dead. Thought if I laid on him I might hear what was going on inside. But I think he's alive. He was moving his hands a bit before and groaning.'

A noise came from the direction of the dish mop. Hunter could hear it now the ambulance had turned off its siren. He leaned down to catch what the old man was saying.

'Get the little bugger off-a-me,' mumbled Joe. 'Can't bloody breathe!'

Hunter pulled his son off the old bloke's back real quick, the dead animal which had been squashed between the two bodies coming away with them. Blood, guts and fur were everywhere. All over the boy. All over Joe. But that wasn't what was holding Travis's attention. There was more blood here than could just be attributed to the damned rabbit.

Joe tried to roll over. Fell back face down. 'I can't,' the old man mumbled. 'Hurts.'

'Just stay there, Joe. The ambos will be here in a sec.'

'What's he done?' Tammy was leaning over Trav's shoulder. 'Are you all right, Billy? Crikey, you had me scared! Crap, that's a huge cut on the old bloke's head. Can you hear me, Joe?'

Joe could hear her all right. Those dulcet tones he'd never thought would drift around his ears again. So beautifully pitched, with the lilt of huskiness curling at the end of the sentence. 'Mae?'

'Good Lord, he thinks I'm my grandmother.' The voice sounded surprised.

Joe couldn't work out why. It *was* Mae, wasn't it?

'Tammy, move over. The ambo's here. He's wanting to get through to Joe.' That was Travis Hunter. Funny, in the few times he'd spoken to the bloke, he'd never heard him sound so agitated and stressed. The man was usually like a refrigerator. Solid and cool.

'Sorry. Here let me help you with that case. Trav, do you want to go check on Billy? The other paramedic's over there. I'll stay here and answer this one's questions.'

There she was again, Mae. No. The man called her Tammy. Who the fuck was Tammy?

'And you are?' the ambulance officer asked.

'I'm – well, I'm actually his niece, but he doesn't know me. He doesn't like people. Especially family.'

Aha, so that's who she was. Of course! Tammy from *that* place. How the hell did she get up on top of *his* hill? The bloody cheek of her! Mae . . . no . . . *Tammy* was talking some more to someone with a calm, male voice. Then there were cool hands on the back of his head, over his body, thoroughly checking here, there and everywhere.

'We're just going to examine you a bit more before we turn you over, Mr . . . ?'

'McCauley. Joe McCauley.' Her again. So Mae remembered him, even after all these years? Damn it, it wasn't Mae. Tammy. It was *Tammy*.

'Is he going to the hospital at Narree? Geez, he's not going to like that. Is he going to be okay?'

Of course I'm bloody well okay, thought Joe. Just a little bump on my head. Can't move me left leg either, but I'm not telling you lot that. I'm fine. You can just sit me up and then bugger off, all of you.

'Yes, I suppose I can get some clothes and stuff sorted for him. As I said he's practically a hermit. Will he be there a while?

What? Leave home? Go to *town*? No way. Who did this Tammy woman think she was? Be buggered if she was just going to step in and take over! He tried to roll onto his back but firm male hands made sure he stayed put.

'No, Mr McCauley, not just yet. We need to make sure we *can* turn you over first. Just give us a few minutes more, okay?'

Fuck it, thought Joe. Bloody rocking chair. He hadn't meant to go that far forwards but he'd been so excited seeing it was a hare not a rabbit and the kid had popped up at the same time he'd squeezed the trigger, and he'd been trying to miss the boy, hit the hare . . . and then he'd been so damned wobbly lately. He'd really fucked it up. What in the devil's name had he just done?

Tammy cast a worried look across at Trav and Billy and was relieved to see the boy appeared none the worse for wear. A little wide-eyed at the whole drama and covered in all sorts of muck, but that was all. He was sitting on the ground with a hand on an old border collie, who was lolling ecstatically at his feet, tongue hanging out, mooching and begging for a scratch.

Hunter was crouched in the dirt beside his son. Not touching him, just watching the boy. Tammy found that kind of sad. Surely he'd want to cuddle him – especially after all this? Heck, she'd thought Billy was dead the way he was lying over old Joe. Thought the old man had somehow done both himself and the boy in.

She turned back to her uncle. Thanks to the ambos he was now loaded onto a stretcher, a pad strapped around his forehead to staunch the bleeding of a nasty cut. There seemed to be no other obvious injuries apart from the fact he was having trouble with his left leg. The taller of the paramedics muttered about a possible broken hip, but they couldn't be sure without an X-ray. They'd given him a green whistle-like thing to suck on, which apparently contained a painkiller, but that hadn't seemed to make much difference.

'If you think I'm gettin' in that bloody ambulance you're gunna be sorely disappointed!'

'Now, now, Mr McCauley. You need to go to the hospital to be checked over.'

'I'm not goin' to some bloody hospital to be poked and prodded by the likes of you. Get me offa this thing right now!'

'Sorry, Mr McCauley, no can do. You need help and you need it now.'

'Don't you Mr McCauley me, you young whippersnapper. If you think you're so bloody clever just fix me up and leave me here then. I've got me dogs for company, I'll be right as rain.'

The old man suddenly gasped as the stretcher hit a boulder. He grabbed at his green whistle and sucked back on the painkiller like his life depended on it.

'Sorry about that, Mr McCauley. That's probably why you cut your head. Those rocks are big and sharp. Now, we just need to adjust this bandage on your head again. It's not quite right.'

Tammy moved up behind the paramedic to peer over his shoulder. The bandage wasn't holding the blood and the wound was weeping outside of the gauze. Nothing like a head wound to turn everything claret.

'*You*! What the bloody hell are *you* still doing here?' said Joe as he spotted her looking down at him. 'I don't need you up on my hill. Jigger off back down to those irrigated flats where you belong. Get the hell off my farm, you –' The old man gasped something and grabbed again for his medicinal whistle.

... land-grabbing little fucker. In her head Tammy finished the sentence with him; she was thrown back to the age of six. She could almost taste the Tabasco sauce on her tongue. She quickly stepped away from the stretcher. The paramedics were giving her sympathetic looks and she could feel the colour starting to steal up her neck. How embarrassing and unfair to be thought of like that.

She had all the land she could deal with right now. She didn't want anything off this horrible old man, except maybe acknowledgement he was family. But the way he was carrying on, why the hell would she want that?

A hand clamped down hard on her shoulder. Travis. 'You all right? I'm sure he doesn't mean it.' His voice was low, only for her ears. 'He's a bit out of it. Pain, pethidine – probably some shock.'

She shifted a little under his warm touch. It felt nice. Quiet and firm.

'Yes. I'm fine.' Was she? Really?

'I told you, Mrs Murphy. Get the fuck away from me.' Old Joe was trying to sit up, impeded by the straps on the stretcher. 'I know your type. Always want, want, want and you only take the best of what's given. So why do you want a gravelly, godforsaken piece of ground like McCauley's Hill? You just piss on off outta here. Get back to that lah-di-dah farm of yours and don't come back. I don't need nobody but this here green stick. It's good shit.'

Suddenly the old man's eyes rolled back in his head and he was gone. Out for the count.

The tall ambo held up a needle and sighed. 'Didn't want to do that, but by God he's a stubborn old bugger.'

Trav laughed quietly and with one last pat of Tammy's shoulder, his warm hand was gone, leaving a searing sense of loss.

'You okay, miss? I'm the new ambo from Lake Grace, by the way. Dean Gibson.' The paramedic stuck out his hand then realised he was still holding the injection he'd used on Joe. 'Argh, sorry.' He dropped the needle into the disposal box in the back of the ambulance then tried again. 'Dean Gibson. And you are?'

'Tammy McCauley. And this here's Travis Hunter and his son Billy.' Tammy pointed across to the child.

'Nice to meet you. I thought the old bloke said your name was Murphy.'

'My married name is Murphy.'

'Oh! So you're married.' Dean looked pointedly at her naked ring finger, his disappointment apparent though he'd tried to hide it. She felt . . . what? Flattered? Vindicated that a red-blooded male thought she was attractive while the man she'd thought loved her called her a frigid bitch?

Maybe try horrified. Was this now what she'd have to deal with? The unwelcome advances of men who didn't interest her in the slightest? Oh dear. And he really did look like a nice man. A nice *ordinary* man, who did absolutely nothing for her.

Travis stepped up to grab Dean around the shoulders and push him back towards the ambulance. 'Good to meet you, Dean. You and your mate there'd better get the old bloke loaded and to the hospital, don't you think?'

'Yes, right. Best be off.' Dean threw another look at Tammy as Travis propelled him on his way.

Tammy moved to where Billy sat in the dirt, still playing with the dog. The border collie was lying on his back, legs spread wide, paws drooping like unworn socks. His tongue was lolling this way and that in ecstasy as Billy rubbed along his belly.

If only her life could be as simple as a dog's.

Chapter 14

Tammy stood in front of the old miner's shack, took a deep breath and mounted the front steps. She grabbed the handle of the wooden screen door that sheltered the inside of the house from prying eyes and slowly drew it open, hesitant to enter a space that was not her own.

She walked inside slowly, Billy following close behind. The screen door sprang shut with a whack and Tammy jumped. The boy silently took her hand as though he too was unsure of himself. She took another step. If she and Billy didn't do this, what was Joe going to have with him at the hospital? She should just get on with it.

The hallway was floored with hardwood boards; an old Axminster carpet runner lay on top in a vain attempt to hide the wear on the fading varnish. Turning to the left, she opened a door and took in the 'best room' – the lounge or parlour of the old house. The faded flowery wallpaper was peeling.

Unfamiliar ancestors glared from ornate photo frames. Overstuffed club chairs were parked formally at the fireplace and a tattered chaise longue sat with decayed elegance in the corner. There was an antique auto-trolley parked in the middle of the far wall, laden with a blackened silver tea service. The handworked doily spilling over the edges was spotted with brown rustlike stains. The air smelled of age and damp. She shuddered. Only dust, ghosts and memories inhabited this room.

Tammy pulled away, nearly stepping on Billy, who was right on her heels. The boy hurriedly moved back and she quietly closed the door. She swung around and saw the hall table and the phone Billy had used to ring 000. Thank heavens they taught that sort of thing at school these days.

Beyond the table was another door, slightly ajar. She pushed it back to reveal a bedroom with an old featherbed, black iron bedsteads standing sentinel at the head and foot. The bed was covered with a beautifully handworked bedspread. Once cream, the bedspread was now riddled with grubby dirt and possum poo, which had fallen through the parting tongue-in-groove ceiling boards. Except for the shadow of an old cedar chest of drawers, the room was bare. No one – at least of mortal soul – inhabited this space either.

Where the hell did old Joe sleep?

Within four strides she was back in the hallway and into the next set of rooms. She peeked shyly around the door. An antique cream wooden and flywire-encased cot, which looked for all the world like a huge meat safe, sat adrift in the centre of the small space. Forgotten, unloved, untouched. A cot full of dreams that never came true.

Tammy couldn't help but wonder what the story was. Did her Aunty Nellie get pregnant but lose the baby? Why didn't they have kids? They obviously wanted them, judging by the contents of this room. She couldn't suppress another shudder. The whole house reeked of loneliness and she despaired for the old man who was so dead against leaving this place in the back of an ambulance.

'Geez, it's not much chop, is it, Tammy?'

She started. She'd forgotten Billy was with her. He was staring all around him, eyes wide, like he was trying to work something out.

'No, mate, it's not.' So he felt it too. The despair, the loss of all hope and love.

She looked around the small kitchen. A functional table sat against the far wall. A single wooden ladder-back chair was parked at the end. And still no sign of where Joe slept.

They moved on, down a small step and into the closed in back verandah. To the left a loo, which Tammy was glad to see, as she'd feared the old man was still relying on an outside toilet. To the right was a shower and ancient twin-tub washing machine. In front of them under some louvre windows was a camp stretcher, swag laid out on top. An old-fashioned eiderdown was perched at the end of the swag. *Finally* they had found where the old man slept. And it was pitiful.

A small gentlemen's wardrobe was standing with its doors slightly ajar. Billy walked over. Inside, neatly folded, were some work clothes, a couple of pairs of faded plain pyjamas, rolled black socks and jocks and singlets. All white.

Packing was going to be easy.

'Right, Billy, we need a bag. Can you have a look around and see if you can find anything suitable? I'll pack up his clothes.'

Tammy rolled her shoulders and moved towards the wardrobe, laying bits and pieces out on the eiderdown. Then she looked down at their threadbare state in dismay. There was no way she could send the pyjamas to the hospital. Brought up by a woman who kept a couple of new nighties up in the cupboard 'in case I have to go to hospital', she just couldn't send these with her uncle, even if he didn't want to admit they were related. She'd have to stop in town and buy him some new ones.

She put the PJs back in the cupboard. Hunting around under the bed she found some old slippers which would do the job. She moved into the little room that held the shower, collected some toiletries from under the vanity basin and put them on the bed too.

'Find anything, Billy?'

'What?' The boy appeared in the doorway.

'That would be "pardon me". Did you find anything?'

'Nah. Nothing I can see except these shopping bags. Will they do?' Billy held up a bundle of white plastic.

Good Lord. Surely they could do better than that. He'd be at the hospital looking like an old hobo. Her mind whispered, But that's what he really is, Tim Tam!

Bugger it. She'd buy him a cheap overnight bag too.

'We'll load the stuff into those bags for the minute, Billy, and buy him something nicer when we get to town. I won't have anything at home; Shon's probably used it.'

Billy looked at her.

Tammy shrugged. 'He's left me.' Not knowing why she felt so comfortable saying this to an ten-year-old boy yet was unable to ring her best friend Lucy and tell her about it.

Billy nodded, just the once, and then got to back to work. Ah. That was why. Lucy would have wanted to know the ins and outs of everything; and Tammy wasn't ready for that. She needed to come to terms with the fact that her marriage was finally over.

'I'll carry these bags out to the truck.' Billy's quiet voice broke into her thoughts. He'd loaded the pitiful pile of clothes into a couple of bags. 'Dad's out there waiting. He'll be wondering what we're doing.'

'Right. No worries. I'll just –' Tammy waved her hands around, not really knowing what it was she was going to do, but recognising she needed a minute to herself. She was standing in her uncle's house and she felt like an alien. Unwanted, unneeded, an intrusive presence in the private world of Joe McCauley.

She moved to close the cupboard doors and walk away from the camp bed, but spotted something which made her halt in her steps. A photo frame, propped up by the bed, on a rickety table beside an old-fashioned alarm clock with bells. It held a photograph of Joe's wife, Nellie. Tammy reached to pick up the cheap frame. Mission brown plastic bordered a photo of a woman who was smiling into the camera. Wearing a dark green cotton dress, she was broad across the shoulders and had a large, squarish-looking bust. A straw hat shaded the woman's eyes but Tammy could see deep creases around her temples, and her smile was a mile wide. Such a lovely, comforting looking woman.

If only she could have known her.

If only Nellie could have made it all better for both of them. Her husband and her great-niece. 'Tammy . . . ?' Hunter's voice came echoing down the hall.

'Coming!' She hesitated a moment, glancing again at her aunt, before she tucked the photo frame under her arm. The alarm clock followed. The old bloke might want a few familiar things around him. She took one last look at the camp stretcher he used for a bed, shook her head and moved back through the house. She met Hunter just as he was removing his boots to come in the door.

'Oh, there you are,' he said, leaning down and pulling his boots back on. 'We'd better be going. Do you want me to drop you at your place to pick up your ute?'

'Umm . . . not sure.' She wondered if Shon was gone. 'I'll ponder that for a minute and let you know.'

Travis gave her a slightly bemused look. Tammy could just about hear him thinking: Women!

He turned to yell at his son. 'Billy! Grab those dogs and tie them up, will you?' He swung back to Tammy. 'I'll come over and feed them while Joe's away.'

'I'm sure he'd appreciate that. He wouldn't want me to do it.'

'Want to tell me about that?' Trav raised one eyebrow, and slung her half a smile.

Tammy felt her tummy curl up into little knots, and it wasn't all due to the family feud. A half-smile that made a man look so delicious should be deemed illegal.

She got her thoughts back on track. 'He and my grandfather never got on. Something to do with my grandmother. I was never told, just something I heard once made me think perhaps both brothers were in love with her.'

She remembered a conversation one day in town. It was a Friday afternoon and Mae had just walked out of the hairdressers to meet her teenage granddaughter in the street. Mae looked beautiful, hair all tinted, falling in waves. Nellie was walking in, and she looked awful. Dowdy, hair in dire need of a perm, a cut, anything to give her a bit of style. Or so Tammy's grandmother had said in the car as they were travelling home. 'I can't understand what Joe saw in that woman.' There was a churlish note to her voice, like she was miffed, which set

Tammy to wondering: Why would her grandmother care who Joe married? Her grandmother had gone on, 'Tamara, always remember that land means *everything*. Money, power, security. Love doesn't necessarily make for a comfortable life.'

Trav's voice came crashing through her memories. 'Is that all?' he asked. 'I overheard Joe calling you a land-grabber.'

Tammy tried a smile to prove she hadn't been hurt by the old man's words. She could feel the ends of her mouth turn up, but inside she was cold, remembering her earlier argument with Shon. Bloody land. It made you but it could also break you.

'Montmorency Downs once included McCauley's Hill. When my great-grandparents died, they left the arable land to my grandfather and the marginal hill country to Joe. At the time Joe was working away, falling trees up the bush. That was his job and he was only home on the weekends. My grandfather, on the other hand, had leased the low country off his parents when they retired and was working it, all day, every day, milking cows. It seemed fair the way my grandparents explained it when I wanted to know why Joe hated us. Now, well, now I'm not so sure.' She remembered the state of the house she'd just been in, and compared it with the more stately and opulent homestead down at the bottom of the hill. The antiques, a legacy of five generations, crowding the rooms at Montmorency; the single wooden ladder-back chair in the kitchen behind her.

'Dogs are done, Dad.' Billy arrived at their side.

'Righto, boy. Let's move then.'

Tammy glanced one last time at the house. The rocking chair, the culprit of all the commotion, lay discarded on its side. The rifle was nowhere to be seen.

'Trav? The rifle?'

'Locked it up in his gun cabinet. Found one in the shed.'

'Right, thanks.' Although Tammy wasn't sure *why* she was thanking him. It wasn't like she had the right to thank anyone on Joe's behalf. She jumped into the ute beside Billy as Trav piled into the driver's seat and took off.

As they drove down the road to Tammy's, Trav lifted his eyebrow. 'Decision time, Ms McCauley. What's it to be? Our company or your own?'

Tammy took a look down the drive. Shon's twin-cab was nowhere to be seen. Good. But at the moment, her own company sucked.

'I'll ride shotgun with you boys, if you don't mind.'

A clap from Billy beside her sealed the deal.

And Trav turned to her and half smiled.

Tammy amended her thoughts on that look being deemed illegal. By the feel of her tummy, outlawed was more like it.

Chapter 15

'What's wrong with plastic bags?' Trav asked, perplexed, as he watched Billy and Tammy load Joe's things into a new overnight bag. They'd stopped off at Drapers Emporium on their way and were now standing in the hospital car park.

'*Dad*! You can't send him to hospital with plastic bags. He'll look all different from the others.'

'The others? What others?'

'The other patients.' Billy stopped short of rolling his eyes. Trav was about to tick him off for his attitude, when he could have sworn he saw Tammy rolling her eyes as well.

'Right. The others. I get it.' Of course he did. But when had he, Travis Hunter, ever worried what anyone else thought of him? Since Kat left you with a two-and-half-year-old son to raise, you hard-arsed bushman.

'Let's go find out what old Joe's done to himself,' said Tammy as she zipped up the bag. 'I reckon he'll still be in casualty. The

Narree ED has never been known for its ability to fast track its patients.'

Travis moved to take the bag from Tammy, but stopped when she threw him another killer look. She took off across the car park.

He stuck his hands in his pockets instead and strode towards the front entrance after his son. Where was this desire to help a woman he didn't even know coming from? He'd never had it before. Well, not since Kat left.

'Mr Hunter? Mr Hunter! Beatrice Parker's my name, and tracking you down is my game.'

He swung around and met clear space and fresh air.

'Down here, Mr Hunter, down here.'

He shifted his line of sight south a couple of feet and was rewarded by two twinkling blackcurrant eyes staring up at him.

'What are you doing here?' asked Beatrice. 'Not hurt, are you? What about your boy? He all right?'

An Uzi couldn't have spat questions faster. 'Nope. Just visiting.'

'Well, I'm here to cheer. You look like you need a bit of jollying along. Was that Tammy McCauley who went in just in front of you? There's a likely sort of nancy to fancy.'

'She's married, Mrs Parker.'

'Not for long. I just met Mrs Sellers. She sells craft on a stall here at the hospital for the church, and she's been texting . . . or was it sex-ting?' The old woman put a finger under her chin in studied thought. 'All these odd words they're putting in the dictionary these days, I don't know. How's a woman supposed to keep up with it all, I ask you?' The blackcurrant eyes widened to the size of sultanas.

'Anyway, she's been chatting to her husband Rob on one of

those fancy iPhone thingies. I really need to get one of those. Did you know you can play Scrabble on them? Now where was I? Oh yes, Rob. Anyway, he's just been buying a sausage roll at the corner store, although I think the roadhouse makes them better . . .'

Trav was still back at sex-ting. What the hell? '. . . and he was talking to the alcohol deliveryman, from the pub? And *he* said, Shon Murphy's just moved in with Joanne at the Lake Grace Hotel.'

'Is that so?' He'd moved from Scrabble to Shon Murphy.

'Yes, and it's all happened today! Although that man has been dangling the angles all over the place, just like *those* Murphys do, so it doesn't surprise me he's finally hustled for a hussy. So tell me, what's Tammy doing here?'

'Her uncle,' he said, distracted. The bastard was gone?

'*Joe?*' Mrs Parker's jaw dropped. Her mouth started flapping but no sound came out. The sight was enough to make Trav refocus.

'Yes. Joe,' he said as he went to walk away; the damned woman slipped around in front of him and blocked him.

'Those families haven't talked in years. In fact, I don't think Joe's *ever* talked to the girl. What's happened?'

'Don't rightly know, Mrs Parker, but if you'll excuse me, I'd better be –'

'Don't you go getting all tetchy now, son. I'm just worried for Tammy. Donald once told me the whole story, but I hoped Joe might have been able to put it aside, make up with the girl after she lost her family.'

Story? What story? Trav stopped then tried his half-smile. It seemed to work on Tammy, maybe it would work here too. 'What story was that, Mrs Parker?'

He watched as the little blackcurrants went slightly misty, and Beatrice's head dipped, like a confidence was about to be shared. 'We-ell,' drawled the woman as she paused for a deep breath. 'Joe used to work for my father up the bush. It was when Joe was a young fella and he started up there in a logging coupe, cutting down trees by hand with a crosscut saw. He was wanting to earn money to buy some woman an engagement ring. But while Joe was up the scrub, his brother met the same woman. Mae was her name. She married him.' An arthritic hand came up to dab at something which looked suspiciously like a tear. 'Joe was devastated. He never went back to the farm. Never spoke to his brother again that I know of. Didn't even go to their funeral when they were killed in that car accident.'

So Joe had been found wanting too. By Tammy's grandmother. Mae had moved on to another bloke. Bloody women. It only confirmed his opinion once again. Love them and they leave. Love them and you'll get hurt, big time.

'It was a train, you see, that killed Tom and Mae. A level crossing without lights or boom gates, just on the other side of Lake Grace. Bang, and they were both gone, leaving their granddaughter on her own. Oh, she was in her late twenties by then but even so . . .' Beatrice paused, seeming to run out of words.

Trav waited, hoping for more information. He wanted to know what had happened to Tammy's actual parents.

As if she had read his mind, Beatrice sighed, 'And then there was the poor girl's *mother* . . .'

'Dad? Tammy needs you.' It was Billy speaking softly while pulling on his arm.

'What?'

'Tammy. She needs you, c'mon.' His son was dragging him in the direction of Casualty, leaving Mrs Parker staring after them.

'Bye, Travis,' called Beatrice. 'Happy hunting!' As he glanced at her, he could have sworn the old woman winked. It was that flutter of her right eye again. Maybe it was a tic. Maybe it wasn't. Whatever it was, it didn't really matter because up ahead all he could hear was Joe McCauley's voice:

'*Fuck off*! Just get me out of here!'

Tammy was standing beside the curtain to the cubicle, her back to the heavy plastic doors that led to the rest of the hospital. Joe was sitting up on a trolley bed facing her, a hospital gown round his middle baring a grey-haired and wrinkly chest. He was yelling his head off.

'I'm not being admitted into no fuckin' hospital. You just put me back in that ambulance and take me home!'

'But Mr McCauley, you have a broken hip.' This was from a registrar clutching X-ray films, standing a safe distance from the bed. 'And you need an operation to give you the best chance of recovery.'

'I don't give a shit what you think. There's nothing wrong with me. I've just got a few bruises.'

'Mr McCauley,' said a nurse, who stepped out from behind the registrar. She was employing her very best 'difficult patient' voice. 'The break is high up in the hip socket. We need to operate to set it in the right place, so you can walk properly again. The orthopedic surgeon told you that.'

'You're not getting your mitts on my body, you damned hussy! There's nothing wrong with me. Take me back to my –' Joe stopped when he spotted Hunter.

Tammy, the registrar and nurse all turned to see what had caught his attention.

'Trav, maybe you can make Joe see some sense?' Tammy interjected. She had her arms folded across her chest.

'Tell them, Hunter. Tell them I'm fine,' said Joe, glimpsing a chance of redemption. 'See, he's a bushman, he understands. You can't shut me up in this place. All these walls and people and sterile things and no fresh air.' His voice went from full throttle to a pitiful whine. 'You just *can't*.'

Trav shifted from one foot to the other. Why was he the one they were all looking at for the answers? He felt like a wild dog that'd just been cornered. How the hell had he got himself into this situation?

He could relate to what the old man was saying, sure he could, but looking at the registrar's face was enough to tell him the break wasn't good. How to get that through to old Joe though? There was a chance to fix things and if the old bloke wanted to remain independent, well . . .

Travis sighed. A man had to do what a man had to do.

'Joe.' Trav drawled it out slow but steady, all the time keeping his eyes on the old bloke's face. They conducted a silent conversation.

Be a man, McCauley. Stand up and be a man.
I'm old and I'm fuckin' scared.
It'll be right. We'll take care of you.
I don't need taking care of!
You do.
Don't want to have to rely on anyone.
Stiff shit. You're going to have to.

It took a few moments but then, finally, movement. Old Joe's nod was almost imperceptible and Trav was sure he was the only one who caught it. He looked down at his son. Billy was standing by his side, a small smile on his face. He'd got the message too.

Not so the nurse. 'Mr McCauley, you must have this operation –'

'All right!' snapped Joe, still looking at Hunter.

'What?' The nurse was taken aback. 'What did you say?'

'I said all right. What, are you deaf as well as dumb?'

'Uncle Joe.' Tammy's voice held a warning.

'Don't you Uncle Joe me, you –'

'I know, I know, you fucking land-grabber,' said Tammy, arms still folded. 'You've made that perfectly clear. And I'm not so keen on you either. Be as rude as you like to me, but these people here' – she swung her arm out to encompass the medical staff – 'they're here to *help* you. The least you can do is be polite.'

The tense silence that followed was broken by a doctor entering the cubicle. Trav assumed he was the orthopaedic surgeon. Long, thin, bare fingers stroked a clipboard as he contemplated his notes. 'I've spoken to theatre,' he said, unaware of the atmosphere around him though he could have cut it with one of his scalpels. 'We can go in as soon as the operating suite is free.' He looked bored – and a little arrogant too. 'Now, Mr . . . ?'

'McCauley. It's Mr Joe McCauley,' said the nurse, simpering at the new arrival. The registrar had muttered something and disappeared. Must have known he was out-gunned, thought Trav.

'Joe, we need to operate on your hip.' The man spoke slowly and deliberately, like he was addressing a child. 'You'll have to be in hospital a short while but then you should be right to head home to . . . ?'

'Lake Grace. McCauley's Hill, Lake Grace,' said the nurse. She really wanted to please.

'Do you live on your own, Joe?'

'Nup. I've got me two dogs and cattle.'

The doctor looked up. 'No one else? A wife? Partner? Friend?'

'Nup. Don't need nobody else. Just me dogs and cattle.'

'They're not likely to be able to look after you though, are they? While you're recuperating?'

'I don't know 'bout that. Boots and Digger'll do well enough.'

The doctor ignored Joe and spoke to the nurse. 'He'll have to go into the Lake Grace nursing home for some respite care after here. Can you organise that?' The man spoke like it was a rhetorical question. He smiled his smarmy grin and the nurse melted like a Mars Bar on a hot dashboard.

'Now you just wait a cotton-pickin' minute! I ain't goin' into no bloody nursing home! I'm going back to me hill,' said Joe, sitting up straighter, then quickly lying back down with an agonised look on his face. The old man was starting to shake so bad the bed was rattling. 'I'm goin' home! Tell them, Hunter. I'm going home!'

'Mr . . . ?'

'McCauley.' The nurse piped up again.

'Right. McCauley. Well, you won't be able to look after yourself for a while following your discharge from hospital. I'm sorry but it *will* have to be the nursing home.'

Joe looked terrified.

Trav felt something crawl up his leg. A hand tug on his shirt.

Billy.

'We'll look after him.'

Trav looked around. Who said that? Then he realised *he* had. Shit.

'Trav?' said Tammy. 'Are you sure?'

No, I'm not fucking sure, he thought as he opened his mouth to speak. He hadn't talked this much in months. 'He can go home to his hill. Billy and me – we'll look after him.'

The sheer relief on Joe's face was worth it.

'I'll help,' added Tammy, quickly turning back to the doctor.

Joe's face turned thunderous.

Trav frowned at the old man. You want the nursing home, bucko?

Joe had the grace to look discomfited.

'Great. That's sorted then,' said the surgeon. 'Scratch the nursing home. Some time in hospital and then home with these good people taking care of you.' He flicked a glance towards Trav, then looked Tammy up and down. Trav could see by his expression that the doctor liked what he saw.

Trav moved a step forwards, then wondered why.

'I'll be off to gown up for the operation,' the surgeon announced. 'I'll see you in theatre, Joe. Now, nurse, have you got a few spare minutes?'

The pair walked off without looking back, heads together, legs moving in perfect synchronicity. And Trav couldn't help but wonder if they'd be passing an empty broom cupboard on the way to the theatre.

Chapter 16

Joe leaned back into the pillows, wanting the crisp linen to swallow him whole, magically transporting him back to McCauley's Hill. He wanted to be sitting in his rocking chair on the verandah of his house, perusing his kingdom, judging the weather by the look of the mountains, wondering at the beautiful day.

How the hell did he get himself into this situation? All he'd done was try to shoot the damn rabbit which ended up being a bloody hare. If that bugger of a kid had of stayed out of the way he mightn't have jerked the gun to try and miss the boy and over-balanced the fucking rocking chair. If only he'd built that verandah rail, then he mightn't have toppled off the deck, clocked his damned noggin on the way down and landed in this whole friggin' great mess.

He sighed and tried to will his body to stop shaking. He felt exhausted. They'd stitched up his head – only a couple of loops and they'd given him a bit of local anaesthestic to numb the job. The pain in his hip was awful though. It wasn't so bad if he stayed still, but all those X-rays and the doctors prodding and poking at his hip had stirred it up. Now a bloody operation. He'd never been operated on in his *life*.

And the bastard surgeon had the gall to tell him he couldn't go home afterwards! Who the hell did he think he was? Just 'cause he'd been to uni longer than most people stuck at a job these days didn't mean he had the God-given right to tell Joe McCauley what to do.

'That was nice of Hunter,' said a female voice.

It was *her*. Maybe if he just kept his eyes shut and concentrated hard he could pretend she was her grandmother.

'He didn't have to do that, you know.'

No, Hunter didn't have to offer to help, to stop Joe's worst nightmare from happening – being locked up in some nursing home in town. But his neighbour understood. He was just like Joe. A loner, a bushman, a jilted lover, a boundary rider on the edges of life who'd just retreated into himself. It was comfortable there. At least on your own you knew who you were dealing with. There was no putting yourself out there to be used and abused. Only one difference, though. A big one. Hunter had a son.

What the hell? He was supposed to just be listening to her voice, not her words.

She's right; he didn't have to do that, Joey! And there was Nellie, as always turning up like she was his bloody conscience or something. Didn't the woman have better things to do up there in Heaven? He flicked his finger, unconsciously trying to push Nellie away.

The girl spoke again. 'It'll all be okay. We'll work it out.'

And it was funny, he believed her. This girl, who by rights could and *should* have been *his* granddaughter – a chit of thing with a useless runaway husband who couldn't keep his pecker in his pants according to the stock agent. Her and Hunter and that damnable kid. It just might work out. It had to. There was nothing else for it. He'd have to put up and shut up if he wanted to stay on his hill.

He opened one eye. Took a peek. Yep. She even looked like her grandmother.

※

Tammy sank down into the nearest chair. What a mess. At least Joe's bed had stopped rattling. The old bloke had been shaking so hard she'd thought the trolley was going to work its way out of the cubicle.

To be so scared. So alone. It was just dreadful.

She shuddered. She knew how he felt.

'I'm going to find some coffee,' said Trav. 'Caffeine's good in these situations. Want some?'

What type of situations? Seeing someone so terrified their bones were shaking in terror? Someone so obsessively defiant about being a hermit, forced to admit they might actually need some help?

'No, thanks. I'll grab some water.'

'Coffee is good.' He was persistent, she'd give him that.

'So is chocolate. I'll have a hot chocolate then, if you're offering.' She couldn't even pay for it. No wallet.

She watched as Trav walked off, Billy hurrying along at his side. The child was like a little puppy looking up at its owner, trying to please but not knowing how. She sighed. If only Travis would notice him.

She turned back to Joe. He'd closed his eyes. She supposed

that was one way to indicate he didn't wish to talk to anybody. Particularly her.

'That was nice of Hunter,' she ventured.

Silence from the bed.

'He didn't have to do that, you know.'

A flutter of a finger. Not much, but still – she was encouraged. 'It'll all be okay. We'll work it out.'

Joe opened one eye. Looked straight at her. Barely dipped his head. Shut the eye again.

That was all she was going to get. But, she guessed, something was better than nothing.

⁂

A nurse, a different one this time, hustled in, followed by a hospital porter. 'Time to go, Mr McCauley. We need to get you prepped for the operation.' They fussed around, pushing things, pulling things, getting the trolley bed ready to travel. When they were done, the sister smiled at Tammy. 'You'll need to go to the desk and check out how long this'll take. Maybe find the hospital Quiet Room or a coffee at the café? Mr McCauley, say goodbye to your . . . ?'

Tammy looked down at her Redback workboots. Studied the dried cow-shit patterns swirling across the well-worn leather. She didn't want to witness the nurse's pitying look when Joe let loose with a new string of profanities.

'Ahem . . .' said Joe, clearing his throat. 'Great-niece. She's my niece.'

Tammy's head shot up in surprise.

But Joe was already on his way out of the cubicle. The last thing Tammy saw of the old man was a hand, slightly lifted, index finger pointing to the ceiling, the classic country wave – gidday, goodbye, be seeing you soon. She was amazed. She'd expected it to be the middle finger.

'He's gone in?' Travis was back.

'What? Sorry, yes. We have to move out of here, though. They need the cubicle.'

Trav handed her a cardboard cup. The contents smelled divine. 'I stuck a bit of sugar in there too. Thought you might need it.'

The man surprised her at every turn. He might look like a wild man; a hard-arsed son-of-a-bitch from the back of beyond, but he sure knew how to turn it on when needed.

'Thanks. Very thoughtful.'

Trav seemed to wince at the last word. Okay, so he didn't want to be thoughtful. Or at least he didn't want *her* to think he was thoughtful.

'Hey, Tammy. Want some of my Kit-Kat?' said Billy, offering her a bar of chocolate.

'Thanks, mate, you're a legend.' At least his son had no problem with thoughtful. 'Just what I need today, a triple dose of sugar.' She took a sliver of the bar and sunk her teeth into it. Yum.

Her phone bleeped in her pocket. A text message. Damn. She hadn't turned it off as she came in.

It was Lucy.

'I'd better go and answer this.' She waved the phone around. Trav had moved to pick up Joe's new bag. The old man hadn't even realised it was his. Just as well. Another subject to cop verbal abuse over. Well, she was used to that, thanks to Shon.

'We'll find out where to wait,' said Trav. 'Meet you in the

foyer.' He walked towards the big island reception area in the ED, followed by his son.

Tammy headed out the emergency ward doors into the fresh air of the ambulance bay. Two ambulances were parked having just dispatched their patients. Rob Sellers was standing there talking to the new paramedic, Dean Gibson. Damn it. She'd gone to school with Rob's wife Susan. She didn't need to run into these two.

'Tammy! How are you, mate?' Rob called, walking over to her and hauling the other bloke with him. 'You met the new ambo yet? Deano, this is Tammy. Tammy Murphy. I mean, McCauley. What are you calling yourself these days?'

'McCauley. And I've met Dean. He brought Joe in,' said Tammy trying to smile.

'How's the old fella going? Heard him carrying on from out here! He's a crazy old bugger,' said Dean. 'Abusive too.'

'Well, you'd be the same if you'd broken a hip!' Tammy snapped back, wondering what had got into her. The old man had been abusing *her*, for goodness sake.

'Sor-ry. No offence,' said Dean looking uncomfortable. 'Judging by what went on earlier, I didn't think you two got on.'

'We don't.'

Rob was looking from one to the other. 'Dean, maybe you'd better move that ambulance out of the parking bay. I think it's blocking the traffic.'

As Dean edged away, Rob slung an arm around Tammy's shoulder and walked with her.

'Hey, go easy on old Deano. He's just trying to be nice.'

Tammy sighed. The cup in her hand slopped from side to side, lukewarm milky brown liquid dripping onto her fingers. 'Yeah, I'm sorry. It's been one of those days.'

'I heard about Shon. You okay?'

'Yes, I'm fine,' Tammy said, sucking some chocolate off her thumb, not even wondering how Rob knew. That was the bush telegraph for you. 'In reality, it's been over between us for a long time. A couple of years in fact. I've just been burying my head in the sand. He didn't love me any more. Loved someone else better. That's all.'

'That's no good,' said Rob. 'Tammy –' He stopped, hesitant to go on.

'Spit it out, Rob.'

'Well, it's just that it'd be hard for him too, mate. You know, living up to the McCauleys.'

'How's that? There's none of us left to live up to!'

'But there's the property. The name. The whole "first settlers in the district" kind of stuff. Shon's a bloke always looking for the next best thing. An opportunity to better himself, and he found that in you. Guess he didn't bet on having his balls cut off in the process.'

Tammy stared at Rob, hard. Susan and he had been her good friends for years and it was testament to her respect for him that she didn't deck him right then and there.

Rob was shaking his head. 'That came out all wrong. Look, I'm not saying what he's been doing to you is right. I'm just saying that –'

'I'm hearing you, Rob. You're saying I'm a ball-breaker?'

'No, I'm not. I'm saying a man needs to be the one to provide for his wife and family. He needs to be able to achieve and feel like he's done it himself. Shon stepped into *your* life, on *your* farm, worked for *your* grandfather and then for you.'

'*With* me,' Tammy corrected.

'Well, yes. But it's still all yours, isn't it? A man's got an ego, Tammy. He needs to be the provider. In most cases, anyway.'

Tammy thought about that as she took another swig of her drink. Ugh, it was cold. Like her heart towards Shon.

'Good riddance to bad rubbish is what I say.'

Rob laughed and nodded. 'Yeah, you're probably right. He always was a bit of a knobhead. You were too good for him, anyway.'

'You old reprobate.' Tammy laughed. 'Thanks, Rob. I kind of needed to hear that last bit from someone today.'

'You're welcome. It's perfectly true though. Regardless of the whys and hows and whether he's running around without balls' – and here Rob smiled at her before going on – 'the man *is* a user. Just remember that when he comes crawling back.'

Tammy's phone beeped again.

'I'd better let you get that,' said Rob looking down at the mobile. 'Might be your new boyfriend.' He nodded towards Hunter's ute and gave a cheeky wink.

'Goodbye, Rob.'

'Goodbye, Tammy.' He was grinning wickedly, then his face turned serious. 'And remember what I said, about Shon. Doesn't excuse anything, but sometimes it helps to have another way of looking at it.'

Tammy nodded and walked off towards a park bench on the lawn outside the hospital. Good old Rob. He might be an earnest and kind man but she'd be darned if she was having any sympathy for Shon Murphy today.

She sat on the bench, put her cup down beside her. She wondered how many people had sat on this very seat struggling to understand the curve-balls life had sent them.

The air around her was dank with humidity, making her feel sticky and hot. And cranky.

She toggled the phone to bring up Lucy's messages, one after the other.

Ring me!
Ring ME!
RING ME! IT'S URGENT!

Chapter 17

'I think Shon's moved in with Joanne!' Lucy's voice screeched down the phone before she'd even said hello.

'Well, yes.'

'What do you mean "yes"? Last time I saw he had his boots under your bed, the bastard.'

Tammy wasn't entirely sure if Lucy was indignant on her behalf or whether she was just unhappy she didn't have the heads-up on the gossip. 'He left me. About three hours ago in fact. I'd decided to try to make him leave but when I got home he was going anyway.'

'Well, at least that made it easier for you. He's moved into the pub. His beer fridge is sitting outside the accommodation donga and a lounge chair followed by a mattress went in the door to one of the rooms.'

Tammy felt sick. It was actually happening.

'Are you okay?' Lucy's voice came down a couple of octaves.

'Sure. I'm fine.' But even Tammy could hear her own voice wobble.

'Are you sure? I can come over. I've finished my shift.'

'No, Luce, I'm okay. I'm not home anyway. I'm at the hospital.'

'So you're not fine! I'll be there in half an hour!'

'No, it's not me, silly. I'm fine, I told you. I'm here with Joe.'

'Jo? Oh, for heaven's sake, you haven't taken a machete or something to her, have you? Honestly, neither of them is worth it, Tim Tam. He's a loser. A lying, cheating loser. And she's nothing but a cock-teaser.'

'Lucy Granger, you're asking for Tabasco on your tongue.'

'Tabasco, my aunt's fanny! I'm just saying it how it is. About time someone did.'

Tammy sighed. She had no idea so many of her friends had an opinion on her marriage which didn't include happily ever afters. 'As I said, I'm here with Joe. Joe McCauley.'

'Hooley *dooley*! You're kidding, right?'

'Nup.'

'Why?'

'He's broken his hip. Fell off the front verandah while trying to shoot a rabbit.' And just missed killing a little boy, she added silently. The whole town of Lake Grace didn't need to know that, and they would if she told Lucy.

'Oh my aunt's fanny!' Tammy held the phone away from her ear. Lucy's screeches tended to give you temporary tinnitus.

Finally Tammy decided to cut through the semi-hysteria. 'Ummm . . . excuse me, Luce? Lucy? *Lucy*!' Her friend paused in mid-stream. 'Joe's in surgery now. Trav's just finding out how long things are going to take.'

'Trav? As in Travis *Hunter*?' Another screech.

Tammy couldn't help but give a little laugh. 'That's the one. Him and Billy.'

'My oh my, I want to know all the juicy details of this one, Tim Tam. In one afternoon you have managed to ditch one bloke and pick up two others. Two *elusive* others. Three, counting the boy. I knew you were good but this just about takes the cake.'

If only that was true. She momentarily relived the scenes back on the hill and in ED before Trav had arrived. The look on Joe's face as he'd flung his insults at her. 'Tammy? Tammy! Are you still there?' Lucy's piping voice brought Tammy back to the hospital park bench.

'Yep. I'm still here.'

'You sure you don't want me to come across?'

'No, Luce, it's fine.' The last thing she wanted was her highly excitable friend muddying the waters any further.

'I'd better go, mate. I've got to find Trav and Billy and see how long old Joe's going to be. Luckily I organised the relief milkers to come in tonight so I don't have worry about the cows.'

'Well, if you need me you know where I am,' said her best friend.

'Thanks, Luce. That means a lot.' And then Lucy was gone.

※

She found Trav and Billy in a square cubicle labelled Hospital Quiet Room. Trav was staring out the window, while Billy was rolling around on the floor pushing a Matchbox car he'd snaffled from a small toy box in the far corner of the room. It was amazing how kids could amuse themselves with four wheels.

'Vroom . . . vroom . . . vroom.' Tammy watched as Billy tested how far he could flick the car with his index finger, and how quickly it would travel if he ran it off the seat of a tilted chair. The young bloke didn't seem too worse for wear after his shooting ordeal. Kids were so resilient. She wished she could say the same for adults.

Her eyes moved to the man who was intent on the scenery beyond the building's walls. A flowering gum stood directly outside the window. Elegant and flourishing branches spread wide to capture space and love and care in the green lawn. Beside it was a tall spotted gum. Tall and alone, its leaves crept up the trunk. This is my space, keep out, it seemed to say to the other tree.

'What's happening with Joe?' asked Tammy.

'He's in surgery now. They couldn't say how long. It depends on the severity of the break,' said Travis, moving his legs to find a more comfortable place to rest them.

Tammy couldn't help but notice how his worn clothes moved with him, like they were glued to the muscles lurking underneath the fabric. The blue flannelette shirt beneath a soft windcheater looked like a safe place to cuddle into. She shook her head. What was she thinking?

'Joe's going to have to go into the nursing home for a while,' she stated in a flat tone. She'd been pondering it while walking around outside.

'What the hell?'

'But, Tammy, you said –?'

'I know what I said, but seriously, how are we going to cope? I've got a farm to look after. Trav, you've got a job. You're barely home long enough as it is.' For a little boy who desperately needs you, let alone an ungrateful, abusive old man, she added silently to herself.

'I can help!' Billy got up, dropping the car. 'Dad?' The child swung towards his father, a begging note in his voice.

But his father ignored him. Instead his vivid eyes were boring into Tammy's. He sat up straighter in the chair. 'Joe is not going into a nursing home.' The words came out firm, a full stop after each syllable. 'I had to put my mother in a home. I had no option; she is entirely immobile and . . .' He blushed. 'She can't use the toilet properly'. Here we do have a choice and I'm not doing it to Joe.'

But Tammy wasn't ready to back down.

Pulling herself up to her full height and jutting out her chin she shot back, 'Then how the hell do you plan to see it through, Travis?'

Billy started hopping from one leg to the next in agitation. 'But Tammy, you said you'd help!'

'Billy.' One growl from his father was all it took to have the young boy back down on the floor.

'He's going to need specialist care. Things to help him to do stuff on his own. Meals. Watching over. We can't do that for him,' Tammy said, sitting down on the nearest chair, arms folded, legs crossed.

Trav just sat and considered her for a moment. Then turned his head to look back out the window. Silence rebounded around the room. It wasn't a comfortable silence, by any means. Not like when she and Trav were working on the fence. Billy lay on the carpet looking sulky and bereft, as though he'd lost his most loved toy in the whole world.

She went to go on but Trav just shifted his gaze and shot her a glare as loaded as his son's. Don't say a word. It irked her that she understood that look.

Seconds ticked by, then minutes. Finally the man at the window turned his head and faced her.

'I'll cut back my hours of work. We've got a few months before the wild dogs will be after newborn lambs and calves. Not much activity around at the moment for the bigger sheep. We'll find out if the occupational therapy people can sort out some stuff for him to take home to make things easier. We'll get some bars put up in his bathroom. We can take turns with cooking or there's always Meals on Wheels. We can get him one of those emergency buttons like my mother has around her neck. He can push it if he goes down again. Billy and me can keep an eye on him.' Trav paused, laid his legs out in front of him, put his hands back behind his head. 'And you too,' a cock of his head, an arched eyebrow – a challenge. 'That's if you're up to it?'

It was the longest speech she'd ever heard the man make and he'd covered everything. The baton had been passed to her for an answer. Billy's head swivelled from his father to Tammy, like an automated clown at the carnival. Hope in his gaze.

Tammy stared at Trav. Both man and boy's eyes bored into her. She felt herself wilt under their scrutiny, their expectations. Could it really be done?

Trav must have sensed her indecision. He leaned forward in his chair. 'Tammy. There is no way you can cage your uncle in a nursing home. He's like me. I *have* to be out in the scrub otherwise I'll go nuts. Back when I was young, at school in Burra . . . it was like they'd stuck me in a cage. Blokes like Joe and me don't cope with walls and . . .' Trav threw his hands around, obviously trying to find the right words, 'and people. We don't cope with folks real well, no matter *who* they are. Joe's a man of the bush. A free spirit who loves the land and the environment with a passion that is rarely seen these days. You can't lock a bloke like that up in a building and expect him to conform.'

'He'd just curl up and die,' added Billy from the floor.

Tammy looked down at her boots, up at the ceiling and then out the window at the gum trees. One shared its shade and beauty by spreading its leaves to encompass the surrounding space, the other kept to itself.

And she felt shame, that she'd only been thinking of what was right for *her*. She was his great-niece after all. Even though he abused her and obviously hated her guts, maybe this was their chance to get to know each other, bury the hatchet. Be a family?

Maybe.

Chapter 18

It was late when Tammy got home. So late the relief milker had long since left. The dairy was in darkness, and the cows safely tucked up in their paddock for the night.

'Thanks for the ride, Luce.'

'You sure you don't want me to come in for a cuppa? Perhaps I can talk you into *trying* pole dancing. It might make you feel better?'

'No, I'll be fine.' Tammy smiled at her friend. 'Thanks for caring though.'

Lucy had arrived at the Narree hospital some time after six that evening. Obviously it was killing her not knowing what was going on. She seemed surprised to find Joe still in recovery and the others in the waiting room, Tammy absent-mindedly reading a magazine and Hunter looking out the window. The only sound to disturb the peace was the 'vroom, vroom, vroom' from the young boy who had spent the last three hours making roadways on the floor.

'Hi, I'm Lucy,' she'd said moving forwards, fingers out to shake Hunter's hand.

Hunter reached over half-heartedly to return the gesture before slumping back into the chair.

Lucy shot Tammy a look, dropped her hand and gave a small harrumph.

Tammy smiled apologetically and motioned her friend to meet her outside the room.

'What's up his ringhole?' asked Lucy, straight to the point as usual.

'He's pissed off with me.'

'Why?'

'Joe needs time in here and then some respite care at the nursing home recovering.'

'He's not going to like that.'

'That's the point. He didn't like it and so wild man in there offered to look after him at home.'

'Right. And the problem with that is . . . ?' Lucy paused and gave Tammy the evil eye. 'You *did* offer to help, didn't you?'

'No, well yes. No. Ummm . . . yes, I did offer but . . .' Tammy stopped and then went on in a rush, 'How the hell can I do that, Luce? Look after him, I mean. I've got a farm to run, cows to milk.' She blinked back a couple of tears. She would not cry over Shon Murphy, not any more. She'd wept enough tears on his behalf over the last few years to fill the Lake Grace dam. She swallowed hard before going on. 'My husband's just left me and what's more,' another gulp of air, 'Joe hates my guts. He's spent most of his time today yelling abuse at me in front of half the town. Why would *he* want *me* to look after him? Correction, why the hell would *I* want to look after *him*?'

Lucy stood there a moment, silently contemplating what she was going to say, which made Tammy pause. Lucy never ever contemplated what she was going to say.

Tammy took a few more steadying breaths. A woman with a food trolley came trundling past, adeptly dodging the two friends. A clock donated by some long-gone benevolent forefather ticked on a wall. Someone in a room nearby laboured over a phlegmy cough that went on and on, rocking and rolling around the now empty corridor. Still Lucy wrestled with her answer.

Tammy waited.

Finally, just as a loud speaker announced the visiting hours, Lucy spoke. Unusually her tone was sombre, her voice pitched low – almost a murmur, not quite a whisper. Tammy had to lean right in to hear it over the mechanical voice spruiking about visitors do's and don'ts.

'You'll look after him, Tammy, because he's family.'

*

The homestead at Montmorency was as sombre as a gravesite, as dark as an after-hours hotel. She stood and contemplated the old place long after Lucy had headed back to Lake Grace.

Why was she here? What was it all for, working her guts out to keep the place going? She didn't have much to show for it. Sure she had the farm, her heritage, the legacy of previous McCauleys. But she had no one to hand that hundred and fifty years of history on to. And now she had no husband to share it with, to make babies with, who would love and cherish the place as much as she did.

The house stood silent. Empty.

She walked down the path towards the back of the house. On the screen door a note was fluttering in the slight breeze blowing off the mountains behind her. The wind was chilly now; there'd been a westerly change. Not like the humidity which had swamped her in a giant wave outside the hospital.

She took the note from under the peg that was used specifically to communicate with her workers.

Gidday Tammy,
Hope your uncle is ok.
Cows in billabong padock.
Seeya later tomorra. Going ta Bairnsdale for darts 2night.
Ta,
Jock & Barb

Jock might not have been able to spell but both he and Barb were brilliant with the cows. Good relief milkers were like gold around these parts and she'd hit the mother lode with these two.

Jock and Barbara were retired dairy farmers and old friends of her grandfather. They had come into her life again two years earlier when they were looking for a house to live in after they'd finished up at their last share farm. Tammy had gladly installed them in the spare home on their run-off block. She'd thanked God many a time that in return for their own house, plus meat and a small amount of remuneration, they'd agreed to relief milk and help her out when she needed an extra hand on the farm.

She unlocked the door and walked straight into the paintings she'd bought from the gallery in town. Jock must have taken them out of her ute. He knew where she kept the spare key to the house and he was a thoughtful man. Not like Shon, who would have dumped them in the dirt against the side of the shed.

She picked up the wrapped packages one at a time and wrestled them into the formal lounge room. It still looked like a tip after Shon's exodus. She checked out the walls. Lots of dead relatives and landscape prints. Nup. Not in here.

She dragged the prints into the family room with its saggy, worn leather chairs and dining table piled high with mail and farm journals. Last week's papers, *The Weekly Times, Stock and Land* – Shon liked to keep on top of what was happening in the farming world. Tammy would have liked to as well but she rarely had the time. And like most dairy farmers, once she sat down she inevitably fell asleep.

A Coonara heater stood solidly in the fireplace. On the mantle bride and groom beamed from their wedding photo. Correction: she beamed at the world, Shon just looked smug. The cat who had finally got the cream.

Tammy hauled down the picture, throwing it onto the floor, face first. It was destined for the big skip-bin at the dairy.

She dusted her hands together and unwrapped one of her new purchases. And there was the angel in all her glory, standing on the edge of a cliff, leaning into the wind. Scenting freedom. The second print was next. The sphinx-angel flying. The expression on her face was still one of happiness and love, just as Tammy remembered. She herself yearned for those feelings.

She went to the kitchen and riffled in the pantry until she found a few solid hooks, measuring tape and a hammer. Back in the family room she marked the right spots and hammered three hooks into place. Then she wrestled the prints up on the wall. Hands on hips, she stood back and studied the results of her labour.

The prints looked perfectly at home. They belonged there.

Now all she had to do was wait for Alice to get number three and the set would be complete. In the meantime she could start doing what the pictures were surely telling her to do. Get her life back. One step at a time.

Tammy walked over to the answering machine, which was flashing a message, something she hadn't noticed when she first came in. Hitting the replay button she heard the voice of one of the irrigation district's water planners.

'Hi, Tammy. Just ringing to let you know your irrigation water has been brought forward to start at ten o'clock tonight. Any queries, ring the Irrigators' Line. Thanks.'

Damn! In all the drama of Shon leaving and Joe's accident she'd forgotten about the water. She checked her watch. Nine-thirty. She'd better head to the paddock and set things up to irrigate, especially now it was coming earlier than she expected. She could check the cows while she was there. Some people in the district had been having trouble with bloat, thanks to the out-of-the-ordinary amount of humidity they'd been getting this season. The sultry conditions were conducive to producing heaps of clover in the pastures. The hollow stems of the plant caught lots of air, which fermented in the rumen and caused the cow to almost strangle.

That afternoon, before he milked, Jock would have sprayed the overnight pastures with anti-bloat oil mixed with water using the boom spray. All the same, it didn't hurt to check.

Tammy grabbed a quick drink of water then headed back out the door, shrugging into a short coat as she went. The wind would be damn cold on the motorbike.

After turning the four-wheeler's engine over and pulling on a helmet, she swung the vehicle out of the yard and headed up the laneway towards the Billabong paddock.

She found her big no-nonsense spotlight in the old milk crate strapped to the front of the bike. Plugging it into the power, she swung it out across the paddock. A couple of cows moved into view. They were sitting down, not doing too much. A few more passed through the beam, then they were gone, and the light slung itself across an empty paddock.

Where was the rest of the herd?

Tammy pivoted her spottie back and took a closer look at the small mob standing in the light. They were staggering sideways, looking for all the world like they were trying to belch.

Tammy swore and focused the torch back on the cows not doing too much. Realised they were stock still. Legs stuck straight out, parallel with the ground, stomachs distended like big round balls. Big, round *dead* balls.

Fuck!

She spun the four-wheeler on a fifty-cent piece and roared up to the gateway that led into the Billabong paddock. Grabbing a Dolphin torch from the carry-all, she leaped over the gate and ran down the hump of the delver channel to where the cows lay – on the wrong side of the electric fence. Three of them. Stone cold dead.

Fuck! Fuck!

The bastards had got through the electric tapes which acted as a gate into the next paddock. Tammy hurdled the remaining tape that sat a foot off the ground and into the offending pasture.

A couple of older cows were propped on the delver channel bank, head up on the high side, bum down on the low, mouths open, trying to belch. That they'd had experience with bloat before was obvious and, even though she was in a panic, a tiny part of her brain applauded them for their ingenuity.

Further across the paddock, at least four cows were staggering, heads out, mouths open and in extreme pain. Two others were down but still moving. Not dead. Yet.

She hurdled back over the tape, ran the delver again, leaped the gate and rushed back to the motorbike, hoping her pocket knife lay buried in the milk crate among baling twine, irrigation pipe plugs, poly-fittings and cattle tags. It wasn't there.

Fuck!

Tammy jumped back on the bike and took off towards the dairy, spinning wheels and throwing dirt and gravel into the air. The spotlight jumped crazily up and down on her lap, still sending out light beams on the water pooling in the irrigation channel to her right. She ignored it. Her eyes and mind were set on the dairy.

She had to find a knife.

Chapter 19

Travis Hunter was tired. Plum tuckered out. Whoever said sitting around waiting didn't bugger the hell out of you had never sat in a hospital.

He looked across at his son. The boy was sound asleep, head slightly cocked back and tilted to the side, resting on the ute's window. His mouth was open and a delicate snore wheezed from his throat every second or third breath. The boy had done well. Not too many kids would have taken an afternoon and a night sitting around a hospital with such grace, let alone good behaviour.

Trav sighed and rubbed the back of his neck. He could see McCauley's Hill. Only a few miles to go, then home and bed.

Old Joe had come out of his operation okay. Groggy, in pain, but still slinging abuse at anyone who came within earshot. Demanding to be allowed to get up and walk out that hospital door. Finally someone had given him a shot of painkiller, which sent him to sleep. Trav never thought he'd be grateful for drugs. But tonight he was. It'd been awful to watch.

A light out to his left caught his eye. It was bouncing a few feet above the ground. A motorbike, perhaps? Trav checked where he was. His mind had gone onto auto-pilot and numbed out all geographical markers a half-hour back. It was a wonder he'd even caught McCauley's Hill. Although the hulking great monstrosity *was* kind of hard to miss. He must be level with Montmorency Downs because just up ahead of him was the section of boundary fencing, replaced after an accident that killed a young girl.

The light bounced some more, then stopped. Hovering. Trav pulled the ute over to the side of the road and turned off the headlights. He checked his watch: nine-forty. Late enough, especially for a dairy farmer. What was going on? Her fool of a soon-to-be-ex-husband causing mischief? Although by the sounds of what Mrs Parker had said, he'd have better things to be doing at this time of the night. Trav shuddered. Joanne Purvis certainly didn't do it for him.

Was the light moving once more? No. Not quite. A light was moving, but it wasn't the same one. This one was dimmer but no less energetic. Bounce, bounce, halt. Swing around. Bounce, bounce, halt. Swinging the other way. It was heading back towards him, moving faster, bobbing across the air like a ball in motion. Then the stronger light was back, zooming across the blackness of the night. Weird. It might pay for him to check it out. Casting another look across at the sleeping Billy, Travis started the ute again and headed towards the gate of Montmorency Downs.

He peeled off the road and up the gravel into Tammy's farm. Cautiously at first, simultaneously watching the light. Suddenly it struck him: the brightness was coming from the headlight of a motorbike that was belting towards the homestead, flat out roaring towards the dairy, which he had in his ute's headlights. He brought the vehicle to a halt outside the milk-room roller-door, the access for the tanker to collect the daily load of white liquid gold.

The motorbike screeched to a halt beside him and Tammy flung herself off it, running towards the air-space between the milk-room and the dairy itself. He was sure she clocked him in her peripheral vision but she didn't stop. 'What's up?' he called. Silence. He moved into the gloom after her and was suddenly blinded as a brilliant floodlight came on somewhere above his head. A sensor light. Tammy hadn't tripped it off, but something he had done sure had.

She appeared again, helmet still on her head, a cracker of a knife in her hand. Now he understood why she hadn't heard him. The helmet. But to come at him with a knife? And she still kept coming, knife in the air. She was crying. He shot a glance towards the still-running ute. He hadn't wanted to turn it off in case the boy woke up. He calculated his chances of making it inside the cab before she got to him. Not a chance. He'd have to face her down. Like a wild dog.

She was saying something. 'Travis. Hunter!' And then she was in front of him, the dagger glinting brightly in the glare from the floodlight. His arm was moving to block the blow, knock the knife from her hand. She spoke again, 'Help me! The cows.'

Cows? 'They've got through the tapes into the next paddock. Three dead, another just about. Others are staggering. It's bloat.' Then she was gone, back on the bike, roaring out of the yard.

Trav let out a huge sigh. To think he'd thought . . . ? Hell, he must be *really* tired. He slung a glance up towards McCauley's Hill. Visualised his bed. Warm, comfortable. And then he thought of the face of the woman who'd just lit out of the yard like all the demons of hell were on her tail. The tears. The look of devastation. He ran back to his ute – his son was still sleeping – got in and took off after Tammy.

&

When he found her she was down on her knees, like she was praying. That wasn't going to do her much good, he thought, looking at the mayhem in the paddock. Cows seemed to be suffocating all around him, not to mention the couple on the ground already dead.

Again he left the ute running to keep the boy asleep, climbed through the fence and set off across the paddock towards her. When he got there she was kneeling in the most disgusting mess of fermented green stuff he'd ever seen. The contents of a cow's first stomach – the rumen. She'd used the knife to puncture the cow's side in the centre of a triangle between the last rib and the hip. Tammy had her hand through the slit, inside the cow, and was pulling more and more green muck out of the stomach. 'Can you do this for me while I do another?' Her tone was urgent, her breath came in short pants. 'You just need to make sure the air keeps coming out the gash and the hole doesn't get blocked by all the fermenting grass.'

Trav nodded, kneeled down in the muck beside her and took over the job. The stink was putrid, but he'd smelled worse – far, far worse – in his line of work. Tammy had moved quickly to the cow she obviously judged as the next worst. This one was still standing. He watched as, by the light of the torch, she assessed where to stab with her knife. Then a dull *thunk*. A hiss of air, like a football being let down or a deflating car tyre. Almost instantly the cow could breathe again. The gagging mouth seemed to close and the need to belch didn't appear so urgent.

It was a few more minutes before Tammy spoke. 'I'll have to get them all up to the yards at the dairy and give them a drench of bloat stuff. And then there's these two to sew up. I'll have to call the vet.' Her voice seemed to catch on the end of the word 'vet'. Trav couldn't imagine what the bill was going to be. 'Can you help me?' she asked.

And he wondered, as well, how much that particular plea cost her. He could hardly turn his back on her now, could he? 'What do you want me to do?'

⚘

The vet had been and gone. Billy had slept through the lot and was now sitting in Tammy's family room watching late-night telly. Not the best place for an ten-year-old to be at two in the morning but, hey, he couldn't do much about it.

'So what happened, exactly?' Trav asked, curious.

'The fence must have a short in it. There are electric tapes in all those paddocks along that side of the farm. It's cheaper and easier than hanging gates. Especially when I've only got a single electrified wire separating one paddock from the next.' Tammy sighed loudly as she set some solid chunks of fruitcake on a plate. 'I swear cattle have a sixth sense when it comes to knowing there's power down in an electric fence.'

'But don't you use bloat oil or something? Spray the paddocks before they're grazed?'

'Yes, but they have to be sprayed just before the cows go in or it's a waste of time. Jock would've sprayed the paddock they were *supposed* to be in, but not the one next door. And rightly so. It's my own stupid fault. I should have run the volt meter over those fences, damn it.'

Travis thought about that. The woman couldn't be everywhere doing everything. 'You weren't to know about the fence just like you weren't to know about the cows getting into that clover. You've been a bit busy.' Trav tried his half-smile. He'd been using it a bit lately. He'd found over the years that it worked with most women. Made them smile back at least.

But Tammy was oblivious, intent on pouring boiling water into the cups and splashing in some milk. He felt something kick deep inside his gut, and was shocked to realise he was irked. And disgruntled. And that pissed him off even more. So he sat back in the chair of this grandiose house with its stiff air of formality and tried to make himself feel comfortable. Told himself it didn't matter that this woman hadn't noticed his attempt to make her feel better about herself. They sat and drank their tea in silence. The only sound to disturb the night air, other than the quiet slurps of hot tea, was the TV murmuring to a young boy in another room.

'We'd better go, it's late.' Trav got up and looked unnecessarily at the clock. He'd been watching the second-hand tick around for the last little while, not sure what to do, what to say. He couldn't make inane comments like, 'Nice house you've got here.' It wasn't his thing. Plus, her house was a tip. All kinds of shit spilled from drawers everywhere.

'Right. Yes,' said Tammy, looking uncomfortable. She got up too and stood watching him, her arms folded across her chest.

'Billy! In the ute,' he called to the boy. Billy jumped up immediately, turned off the TV and scooted on outside.

'He's a good boy,' said Tammy, watching him go.

'I know,' said Trav.

'Do you? Do you *really*?' She was giving him a weird look.

It was late, he was knackered, and clearly so was she. 'I'll see myself out,' he said, finally.

At the car he helped his son into the passenger seat.

'Thank you,' a voice said behind him. Trav spun round. Tammy stood in the shadows of the big old house. 'Thanks for your help,' she said again. God, that voice was a doozy. So sweet and sexy, playing around his ears like a song of seduction. And it seemed she had no idea of its power. Her brow was slightly scrunched in a look of despair. Her vulnerability made his toes curl with the desperate need to soothe. His hand went up, without him even knowing it was in the air, like he was going to tuck a piece of Tammy's hair back behind her ear. The silky strands were weaving around crazily in the breeze. But he realised what he was doing before he made contact and his hand fell.

He glanced at Tammy to see if she'd noticed. Her face was still sad. From nowhere came the urge to kiss her. To wipe all the misery away. Make her forget the past few hours, in fact the whole day. Unconsciously he felt his body lean forwards towards hers. But then he pulled back. What was he thinking? She was hell on wheels normally. A fiery piece *who was still married.*

Abruptly he got into his ute, gunned the engine, tipped a hand to an imaginary hat and took off, leaving Tammy standing alone in the moonlight, still rocking back and forth, arms crossed. As he made his way down her drive towards

Hope's Road, Trav wondered just what it was with this woman, why she made him feel so protective. He watched her in the rear-vision mirror as he drove away, until she became a dark shadow that blended with those of the old homestead.

Chapter 20

'I'm not having no fucking grab bars and what-not in my shack. What do you think I am, a bloody cripple?'

It was a week or so after the operation and why in the heck Tammy had agreed to help organise Joe's return home, she would never know. The nursing home option was looking mighty good at the moment. The old man was in full flight.

'And as for having other people on me place, you can bloody forget it!'

'But Mr McCauley, as I have been trying to inform you,' Susan, the aged care coordinator, insisted, 'you are entitled to a post acute-care package for six weeks that includes home help, visits from the district nurse and Meals on Wheels.'

'But I don't want it!' Joe slumped back on the hospital pillows, exhausted from all the yelling.

'Maybe you'd better rest, Uncle Joe, while Susan and I sort things out.' Tammy was rewarded with an icy glare. She wasn't sure if that was for calling him uncle or all the other stuff Susan was trying to force down his throat. A *care package*? It sounded like they were talking about a holiday, or a home loan. But at least he'd stopped yelling. That had to be a bonus.

Tammy shuffled the aged care coordinator out the door, and into the passage. 'You'll have to excuse my uncle, Susan. He's having trouble adjusting to the fact he needs assistance.'

Susan patted Tammy's arm. 'No worries. We get this all the time. It's a terrible shock to lose your independence. Makes the oldies lash out at everyone they love.'

And Tammy suddenly realised Susan thought that she, Tammy, needed comforting. 'Oh, no! You've got it wrong. *I* get this all the time. He doesn't love me. He hates me, actually.'

Susan smiled. 'Now where did you get that idea from, love?'

'What idea?' Travis Hunter loomed up beside Tammy, making her jump. How on earth did the man approach so silently? He was like an apparition.

Susan looked at Trav questioningly and he stuck out his hand. 'I'm Travis. Joe's next-door neighbour. Soon to be part-time carer.'

Tammy glanced up at him in shock. The man was volunteering information? Then she noticed he was smiling that half-grin and Susan was melting like ice-cream. Oh, good Lord. *Please*.

Tammy pushed Trav towards Joe's room. 'Go talk man-to-man stuff with the old bugger. He doesn't want anyone helping him, no bars in the bathroom, no aids, no home help, no district nurse and definitely *no* Meals on Wheels.'

'I can understand that. Mum had them once. Those meals are terrible.'

Trav disappeared through the door and Tammy found herself apologising once again to Susan.

'So what do you want to do?' Susan was now looking down at her clipboard, a little rosy flush on her cheeks. 'Shall I give him *everything* he's entitled to? Only some? Or nothing? But if you're going to say nothing I urge you to reconsider.'

Tammy didn't even have to think about it. 'We'll take all of it. Even the meals. We can always cancel if we find we don't need something.'

Susan ticked all her boxes and scrawled some notes down the bottom of the page. Tammy wondered if they included *Abusive old man and dysfunctional family situation – BEWARE*.

Finally Susan snapped her pen into a holder hanging around her neck and rammed the clipboard under her arm. 'The occupational therapy people will sort out what aids he requires – a toilet chair, walker, et cetera. They'll also need to measure up for grab bars. We'll give you a ring to sort out a time. They're pretty busy.'

'That's okay. We might be able to fit them ourselves.'

'Right,' said Susan. 'Here's my card if you want to call me. I'll be his care coordinator from now on. Ring if you need anything.' But before she stepped away, Susan seemed to take a deep breath. Was she going to tell her they were all wasting their time and he should be in a nursing home after all? 'Love?' said Susan.

Tammy couldn't stand it when people called her love or darling. They had to earn the right to use those words.

Susan put her hand on Tammy's arm. 'He does care about you, you know. I can see it in his face.'

Tammy ducked her head. Mmmm . . . If only she could believe that.

At the sight of Boots and Digger running excitedly in circles, tears welled up in Old Joe's eyes. *I should have smuggled one of the dogs into the hospital,* Tammy thought. *Maybe that would have made it easier to manage the bloke.*

As the old man carefully climbed out of Trav's ute, Boots threw himself at his master, causing him to totter on his walking frame. On the advice of the occupational therapists at the hospital, Trav had hurriedly brought in a few bucketloads of dirt and gravel with the tractor and made a rough-looking ramp next to the steps up to the verandah. They put the old man into a wheelchair and pushed him up to his usual spot, looking out over the eucalypt bush, blue-grey mountains and verdant green flats. Joe breathed in the fresh late afternoon air and sighed. A deep, gentle, happy sigh. 'Ah, this is the life.' After a week of pain, anger, confusion and frustration, his face finally relaxed, making him look ten years younger.

'Can I get anyone some dinner?' Travis was calling from the back of the house, where he'd disappeared with Joe's bag.

Beside Tammy, Old Joe grunted. She'd made the casserole and left it in Joe's fridge while Jock had been doing overtime, trying to make up for the bloat incident. She didn't even want to think about that night. She'd lost nearly six thousand dollars' worth of cows in one go. But then again, it could have been a whole lot worse — and would have been without the help of the man now in the kitchen. 'I'll have some tea. What about you, Joe?' The old man waved his hand in the air, a negative response.

'Joe'll have some too,' she called out to Trav.

The old man frowned at her but to Tammy's surprise didn't say anything. There seemed to have been a truce drawn somewhere in the last week or so. The last big argument she and Joe had was when she was unpacking his clothes at the hospital. 'I don't need no fancy new pyjamas! What's wrong with the ones I had?'

Billy had weighed into that argument, thank goodness. 'Mr McCauley,' the young boy's voice had quavered first up but then gained strength, 'you can't be in hospitable with those awful PJs you had. People'd laugh at you for being different.'

'It's "hospital" not "hospitable",' Joe's voice was gruff. 'And I don't care if people laugh at me for being different. I've been different all my life. Nothing wrong with that, boy.' But the old man's tone was softer than Tammy had ever heard before.

Under Billy's earnest gaze, Joe finally took the proffered blue-and-brown striped pyjamas, mumbling, 'Fucking stripes. Always hated stripes.' He then glared at Tammy. 'And different, he says. These pyjamas is bloody different. What happened to plain old blue *or* brown, I ask you?' But there had been a tear in his eye that he'd swiftly dashed away. Maybe he realised they were only trying to help because since then he hadn't been anywhere near as frosty or horrible to her.

Beside Tammy, Joe leaned down, searching for Boots's ears to ruffle. He breathed in the damp mountain air that was starting to waft across from the slopes. 'Going to be rain in the next few days,' he said, sniffing hard.

'How do you do that?'

'What?'

'Know about the rain.'

She could tell he was about to shut her down with some smart-arse comment. Then he stopped, shrugged. 'Don't rightly know how. I just know.'

'But what did you take into account to make that observation?'

'The smell on the breeze; studying them hills. See how they look like they've picked themselves up and moved in closer to us? Like they need protection from something? And they've turned a real dark blue.'

Tammy took a closer look at the mountains. He was right. They did seem like they were scared.

'And the birds are flying low rather than up high like they do in fine weather,' Joe's voice rumbled on beside her. 'Then I take in the paddocks on Montmorency Downs. You've just irrigated, am I right?'

Tammy nodded. 'Yes. I finished yesterday.'

'And it usually rains within a day or two of you finishing.'

She glanced down at the old man and saw two twinkling cornflower-blue eyes staring right back at her. 'Holy hell,' she said in wonder. 'You're making fun of me, aren't you?'

※

They were all seated around Joe's table. Tammy and Billy had the only two chairs, having dragged another one in from the front lounge. Trav was sitting on an upturned twenty-litre drum he'd rooted out of the shed and Joe was perched on his new wheelie walker. If anyone had been peeping through the window it would have looked like any regular family sitting down to dinner. Mum, dad, son and maybe granddad. Very congenial. It was anything but. The tension in the air was palpable.

Billy was on edge as if he was trying to second guess what he was supposed to do. Joe was shooting dagger looks at all of them, like it was him against the rest of the world. He obviously just wanted them to leave him alone. And Travis? He was silent and brooding. As if he was finally realising what a big job it was going to be to look after this irascible old man.

Their next big problem was how to get the patient to bed. He couldn't sleep on the camp stretcher in his swag any more. It was too low, and he'd never be able to get into it, let alone out of it. Tonight they had to install Joe in the bedroom where he should have been sleeping in the first place, and somehow fix the gaping hole in the ceiling to stop the possum shit from falling through.

Then there was the problem of bathing. How were they going to get Joe into that shower? It was the size of a dog kennel. His walking frame barely fitted between the walls.

Suddenly a car door banged shut and they all jumped out of their skin. 'Who the fuck is that?' the old man muttered.

'Hi all!' yelled Lucy from the verandah, where she was obviously kicking off her shoes. She bounced inside, and down the passage to the kitchen doorway. 'I've brought your groceries, Joe. Thought I may as well bring them on up rather than leave them by the gate. It's not like you can drive or anything –' Lucy stopped and took in the four pairs of astonished eyes staring at her. 'What? What have I done?'

She looked puzzled for a moment then flung a hand to her head. 'Haven't you seen anyone with coloured hair before?'

Tammy was the first to recover. 'Luce. Oh, Luce . . . what *have* you done?'

Lucy grinned wickedly and spun in a circle. 'Like it?'

'Ummm . . .' Trav went next. 'Well . . . it's colourful.'

'I couldn't decide.' Lucy patted at the halo of pink, blue, red and brassy yellow streaks. 'As long as I don't look like a chook. Couldn't bear to look like something that shoots bumnuts.'

'No, not a chook,' said Billy. 'Maybe a clown?'

Lucy laughed. 'Clown I can deal with! Anyway, it makes a statement. And the oldies at work love it. They figure they're not the only ones going slightly senile.'

Outside, another car door banged shut. 'Fuck! What is it with this place lately?' growled Joe. 'As if I haven't got enough to deal with here with you mangey bastards.' He looked at Lucy before adding, 'And clowns.'

A woman's voice rang out on the verandah. 'Oooo, Dean! You are a sweetie! I couldn't have done that without you coming to my rescue.' A low male voice murmured back. 'Oh no! I'm sure my little red car would never have made it up that hill without you.' Tammy heard Trav's groan. 'Who the fuck is *that*?' Joe yelled towards the outside.

'Ah, *that* would be me, Mr McCauley.' Dean Gibson clumped through the door before holding it open for another person.

'And me!' said a voice behind him. Jacinta Greenaway sashayed into the room. She wore a low cut lacy crimson top. A pair of cut-off denim shorts encased her trim bottom. Long tanned legs and bare feet with bright pink toenails finished the Project Barbie look off.

'Who the fuck are you two? And what the hell are you doing on my hill? *In my bloody house?*' thundered the old man. Dean took a step backwards, but Jacinta stood her ground. 'Hello, Mr McCauley,' she said sweetly. 'How do you do? I'm Jacinta Greenaway, but my *friends* all call me Cin.' The inference was clear. Joe could be her friend too if he liked. 'I heard you'd been in the wars, so thought I'd drop over some big, fat chocolate muffins. There's nothing like chocolate to set those feel-good endorphins loose.'

A big box covered in cellophane appeared on the table, perfect brown muffins dripping with chocolate buttons sitting snug inside.

Tammy watched, incredulous. Old Joe – the abusive, belligerent old codger – became melted butter within seconds. 'Harrumph.' The old man cleared his throat. Nice words were obviously sticking in his gullet. He had another go. 'Well, then . . . thank you.'

'Oh you're most welcome, Mr McCauley. It must have been a *terrible* ordeal for you. Would you tell me *all* about it? I understand you were extremely *brave*!' The girl fluttered her eyelashes at Trav, who was watching the whole show, dumbstruck. Tammy wasn't sure who Cin thought was 'extremely *brave*!' – Trav or Joe.

Suddenly Trav snapped out of his trance and abruptly gestured at Billy, who jumped from his chair and offered it to Cin.

'Oooo, Billy! Thank you. How lovely.' Cin sat down and then pulled the chair closer to Joe, leaning across the table, her full breasts perched within spitting distance of the old bloke's mouth. Tammy could swear he started to drool. She grinned and met Trav's eyes across the table. He was smiling too. At her, not Cin. His half-smile. The one that had just recently started turning her stomach inside out.

'So, Mr McCauley, how did you hurt your hip? Tell me the *whole* story, right from the start,' Cin's voice twittered somewhere to Tammy's right. A tiny part of her brain was saying she should swing around and talk to Dean Gibson, who still lingered in the kitchen. Be polite. Apologise for her behaviour towards him at the hospital. But her whole being was focused on Travis Hunter and his half-smile. His eyes had darkened from their usual vivid bright blue to the same navy of the mountains before rain. Tammy felt her mouth drop open slightly. Found she was breathing in small gasps. She felt herself leaning towards him. Saw him do the same. Oh good God! He felt it too. This pull, this attraction, this –

'And so, Tammy, I was just calling by to see if you were free next Friday night. Rob Sellers told me where I could find you.' Dean's voice broke into her thoughts. 'I met Jacinta down near Joe's gate – she was looking for Travis.'

The spell was broken. Just like that. Tammy pulled herself back from Trav. Disappointed, she turned towards Dean. 'Huh?'

'Oh, and I thought I'd check to see how your uncle was too, of course.'

'Well, as you can see he's good.' He was far from good but that answer would do for now while she pulled herself together and got her mind out of Travis Hunter's pants. Geez! What the hell was she thinking? He was the wild man from the back-of-beyond. And her own husband had only just removed his jocks from her drawer!

'And so, what about next Friday night? Would you like to come with me? I think the dance starts about eight-thirty. We could do tea beforehand.'

'Oooo yes, let's!' Cin chimed in. She turned to Joe. 'There's a dance on, Mr McCauley, to raise money for the ambulance station. A new defibrillator or something.' Cin clapped her hands together like she'd had some divine inspiration. 'Travis, let's *all* go!'

'What about me? Can I come?' This was from Lucy in the corner.

'Of course you can!' gushed Cin, swinging round. 'We'll find you a date too –' She stopped and gulped, taking in Lucy and her hair for the first time '– somewhere.'

Dates? A dance? Oh good Lord. Tammy glanced across at Trav, who'd gone pale. She was being asked out. By Dean Gibson. 'Sorry, Dean, need to look after Joe –'

'Can't, Cin. No one to look after Billy –'

Jinx again. They both stopped and stared at each other, then looked away.

Lucy was pouting.

'Well, I think we can sort that one out pretty quick smart,' said Joe, speaking into the uneasy silence. 'I'll look after Billy, and he can look after me.' He glanced at the boy, who had remained as quiet as a mouse. 'Right?'

Tammy's heart went out to the child, whose eyes were now swinging wildly from his father to each grown-up in the room. She could almost see his mind whirring: he and Joe spending some time together alone? The boy looked like a cornered animal. Then Billy stared straight at the old man. 'Yes, sir.'

'Yes sir, what?' Joe was unrelenting.

'We can look after each other, sir.'

'Splendid!' Cin cried, clapping her hands. 'What fun!'

'Ripper!' said Dean. 'I'll come out and pick you all up!'

'Oh, my aunt's fanny!' Lucy was grinning.

'Just great,' murmured Tammy.

'Fuck,' muttered Trav.

Chapter 21

Tammy stood in the doorway contemplating the gaping bedroom ceiling. Outside, she could hear Travis calling the dogs to their kennels, the faint drone of two vehicles as they made their way down Hope's Road – Lucy, Dean and Cin were heading home. Crockery was clanking against the sides of the stainless-steel sink in the kitchen as Billy did the dishes. And she assumed Joe was where she'd left him, tucking into his third chocolate muffin. She surveyed the width of the gaps. They'd have to find some planks and do a quick fix.

Tammy moved outside and met Travis coming up the verandah steps. 'We're going to have to mend that ceiling otherwise Joe will be swallowing possum or rat poo while he snores.'

Trav nodded. 'I've been for a scout around and found a few spare lining boards up in the roof of the old barn. Want to come give me a hand to slide them out of the rafters?'

Tammy agreed and followed him out towards the sheds. The night was clear and brilliant under a bright fullish moon as she walked in Trav's footsteps. She couldn't help but marvel at how good his butt looked in a pair of Wranglers. 'Enjoying the view?'

Tammy could feel a blush steal up her neck. She looked up but Trav was still walking and waving his big torch out across the mountains, glowing in the moonlight. 'Looks pretty special, doesn't it?'

She glanced down again and pursed her lips in thought. Yep, the way the denim cupped his bum cheeks looked mighty fine to her.

Travis suddenly stopped and turned. She ran straight into his broad chest. Her knees went out from under her and his arms came around her slim waist to catch her fall. 'Geez, Tammy. Get a grip. Those mountains aren't worth two McCauleys landing on your arses.'

But Tammy was lost in the folds of a navy-blue King Gee workshirt. The smell of the man was sublime: all wood smoke and manly deodorant mixed with the scent of warm skin. The feel of his arms around her was making her nerve endings fizz like freshly opened lemonade. His hands travelled down past her elbows, his clutch fierce when steadying her but at the same time almost like a caress as he checked she was okay. The touch of his fingers dancing across her arms burned like a peppering of hot rocks.

Then all the heat was gone, leaving her to think she'd imagined the way her body fit Travis Hunter's like a second skin. He'd pushed her away, but not before she felt the warmth and hardness centred in the man's groin. He obviously felt something too. She couldn't see his face in minute detail due to the shadows of the night, but she could sense the steel in his glare. He stood for a moment and stared down at her in contemplation. But then he spun on his heels and stalked off, leaving her to gaze after him.

Tendrils of unease ran through her body. Why did she feel so attracted to this bloke? Shon, even in his earlier charming years, hadn't had this effect on her equilibrium. Never had she felt she would combust with heat at the slightest touch. With a wary eye, Tammy watched the man who was now entering the barn. She didn't need any more problems or emotional upheaval in her life. It was complicated enough.

The silence surrounding them as they wrestled some planks down from the rafters of the shed was as tense as twine on freshly baled hay. Tammy gladly moved away to an old workbench in a lean-to and riffled around to find some nails, hammer, tape and a saw. If she kept her head down maybe Travis Hunter would disappear in a puff of smoke. *Pffit!* Then she wouldn't have to deal with him again.

But she couldn't help but feel disgruntled when Travis headed off with his torch without a backwards glance to find a ladder. Like it didn't really matter that he'd left her there by herself in the dark. She stalked outside into the moonlight, carting her tools, and stood and waited for the man to reappear. She'd have to help him wrangle the planks inside. At least there would be seven foot of timber between them this time.

Travis reappeared with the ladder and picked up the end of the lining boards with his spare arm. They carried the planks to the offending room, shoved the bed to one side and nailed the extra boards up on the ceiling to cover the gaping holes, all in complete silence. Tammy darted a surprised look at the man as he hammered in nails with ferocity. Baltic pine wasn't *that* hard.

She searched around and found some fresh linen in an old wood box in the far corner of the room. The camphor nearly knocked her out, but she supposed it was better than the smell of possum shit. 'We'd better make the bed up for the old bugger,' said Tammy, in an effort to ease the tension. 'He won't be able to do it himself.'

She and Trav made the bed, moving around, trying not to touch one another, not acknowledging this *thing* that seemed to be zinging between them. They kept the double mattress between them most of the time but the problem was when the man's muscled, tanned hands smoothed the sheets, then the blankets, all Tammy could think of was those same hands on her waist, her arms, as he righted her fall outside. Caressing her body like she was his. All she could dream of was Trav's broad shoulders, his strong and muscled body naked in that bed with her. Making love to her. Giving her that half-smile as he thrust into her. Her wet with desire. For him. Oh good Lord. She could almost feel –

'I'm not sleeping in that bed!' Joe's yell from the kitchen interrupted her daydreaming.

'Well, I know you don't want to but where else are you going to sleep?' Tammy called back, her voice surprisingly steady, as she pulled her mind out of the sheets and away from Travis Hunter. 'I don't see you fitting into that meat-safe cot.'

'Ha, ha, ha. Very funny, girl. Don't be impertinent!'

Impertinent? He was saying *she* was impertinent? Tammy stifled a giggle and dared a look across at Trav.

'Obviously, his good humour departed along with Cin's skimpy sandals,' Travis whispered.

Tammy shoved a hand across her mouth, trying to stop herself from giggling more. She glanced at Travis again. *He* was doing the same. Their giggles erupted into chuckles. Then full-blown laughter. Trav threw the pillow he'd just covered at her, trying to get her to stop. She buried her face in it but still the laughter kept coming. Unbottled, unfettered, hysterical laughter that was just bubbling to the surface – the tension, the stress, the worry, the events of the past few weeks set to blow like a champagne cork.

'Are you laughing at me, girl?' Joe yelled, really pissed off.

'Me?' called back Tammy. 'No, I'm not laughing!' But she found she couldn't help herself until Trav strode around the bed and pushed her onto the big, soft mattress. He held her down, covered her with his strong and hard body, placed his hand over her mouth as tears poured from her eyes and laughter rumbled uncontrollably through her chest. She bit at his hand, and shook her head to dislodge it. Caught the look on his features and stopped. He stared down at her like he was doing battle with himself. His face had sobered, his eyes turning dark with hunger as they drank her in. Desire chased laughter away.

His soft lips came down sure and straight on hers, which were by now rising to meet him, all hilarity swept away by the look in his eyes, the feel of his body, the strength and sureness of his intent. Oh God, it was *really* happening.

Their lips met just as Joe's voice exploded from the kitchen. 'I tell you. I'm not being told what to do by you pair of fucking morons! Here, boy, help me up! I'm going in there to give the pair of them the what-for!' The sounds of a scraping chair being moved out of the way followed, along with deep grunts of pain as the old man struggled to his feet.

And still Trav kissed her. Long and deep. Tasting, exploring, claiming. His warm lips moved softly and she was lost. In the moment. In the kiss. In Travis Hunter.

Then he was gone. Again. Cold air was all that caressed her body. Tammy wasted precious moments lying there wondering what had just happened.

'What are you doing lying on my fucking bed?'

Tammy sat up, hoping her cheeks weren't as hot as they felt. 'Just testing it out for you. See . . .' She gave the mattress a couple of bounces. 'The springs are still good and I'm sure you'll be very comfortable.' Then she got off the bed quickly, refusing to look at the silent man on the far side of the room.

'Harrumph! I'll sleep in me swag. Like I usually do.'

'You can't get down there and you won't be able to get up,' Trav said from the shadows.

'I'll fucking well give it my best shot!'

※

'It's the bed or the nursing home,' said Tammy ten minutes later, after she'd watched Joe try to lower himself to the camp stretcher at least a half dozen times.

'And that'd give you great pleasure, wouldn't it?' snarled the old man, out of breath. He tried again, and again, but eventually gave up, exhausted.

Tammy watched in silence until he stopped, then held the door open to allow him to clump back into the kitchen where Travis was helping Billy dry the dishes.

'So the bed it is, McCauley?' Travis's tone was wry.

'Harrumph!' The old man stomped his walking frame towards the front room.

'Happy little camper,' said Trav, shooting a glance around at the others in the kitchen. When he reached Tammy she watched as his eyes paused and seemed to take in her whole body in one gulp. And her mind shot back to the scene on the bed, the look in his eyes, the reluctant hunger, *that* kiss. Tammy could feel the heat start to rise from her crotch.

Across the kitchen, Travis's Adam's apple quivered in his throat as he swallowed. 'Right then. We'll get Joe into bed and then be off. C'mon, Billy.'

'But, Dad, we haven't put the stuff aw –'

'I'll do it,' said Tammy quickly. 'I'll put it away, Billy. Off you go.' Anything to get this man out of the kitchen, the house. And the rate Travis Hunter moved through the door after Joe, she guessed he was feeling exactly the same.

It had been five days since her uncle had arrived home to McCauley's Hill and he'd been one difficult patient.

'I'm not fucking eating that stuff!' yelled an indignant Joe, pointing to the offending food, now sitting in a nearby dog bowl. 'Look! Even old Digger won't touch it and he eats *anything*!'

Tammy wondered if Travis was experiencing the same kind of behaviour. But she couldn't ask him because she hadn't seen him in five days. Or, more accurately, one hundred and eighteen hours and forty minutes. Not that she was counting. Somehow they'd managed to instinctively avoid each other. Travis came first thing in the morning to make sure Joe was up and about and then at night to see the old man into bed, leaving her to do the lunchtime and before-afternoon-milking run. Nothing had been verbally organised, it was just the way it had worked out.

'I'm not eating it,' the old man said again, crossing his arms for emphasis. Tammy peered at the contents of the dish. A couple of very thin slices of grey meat, one lonely boiled potato and peas. Lots of peas. All floating in a brown broth that she supposed, at a stretch, could be called gravy.

She tried to inject a bit of enthusiasm into her voice. 'Surely they delivered more meals? Susan said they would bring enough food for a week.'

Joe pointed towards the kitchen. 'Go look. Tell me what you see.' He folded his arms and turned back to his kingdom, lips in an angry sulky line.

She kicked off her Redbacks and walked inside, clocking the bedroom on the right as she went. Try as she might she hadn't been able to stop thinking of Travis. What was it that drew her to him? He was so different to her. There was something about the man that made her think of circles and ovals rather than squares and rigid lines. A man who moved with the environment, the seasons, never on a set path. Wild. Dangerous.

She, on the other hand, was a perfectionist. A neat, tidy, worrying, perfectionist – someone who liked neat edges. Someone who had goals and targets to meet. Milk figures to aspire to; pastures to perfect. Her day was set out like a Rubik's Cube in precise boxes. Well ordered. Careful.

He was like pepper to her salt. No, that wasn't it. A wire to her strainer post? That wasn't it either; he'd be going through her then. She could feel her face flush with heat at the thought of *that*. Oh hell, face it, McCauley, he was just *hot*. Really, really hot.

Tammy let out a sigh that would have rivalled an asthmatic's wheeze. She needed to focus.

'What did you say, girl?' came from outside. 'It's not my fuckin' fault those stupid people can't cook! They should've taken lessons from my Nellie. Now, there was a woman who could make a man drool.'

Tammy glanced at Nellie and Joe's wedding photo on the wall.

'She could cook a bread and butter puddin' that would make your insides just sit up and beg for a second helping,' yelled Joe.

A bit like Travis Hunter's kisses, thought Tammy as she stared at the bed again. She'd sure like another serve of them. Those soft lips, the strength of the man as he loomed above her, the feel of his body on hers, moving against her, loving her.

'And her Sunday roasts were something else . . .' came floating through the door on the breeze.

Crap! What the hell was she in here for again? Meals: that was it. Maybe it was easier to cook for him herself? Surely he'd put up with that, just like he'd put up with something else she'd found out about. Joe had let it slip Travis had been dropping off venison to him every now and then, since way before the accident. She could well imagine that little meeting, each man silently staring the other down. It would be like granite meeting iron.

She wondered if the meat drop-off was more about checking on the old man than the extra tucker. It had made her see another facet of Travis Hunter. Almost against his will, he seemed to want to care and protect the vulnerable, although why he didn't see his own son in that light confounded her.

Tammy forced her mind back to the job at hand, resolutely moving towards the kitchen and its freezer. She already had enough turmoil in her life. She needed to put all feelings and thoughts of Travis in the same sort of cold storage as the food. He . . . it . . . whatever had happened between them was never going to happen again. She needed to make sure of that.

Chapter 22

Trav was in trouble. The clock was inching its way towards six-thirty and he couldn't find a shirt to wear. To make matters worse Billy was watching him with a mystified look on his face as he rushed from ironing board to cupboard. 'Well, what do you think?' He stood there in his Wrangler jeans and a paisley brown and green swirled shirt. Something that had looked fine ten or so years earlier.

Billy was frowning.

'What?' Trav peered down. 'It's the shirt, isn't it?' It was ridiculous.

Billy nodded, hesitantly at first, then really hard.

'Right.' Trav ripped off the offending article and threw it at the bin. He strode back to the closed corner of the old shack, which took the dubious title of 'the main bedroom', and retrieved another shirt of pale green with RM Williams picked out in blue thread. 'It'll have to be this one then, that's all I own.' Trav cursed himself for not thinking ahead. If he'd had time between working, looking after Billy and helping Joe, he might have headed into town and shouted himself some new clothes. Actually tried to impress Cin.

Who was he kidding? It wasn't Cin who Trav wanted to impress. It was the other one. The one who was all woman in her buttoned-down shirt and tight RM Williams jeans. The one with the firm body who only ever showed a hint of cleavage, but who had a voice sexy enough to get his heart pounding and his blood pressure well and truly up.

Her luminous big brown eyes had stared up at him in his dreams for the last fortnight. And who could ever forget that kiss? That beautiful, soft, deep kiss that went on forever and ever. Until it was interrupted by a belligerent old man.

'Dad. I think that's good.'

Trav hit the earth with a thud. His son was standing in front of him. 'What?'

'It's good. The shirt, I mean.' Billy seemed to struggle for a minute before rushing on, 'You look great. Ms Greenaway will love it.'

Ms Greenaway? His date for tonight. 'Fuck!' he muttered, immediately feeling resentful about the dance all over again.

The boy flinched and that kicked Trav in the gut. He couldn't get it right. Guilt was like an open maw of shame that clamoured to take hold of anything that was good between him and his son. The child was turning away, his shoulders slumped. Just like Trav used to do when he was a child, when he'd buggered up with *his* dad. Same look. Same slouch. Same defeated stance. 'Thanks,' he said quickly to Billy's back. The boy half turned. 'Didn't mean to sound cranky, I'm just a bit . . . like . . . ummm . . .'

'Nervous?' offered Billy, daringly.

'Yep. Nervous.' Trav said, reaching out a hand. He touched the boy's head, instinct guiding him. The red hair was soft, so soft, and spiralling like a curly retriever's. Trav quickly took away his hand and shoved it into his pocket. As he walked towards the door, he missed the look of wonder on his son's face.

⁂

Old Joe was in fine form. He'd have no fucking babysitters tonight. They'd all be partying in town at the dance and he, Joe McCauley, would finally have the hill and his whole kingdom to himself. At last. Well, except for the boy. Joe was figuring he shouldn't be too much trouble. He might even get to sleep on the old camp bed, seeing there'd be no busy-bodying bastards to look in on him. And the boy could sleep in the bed. There, even Nellie couldn't disagree with that one. She'd love it, finally a child in the house, warm and snug and safe in her bed at long last.

The woman had been having a bit to say lately. All in his mind, of course. He wasn't far enough off his rocker to think she was really there. But still – that night when he'd arrived home from hospital and slept in *their* bed, the first time since she'd died – he'd felt her. Nellie's soft body had rolled into his back like she was shoring up his rear defences, just like she always did before she fell asleep.

And he could have sworn he'd smelled her the next morning in the early hours, just before dawn. Roses. Lavender and roses. An interesting mix, which on Nellie spoke of comfort and safekeeping. Home was what the old woman was to Joe.

Mae Rouget had been all class and fun, but Nellie had been steadfast strength and love. He missed her something terrible.

'I've brought Billy.' Hunter was on his verandah. Joe hadn't even heard him pull up.

The old man quickly pulled his grumpy face on. 'Right. Well. C'mon over here, boy, give us a look at you.'

Billy shuffled across the verandah boards, clutching a small rolled canvas swag. On his back was a pack filled with stuff, and he had what looked suspiciously like a worn-out teddy peeking out from under his arm. Joe chose to ignore the bear. 'Stow your swag and pack in the kitchen and come back out. Bring a chair with you.'

'I'll be going then,' said Travis, his eyes following the boy through the door. He looked back at Joe. 'Thanks for this.' He stopped a beat then added, 'I think.' The dog trapper's grin was rueful.

'You're welcome. Now go. I can see Gibson's car's going down the girl's drive.' *His* smile was sly. 'Happy hunting, Travis.'

⁂

Tammy was looking for her shoes when the doorbell rang. She hadn't heard the car as she was buried in the wardrobe trying to find the scrappy things that the shoe-shop woman had assured her were sandals. More like fine strings of leather hanging off a three-inch heel – *and* they'd cost a fortune. A bit like the peacock blue and green dress she had on.

She'd fallen in love with it, although it wasn't as demure as she was used to. Thinking of sexy Cin and the wolfish Joanne, though, she'd gone beyond her comfort zone and bought the damnable scrap of floating layers of chiffon. When the saleswoman assured her it covered all that it needed to, she hadn't realised just how *little* it actually did.

She pulled the bodice up a bit more, and watched in the mirror as it obeyed gravity and snuck down again, relentless in its intent to show off more cleavage than she was comfortable with. The doorbell pealed again.

Shit. Not only was the bloke persistent, he was on time. She should have guessed. 'Coming!' she yelled into the wardrobe, then realised he'd have no hope in heck of hearing her; her bedroom was way up the other end of the house. She half ran – trying at the same time to pull on her errant sandals – then limped down two passages, around a few corners, through the kitchen, dining room, and across the closed-in verandah to the back door. She quickly did up the tiny buckles on her shoes, then opened the door.

'Dean. Hi. You're on time.'

The man was staring at her like she was some strange apparition. 'Yes. I'm always on time.'

Of course. Silly her. Then she realised he was looking at her funny. 'What's wrong?' Her hand flew up to her ears. Was it cowshit? Hadn't she scrubbed it all off? 'Have I missed something?'

'No. No! Nothing at all. It's . . . well, Tammy, you look stunning!' His eyes moved from the tips of her blow-dried hair, over her lightly made-up face and down to the hem of her skirt. Where he stopped and frowned. 'Do you think they . . . maybe could have . . . well, possibly should have . . . made that dress a bit longer?'

Tammy looked down. Saw that in her flight through the house, the dress had ridden up and now barely covered her thighs. Shit. 'Do you think I should change?' she said.

'Oh my goodness, no. No! Together we'll be the belles of the ball!'

She finally took a look at what Dean was wearing. A pair of black slacks, pressed pleats rigidly dissecting each leg into two, topped with a brown and green swirled paisley shirt. The shirt hid a singlet, a white 'wife beater'. On a man in his thirties? In the bush? She could see a bit of it poking out near his neck, where in shaving he'd missed a run of hairs. The singlet and shirt would have been hip ten or twenty years ago, but right now?

It looked hideous.

She gratefully turned her face away from the paisley as she saw Trav's ute arrive. It rumbled its way past the dairy and pulled to a stop outside the garden gate, just behind her own four-wheel drive.

Travis Hunter slowly appeared, bit by delicious bit: first, a pair of tooled leather cowboy boots (Ariats if she wasn't mistaken. She'd forgotten he was a station-boy from way back). Then came a long pair of denim clad-legs (Wranglers). Followed by strong, muscled arms covered by a gorgeous, soft and worn celadon shirt with its distinctive RM Williams bull-horns logo, sleeves rolled to the elbow. The shirt clung to him, showing the outline of a bluey singlet underneath. He looked freshly showered, his hair all rumpled and softly curling at the tender nape of his neck. The buzz cut was growing out.

'Deano.' Trav's greeting to the other man was brief. Then he was standing at her back door, drinking her in like fine wine. And Tammy forgot all about paisley vs celadon. She forgot all about white wife-basher singlets vs the tough Bonds blue. She literally forgot about everything other than this man.

Because close up he looked good enough to eat.

And Trav was taking in *her* whole body. Absorbing her – her hair, her face, her eyes, her mouth. His gaze moved down to the indecent amount of cleavage and her nipples standing on high beam, across her flat belly, down, down, down and appearing to take forever as he soaked in her long legs, finally stopping at her barely-there sandals and their tall, sexy heel. 'You look great,' he managed.

'She looks more than great, Hunter. She looks sensational!' Dean moved in to claim his date around the waist with a possessive arm. 'Are you ready, sweetheart? We've got a party to go to!'

Tammy adroitly stepped out of Dean's clasp and half-turned to go inside again. 'I'll just lock up.' And catch my breath, slow my heart and forget how I nearly made a fool of myself by falling all over Travis Hunter out there.

Dean spun and moved back down the path towards his car. 'Okay, I'll warm up the old bus for you, love,' he called over his shoulder.

She grimaced, then went to move off to find a key. A hand came out and grabbed her arm.

Travis. 'You look stunning,' he murmured. His blue eyes bored into her brown ones. He took a stronger hold. 'Beautiful.' Then he leaned in and placed a soft kiss on her mouth. A question, an exclamation mark, a full stop. He drew back, let go of her arm, cast her a look of rueful apprehension and then turned towards the car that was now bumping down the drive. Jacinta's shiny red convertible, rear spoiler jumping as the tyres hit the potholes in the gravel, mag wheels being spattered with spots of cow-shit.

High up on his hill, Old Joe was naming star constellations to an avid listener. The boy was gaining confidence with every question.

'Which one's Jupiter? How many moons does it have? What's the Milky Way made up of then? And are we part of it all? You know, the whole university?'

'Universe, boy. Not university.' Joe swung an ancient-looking telescope this way then that, sharing with him the knowledge of nearly ninety years staring at the night sky.

After a while, Billy's attention was distracted from the heavens by a glint of water in Backwater Creek. 'Why is that thing there, Mr McCauley?' He was pointing to the slabs of bark that you could vaguely see in the moonlight.

'Ah, that's the remains of old Cec's hut.' At Billy's interested look, Joe went on. 'He was a prospector years and years ago, before I was even born, hunting for gold in these hills. Looking for a pocketful of gold and a handful of hope.'

'Is that why our road's called Hope's Road?'

Joe stared out across the flats, contemplating his answer for a few seconds. That was a loaded question even if the boy didn't know it. 'Yep. We're all looking for it in one way or another I guess.'

They took more turns peering through the eye-piece up at the sky again until it was Joe's go with the telescope. He swung it back to earth, just for a few minutes while Billy was distracted by Digger gnawing on a bone.

The scope brought Montmorency Downs into his sights. The old diesel ute of Hunter's sat hard-up against Tammy's vehicle. It looked good, Joe thought. Like it was supposed to be there. Not like that other solid yet slightly tizzy number – it was a townie's car, for sure. Must be Dean Gibson's. Nice enough bloke, but a bit wussy. And Joe didn't just mean the car.

The telescope swung to the back door, where all the action appeared to be happening. The car went with the shirt Gibson was wearing. Joe could see sloping shoulders wearing a solid patch of garish colours. Even *he* wouldn't be seen dead in that get-up.

He moved the scope over Gibson's head – and sucked in his breath. Holy Lord. She was as beautiful as her grandmother. Shoulder-length brunette hair feathered around a sweetheart face, long aristocratic nose, high cheekbones, deep brown eyes. There had to be French versus Egyptian somewhere in the Rouget genetic lineage.

And for fuck's sake, look at that dress! It barely covered her bottom. He went to rise out of his chair in indignation, landed back down with a thud. Holy hell, that hurt.

He returned the telescope to his eye, refocused it on the old homestead once more. Gibson was gone, down the path towards his flash car. And Travis Hunter was now standing there, his shoulders square. He was talking. Then he was leaning forwards. Moving in. Then he was kissing Joe McCauley's great-niece right at her own door.

Joe sat back in his chair, telescope dropped to his knees. Oh, my aunt's *fanny*!

Chapter 23

Lucy Granger was perched on a concrete planter box, her hair a mess of multi-coloured hot-roller-assisted curls as the foursome pulled up outside the pub.

'Geez, I thought you were never going to get here!' She bounced up to Tammy. 'C'mon. All the seafood will be gone! Joanne's so tight-fisted she never lets the chef order enough.'

Then Lucy took in her best friend's outfit. She slowly let out a wolf-whistle. 'Holy crap, Tammy. You look unreal. Totally hot!' She spun to Trav who was standing behind her. 'Doesn't she look hot? Man, if I felt like some time on the other team . . .'

'Well, luckily you don't,' said Dean, coming around the car bonnet and taking Tammy's hand. 'Do you?'

'Well . . .' said Lucy looking thoughtful. 'It's an idea. I wasn't able to rustle up a date for tonight, not one under the age of seventy anyway. In fact, Dean, I've had some very . . .

interesting ... relationships in my life. I don't like to label myself either way.'

Tammy rolled her eyes. She'd heard Lucy's tales of university experimentation, though she wasn't entirely sure how far to believe them.

'C'mon,' said Cin, for a change looking demure in a black cocktail dress with a simple Jacqueline Kennedy cut. She stood, smoothing the car creases out of the knee-length frock. 'I want a salt and pepper calamari and it'll all be gone if we don't hurry up.'

'That's what I was just saying,' grumbled Lucy. 'No one ever listens to me.'

Tammy disentangled herself from Dean and threw her arm around her best mate, dragging Lucy towards the pub lounge door. 'Of course we do.' Then she whispered, 'You can have my date if you want.'

Lucy laughed as she slung a look back across her shoulder at a disgruntled Dean standing with Cin on the grass verge. 'No way, Jose. That shirt is god-awful, not to mention the pleated pants. What was he thinking?'

'Not much, obviously.'

'Well, he's hardly likely to attract a woman in that get-up. Hunter, on the other-hand ...' Lucy paused on the hotel doorstep, checking they were still alone. 'In my next life I'm going to come back as a wild dog. To be caught by a man like Travis Hunter would be,' Lucy's eyes turned dreamy, 'incredible. Totally amazing. But, I'm dreaming ... and besides, he's too much the strong silent type for me.'

Lucy's grin slipped as she moved in for a better look at the flush claiming Tammy's face. 'Oh, my aunt's *fanny*! You like Travis Hunter? You want the dog trapper, don't you?'

'Him? What utter nonsense!' Tammy flapped her hands in the air in agitation. 'C'mon, let's go get you some poor dead marine creature.' She moved to drag Lucy through the lounge door to distract her somehow. 'And remember I'm relying on you to give me some protection from that bitch behind the bar.'

Lucy stopped again, her face serious. 'You sure you want to do this? We could go somewhere else?'

'Like where?'

'Oh, I don't know. The roadhouse for a sausage roll? The corner store for fish and chips?'

'Go raid some of the yabby nets the kids throw into the lake? Cook the muddy suckers on the barbecue in the APEX park?' finished Tammy.

'Muddy suckers? The kids or the yabbies?' asked Lucy, grinning.

Tammy winked. 'It'd have to be the kids. I can't stand crustaceans.' They both laughed before she went on, 'No. It's fine. I've got to face Shon and Joanne together some time. May as well be now.'

'You sure?'

'Of course I'm sure.' *Not.* Tammy tried to soothe her thumping heart and plaster on a reassuring smile. 'Let's get some tucker and then go find a party.'

※

As it turned out, neither Joanne nor Shon were to be seen in the Lake Grace Hotel.

'Must have the night off,' whispered Lucy later after she'd consumed a whole basket of prawns.

Tammy's chicken Maryland still sat on its plate, barely touched. 'Yeah, probably ensconced in a lovers' boudoir in Lakes Entrance or Batemans Bay,' she muttered back.

'Come along, kiddies,' called Dean from the other side of Tammy. 'We've got a dance to attend and it's now eight-thirty-five by my watch. We're running late.'

'Oooo, yes!' Cin clapped her hands and bounced in her seat. The creamy strands of pearls that covered any sign of her bosom slapped up and down.

'Doesn't he know you never get to these things on time?' Lucy murmured. 'This is the bush. Dairy farmers are *always* late!'

This time Trav answered. 'Don't think "late" is in old Deano's vocabulary.'

Tammy looked across at him. He had barely said a thing all night, preferring to just stare at her every now and then.

'C'mon, Tammy,' said Dean, catching her under the elbow and lifting her up out of the chair. 'Let's get this show on the road. Although . . .' He frowned down at Tammy's plate. 'I don't see how you're going to have any energy to dance. You didn't eat a thing!'

'You know women these days, Deano,' said Trav, moving to Tammy's other side. 'Always worried about their figure.' Then he turned to her, his half-smile and azure eyes seeming to say, 'But you don't need to.'

※

The music was just cranking up when they arrived. Barely a dozen cars were parked outside the hall. 'That's weird,' said Dean looking around. 'Everyone I spoke to in Lake Grace this week said they were coming.'

'They'll get here,' said Lucy, rolling her eyes towards Tammy. '*Eventually* . . .'

The group lined up at the old-fashioned ticket-box just inside the entrance vestibule. Beatrice Parker took their money. 'Nice to see you all here,' she said with a cagey smile. 'Who is with whom?'

Dean grabbed Tammy's arm again. 'This gorgeous woman is my date for tonight.'

Tammy tried surreptitiously to wriggle out of his clasp but to no avail. Deano held on tight.

'Oooo . . . and this handsome fella is mine!' cried Cin, grabbing Trav's hand.

But Beatrice wasn't paying any attention to Cin. Her disapproving eyes were on Tammy's dress. Her gaze didn't have to travel far to look the scrap of material over. Tammy tried to pull the skirt down, which in turn pulled the already low-cut top in the same direction. Inwardly she cursed herself yet again for buying the damn frock.

'Mrs Parker? Earth to Mrs Parker?'

Beatrice tore her eyes from Tammy to stare at Lucy, who was waving her fingers in front of the old lady's face. 'You wouldn't happen to know of an available woman willing to try out being a lesbian?'

'I *beg* your pardon, Ms Granger?' said Beatrice, now completely distracted from Tammy. 'Did you say *lesbian*?'

'Oh no, Mrs Parker,' Trav interrupted. 'She said thespian. She's giving away pole-dancing for the dramatic arts. C'mon, Granger.' He grabbed Lucy with one hand and Cin with the other and towed them into the main hall. Tammy and Dean shrugged at a skeptical-looking Mrs Parker and moved quickly to follow the others.

'I would have sworn that Granger girl said lesbian,' the old woman muttered to herself. 'And as for that dress on Tammy McCauley! She's turning into a hussy, just like her grandmother.'

Tammy, who'd heard it all, walked quickly away.

※

Slowly more and more people started to arrive at the hall until the dance floor, which encompassed the whole centre of the old rectangle weatherboard building, was jammed with bodies. Some were dancing ballroom style, fox-trotting around the edges. Others were just shaking their limbs to the raucous music that was getting louder and louder as voices rose in competition.

Tammy hadn't lacked for partners. Every dance, someone plonked himself in front of her and asked for a turn on the floor. Neighbouring dairy farmers, old friends of her granddad's, tradies from town. She was aware of Dean getting more and more disgruntled as once again she was carted away by another partner. 'Next one's for you, Dean,' she called as Rob Sellers took a drink from her hand and dragged her along with him to swing to the Pride of Erin. Dean's grimace was her answer.

One of the few men in the hall who hadn't offered to dance with her was Travis Hunter. And Tammy was surprised at how much that hurt. She had been aware of him the whole night, knew exactly where he was at any given time. She was so *attuned* to the man – it was both startling and disconcerting. She didn't need to be mooning over the dog trapper and found herself getting more and more annoyed by how much time her mind devoted to tracking his every move.

Finally she ended up on the dance floor in the arms of Dean Gibson. The man was courteous, kind and had great rhythm, but there was one huge problem. She didn't feel in the least bit attracted to him. In fact the scent of his mouthwash was a real turn-off, as were the sweaty hands sitting hesitantly on her waist. Then there was the musty smell coming from that damn shirt. Every time Deano tried to pull her in close she backed away. It became almost a duel of strength, one which Dean eventually won. Tammy suddenly found herself hard up against the paramedic's chest, his arm around her waist, hand moving up to caress her back. She tried to move away but found she couldn't.

'Excuse me, may I cut in?' The voice came from close to Tammy's left ear. Startled, she swung around, causing her partner to lose his grip. She was just in time to see Trav deftly slip in and shoulder a scowling Dean out of the way.

'Thanks, Deano,' he said. And then she was away, being twirled across the floor with surprising grace. The dance was a fast foxtrot and, as she was whizzed around the corner, she was shocked by how different Travis's hands felt to Dean's.

The grip on her waist was firm and sure. He held her body just slightly distant from him, far enough away to look down into her face, near enough to feel intimate. His vivid blue eyes were alight with humour and mischief. 'Don't think I'm the most popular man with old Deano at the moment.' He gave a wicked grin. 'You dance well, Ms McCauley.' He swung her around another corner, pausing to flick her under his arm, before pulling her back in close in a classic ballroom dance pose.

'And you too,' said Tammy. She was surprised at his dexterity on the dance floor. 'Who taught you to move so well on your feet? Those wild dogs up on that fence?'

'Nope. My mother. She made me take ballroom dancing lessons. A dance teacher was in town for a while when I was at school and I think Mum figured it might give me some culture.'

'And did it?'

'Nope. Just made me more nimble on my feet – good for avoiding a flogging.'

Tammy laughed softly. This man was *good*.

Suddenly the music changed to a more melancholy song. It was slow and intimate, with every note dipped in romance. The tune and lyrics thrummed with the need to pull a loved one closer and the couples moving around them slowly came together.

It was then that Tammy found herself in a whole lot of trouble. Trav had reacted almost instinctively to the change in rhythm, pulling her into his chest, tucking her head under his chin. She was instantly aware of him. His smell, his feel. Her whole body pulsed with heat and suppressed flames of desire erupted to life. The slivers of cotton and chiffon that kept their bodies apart became almost negligible. The hall, the music, the people around them, all seemed to flee her consciousness. They were alone. Moving as one to something beyond the music. The roaring in her ears grew louder and louder, and her whole body felt like it would simply explode from the heat flowing through it. They may as well have been naked. The feel of the long and hard muscles resting against her skin sent tiny quivers of erotic need thrumming through her body. She felt a hand move gently to stroke her back. It felt so natural, so infinitely *right* to be in this man's arms.

And then abruptly it was over. Trav was pushing her away as if he wasn't sure what had just happened. 'Thanks for the dance,' he muttered, before fleeing the floor, leaving her standing alone.

Bereft.

The last she saw of him was the back of his head disappearing through the side hall door.

Chapter 24

Tammy was up on the dance floor doing the 'Nutbush' with Lucy, Cin and Susan Sellers when a very drunk Shon Murphy sauntered in the door of the Lake Grace Hall. Tammy had been glad of a dance with the girls. After Trav had disappeared, her whole evening had gone pear-shaped, what with wondering what she had done wrong, trying to keep Dean out of her personal space without offending him . . . and now this.

Shon made his way towards the bar, before stopping when he caught sight of her. 'What's my fucking wife doing here dancing half naked?' he yelled across the hall, causing everyone within earshot to fall silent. 'Hey! Tammy Murphy! Get your frigid arse over here!'

The young boy operating the karaoke machine was stunned into pressing the off button. The music stopped. The crowd around the edges of the hall shuffled their feet, nudged each other, pointed.

'I said get over here!' Shon roared again.

Tammy stood stock-still in the middle of the hall, Lucy on one side, Cin on the other. Both women had their hands on her arms, holding her back from moving a step in any direction. Susan Sellers stood behind her, shoring up the rear.

'She'll be going nowhere, mate.' Travis's voice came from Shon's left. He walked up and stood in front of Murphy, facing him down. Trav's shoulders were back, his head was up and he looked unperturbed by the huffing and puffing red-faced menace standing in front of him. 'And I'd like you to do all of us a favour and turn around and walk right back out that door.'

'That might be for the best,' said Rob Sellers, coming up on Trav's right flank, desperately trying to look amiable but threatening all the same.

Dean Gibson scrambled to his feet from a nearby chair. He'd been watching Tammy dancing while devouring one of Beatrice's delicious cakes. 'I second that,' he squeaked around a mouthful of cream.

'Who the hell are you? I know him and him,' spat Shon pointing to Trav and Rob, 'not *you*.'

Dean tried to swallow the cream that was threatening to tumble from his mouth. 'Ummm . . .'

'Dean is the new ambo,' said Trav, nice and slow. 'And if you don't leave now he'll have to patch you up, so I'd go easy on him if I were you.'

Shon dipped his head up and down like a bull deciding whether to charge. From twenty feet away a mortified and fearful Tammy watched. She saw flashes of his face as he sneered at her and her friends, as he took whatever he wanted and spat on the rest, as he swung his arm back and –

Dean leaped back three feet. 'C'mon, boys . . .' He attempted to inject a soothing note into his voice, arms out in front, palms down. 'Let's sort this outside.'

'Too fucking right we'll sort this outside,' roared Shon. 'Who are you to tell *me* what to do, boundary rider?'

The silent crowd drew back with a collective breath – and then leaned in to watch what was going to happen next.

'Shon Murphy! You should be plain Jane ashamed of yourself!' A voice could be heard from beyond the standoff. Beatrice Parker came tottering up to the little knot of men, the diminutive figure leaning on her walking stick, pushing past Rob Sellers and inserting herself between Shon and Travis Hunter. 'Speaking about your wife like that!'

'Ex-wife,' chorused Dean and Rob. Trav didn't say a word. He was too busy staring Shon Murphy down.

'Whatever,' said Beatrice, flapping her arthritic hands in dismissal. 'Stop this nonsense at once, you hear, dears. I won't have my dance all mucked up. You can head back to wherever you came from, Shon Murphy, and sleep off that drink or throw up in the sink. We've got a defibrillator to raise money for. So come along. No more.'

And she grabbed hold of Shon's arm, and towed him through the hall, and right out the double front doors. The night air was filled with his threats but it was to no avail.

'Say hello to Joanne,' Beatrice called outside the hall. 'I'll be in to get a donation towards the defibrillator from the hotel when she's well.'

The little elderly lady then walked back inside, clapped her hands and motioned to the karaoke boy to crank the music back up before making a beeline towards Dean, Rob and Trav who, seeing her coming, hastily fled towards the men's toilets.

'Pikers,' muttered Susan Sellers from behind the girls.

'Cream puffs, more like it!' said Lucy, looking around and wondering why no one was laughing.

※

'Are you all right?' A deep voice came from the hall doorway. Tammy was leaning over an old horse-hitching rail outside, trying to calm herself. Shon had scared the crap out of her. More memories of being down on the ground spun like a kaleidoscope before her eyes. Shon looming over her with his fist in the air . . .

'Hey. It's okay.' Trav was right beside her now. 'He's gone and no harm done. He's probably fallen unconscious after vomiting on Joanne's silk sheets. She'll give him curry for that.'

Tammy attempted to laugh. She really *wanted* to laugh at the fact her ex-husband had made a fool of himself – and her – in front of their whole community.

Instead the laugh became a sob and she found herself crying, the grief coming from deep inside her belly. How had their marriage resulted in this? It had been so *good* at the start. Love and hate – they really *were* aligned close together and Shon's violence, she sensed, was born from supreme frustration, his inability to get or be what he wanted. She just happened to be the whipping post, the thing he perceived to be in the way of achieving his dreams. Plus, the drink didn't help. She couldn't really put her finger on when *that* had become a problem. But none of it was an excuse for treating her like this.

Trav's arms came around her, firm and secure yet again, but this time there was an unspoken question at the same time.

Perhaps he wanted to comfort but didn't want to intrude on the end of a marriage.

Or was it that he didn't know what he wanted himself? The man confused her completely. Their obvious attraction kept bringing them both to this point, and each time the mixed messages drove them apart. What the hell did he want? She couldn't do this seesaw of emotions, not now, not yet and maybe not ever.

'No – Trav. I can't.'

He lifted her chin. 'Can't? Or won't?'

'Can't. Won't. Does it really matter?' The sobs were coming freely now and she wasn't sure they'd ever stop. She moved to break away. 'It's not you. It's me. I –'

'It's okay,' Trav said, his arms quickly releasing her. 'It's fine.'

There was that incongruous word. Fine. It wasn't fine. Not the way he was saying it anyway.

His warm body was moving away, leaving her cold, lonely, heartbroken. 'I've been there, remember,' he said.

And then he was gone.

※

At midnight they'd all driven home pretty much in silence. Even Cin had the good sense not to say too much on the trip back to Montmorency. After pulling in the drive, a brooding Trav had *shaken* Cin's hand goodbye, thanked Dean for the ride, nodded tersely at Tammy then jumped in his ute and roared out of the drive.

Cin stared after him, blinking back tears.

'Well, then . . .' Dean coughed and cleared his throat. 'Thanks for a lovely night, ladies. We should do it again some time.'

Both women glared at him before Cin walked towards her own car in silence. She flung them a half-wave, got in and took off, spinning the wheels as she high-tailed it out towards the main road.

Dean turned to Tammy. 'Well, the supper was really nice . . .'

She had to give him credit. He really tried. 'Dean, thanks a lot for the ride, the date. I think I'll just wander in and go to bed,' Tammy said, putting her hand up to fake a yawn. 'I've got to be up at five to milk so you won't mind if I don't invite you in.'

'Oh. Okay,' he said, sounding disappointed. 'Ummm, Tammy? I meant it. Maybe we can do it again some time?'

She gave the man a small, sad smile.

'Maybe. Good night, Dean.' And she leaned forwards and kissed him on the cheek before turning and making her way down the path, into her big, old silent house. To be alone with the feelings of loss, sadness and grief that were swamping her mind.

Chapter 25

In the light of day Tammy decided she wanted nothing more than to drive into Narree and buy that plane ticket to the Great Barrier Reef. Warmth, peace and quiet. Far away from Montmorency Downs, Lake Grace and the problems mounting up around her.

It was autumn and thus, on a dairy farm, time for maintenance – sowing new pasture and fencing and putting in stock troughs and irrigation outlets and renovating delver channels – the list went on and on.

Buying the run-down run-off block two years earlier had doubled her workload. The whole place needed fixing up – which was why they'd bought it at such a good price.

She walked around the hayshed and headed towards the house for her lunch. Well, it was breakfast really, because a slice of toast at five am, when she was running out the door to bring up the cows to milk, probably didn't cut it.

The day was lovely. The sky bright and blue. The sun not too hot, not too cold and there was the scent of the hay in the shed on the slight breeze. Nothing made you inhale more deeply than warmth, fresh air and the smell of hay. It was a shame she wasn't in a better mood to appreciate it. She was tired and cranky because of the night before. The dance. She didn't want to remember really.

As she turned towards the homestead, something caught her eye up at the house. A flash off a windscreen glinting in the sun. There was a ute in her driveway. A twin-cab parked close to the garden fence like it was staking its right to be there.

Shon.

Tammy's heart sank right through her boots.

What the hell did he want?

※

He was sitting in the kitchen, feet up on a chair, lounging back like he owned the place. The odour of stale alcohol floated around him.

'And so, the lady of the manor returns. Whose bed did you end up in last night? Or do I need to ask?' His sneer crowded a red vivid face. 'That paramedic looked like he was all for jumping your bones. Him or maybe even Rob Sellers? He was pretty quick to leap to your defence.'

'You leave Rob out of this,' said Tammy, stung her friend's loyalty to *his* wife was being called into question.

'So the bitch bites back. Interesting.'

Tammy wondered how she could have ever thought she loved this man. It was incredible how much he seemed to hate her. Her mind spun back to her conversation with Lucy, the day she knew her marriage was over.

'When did it all go wrong? What did I do?' she'd asked.

'You didn't do anything. He's got a lot of problems, Tam, and none of them came from you, no matter how he blames you for them.'

Now she asked, 'Why are you here, Shon? Because you sure as hell aren't welcome.'

'When was I *ever* welcome?'

'Oh for goodness sake –'

'Fuck off, you stuck-up frigid bitch.'

'Well, gosh. Am I frigid or am I seducing my friend's husband? So confusing.'

He jumped up from the table and came towards her. The look on his face truly dreadful.

Tammy stepped back and sped right out the door, Shon following her – chasing her. She flung a glance over her shoulder, then grabbed the long shovel that was still leaning against the back of house – her snake shovel. What better use for it than now? She swung back around towards the man, spade held across her body protectively.

With his thick shoulders thrust back, head up and forwards, moving relentlessly towards her, Shon looked like a charging pig.

'Stay away from me, Shon Murphy. Say what you want and then clear off, you hear!'

'You think you can stop me taking what I want with a *shovel*?' He started to laugh. Big, masculine guffaws that, years ago, were one of the things she loved about him. All in or all out. That was Shon Murphy's motto.

'What. Do. You. Want?' Tammy spat it out.

Shon sobered up quick. 'Half the farm.' His eyes were

calculating. He crossed his arms and slouched nonchalantly to one side, like he had her right where he wanted her. 'I'll take the money in two instalments. Half now. The rest in twelve months. It's the least I deserve after putting up with . . .' and the man went on and on, his grievances boiling to the surface in one big seething cauldron of rage.

Barely listening to him rant, Tammy sucked in a breath, stunned. Half the *farm*? In *instalments*? Like hell.

'No.'

Shon's irate voice ground to a sudden halt. 'What do you mean, "no"?'

'The farm belongs to me. The run-off block belongs to both of us. I'll pay you out for the block, but that's all you're getting.

'I worked my arse off here,' he snarled.

'*Ha!* That's a joke. Sitting around drinking and playing *lord of the manor* isn't "working", Shon Murphy!'

'Why you little –' And he was coming towards her, thrusting aside the shovel like it was a twig, meaty fist in the air . . .

⚜

The morning's fun had started not long after Hunter's ute disappeared down the hill. The dog trapper had arrived to tell Joe that he needed to check out a line of traps. Could he have the boy for the day? Which was interesting in itself. Hunter had never worried about leaving the boy on his own before.

And Travis hadn't seen the look of glee on his son's face. He didn't know about the conversation from the night before. Joe had told Billy he'd show him how to set one of the rusty rabbit traps hanging in the shed. 'Me, I shoot 'em these days,' the old man said to the boy.

'How many of the little bastards have ya shot?' asked Billy.

Joe blinked at him for a minute, not sure if he should say anything about the swearing – after all, the child *was* a boy.

Then Billy added the clarification he thought Joe must be waiting for: 'Honest to goodness. Man to man, like.'

Joe had grinned and said, 'Shitloads. I'll show you how to do that tomorrow too, if you like?'

'If I *like*?' yelled Billy. 'Awesome. Totally awesome! Stuff the Cheeseburger. With you on board, my family is now the size of a McFeast. I just need a mother and I'll have the whole Big Mac!'

Joe had shaken his head. He had no idea what the boy was talking about but he was happy, that was the main thing.

And then, just to add a bit more excitement, Joe suggested that Billy might like to have a go at driving his tractor.

The kid had bounced up and down with glee. 'You mean you'll teach me all that? Like a real granddad would?'

Joe had nodded, feeling unfamiliar threads of satisfaction unravel through his body. It was a strange feeling, this making someone happy.

'Move it, boy,' he said when Travis left. 'Get some brekkie into ya and we'll get cracking. Got to feed them cows today.'

'But Dad said he'd do it.'

'I know what your father said,' Joe grumbled. 'But since when does a learned man of nearly ninety years have to listen to a young whipper-snapper like him?' The old man's grin was conspiratorial.

'Ummm . . . He'll be *ma-ad*!'

'Travis Hunter doesn't scare me,' said Joe with a scoff. 'Tammy does, though, a wee bit.' The old man then looked rueful. 'When she gets that glint in her eye, like she doesn't give a bugger what you say, she's going to do it her own way and to hell with the rest of 'em.'

Billy looked thoughtful, like he was trying to work out whether he should say something or not.

'What?'

The child shook his head, smiled and then asked very politely where to find the toaster.

So then the day started in earnest. It'd taken a while but they'd got over to the shed eventually, a small boy gambolling along with two dogs at his heels, an old man moving slowly but surely on an aluminium walking frame.

Billy had found a chair in the shed for Joe to sit on, and the man had sunk into it gratefully, though he did his best not to show the boy just how much of an effort it really was to be out there.

When Joe gave him the nod Billy hopped up onto the tractor, bouncing excitedly on the seat.

'Now settle down, boy, and listen to me carefully. The key is there on the right. Clutch at the left foot, brake at the right foot. Gearstick in the middle. Throttle to the right of the steering wheel, on the arm. Ya driven your dad's ute before?'

Billy nodded, though Joe could tell he wasn't really paying attention.

'Okay, now start her up.'

The tractor rumbled to life. The cat shot out from under the massive back rubber wheels, squealing. Both dogs started to bark excited yelps.

'Clutch in, gearstick engaged, clutch out and go,' yelled old Joe, not sure Billy was hearing him over the din. Oh well.

If he'd driven Hunter's ute, he'd work the clutch and the gears out on the tractor quick enough.

'Way to *gooo*!' Billy yelled at the top of his voice. His little foot depressed the clutch, his fingers crunched the gear, and he was off. Bunny-hopping. Tractor roaring. Dogs dancing around the front tyres, yelping, barking, running from side to side with glee. Joe watched the cat shoot up the drainpipe and onto the rafters, then turned at the sound of a yell.

Billy. Still heading straight ahead on the tractor. Poleaxed into position. Staring at what was ahead. The side wall of old Joe's house.

'*Stop*, Billy! Turn the wheel! Turn the fucking steering wheel, you idiot!' Forgetting his bad hip, Joe went to jump up, intent on running after the tractor. He sat back down with a thump. '*Fuck!*' The old man grappled for the walking frame, wincing and chomping down hard on his bottom lip with the pain. The tractor was moving closer and closer to the house, until even the dogs started to look worried.

'For crying out loud, Billy! *Turn the wheel*!'

Finally the boy heard him and hauled hard on the big, round metal circle. He heaved down, and tried with all his might to get the tractor to turn. The machine slowly responded and the smaller front tyres missed the house wall by inches.

Joe slumped back into his hard chair in relief and closed his eyes. Then opened them again as he realised the sound of the motor wasn't stopping. In fact it was moving away. Billy and the tractor, and his dogs, were all chugging off into the distance, towards the hayshed. Billy was yelling something back at Joe.

The old man cupped his ear to try to catch the words.

'How do I *stop*?'

Chapter 26

Old Joe was sitting back on his verandah with the boy safely by his side. His heart was slowly returning to its normal rhythm. Christ, Billy had scared him, although he had to give it to the kid – he'd had the presence of mind to haul down on the steering wheel and drive in circles until Joe had reached him. That had taken a while, clumping along on that damnable frame. Then it was just a matter of yelling and gesturing until the child understood what knob to pull out to make the tractor stop.

After a few practice sessions up and down a very *big* paddock, Billy had mastered the art of driving in first gear. All farm buildings – including the house – and fences were still intact and the tractor, while not parked to Joe's normal standards, was *pretty much* in the shed.

They now had Joe's beloved .22 rifle out of the gun-safe and on his lap.

'Now, boy, you need to be real careful and respectful of guns. These things can kill people . . .' Joe stopped. The two of them shared a look, remembering that terrible day when Joe thought he'd shot Billy and Billy thought Joe was dead.

Joe moved uncomfortably in his chair and instinctively pulled the gun up to his eye. Just taking a look to see what bunnies there were around. Instead, below him, down on the irrigated flats of Montmorency Downs, Joe spotted a man he'd hoped he'd never lay eyes on again. Shon Murphy was coming out the back door of the homestead after Tammy. A meaty fist swinging through the air.

'Holy *shit*!' yelled Joe.

Billy jumped two foot in the air.

'Get the ute! Get the truck! Get the fuckin' tractor, boy! Get something and get me *down there*!'

Billy looked at Joe like the old man had finally flipped his lid.

'*Now*, Billy! Get me to Tammy's! Move, boy, *move*!'

Billy belted down the steps, ran to the small open carport where Joe kept his old banged up Triton ute, got in and started it up. Joe watched him zip through the get-moving procedure – clutch in, gearstick, clutch out – the whole caboose he'd just been practising out on the tractor.

He bunny-hopped out the front of the shed, tumbling some boxes which had been stacked there. Pulled up with a screech of brakes and a stall at the rough ramp which led up to the verandah, where the old man was waiting.

Once Joe was safely on board, and with a decidedly jerky take-off, they headed off in first gear, engine screaming, straight down the hill.

Joe didn't have time to register the fact he was on the property he'd vowed never to set foot on again, didn't even clock the fact he was on a driveway he hadn't seen up close in decades.

He only had eyes for one thing.

The figure of a woman holding what appeared to be a shovel. 'Stay in the car, Billy.' He wanted the kid safe.

'*Stop right there, Murphy!*' Joe was yelling before the ute stalled to a stop. He was intent on the man who had a handful of his niece's button-down shirt in one hand, a fist back behind his shoulder, frozen in mid-swing.

'What the –?' spluttered Shon Murphy. 'Who the fuck are you?'

Tammy bucked and kicked, struggling to get herself free from her distracted attacker's grasp.

Joe swung his legs out the door and stood up, as proud and as tall as his hip would let him. 'I'm Joe McCauley. And that there is my niece.'

Shon effortlessly deflected Tammy's desperate struggles and started to laugh. 'So you've come to watch the show? You couldn't stand her – *or her grandparents* – either!'

Joe shuffled forwards, hands behind his back. 'Get away from the girl, Murphy.'

'She's my wife! You can't tell me what to do. Get in that bomb of yours and piss off.' Shon turned to take a better hold on Tammy's shirt. 'And take that shit of a kid with you.'

'Let the girl go, Murphy!'

'You still here?' Shon spun back and took a menacing step towards old Joe, dragging Tammy with him. She kicked out with her boot, missing her attacker by inches. Billy cringed at Shon's seething face.

'Fuck off, old man.' Shon's voice was rising to a shout. 'This is nothing to do with *you*.'

'It has *everything* to do with me. This here is McCauley land, and we don't want no bloody Murphy desecrating it any more. So take that fancy ute of yours and piss off!'

'And how's a tottery old man, a snot-nosed kid and my useless wife gunna stop me?'

'She's not your wife! Not any more!' yelled Billy from inside the ute. 'You don't deserve her, you mean horrible man!'

'Billy!' gasped Tammy, as Shon took another step towards the Triton, giving her the chance she needed to wrench herself out of the man's grasp.

'The boy's right.' Joe shuffled forwards a bit more, away from the ute – and brought the .22 rifle out from behind his back. 'You, Shon Murphy, don't deserve her and you have no right to be here. No right whatsoever.'

He levelled the gun somewhere over Shon's left ear.

Shon moved backwards, his hands up defensively. 'You can't threaten me, McCauley! I'll report you to the coppers. Pointing a gun at a man is an offence.'

Joe laughed, which made him stagger sideways slightly, gun swinging a little away from Shon. 'Pointing a gun at you?' The old man levelled the rifle again. 'Wouldn't waste a bullet on a piece of shit like you. But . . .' He looked contemplative, flipped the safety catch, pulled the trigger.

Bang!

'*Joe!*' yelled Tammy.

'*Fuck!*' shouted Shon.

'. . . that duck over yonder looks mighty tasty,' finished Joe, peering at a spot beyond Shon's ear. A wicked grin lit up his face as he ejected the case and quickly reloaded. Aimed it again.

'*Fuck*! You're mad! You're all fucking mad!'

'Possibly,' said Joe mildly.

Bang!

Shon took off running, across the lawn towards his ute. He leaped the fence like a SWAT member and scrambled in the passenger-side door of the twin-cab. They could see him through the window, wrestling with the gear stick as he clambered his way across to the driver's side. He gunned the engine and swung the ute around in a wide circle, winding the window down as he went.

'I'll get you, you bitch!' he yelled to Tammy through the window.

Bang!

'*Fuck!* Stop shootin', you crazy old bastard!'

'You talkin' to me?' Joe called.

Bang!

'I'm calling the police!'

'Geez! The ducks are fat around these parts,' roared Joe, as he ejected the spent cartridge again. 'And lazy and slow.' He reloaded. 'Real slow in fact.'

Bang!

Shon scrambled to do up the window and sped down the drive.

Joe's laughing hiccupped to a stop. He dropped the gun and began to fall sideways, the effort of holding himself erect suddenly too much.

Immediately Tammy was right there beside him, propping him up. Billy leaped from the ute onto the ground and gently picked up the gun, handling it with extreme care, just like Joe had told him earlier.

'Are you all right?' Tammy asked quietly, bearing most of the old man's weight.

'Yep, fit as a fiddle,' mumbled Joe, blinking back tears, resting against the girl who looked and sounded so much like Mae.

'Geez, Mr McCauley! That was *awesome*!' said Billy.

'Argh, don't know about awesome, boy, but he sure turned tail and ran, didn't he?' Joe stopped and gazed up into Tammy's brown eyes. The girl might look like her grandmother but she was a McCauley through and through. Tough, strong and determined. 'I reckon he'll think twice before he comes sniffin' around here again.' He pulled himself upright. 'Get me back in that there ute, girl.' Joe cleared his throat. 'That's if you don't mind . . .'

'Mind? I don't mind at all,' said Tammy, allowing the old man to use her hands and arm like a crutch. The pair limped the few steps to the ute. Joe slowly swung around and sat down with a sigh. Getting rid of Murphy had sure taken the stuffing out of him. As had Billy's antics with the tractor this morning. *Where had his quiet, solitary life gone?*

'Righto. C'mon, Billy. Let's head home. We've got some shootin' to be doing. Bunnies to be having.'

'How about I drive you both back?' suggested Tammy. 'Billy's not supposed to be driving on the road.'

Joe was about to agree, until he glanced across and saw Billy's downcast face. He bit back a sigh. 'The lad did a good job of getting us here. I guess he should be able to drive home.'

Billy's face lit up and he scrambled for the driver's seat.

Tammy shook her head and moved to help the old man shut the door. She leaned through the open window, elbows resting on the sill.

Joe could see her struggling to say something and thought he'd beat her to it. 'The place still looks good.' He smiled as he took in the old house, his former home, which was sprawled out before him as solid as when it was built more than a century back. 'Real good.'

'Thanks, Joe.' She leaned in further and placed a warm and dry kiss on his wrinkled cheek. It felt lovely.

She pulled back, a small grin on her face. 'I'd best be going to gather up those dead ducks. Find a nice recipe to cook them.'

The grin became wider and she lifted a hand in salute. Billy started the ute and muttered to himself. 'Clutch in, engage gear, handbrake off, clutch out and . . .' The ute jumped forwards.

'Back, boy. *Back*!' yelled Joe, as the rear end of Tammy's vehicle loomed large in the front windscreen.

Billy slammed on the brakes. The old Triton stalled and stopped.

Joe let out the breath he'd been holding. Tried to make his voice sound smooth and reassuring. 'Right now, boy. Try again. Engage reverse gear, back away from Tammy's vehicle and *then* go forwards.'

'Right,' muttered the child. 'Reverse first . . .'

And they were off. Backwards. Stalling to a stop. Then forwards, in first gear, down the drive and out the gate. They turned left, heading up Hope's Road for the hill. McCauley's Hill.

Suddenly the ute lurched to a near halt, engine still roaring, then the vehicle leaped forwards again. Tammy heard a faint '*Yahooo!*' on the breeze as the motor moved up a gear. Billy had finally hit second.

Tammy watched them, a hand in the air, a whisper on her lips.

'Thanks, Uncle Joe.'

Chapter 27

The week passed fast. Tammy was flat out milking cows, doing farm work, checking on old Joe – making sure he was getting the right food to eat, the correct treatment to ensure his hip healed well.

The cows due to calve in late autumn had started to drop their babies, adding to her workload. She was checking on them both day and night, which wasn't helping with her mood either. She'd never been one to handle broken sleep without getting grumpy.

And for the past week, as predicted by those bloody currawongs, it had rained and rained. The farm was so goddamned wet. The ground was pugging and her paddocks were a boggy mess. The Lake Grace Weir was close to capacity, which made her keep a wary eye on the weather. With Montmorency Downs sitting so close to the river, she didn't need a flood on top of it all.

A barrage of phone calls kept coming from Shon, each one more urgent and abusive than the one before. He wanted his money and he wanted it *now*. Apparently Joanne and he were going halves in another hotel, or so Lucy had heard. Not that Tammy cared. She was too busy trying to run the farm and worrying about how in the heck she was going to buy him out to concern herself with where he was going to spend the damned money when he got it.

If he got it.

She'd been to see a solicitor in town. He'd told her to just sell up and distribute the money as decreed by the court. He didn't seem to understand. *Sell her farm?* A fifth-generation property handed down through the McCauley family? No way, not if she could help it. She just had to find the money, courage and energy to fight it. Somehow. Shon's anger and abuse had worn her down. He was determined one way or another to ruin her.

In an attempt to stay sane she'd given in and gone pole dancing with Lucy.

*

'Shon still bugging you?' Lucy said one night while they were hanging upside down from a stainless steel pole. Her friend was looking more drawn and ragged every day.

'Yep,' came Tammy's reply from underneath a curtain of hair.

'So what are you going to do about it?'

Tammy flipped herself back against the rod and slid downwards to the floor. 'Nothing at the moment. Too busy on the farm.'

'Tammy! You can't do nothing! He'll take it *all*! And then where'll you be?'

Tammy looked across at Lucy who'd landed heavily beside her. 'Well, he's already taken the last of the inheritance I got from my grandmother.'

'*What?*'

'I went to the bank yesterday. The third print in that set I bought after Shon left is due to arrive soon. Thought I'd better be prepared. Plus I needed to top up my operating account for the farm.'

'And?'

'He's buggered off with all the money. A week or so before he left I asked him to take a withdrawal form into the bank to get Mae's money so I could reinvest it elsewhere. I forgot about it with all that was going on and now it's gone.'

'The bastard!'

'I know.' Tammy sighed, and pulled at her hair in exasperation. 'And now I'm so tired. I'm over the whole lot. I need to run away to an island and forget it all!'

Lucy snorted. 'What you *need* is a good solicitor! A woman who doesn't mind getting her hands dirty. Someone who'll fight the battle with Shon for you while you manage the farm.'

'Any suggestions would be gratefully received at this stage, believe me. Shon and his solicitor are pushing really hard for settlement.' Tammy snatched a drink from her water bottle and squirted some water into her face. Damn it, this pole dancing sure made you sweat.

'Leave it in my capable hands. I'll find you someone even if I've got to go to Melbourne to get them,' said Lucy looking fierce. 'But why can't you pay him out and just get on with it? Surely you've got enough collateral with the farm and the run-off block?'

Tammy sighed. 'To buy the block we had to mortgage Montmorency Downs. To keep Montmorency, I have to sell the block. If I sell the block I don't have anywhere for Jock and Barb to live. The deal was that they'd have a place of their own. I offered for them to move in with me, into the old part of the house, but they won't. And I can't afford to pay them wages if they live off-farm. So I lose both the block and my workers.'

'But you could cut back, reduce your cow numbers and still trundle along on your own, couldn't you?'

'Nup,' said Tammy, shaking her head. 'The farm's in too deep. Shon took some of the money we borrowed when we bought the block and had a play on the stock market as well. The shares didn't do so well . . .'

'The man's an idiot. What does Joanne see in –' Lucy stopped short.

Tammy smiled. 'Yes, I know. What did *I* see in him? But he wasn't always like that.'

'You want to make a bet?' muttered Lucy as she swung back upwards on her pole.

Tammy gave her friend a sharp look but chose to ignore the last comment. 'Anyway, I need to keep the cow numbers up to get enough milk to pay the bills. I need the extra land to sustain the cows and Jock and Barb to help me. So there you have it. I'm damned if I do and damned if I don't.'

'Not if I've got anything to do with it,' said Lucy. 'I'm finding you a bitch of a solicitor – and fast.'

⁂

A few days later Tammy found herself sitting in front of a female solicitor, a practitioner from Melbourne who visited Narree once a month. Hilary Stratton was a silver-haired woman who looked and acted like a frumpy middle-aged shark. Obviously her parents hadn't believed in dental work, if the row of huge teeth protruding from a squared-off jaw was anything to go by.

But she knew her stuff. My word she did.

'And so, Ms McCauley, how long had you been married?' Her eyes focused on a pad of paper, placed perfectly in front of her, rather than on her client.

'Ten years.'

'Any children from the union?'

'No . . . no . . . there weren't. We would have liked them but –'

'What did you both bring to the marriage in the beginning?'

'Well, just ourselves really.' Tammy stopped. The woman opposite her was frowning at the piece of green legal paper sitting on the big desk between them. Her pen wasn't moving. She was probably wondering what Tammy was doing here if they didn't have anything to fight over. Tammy took a deep breath and went on, 'But then my grandparents died soon after we married and I inherited the family property – Montmorency Downs. We bought a run-off block two years ago, after taking a mortgage out on the farm.'

The pen started moving once more. 'So what contribution did you both make in the last decade to the accumulated wealth of the marriage?'

'What contribution?' Tammy paused again. 'Well, he worked on the farm since we married and then after my grandparents died . . .'

And so it went on, until there was nothing more to tell and Tammy felt like a wrung-out sponge. She sat back in the chair.

'Well, Ms McCauley, on consideration of what you have told me today, my advice to you is simple.' Hilary Stratton put down her pen and looked up at Tammy for the first time, peering over her bifocal glasses.

'Yes?' said Tammy, leaning forwards.

'Do a property settlement and put everything on the market ... That's unless you can afford to buy out your husband's interests in the marriage some other way?'

Tammy reeled back. 'Sell Montmorency Downs? But –'

'My dear, even though Mr Murphy will most likely only be awarded no more than twenty per cent of the value of both properties, due to the fact you can't afford to pay him out, you will have to liquidate the assets.' The woman peeled off her glasses, seemingly unaware of the blow she'd just struck. 'If a party in a property settlement in dissolution of the marriage is awarded a cash settlement he or she can force the sale of the properties in question in order to liquidate the assets.'

Tammy sat stunned. Is that what a hundred and fifty years of history was labelled? Just assets?

'Of course you will get the bulk of the proceeds of the sale.'

She didn't want the money. She just wanted the land. Her land. Her family's heritage, her heart, her soul. Home.

'*My aunt's fanny!*' shrieked Lucy. 'She said sell *up*? Get outta here! She was supposed to be a total bitch.'

'She was. And apparently it's all "very simple" seeing there are no children,' said Tammy taking another bite out of her chicken and avocado sandwich. It tasted awful. She spat it out into her napkin and pushed the plate away. 'If I can't raise the cash another way, it's liquidate the assets, pay him out and move on.'

'So, what are you going to do? I mean, I wish I had the money to give you,' Lucy held her hands out towards Tammy. 'I really do, but I'm doing overtime just to pay off my little house, let alone a whole farm!'

Tammy took Lucy's chubby fingers and gave them a squeeze – a silent thank-you. She shrugged, determined not to give in to the tears that had been threatening since she left the solicitor's office. 'Hilary's also going to try and find out what he's done with my inheritance money, but that's only a drop in the ocean compared to what I need. I can't see a way out of this one, Luce. Last time, when the creditors came sniffing around after Grandpa Tom and Mae died, I didn't have as much debt and I had Shon to help me pay the money that was owing. This time . . .' Tammy broke off, unable to continue.

'If only you hadn't bought that other place!'

'Shon really needed it. Wanted his name on a title.'

'And look where that's got you!' Luce stopped.

Tammy was well aware of where Shon had got her.

※

'Here's your medication, Joe,' called Tammy, stomping up the verandah steps a while later.

'And a mighty fine day to you too,' said Joe. 'What's got your gander?'

'Nothing.' Tammy slammed the paper bag down on the wide verandah rail and turned away to calm herself. It wouldn't do any good for Joe to see how upset she was. She gazed out across the mountains and drank in the view. She looked down below McCauley's Hill and saw Montmorency Downs, her beautiful and historic farm. What was the old saying? One generation to make it, the next to use it, the following to lose it. Damn it, she couldn't lose the farm. What would she do?

'Got to get home. Jock's milking for me. Do you need anything else this week? Luce delivered your groceries, didn't she?'

'Yes. The batty Ms Granger has been and gone.'

'Lucy is not batty. She's just different.'

'Argh,' Joe snorted. '*We're* different. *She's* a veritable fruitcake.'

Despite herself Tammy couldn't help but smile. 'A nice fruitcake though.'

Joe paused and peered out across the flats below, as if thinking of something to say. Eventually, 'Yes, well, I suppose you could say that – one with plenty of nuts. You seen Hunter lately?'

Tammy quickly turned, not quite subduing the blush she could feel blooming on her cheeks. She caught a funny look in the old man's eyes before he flicked his gaze away. A knowing sort of look. 'No, why?' she asked.

'No reason. Just wonderin'.'

Chapter 28

It was four o'clock when Trav finally drove out of Grayden Horton's front gate, heading for home. It'd been a busy week trying to juggle everything. This morning he'd been up before daylight and he'd hoped to be home by now, but unfortunately duty called. Grayden ran a sheep property above Lake Grace and he'd lost six pure-bred ewes to a dog over the past week. He wasn't a happy man.

The dog they were tracking was grabbing the sheep on the left shoulder, going for the throat, barrelling the animal down, and then eating the fat off the brisket, leaving the maimed sheep to die a horrible death.

A dog usually didn't live too far from what they were attacking, and Trav should have been able to track it reasonably easily. But this one was doing his head in. Just when he thought he had the bastard all worked out, it would evade him and Trav was back to square one. However, as he swung the ute towards home, he had to admit to himself this was why he loved being a dog trapper. Here it wasn't about maintaining a fence, it was about pitting his skills against an animal's. A wily and clever dog.

Beside him the mobile phone rang suddenly. He pulled to the side of the gravel road and picked it up. 'Hunter speaking.'

'Trav?'

He drew in a deep breath. It was the unmistakable voice of the woman who didn't want to have anything to do with him. He cleared his throat, 'Speaking.'

'Thank heavens I got you. I've been trying all day,' said Tammy.

'What's up?'

There was something desperate in her tone. An edge he'd never heard before, not even on that God-awful night in the Lake Grace hall.

'I've lost two calves, Trav. Heifer calves. I think it was a dog. You should see the mess! It's terrible . . .' Her voice trailed off. Then a soft plea. 'Can you come?'

※

That morning Tammy had swung the motorbike into the calving paddock. She was desperate to get these calves on the ground, and hoping for a good drop of heifers. She had her eyes on the dairy heifer export market, where they were making really good money. And thinking of her discussion with the solicitor, she knew she needed every cent she could get.

The sight that greeted her in the paddock was extraordinary. Two cows, out on their own, one bellowing and carrying on, the other standing over what looked like a lump of red raw meat in the lush grass.

Tammy pulled up in front of the animal that was now nudging at the mound, only to stop and gag. The lump of raw meat was a baby calf. Completely skinned.

The mother was standing over her baby, lowing softly, nudging the sinewy mess, trying to get it to move. Then, as Tammy watched, she took a last deeply mournful bellow, stepped away from the remains of her baby and ambled across the paddock towards the rest of the herd.

Tammy got off the bike and peered at the body, tears pouring down her cheeks. The perfectly formed little hooves were completely clean. Not a mark of grass or dirt. The poor little sod hadn't even hit the ground. The dog had been waiting for it as it left its mother's uterus. *The bastard!*

Tammy spun around and kicked out at the motorbike tyre in frustration. Only to spot another bloody carcass. But this one was still moving, which explained why the other cow was going berserk.

The newborn Friesian heifer had been skinned too. Bite marks punctured the area around its neck, and the hide had been peeled back like a jumper. The poor little baby was still alive.

Running back to the bike, Tammy gunned the engine and sped back towards the dairy to where she kept the gun safe. Grabbing her .22 rifle and some ammunition she roared back to the paddock and the tortured animal. It was still trying to live without a skin. She loaded the gun, pointed it, pulled the trigger.

'So what's happened here is the dog has come in and gone for the neck. See the bite marks?' said Trav dispassionately as he walked around the pitiful remains. 'It's then stood on the back end to hold the calf and skinned it. It's started to eat the poor little bugger straight away but I'd say you've disturbed it and it's taken off.'

Tammy shuddered. It was appalling. And she still had at least thirty cows to calve down. 'So what are you going to do about it?' she asked, trying to stop the slight sound of hysteria she knew was threaded through her voice. She'd been telling herself to remain cool and calm but her vocal chords weren't listening to her brain. She felt like she wanted to murder someone or something! It had certainly driven worries about Shon and the property out of her mind. There was that.

'By the way it's attacking, I'm guessing this isn't the same dog having a crack at Grayden Horton's ewes.'

Tammy gasped. There was more than one dog killing?!

Trav looked up at her with his vivid blue eyes. 'You okay?'

Tammy nearly came undone at the kindness in his gaze. Damn it! Just when she needed him to be prickly so she could hate him, he went all caring and George Clooney on her. All she needed now was that half-smile and –

Trav gave a half-smile in sympathy. 'We'll get him, Tammy. Don't worry. Are you sure you're okay?'

'I'm fine,' she muttered roughly. 'I've had a difficult week and this just tops it right off.'

'Mmm . . . yes, well, you get that.' His voice was flat, the half-smile gone in a flash. The stern look had returned with a vengeance.

Aha! So the wild man was back. Bring it on.

'I reckon he's come from that long ridge line up there past old Joe's place,' said Trav. He waved an arm out towards

McCauley's Hill. 'Dogs are lazy like humans so they travel the easiest route. Long spurs are a favourite entry point. The breeze would be coming up on either side of that ridge so he could smell what's around.'

'I haven't noticed anything amiss. What sort of stuff should I be looking for?' Tammy was desperately trying to match Trav's matter-of-fact tone.

'Dog prints, turds, scratches, drag marks. I'll go for a wander and see if I can spot anything along your boundary. Billy said he saw a dog the other week when he stayed at Joe's, the night of the dance.'

Tammy dropped her gaze, dug a few divots in the dirt with the toe of her boot. She didn't want Trav to see the disappointment and the need, which she knew would be blazing in her eyes. God, she wished she could have said yes to whatever it was he'd been offering that night. How often over the past week had she flogged herself for pushing him away? Round and round her reasoning would go, like a Ferris wheel, until it was all-out war between her brain and her heart. The problem was this *thing* between them wasn't something tangible she could reason with or reject. It was a need. A raw desire for this man that confounded and frightened her.

'So what now?' she asked, trying to keep to the point at hand.

Trav looked down at the meaty lump at his feet. Gave it a shove with the side of his leather boot. 'We need to think like a dog. How would I come in? How would I do this?'

'Will he kill again?'

'Possibly. Depends if he's still around or whether he's taken off to patrol his territory.'

'His territory?'

Trav flung a hand up to scruff at his hair. 'Every wild dog has their own discrete area or territory which they mark with urine. On trees, tussocks, clumps of grass, whatever. They piss on everything to let other dogs know not to cross into their patch. It remains that particular dog's territory until he dies or moves on due to lack of food.'

'How big an area?'

'It varies. Every dog is different. Sometimes it could be twenty to thirty square kilometres or so.'

'Crikey. That's a lot of travelling for one dog.'

'Not really. He could do that in a couple of hours if he really wanted.'

'Should I shift the stock nearer to the house? Would that help protect them?'

'Wouldn't be a bad idea,' said Trav. 'Once a dog's inside the boundaries and killing, you know they've learned the lay of the land. That makes them twenty times harder to catch.'

'So, what can *you* do to help me?'

Trav turned and took in the ridges leading down to Montmorency. 'I reckon I'll try staking him out. Maybe head down here before dawn. If I don't get him, I'll try setting a few traps along Boundary Track and thereabouts.'

'Can I come?' She needed to get onto this right away, tomorrow preferably.

'Sure,' he said, looking surprised.

'I'll meet you at your place in the morning,' she said.

Chapter 29

They were out on Boundary Track past where old Joe's place met the bush. Travis drove his ute with one hand on the wheel, head out the driver's-side window checking for tracks.

'What're you looking for exactly?' said Tammy, breaking the uneasy silence. They hadn't spoken since they'd left her paddock after staking it out until the sun was well up. The dog hadn't appeared so Travis wanted to set some traps.

'The ground is sandy in these parts so it's easy enough to pick out the different spoor. See these tracks?'

Tammy leaned over to look out of Trav's window, acutely aware of the man as she did so. She tried really hard not to touch him but the warmth emanating from his body, his scent of earth and male were intoxicating. They drew her in like a lure. Get your mind on the job, McCauley, she reprimanded herself, pushing back towards her own seat.

Travis, in the meantime, was leaning out the window,

completely oblivious, staring at spoor on the ground. 'That's a wombat, and that's a deer. There's a roo,' he pointed to a longer track, 'and that's a –' Trav suddenly stopped the ute. Got out and crouched on the ground.

He glanced up at Tammy who was lying across the seat again, looking out the doorway at what he was pointing to. 'That's a dog. The thing is, where has it gone?'

He stood up, looked around a bit then went to hop back in the ute, watching as she scrambled to reach her own side once again. He gave a small grin. 'I'm not contagious. In fact, I hardly ever bite.'

Tammy's brain went into meltdown imagining Travis Hunter biting her all over. 'Right,' she said, not knowing what else to say. She could feel a red-hot flush claiming her face at the way her thoughts were heading.

'Let's follow these tracks and see where they go.' Travis was back in the ute and had the vehicle moving, eyes focused on the ground outside his window.

Just as well he's distracted by that spoor, thought Tammy. She'd have a tough time explaining this furious blush away.

Travis tracked the dog to an intersection of Boundary Track and Tin Pot Creek Track. There he lost the spoor. He got out again and walked around.

Tammy bailed out of the ute with him this time but stayed a respectful – and respectable – distance away. 'What're you looking for?'

'Any sign, like prints, dog shit and scratches in the earth where the ground had been torn up by a dog's back feet,' said Travis as he wandered around. 'The idea is to look and *see*, not just look.'

He was so intent on his job, Tammy couldn't stop herself watching him as he poked around. His body looked at one with the bush, his worn and crumpled clothes blending in among the scrub. His head was down, eyes focused on the dirt as he gracefully moved to this spot then that. It reminded her of the way he danced, movements that were methodical but with a hint of unexploded energy, some wild passion held in check. She was so attuned to what he was doing she knew immediately when he'd noticed something amiss. 'What? What is it?'

He pointed to an old gum, its lower trunk a bright lime green, wizened and wrinkled at the base like a giant elephant's foot. 'That's a marker tree. Wild dogs mark their territory and the constant spray of dog piss turns the exposed root green.'

He strode back to the ute and let one of his dogs – the male, Tommy – off the back. The mutt ran around and she could see Trav clock that Tommy paid particular attention to the tree, spraying the root with his own piss and then a nearby clump of tussock as well.

Travis called the dog back onto the ute, locked him up. He returned to Tammy, a wicked little grin playing across his face. 'Tracking a wild dog without a dog of your own is like going into a whorehouse without a dick, if you'll pardon my French.'

He looked so contrite at being impolite, Tammy chuckled. The man was an incredible mix of contradictions. Inside that hard body of muscle, which seemed to repeatedly send erotic thoughts skidding through her mind, a wild caveman clashed with a refined gentleman. Maybe one man was what he really was, the other what he thought he should be.

'Have I offended you?' His eyes and brow were now crinkling with concern.

'Hey, I'm a dairy farmer. I think I can handle it.' She was really laughing now. 'Obviously you've never spent time at

Montmorency. A choice swear word or two always helps relieve the stress in the cattle-yards.'

Travis gave a half-grin in return, his watchful gaze pausing to take in her laughing face as if he'd never seen it properly before. His eyes skimmed over her pert nose, high cheekbones and lightly dimpled chin. The intensity of his stare made her stomach do somersaults, while her brain dived into her pants. That hungry look of his made her feel like she was the most desirable woman in the world.

Tammy found herself looking down, suddenly self-conscious. 'What now, Mr Boundary Rider?' she mumbled to the ground.

He moved towards the ute. 'We have something to eat, Ms McCauley. I'm starving.'

I am too, was her immediate and traitorous thought. Just not for food.

※

'So, where were you working on the dog fence?' she asked, a tentative note to her voice. They were both munching on sandwiches; Tammy had just poured two cuppas from a Thermos she'd stashed in the ute. He noticed she didn't ask anything else, just looked around, giving him time to decide whether he wanted to answer or not.

He sat and thought about what to say. How much to share? Above their small clearing, where they sat perched on fallen logs, the sun was bright and warm. The swish of a nearby fern told him some little marsupial was abroad. And still she sat there patient and silent. It all felt so intimate he found himself wanting to say something.

'We started out at Broughams Gate in western New South Wales. It was fine while I was out there by myself. I loved it. It's so isolated being on the edges of the Strzelecki Desert...' Travis paused and took another bite of his sandwich. 'But then I met Kat, we got married and all she wanted was a baby. She wouldn't let up, even though I worried that we weren't ready – anyway, she got her way and Billy was born.'

He heard Tammy suck in a soft breath, but she stayed quiet.

'Well, Kat didn't cope so well out on her own. At Broughams there's only one house, so we moved to Smithville. There are four houses there, so she had a bit more company. I thought she'd be busy with the baby to care for and with a few others around...' His voice trailed off then started again, 'But that didn't work either. She just got more and more resentful of being out bush. She was a country girl. I had no idea she wanted to go to the city, though she was saying by then that she always had... Anyway. So as a compromise we got a house in Broken Hill for her and Billy, and I tried to make it home every second weekend, even though it was an eight-hour round trip.' Travis sighed, tossed the dregs of his cuppa into the bush.

Beside him Tammy waited, wondering what was coming next.

'I got home one weekend... It was a Friday night.'

※

The lights in Chloride Street were just blinking on as Trav swung his LandCruiser tray into the driveway of the little house crouched on the corner. He got out, swung the canvas kit bag over his shoulder and loped towards the back door. The house was silent.

The paper lay curled like a snake on the table. A series of small oblong Post-It notes, stuck on the laminate in a snail-shell-like spiral. The trail of paper looked like it was heading out of control, fighting for space among the slashes and chips in the laminate.

Butter
Vegemite
Toothpaste
Baby formula
Nappies
Bread
Milk

Trav let out the breath he'd been unconsciously holding. A shopping list written by a bored, artistically minded housewife. That wasn't so bad.

'Kat?' he called.

He moved to the lounge door and yelled again, 'Kat, I'm home.'

The house wasn't big and his deep voice came back at him, rebounding off the high, tongue-in-groove ceilings.

'*Katrina?!*'

'Whaaa . . . *whaaa* . . .' A child. Woken by the sudden disturbance.

Trav strode into the nursery, decorated in a soft blue. A big old wooden cot was secluded in the corner, a carousel of bright clowns spinning gently in the breeze coming from the idly turning fan overhead.

In the cot lay a toddler. A screaming toddler.

'Billy, mate. Hey, c'mon little fella. No need for that, little man.' And he awkwardly picked up the little boy, taking in his red, tearsodden face. The swollen eyes had come from more than a few minutes of crying. 'Where's Mum, mate? Hey, c'mon.'

Not knowing what else to do, he lifted the two-year-old up against his broad, warm chest, patted Billy's little back. The boy snuggled in, comforted and lulled by the security.

Now he was really worried. Kat wouldn't have left the toddler. Sure, she'd been a bit weird lately but that was just because she was still struggling with the adjustment to being a mum.

'Trav?'

He swung around.

'Travis?' The voice moved down the passage.

'I'm in here.'

'Oh, thank heavens you're home.' The next-door neighbour, Beverley Spencer, looked relieved as she met him at the nursery door. 'I heard the baby. I'd just come out into the garden and I ignored it to start out with. Then I started thinking I'd seen Katrina heading off down into town a while ago and I realised the crying was coming from here and, well . . .' Bev's voice bumped to a halt as she took in Trav's expression of horror.

'Kat left the child here? By himself? What the –?'

The phone started ringing in the kitchen.

'Here. Let me take the little man. You go answer the phone.' Bev grabbed at the toddler, ducking her head so he couldn't see her face. But Trav had seen a glimpse. Horror, pity, sorrow all blended together.

'Travis Hunter speaking.'

'Trav?'

'Kat! What the fuck –'

'Just stop and listen to me.'

'Kat, you've just walked off and left Billy –'

'I can't do it, Trav. I just can't do it any more.'

'What?'

'I can't be a mother, a wife . . .' Trav could hear her breaking into sobs.

'Kat! C'mon. Come home. We'll sort it out,' he pleaded, wildly searching for something to say to hold her. 'We'll get some help, talk to someone. We'll work it out! Kat.'

A loudspeaker came over the phone announcing a departure of something to somewhere. Trav couldn't hear it properly. 'Where are you, Kat? I'll come get you, hon. Let me come get you and we'll talk this –'

'No! No, Travis!'

Trav was shocked into silence. Kat never screamed, never yelled, not even when Bev accidentally sprayed glyphosate over her organic vegetable garden.

'I'm going. There's nothing you can do to stop me. I don't want you coming after me Trav. I'm not coming back.'

And Trav could hear her crying. He went to interrupt – to say what? He didn't know. Anything to stop her from doing this to herself, to him, to Billy. She overrode him, speaking loudly to stop his begging.

'Look after our baby. One day . . . one day tell Billy his mummy loved him . . . But I have to go. I have to leave to save myself, Trav. Can't you see? I've lost *me*. So many hopes, so many dreams . . . all gone.'

Trav could feel his legs starting to give way under him. Such a strong man, people said. Such a strong, devoted man who adored his wife so much. A lovely thing to see, especially these days with so much divorce going on. 'Kat?'

'I'm sorry, Trav. I'm really, really sorry.' The phone went clunk.

And she was gone.

⁂

Back in the clearing, Travis felt Tammy take his hand. He looked at the tanned fingers threaded through his in shock. He hadn't realised he'd kept talking, telling her the whole story. Geez, he'd never done that. Not even with his own mother; he'd preferred to give her the less painful edited version.

He looked across into a pair of empathetic burned-caramel eyes, urging him to go on. What the hell, he'd said this much now. 'We battled along, Billy and me. I took him out to Smithville, and a girl living there with a bloke helped us for a while. But then they left, Billy turned four and was heading for school. It was just getting too hard. My mother, Diane, she lived in South Australia, offered to take on the boy. She was good to him. Good to us both.'

'It must have been difficult to leave him,' said Tammy quietly. He could see dismay in her eyes, at the thought of him having to leave his child.

'Yes and no. Yes, because I knew the little bugger deserved better. No, because it'd all become too hard. I'm a bloke. We don't do the nurturing thing like a woman.'

He could see she was having trouble with that thought.

'You don't agree?'

Tammy shook her head. 'Nope. You obviously never met my grandparents. My grandmother was not the nurturer in that marriage.'

'She didn't love you?' said Trav, curious.

Tammy considered that for a moment. 'I wouldn't say that. She loved me as much as she could.'

'What do you mean?'

Tammy smiled. 'Well, Mae was a very beautiful woman . . .'

'I wouldn't doubt that,' interrupted Trav, looking pointedly at her. 'The gene's obviously carried through.'

Tammy blushed, seemed to fumble with her thoughts for a few seconds before going on. 'She enjoyed being the centre of attention all the time, and I guess Grandpa Tom and I pandered to that.' Her expression turned rueful. 'It was just easier to play along rather than rock the boat with Mae.'

'Mae? Not Grandma or Nanna?'

'Oh, heck no!' Tammy shot him a look of mock horror. 'That sounds waaay too old. Almost doddery!'

'And Mae didn't do old and doddery?'

'Nope. Well-groomed perfection was my grandmother. Any messy nurturing stuff like hugs and kisses I had to get from my grandfather. When I was growing up I always wished she could let life be about someone other than herself just for one day. But then when you're a teenager life is all about *yourself* too.' She stopped, soft chuckles rumbling through her chest.

Trav wondered if she knew how laughter lit up her entire face. It made her look more beautiful than ever.

She continued, 'We were both so selfish, it must've been hell on Grandpa.'

'He was good?'

Tammy's eyes shone with love. 'He was awesome, and my escape. He taught me everything I know about farming and it didn't matter to him that I was a girl. He was also the one Mae and I ran to when we couldn't get on with each other. Mind you, technically Mae always won those bouts but Grandpa

Tom had this way about him that made us both feel we'd won in the end.'

'How'd he do that?'

Tammy took a few moments to think about it. 'I think he just took all the blame onto himself.' Her face turned wistful. 'I miss them both terribly.'

'I'll bet you do,' said Travis, wondering whether he could ask about her mum but at the same time cursing himself inwardly for his interest. Wasn't he supposed to be staying away? 'My mother had a stroke but at least she's still here.'

'Is that why you came back to Lake Grace? For your mum?'

Travis got up and started to pack up the Thermos and wrappings from their lunch. 'Yes. It was the least I could do,' he said as he threw it all into a toolbox on the back of the ute. 'She deserved the best I could give her.' This was all getting a bit too up close and personal. 'You ready to learn how to set a dog trap?'

Tammy got up off her log and brushed down her jeans. She'd taken his hint the conversation was over. He'd told her more in the last half hour than he'd shared with anyone since Kat left. He just hoped she couldn't see through him now. He liked that his gruff exterior hid the fact that he actually cared a lot. That sort of thing just caused entanglements – and trouble.

'Righto, Ms McCauley, it's time to get serious.' Travis dragged out a couple of rubber-jawed traps from his ute. Clearing an area right beside the marker tree, he set the first one. Snapping a small but thickish stem from a nearby bracken fern, he scored a nick into the square branch and placed it under the trap plate.

'Why'd you do that?' asked Tammy, fascinated.

Trav was relieved they were back on the track. He felt much

more comfortable talking about practical things than touchy-feely stuff. 'To stop any marsupials or birds from setting it off,' he said, as he carefully placed a piece of fly wire over the open jaw and sieved some dirt lightly on top. He grabbed an old board and put it on the trap to protect it.

'Let Tommy off the ute again, will you?' he called to her.

She let the dog go. Tommy ran over to Trav and, at his master's command, pissed over the bark and trap. 'Beautiful,' said Travis. He ordered his mutt back onto the ute tray. Next he removed the board and stood back to inspect his handiwork. 'Hopefully now the wild dog will come back, smell the new dog's scent and re-mark his territory. Snap. Got you, you bastard.'

The woman didn't say anything. He cast her a glance. Any sign of a smile was gone, replaced by an expression that was both grim and haunted at the same time. Travis could feel Tammy's eyes watching him as he kneeled and spent some time poking sticks and twigs into the ground around the hidden trap, trying to make sure the dog would put its paw on the correct spot.

It was funny how she could be so quiet. Most females he'd known in the past would feel the need to fill the peace with chatter. Not this woman. She seemed to respect silence. Know that sometimes it was better to say nothing at all. Where did she learn that? From her grandmother or her bastard of an ex-husband? Speaking of which: 'If this doesn't work I'll bring some of my bitch's piss out here and pour it around the trap. That usually works, especially if the rogue dog is a male.' Travis grinned inwardly, appreciating the irony even if his company wasn't privy to his thoughts.

Tammy stood and contemplated the area. 'You'd never even know we've been here.'

'And that's just the way I like it,' said Trav. He turned to the dark-eyed siren beside him and slung her a half-grin. 'Dogs are a bit like women. The more you *think* you know about them, the less you do.'

'You speaking from experience there, Hunter?'

'You betcha.'

Chapter 30

It was late when they pulled up at the back door of Trav's house, or shack really. The place looked well worn in – like a comfortable, sloppy jumper the owner loved to bits. It seemed to hunker down on its rocky hill, with scrambling wild vines trying to find purchase on the roof and native shrubs shrouding the walls. The vegetation made the place seemed rooted in the soil, one with the bush. Like its current inhabitant, who was on the phone to Joe, checking to see if his son could stay another night.

Tammy couldn't help but wish she lived here. No expectations loomed from the building other than taking shelter. There wasn't a hundred and fifty years of history mocking you in the face like at Montmorency down the bottom of the hill. And in fact, she should be getting back there. Her relief milker would be long gone by now.

They'd spent most of the rest of the day setting and checking traps and talking with other farmers whose properties abutted the state forest. The landowners wanted the government to do more about the wild dog problem that just seemed to be getting worse. 'More tucker around. It's the good seasons,' they'd said.

Tammy wished with all her heart this was a good season for *her*. But it wasn't. There were too many things around her that were spiralling out of control as fast as a tornado, and this goddamned dog problem just about topped it right off.

Trav got out of the ute and moved to the back, unloading their lunchboxes, Thermos and coats. Tammy met him coming around her side. She held out a hand. 'Thanks,' she said. 'I appreciate your help.' To her horror she found tears were welling. She tried to force them back but to no avail. The minute Trav's warm hand touched hers, she was gone.

The sobs erupted, rumbling through her body like thunder. What the hell? Couldn't her emotions have waited until she was alone? She tried to suck it all back in but the disappointment, the despair, the anxiety she was feeling all came tumbling out in defiance of her efforts.

A pair of strong arms came from nowhere to clutch at her body, to draw her in, to murmur into her hair, 'Tammy? Oh Tammy, mate.'

And that just made things worse. Now she was within the comfort of Trav's hug, her sobs became cries, her stream of tears a river. Then she heard him whisper again, his breath sending wisps of her hair curling around her ears, 'I'll get him, Tammy. I promise you I'll get him.' And in her despair she wondered if he was talking about Shon or the wild dog that was destroying any chance she had of keeping the farm. She didn't really care. They all amounted to the same thing. Ruin and despair.

Her whole world was crashing around her and she was falling and falling further than she'd ever fallen before, further even than after her grandparents died. But wonder of wonders: there was someone there to catch her. And that hadn't been the case for years. Maybe it was okay to soak in the comfort for a little while and pretend nothing else existed beyond Travis Hunter's strong arms.

Tammy had no idea how long they stood there with the dark shadows of the tall gum trees holding them within their embrace.

'I'm so sorry,' she mumbled into the warm flannelette shirt. 'I don't know what got –'

'Stop,' said Trav, as he pulled her in closer. 'Sometimes we just have to cry it all out. No rhyme, no reason. It's just the way it is.'

Trav wouldn't know how much was riding on getting those calves on the ground. Why should he? She hadn't told anyone but Lucy about the fix she was in. Not even old Joe. How could she tell *Joe*? What would he say when he heard she was going to have to sell Montmorency Downs, the heritage of the McCauley family, to pay out a Murphy?

You'll have to find a way, her subconscious whispered. Yes, she'd have to find a way. She owed it to the old man. Until recently, he might not have set foot on the place for sixty years but he still loved it. Land was like family.

She went to pull away but he wasn't letting her go. 'Trav –'

'Shhh,' he whispered, pointing towards the canopy of the tall eucalypt tree. They both looked up to the tawny frogmouth owl that was staring down. Big round unblinking eyes observed them. Then with a soft hoot he flew away, spooked by the soft growl from a dog on the back verandah.

Tammy was acutely aware of Trav's hard, muscled body. The length of it was burning into her side like a hot slab of iron.

'How about a cup of hot chocolate?' he said, as he turned back to her, the spell cast by the owl now broken. His look was soft as he gazed down at her. She was vividly aware her own eyes must be swollen and red. In fact her whole face was most likely a blotchy mess.

'Really, I should be going.' But Tammy found herself reluctant to move from the warmth, the comfort of being *with* someone.

'Just one hot chocolate. Here – you're shivering now. I can't send you home like this.' Trav took matters into his own hands and walked her across the gravel, through the gate, along the path, to the back door of the little shack.

'But what about Billy?'

'He's at Joe's.'

Of course. She knew that. Silly her.

'Just a hot chocolate then.'

'Just a hot chocolate.'

Inside, while Trav put the kettle on the old combustion stove, Tammy wandered around the small room that functioned as the kitchen, dining and lounge all in one. On the walls were photos, framed with hand-wrought timber and metal. Big ones, little ones – all landscape shots of arid-looking desert country and a long and ribbon-like chain-mesh fence rolling over red sand dunes that looked like a russet-coloured Loch Ness monster.

'Are these all the dog fence?' Tammy asked, peering at a close-up of an unconcerned shingle-backed lizard clinging to chain-wire.

'Yep. The fence has created its own ecosystem. You often see those little beggars hanging there on the wire just taking in the world.'

Tammy turned to the man, realising she wanted to know more and more about him. 'What other animals did you see?'

Trav smiled as he dished tea leaves into a teapot. A can of Milo stood nearby. He took his time to reply, his eyes seeing something far beyond McCauley's Hill. 'The mighty wedge-tailed eagle. Dozens and dozens of them. All living off the little critters that call the fence their home. They were something to see. Them and the Woma Pythons. They're a big desert snake about twelve foot long that lives in rabbit burrows. Harmless, but endangered, so we had to help them over the fence when they got stuck. First time I saw one of those it scared the shit out of me, but then I learned how to handle them, what to do.'

She moved around the kitchen bench, drawn by the soft reflective tone of Trav's voice and by the passion in his eyes.

'Then there were emus, kangaroos, frill-necked and blue-tongue lizards, sand goannas . . . plus the thunder and sandstorms that could rage around you for hours on end.'

'You loved it, didn't you?' she said softly.

A pair of dreamy blue eyes stared back at her. 'Yes, I did.'

The kettle on the stove started to whistle, startling them both. Together they leaped to turn the gas off, and their arms collided as the supply shut down. Hand met hand. Fingers met fingers. Tammy looked up to see Trav staring down at her and what Tammy glimpsed was breathtaking. An intensity of gaze she hadn't seen since the night of the dance. The night she turned away. But she couldn't turn away now. Not even when Travis Hunter took her hand in his and slowly drew her in. Not even when his head drifted downwards. Not even when, with one last look into her eyes, he gently covered her trembling lips with his own.

Every nerve-ending in Tammy's body seemed to quiver as Travis slowly traced the outline of her mouth, gently at first, taking his sweet time to taste. Then, as he met with no resistance, drinking where before he'd just sipped. Pulling her in tight to his hard body. Demanding yet soft. It was all she could do to stay on her feet.

And then, just when she thought her legs would go out from under her, he was retreating, moving away. She heard herself whimper. But he didn't go far. His warm mouth languidly traced the gentle curve of her neck, nibbling and sucking, seeking and finding the sweet spots. Tammy let out a low moan as he feasted on her skin. Her body swayed in ecstasy. All she could hear was that same roaring in her ears, punctuated by her own little gasps of pleasure. All she could feel were Travis Hunter's lips. All she could see was the softly curling hair where it met the skin of his neck.

Tammy gasped as Trav's mouth reached the pulse at the base of her throat. He paused, hovered in momentary indecision. Then slowly but surely he trailed kiss after kiss along her collarbone, up her neck and back to the softness of her lips.

She felt him push the kettle off the still-hot hob, and take her hand, drawing her towards the doorway of an adjoining room where she could see a double bed. She didn't want this to stop. She found herself looking up into those eyes, usually a vivid blue but now a dark and dangerous navy. He bent his head down to her and she was carried away in his kiss once more.

Tammy felt his hands move from her sides to the front of her shirt. Starting at the waist he undid her buttons, one by one, taking time to explore the body beneath his hands. Her shirt came off, followed by her bra. And then she was gently picked up and laid down on the bed. Trav stripped his own shirt off in one go and Tammy gasped. His chest was broad, muscled and lightly patterned with soft hair in all the right spots. Then he was upon her, kissing and nuzzling her breasts, licking the soft rosy peaks, which had risen to meet his touch.

Nibbling and kissing his way down to her waist, he slowly eased her jeans from her hips, caressing her skin as he went. Tammy thought she was about to die, so strong was her greed to have this man deep inside her.

'Your jeans,' she muttered through clenched teeth.

He pulled the rest of his clothes off, piece by piece, with Tammy watching every move. She'd always thought him sexy but, with his clothes off, the man was more than sexy. He was – oh God, what was he? Tammy couldn't think, couldn't breathe, because he was there. Right there. Right where she needed him to be. His fingers. His tongue. Touching. Teasing. Oh my Lord – she could feel herself rising, heading for a peak. Oh, so close. 'Keep going,' she begged, as she twirled her hips.

'I intend to,' he whispered.

And then she knew she had to have him. 'Trav! Please!'

Trav moved fast, up and over her body, thrusting himself into her with one strong, firm stroke. Moving with her, riding the waves that had started to thrum through her body. She felt herself explode, her muscles clenching around his long, hard thickness. And then it was Trav's turn. Up and over he went, gasping, cursing, riding ecstasy. Trav collapsed around her, and reached to cradle her body into his. Eyes closed. Body limp. He pulled and tugged until Tammy was curled up, spooned into him.

Tammy felt a soft kiss land in the nape of her neck, another on her shoulder. An arm came out to haul the now scrunched-up fluffy doona over them. And then there was nothing other than the soft hoot of a night owl abroad.

Chapter 31

Travis lay on the edges of sleep, wondering three things. Why did his arm feel dead? Why there was a drum roll coming from somewhere? And why was there a bright light on in his bedroom? He opened one eye and spied a waterfall of dark brown hair cascading across his chest.

Then he remembered. And after he glanced at the clock radio, he realised why it was so bright in his bedroom. It was nine am. The only thing he couldn't work out was the drum roll which had metamorphosed into an insistent thump followed by a voice calling, 'Trav. Oh, *Tra-av?*'

Then there was the sound of a sliding door opening, followed by the swish of drapes. A clicking of high heels on the wooden floor and –

'*Travis?*'

He hadn't seen Jacinta since the night of the dance. Now she was at his bedroom door and the expression on her face was a sight to behold. Shock. Fleeting anger. Disappointment. Then, a bright and brittle smile.

'Hi!' she said, waggling her fingers in the air. 'It's a lovely morning out there!'

Only a woman like Cin could attempt to make this seem normal, thought Trav, as the woman beside him struggled to sit up. Then, realising she was naked, slunk back down just as fast.

'Hi,' said Tammy weakly.

But Trav wasn't looking at Cin. He was looking at where the doona now only barely covered that glorious body. A body belonging to the woman he had thoroughly loved last night . . . and again in the wee hours of this morning. He felt himself harden at the thought of it.

'Ahem, well. I guess I'll just go turn the kettle on, shall I?' said Cin. 'Give you time to get up?'

Bugger the Jacintas of the world. He opened his mouth to demand she leave when her words came floating through from the kitchen . . .

'I just called in to say I think there's something wrong with Billy.'

Both Trav and Tammy stared at one another in horror. The bed erupted into action. Within minutes both were dressed and colliding with each other as they tumbled through the doorjamb.

'Oooo, be careful. One at a time!' called Cin, in her best school-marm voice. She was quailed by dagger looks from both parties. 'Oh, well then,' she uttered, hesitating a moment before lifting the teapot in the air. 'Cuppa anyone?'

'What's wrong with Billy?' demanded Trav. 'What's happened? Where is he? Where's Joe?'

Cin looked across the bench in surprise. 'Oh, I didn't mean he's hurt himself or anything. Did he spend the night with Joe?

So you two could . . . ? Well, you know?' Cin waved her arms around and blushed a deep red.

Trav dropped onto a barstool and buried his face in his hands.

Tammy automatically placed a comforting palm on his shoulder. 'And so, Cin, what *exactly* is wrong with Billy?'

Cin looked hard at Tammy and then her gaze dropped to the hand sitting on Trav's flannelette shirt. Tammy quickly snatched it back and moved away.

Cin grimaced and then heaved a huge sigh. 'We suspect he's hearing impaired.'

Trav's head reared. 'He's w*hat*?'

'Hearing impaired. We suspect he's deaf.'

'I heard what you said the first time!' Trav's voice verged on a yell.

Cin dropped her head, concentrated on making the tea.

Tammy could see the woman was chewing her bottom lip and about to cry. She pulled up a stool a respectable distance from Travis and dragged her cuppa across the bench, blowing across then slowly sipping the hot brew. 'What makes you think Billy is deaf?'

'Yeah. Why do you think my son isn't the full bottle?'

'I didn't *say* he wasn't the full bottle.' Cin flushed and looked indignant. 'In fact he's one of the most switched-on children in my class. What I said was, I think he's got a hearing problem.' The woman picked up her coffee and peered at Trav and Tammy through the stream rising from the mug. 'Remember the note, Trav? The one about the school nurse coming to do a check-up on the children?'

Trav nodded reluctantly.

'Well, she came yesterday and checked all sorts of things, eyes, ears and so on. Billy didn't pass the hearing test.'

Trav stood up, combed his fingers through his rumpled hair. 'He's not deaf. He must have been having a bad day. Maybe he wasn't concentrating.' He turned to Tammy. 'You know what he's like. If he's not focusing on you or what you're saying he doesn't hear a thing. Just goes off into his own little world . . .' His voice trailed off as he looked up at the ceiling. Tammy could see him replaying in his mind exactly what he'd just said.

The truth hit.

❧

Trav couldn't think straight. No sleep, chasing wild dogs, finally making love to Tammy — and oh, how amazing was that — Cin bursting in on them and now this? Billy was deaf! It was all too much. He needed air.

He spun and walked out the door of the little house. Down the path. Out the garden gate. Through the bush, following a path barely visible to those who didn't know it was there. Manuka and dogwood bushes snatched at his sleeves, pulling at the material, trying to hold him back. But he ploughed on, leaving their branches to wave in lonely despair.

The words that had just turned his whole world upside down were hammering in his head. Billy was deaf.

His son, Billy, was *deaf*.

And it was all his fault. It couldn't have been Kat's. She was so perfect, so good.

She wasn't good. Look what she did to you and the kid.

His stride ate up the bush as his thoughts drove arrows through his head. She walked out on you both. Just left you to bring up the kid on your own. Hasn't even tried to contact you since. Thank goodness those solicitors handled the divorce or you could still be married to her. You don't even know if she's alive.

Course she's alive. I'd know if she was dead. I'd feel it, somewhere down deep inside.

Would you? You didn't know she was going to leave, did you? Did you . . . Did you . . . Did you?

Then suddenly Lake Grace was in front of him. The massive expanse of water that irrigated around fifty thousand hectares of prime pasture-land in the district of Narree.

From high upon his hill, he looked down on the weir. Sunlight was glinting off the ochre-coloured lake. A small section of his brain noted the fullness of the weir, a rare sea-eagle gliding the eddies to his south, swooping down every now and then to feast on a kill. The misty haze hung low over the looming blue-grey mountains to the north.

But otherwise all Travis could see in front of his eyes was an earnest little boy who looked so like his mother, with his red hair and a smattering of freckles. A spindly, funny little kid who every day reminded Trav of what he had lost and how he, Travis, was failing, even now.

Billy was deaf.

And it was all his fault.

By the time Trav made it back to the house, Cin was gone. Tammy was chopping kindling. He could hear her distinctive voice even as he came through the tall trees a way back from the house. She appeared to be having an angry one-sided conversation with his dog. 'Billy's got a hearing problem. So what? It's fixable.'

The axe came down hard. *Smack!*

'What's his problem with that?'

Smack!

She stood up, stretched her back, looked at the dog like she was expecting him to say something. 'That's right. There isn't a problem.'

She grabbed another block of wood and set it on the chopping block. 'So why does he take . . .'

Smack!

'. . . everything so personally . . .'

Smack!

'. . . and just . . . just . . . walk right on off?'

Trav came up to stand behind her. 'So what am I supposed to do? It's all my fault.'

Tammy jumped in the air, dropping the axe, which just missed her foot. 'For crying out loud! Do you always have to move so quietly?'

'The dog knew I was here.'

'I wasn't looking at the dog, I was chopping wood.'

'You were talking to the dog.'

'I was not.'

'You were too,' he said.

Tammy picked up the axe. What was she going to do with it? 'I'm heading home.'

'You're taking the axe?'

Tammy looked down at the implement then slammed it into the chopping block. 'No. There's some kindling. Although you don't deserve it. Goodbye.' And she went to walk off, shoulders back, but Trav grabbed her by the elbow as she swung past. Spun her around to face him.

'You're angry with me. Why?'

She took a deep breath. 'Too right I'm angry with you, you self-involved, selfish, arrogant, surly . . .' She stopped, seemingly lost for more words, before adding, '. . . bastard.'

'Would you care to explain exactly why I'm a bastard?'

'That child adores you. Idolises you. And you don't give a jot about him. You don't care. You're told he's got a hearing problem and you just walk off? When was the last time you looked at him? Really *looked* at him and took notice?'

'Not care? Not notice him? Of course I do – I'm his father, goddammit!'

'Well, it's about time you started acting like it,' she yelled, before storming off towards her ute.

Trav couldn't believe it. Everything he *did* was for Billy. He called after her, 'I put a roof over his head, feed him, clothe him, send him to school.'

Tammy spun back. 'But you don't *show* him you love him, do you, Hunter? You don't show him you care.'

'I do!'

'When was the last time you hugged him? Kissed him? Ruffled his hair?'

Trav flung a hand up to scratch at his own head. 'I don't kn –'

'That's my point. You don't. That child is crying out for attention. *Your* attention.'

'I do the best I can.'

'Well, your best isn't good enough,' she said before walking towards her vehicle.

'Tammy? Tammy! Don't go. Help me understand.' Trav started jogging after her, aiming to cut her off before she got into the ute. He made it just as she was opening the door. Over her shoulder he leaned in and shut it. She tried to open it again but he wouldn't let her. 'Tammy?' he begged, not exactly sure why he was so desperate to stop her leaving but knew he needed her to stay. To explain why he was doing all this so wrong.

She paused with her head down, still facing the car. He held his breath. 'Tammy, please?'

And still she didn't move. Trav stepped back. But instead of opening the door of the ute, she turned to look up into his face. He was shocked to see tears in her eyes. 'That child needs you, Trav. Especially now. I know what it's like not to have real parents. I don't even know who my father *was*. But you . . .' She swallowed. 'You *are* his father. And through you Billy has a chance to know he is loved.'

Trav stared down into the deep brown eyes. 'Help me.' he said. 'Help me to understand. Show me what I need to do.'

'It's not rocket science. Show interest in the child. Do stuff with him, talk to him, kiss him, hug him, just show him you love him – try being a real dad.'

'And the hearing? Did Jacinta say anything more about that?'

'You have to make an appointment with the audiologist. Get a handle on what you're dealing with.'

Trav hung his head. The poor kid. He felt a small but firm hand come up and cradle him under the chin, lift his head up.

'It's not that bad, Trav. Maybe just a pair of hearing aids? There are thousands of kids out there who are hearing impaired and they're all living full and happy lives.'

'But it's my fault.'

'How the hell do you know that? And who really cares anyway?' She ran her fingers over his cheek and gave him an encouraging little grin. 'It'll be okay. Hearing aids and he'll be right as rain. You just have to learn to be a real dad.'

'But how do I learn? My father wasn't ever one to me.'

Tammy planted a soft kiss on his mouth before getting into her vehicle. 'Billy's a great kid, Trav. He'll teach you. Just open your mind and your heart.'

Her ute started rolling down his drive. A voice came calling to him on the slight breeze. 'And just for the record, that was the best hot chocolate I've ever had!'

Chapter 32

'Tammy? Tammy McCauley?' The words crackled down the phone line. 'It's Alice Stringer from the Narree Gallery. You bought two prints off me a while ago?'

'Oh, Alice. Yes. Hello.'

'I was just calling as I finally might have my hands on the third print in the series.'

'Really? Oh Alice, I'm not sure I can afford the third one at the moment. Something's come up.' Like her husband wanting to take her for half the farm, but Alice Stringer didn't need to know that.

'Oh that's all right. It's not here yet anyway, and I'm sure we can come to some arrangement. I was actually ringing because I thought you might like to attend the official opening of my gallery next Friday evening. The creator of the series you bought has kindly agreed to be our feature artist on the night.'

'That's wonderful for you, Alice! And yes, of course I'll come.'

'And could I prevail on you to put your two prints on show too?' said Alice. 'Just on loan mind you.'

'Yes. Yes, of course.'

'Lovely. Mention it to all your friends. I'm in need of lots of bodies to fill the room for the night.'

'No worries. I'll tell anyone I see.'

Tammy hung up and looked through the lounge-room door at the two pictures on the wall. The sphinx-angel was still gliding the eddies in blissful contemplation. She wondered how that would feel.

The phone behind her rang again.

'Good morning, Tammy. It's Hilary Stratton, your solicitor, speaking. I'm ringing with regards to the proposed property settlement with your husband.'

She should have let it go to message bank. 'Yes, Hilary?'

'As you instructed, I have discussed the realisation of all marital assets with your husband's solicitor. He has in turn advised me that both he and his client are very pleased with the outcome.'

'Outcome? I didn't realise I'd made a decision!'

'You have decided to put it on the market, haven't you? Quite frankly, Tammy, upon further review of your limited options, you have absolutely no recourse other than to sell your property, er . . . Montmorency Downs.'

'None at all?'

'None at all. Not unless you've dug up a treasure chest of money somewhere on your farm.' The woman laughed – an awful braying noise like a donkey. 'As I said, both your husband and his solicitor were very pleased and hopefully we can do this in a hurry. You will, of course, receive the majority of the proceeds from the sale so if we move this along, you'll get paid out quickly. Like I said at our meeting, it's going to be a great outcome all round.'

Tammy sank to the floor. This was really happening. She was going to have to sell Montmorency.

'I'll need you to make an appointment to come in and sign the agency agreement. How about tomorrow? I'm in town for a couple of days this time. We've got a run on divorces in the district,' said Hilary, laughing again.

Tammy couldn't believe the woman could be so insensitive. These were people's *lives* she was dealing with.

'We'll need to get a vendor statement arranged, but I'll organise that. And the real-estate people will want to come out and take some photos, although apparently your husband has already provided a few. But first up we'll need your signature . . .'

Tammy tried to hold back the despair that was threatening to engulf her. 'I'll be in town tomorrow, around lunchtime. I'll call in and sign the form.'

'Great! I'll see you then. And Tammy?'

'Yes?'

The solicitor's voice softened slightly. 'It mightn't seem like it now, but this really is for the best. You should come out of this with enough money to start again.'

But she didn't want to 'start again'. She was losing her family's heritage, her home, her life. Montmorency Downs was going on the market and there wasn't a damn thing she could do to stop it.

After Tammy had left, Trav had headed out to check the line of traps he'd set out at Grayden Horton's place. That had taken most of the afternoon and the sun was dipping down over the horizon before Trav finally made it back to Joe's. He was just in time to see the old man throw a gallon of diesel on a dozy fire contained in a metal drum.

The explosion buffeted the air on the hill with its sudden heat. A black and white dog shot off into the bush in fright.

Peals of laughter came from a deck chair set a safe distance from the flames. Billy was holding a plastic bag in one hand and a can of lemonade in the other and he was rocking the chair backwards and forwards with his boots. 'Go, Joe!' he was yelling.

The old man had staggered back and was hastily dabbing a hanky on his eyebrows.

Trav jogged towards Joe. 'You all right?'

The old bugger spun around to face him. One bushy grey eyebrow was still intact, wiry hairs spinning out in a myriad of directions. The other was, unfortunately, gone. Completely eradicated by the blast.

'Bloody hell!'

'Mmm . . . I was perhaps standing a little bit close,' said the old man, still dabbing his eye with the scrap of material.

'Possibly. Do you need some water on that?'

'No.'

'You sure?'

'Yes. I'm fine. Let's move on. Billy?'

The boy came running, then stopped. Shot a look at his father like he wasn't sure whether to say hello or not. Trav's heart twisted a bit. He wondered if he'd given the same look to his own father. But he wasn't his father and Billy wasn't Trav.

'Hello, Billy.'

'Hello, Dad.' A little smile erupted on his face. 'We've got marshmallows.' He held up the plastic bag.

'And lemonade?'

Billy's face fell, assuming his father disapproved and would take the can of fizzy drink off him.

'Better go find yourself a stick,' said Trav, with a slight smile, 'to toast the marshmallows over the fire. Is that what you were going to do, toast them?'

The boy nodded so hard he dropped the bag.

Trav leaned down and picked it up. What was it that Tammy said? 'Do stuff with him, talk to him . . . just show him you love him . . .'

'Find me a stick too, will you?'

'And me!' said Joe.

'Make sure it's a good one though,' said Trav, reaching out a hand to ruffle his son's hair. Billy moved into the caress like a cat. 'Off you go. And grab me and Joe one of those cans of lemonade too.'

Both men stood with their backs to the flames as the child eagerly scampered up the slope towards the thicket of bush near the rear of the house. Obviously the spot to gather good toasting sticks.

'He's a terrific kid, Hunter.'

'I know.'

'Do you?'

'Not you too.'

'What?'

'I've already had your niece on my case about Billy this morning.'

Joe shot Trav a sneaky glance. 'I'm guessing she wasn't only on your case?'

Trav looked startled.

'I'm up early again these days and I beat you getting the fire going this morning. You haven't even got yours *started* yet.' The old bloke chuckled. 'And my rifle-scope tells me things. Saw a red car arrive. How'd you go with the two women there together? A bit of skin and hair fly?'

Trav was silent for a moment, reliving the look on the young teacher's face when she saw there was someone in the bed beside him. 'No. It was okay. Jacinta just called by with some news.'

Joe raised his remaining eyebrow in invitation.

'Billy failed his hearing test at school. They're saying he might be deaf.'

'Mmm . . . I wondered.'

Trav looked at the old man in surprise. 'You think so too?'

'Somethin's wrong. Makes sense it's his ears.' Joe heaved a big sigh. 'When I was teachin' him to drive the tractor –'

'You were *what*?'

'Teachin' him to drive. Someone's gotta do it and you sure as hell weren't.'

'He's only nine, Joe.'

'Ten.'

Trav thought about that for a minute. Did he miss the kid's birthday? Shit. *No!* Hang on a minute . . . He gave him an Akubra. Trav heaved a sigh of relief.

'How old were you when you learned to drive?' asked Joe.

'About six or seven, I suppose. My brother, Danny, was older.'

'Didn't know you had a brother,' said Joe with interest. 'Where's he?'

'Back home.' Trav didn't want to talk about Danny. 'You were talking about Billy?'

Joe gave Trav a searching look. 'Mmm . . . anyway, Billy couldn't hear my instructions. Caused a bit of bother, but we got there in the end, didn't we, Boots?' The collie had slunk back from the scrub to sit at his master's feet.

Trav glared down at the dog, thinking hard. Why did everyone have such a low opinion of his parenting skills? Probably because you don't have any, his mind whispered back.

'Hunter?' said Joe, appearing pensive, which was most unlike him. 'Can I talk to you straight?'

'Nothing usually stops you,' said Trav.

'As you know, I'm a loner – happy in my own company. I guess it comes from working for a lifetime in the bush. You're the same.'

Trav nodded.

'I thought I'd lost my true love. Her name was Mae. I'm guessing by the fact you and Billy are by yourselves, you did too.'

Trav nodded again.

'Well, life's got some surprise twists and turns and sometimes what we want and what is good for us are two different things.' The old man paused, then sighed and looked out across the fire drum, towards the mountains splayed in the late afternoon light. 'We live on the edges, you and I, Hunter. And to a certain degree Billy and Tammy do too. We all ride the boundaries of life. We ain't real normal-like. But' – and Joe turned with his finger in the air – 'and this is the key point I'd like to make. Between you and me there is one very important difference . . .'

Trav stood waiting, although he had a suspicion of what was about to come.

'Nellie and me were never able to have children. You, Travis Hunter, have a son. A great kid who is crying out for your love.'

Trav went to speak, but the old man held up his hand. 'I haven't finished. I know you're trying to do your best for that boy. Others mightn't see it, but I bloody well do. A single man on his own, working long hours away from home.' The old bloke stopped, grimaced and sucked in a gulp of air before going on. 'But you need to do more. You have to be a proper father to him, otherwise he'll turn out just like you and me.'

'And what exactly is that?' asked Hunter.

Old Joe looked him dead in the eye. 'A lonely, old reprobate bushie who'll be a boundary rider as well.'

Chapter 33

The fire had died down to a stack of glowing coals. Trav could see them throbbing red through the holes in the 44-gallon drum. Someone had cut the name *McCauley* into the metal side of the makeshift heater and it was glowing a golden colour in the light from the fire.

He and Joe were sitting in companionable silence. The stars were gleaming up above their heads. There were so many swathed across the heavens.

'So tell me about this brother of yours,' said Joe, disturbing the peace.

'Not much to tell.'

'You said he's at home. Where's that exactly?'

'Cattle station, north of Yunta in South Australia.'

'So why aren't you there too?'

'He got it. I didn't. End of story.' Trav moved around in his chair, shifted his long legs. The boy asleep in the swag at his feet murmured, then flung an arm out to cuddle Boots, who was lying against him.

'Do you talk to him?'

'No, not much.'

The pair lapsed back into silence once more. In the soft breeze, tree branches laden with eucalyptus leaves whispered above their heads.

A high-pitched howl cut through the night air. A bloody wild dog. Probably the wild dog he was trying to trap.

'Bit close,' said Joe. 'You obviously didn't get him yesterday.'

Trav shook his head. 'No, we didn't. I'll do a stake-out every second day for a while.'

Joe nodded slowly. 'See any other signs of it?'

'Only a few prints. And some hairs caught on the barbed wire of the fence. But I reckon it's having a ball eating all the calf shit once it's in the paddock. The dogs go mad over it because it's full of milk and cream.'

Joe nodded again just as another howl came from the bush nearby. Boots's ears flicked in his sleep.

Trav flung back his head and let out a howl of his own. His sleeping boy stirred but didn't wake. The kid must have been exhausted because Joe nearly fell off his chair in fright. 'Fuck, mate, let me know before you're gunna do that again!'

Trav laughed, then sobered real quick as a responding howl came from the bush. 'He thinks I'm another dog.'

'I don't see why. Sounded more like one of them bloody chipmunks on Billy's DVD.'

'What DVD?'

'The one Tammy gave him for his birthday.'

Trav had never seen it. 'Right. Yes, of course.'

'You don't know what I'm talkin' about, do you?'

'Nope. Got no idea.'

'You've really got to start taking notice of that boy, Hunter. Before it's too late.'

Trav looked down at the child curled up in the green canvas swag. Such an innocent little kid, lying there with his skinny arm flung across an old dog. Billy had done nothing wrong – he'd just been born to a woman who couldn't love enough and a cynical man who'd once loved too much.

'Yeah, I'm hearing you. Loud and clear.'

'What did Tammy say to you about it?'

'About Billy?'

The old man nodded.

'She said much the same. Told me to just try being a real dad.'

'Yeah well, she knows a thing or two about being neglected.'

'Neglected? Tammy? She had two loving grandparents.' After her revelations yesterday maybe it hadn't been a perfect relationship with her grandmother, but it didn't sound like she'd been disregarded.

Beside him Joe's face shut down, like he was regretting he'd said too much.

What the hell was the old man on about? 'C'mon, Joe. Spill your guts. What makes you think Tammy was neglected?'

Joe sat silent, poking the ground with the stick he'd used to toast his marshmallows.

'Joe?' What could be so bad that he felt he needed to hide it?

The old man looked up but his eyes were glazed like he hadn't taken in his question. 'Mae was her grandmother,' he said in a remote voice.

'I know. What happened to her parents?' asked Trav again, but more quietly this time.

Joe's eyes were still unfocused, his mouth a grim slash, as if he was looking back in time and not liking what he saw. 'Didn't ever find out who the father was, but the girl got pregnant just out of school. An end-of-year party to celebrate entering the real world. What an entry that was, a belly full of arms and legs.' Old Joe grimaced again. 'She was a pretty girl too, just like Mae. Big brown eyes, long dark hair. Natalie was her name. Anyway, she stayed with her parents, had the baby, was going to go on to university and do nursing, they said.' Then Joe lapsed back into silence.

'And? Where is she?' said Trav, thinking of Katrina. Another runaway he'd bet.

'In row number 24B, third from the left.'

'Row what?'

The old man glanced across at him. 'She's in the cemetery. She died. Went down to the Narree River to have a midnight swim with some friends just before heading off to Melbourne. Mae was going to have the baby during the week, and Natalie was going to come home on weekends. Or so the stock agent told Nellie.' Joe seemed to take a deep breath. 'The river had been in flood that year. Lots of snags around. The girl dived in, didn't come back up. It was night time, no one could find her. That was it. Gone.'

A chill crept up Trav's backbone.

'They dragged the river, but nuthin'. Found her body a week or two later, somewhere down near where the Narree meets the Gippsland Lakes. Anyhow, Tom and Mae took on the baby and brought her up. And they tried. Well, I guess they did. But they were getting on themselves and grieving. The child ran wild. I used to see her through me scope – she was a real feral bit of gear. But she seems to have made it through all right.'

'Your brother and his wife must have been devastated by it all,' said Trav, thinking of how he'd feel if Billy died. Probably beyond grief. 'Then to have to bring up another baby. Shit. What a big ask. It's hard enough when you're my age.'

Joe stared into the night sky. 'I guess so. To be honest . . .' He turned and looked Trav straight in the eye. 'I really wouldn't know. Never spoke to them.'

Trav digested this for a moment then asked quietly, 'So if you never talked, how did you know all this?'

'Nellie. She'd find out things in town and then there was the stock agent. He was always up for a yarn after Nellie plied him with her cakes. He told her lots of stuff that was going on down the bottom of the hill.' Joe suddenly seemed defensive. 'I told you, I was a loner. Don't know how Nellie put up with me really.' Boots, sensing his master was upset, gently slid from under Billy's arm and came to sit at Joe's side. Right where he could reach his soft ears without bending too far down.

'You mustn't have been too bad, Joe. For an old reprobate bushie, that is,' said Trav, with a gentle half-smile.

'Yeah, well. She was a good woman and I didn't deserve her but she stuck with me. Didn't realise what I had until she was gone.'

'Yeah, tell me about it,' said Trav thinking of Katrina.

Both men stared into the fire as they thought about what they'd loved and lost. Hot burning coals shifted as a log dropped lower into the drum.

'Tammy took me on a tour of Montmorency the other day,' Joe cleared his throat, 'to have look around.'

Travis stared at the old man, shock written all over his face.

'What's wrong with that?' said Joe, sounding indignant. 'Hadn't seen the place for a while.'

'And?' Travis raised an eyebrow.

'She's doing a good enough job.'

'Good enough, hey? You tell her that?'

'Nope.'

'Probably would've meant a lot if you had,' Travis observed.

'She don't need no opinions of mine. And what's more, don't you go saying that I've been talking about her. It's not like me to open me trap and I don't want her thinkin' I make a habit of what's her business to be coming from me.' The old man cast Trav an evil look. 'Or I'll come and do somethin' drastic to you.'

'Like what?'

'I'll tell Mizz Greenaway you've got a different woman in bed every week.'

'I don't think that'll matter too much, Joe. I'm thinking Miss Jacinta's already gone off me.'

'Really? Things go that well with my niece?'

'Yep.' Trav felt a twist in his gut. He swallowed the hard lump of apprehension that had become lodged in his throat. 'She's a great girl. I need to get this dog that's causing her so much grief.'

'That's a pretty good description of Shon Murphy.'

Trav laughed softly. 'You know what I mean.'

'Yep,' said Joe, 'I sure do. You can have a go at *both* the domestic and feral dogs if you like.'

'Dad?' mumbled Billy, opening his eyes. 'Is it home time?'

'Yeah, mate,' said Trav, leaning down to drag the boy from his cosy hole in the canvas. The child came out of the swag all limbs and Trav slung him over his shoulder. 'I'll put you in the ute. Hang on tight.' And the little boy did, his arms sneaking hesitantly around his father's neck.

'And another thing,' called Joe, slowly staggering to his feet.

The old man grabbed a log from a stack he had beside the fire and threw it into the drum. More bright sparks flew through the air around him, some whizzing up into the night sky. Then Joe looked at the father with his boy clinging tight to his back like a koala. Waiting.

'You should talk to your brother. Forever is a long time to live with regret.'

Chapter 34

The radio beside her bed burst to life with a scream of rock music. Tammy rolled over, opened one eye. Surely not. It couldn't possibly be six am.

She slung her legs off the bed and staggered to the bathroom, tripping over the tissue box, which was lying empty on the floor. Shit. Bugger. Blast. Tissues like clumps of snow dotted her bedroom floor.

No wonder her eyes felt like they were seeing through slits. She made it to the bathroom and peered in the mirror. Swollen red lumps stared back at her, ringed by heavy bags of black and cerise. Lucky she didn't have to be anywhere bar the dairy this morning. What in the heck happened?

And then it all came crashing back. The lawyer's phone call. Crying. Milking the cows. Crying. Staggering back to the house. Crying. The wine bottle. A maudlin daze. She was selling Montmorency and Shon Murphy, along with his solicitor, were 'very pleased'.

'I'll bet he's flamin' pleased,' Tammy muttered as she struggled into her milking clothes. On went the old jeans, the flannel shirt, a wind-cheater stained with last night's milk, followed by a peaked cap covered in cow-shit. 'He'll get a share of a multi-million-dollar property. And he knows selling it will just about kill me.'

'Kill who?' said a voice from around the door.

'Christ! What the –?'

'You can't kill Christ.' Lucy entered the bathroom wearing the brightest scarlet Betty Boop PJs Tammy had ever seen. 'He already died. But he came back. Mind you, he went again. Just like most men. Well, that's what I think happened. Anyway, you're a Catholic, you should know.' She peered right into Tammy's face. 'Damn, you look terrible.'

'No shit, Sherlock. What're you doing here?' said Tammy, squinting her eyes to try to allay the sledgehammer knocking around in her skull.

'You rang me, remember? Some tripe about selling the farm. Thought you'd been drinking so I came round straight away. In my pyjamas too. You shouldn't drink on your own, Tammy. Bad form, my girl. Even Betty for company would've done.'

'I wasn't drinking!'

Lucy's eyebrows shot into the air. 'So what was the empty wine bottle doing on the bench? Having a party all on its own? You're a one-pot screamer, girl. I would've thought with your breeding you could do better.'

'And just what is that supposed to mean?'

'Joe. Look at him. He can hold his drink no worries at all. But you, you're hopeless. Remember that night at the Burrindal B & S? You and one of the McDonald boys. Which one was it? Macca? Tys? Maybe it was Sean?'

Tammy shut her eyes. The sledgehammer was really going to town now. What's more her brain felt like it was being squashed in a vice. And yet despite all that, a vivid picture of the McDonald boys, all cousins, snuck into her mind. She could never go past the new section of boundary fence without thinking of Macca and what he'd lost on that fateful day. The afternoon his girlfriend, Patty O'Hara, died when her red ute crashed into a B-Double truck. Bluey Atkins, the rig's driver, had never been the same after the smash. He and his wife had finally sold up their fertiliser and stock feed business. Going to Darwin, they said, as far away from Narree as possible. The whole incident had rocked the district for months.

Tammy shook her head, then wished she hadn't as the hammer went wild. Anyhow, things had turned out all right for him in the end. Macca was with another girl now. Lived somewhere up around Mount Isa.

'Luce, about selling the farm . . .'

'It was all bullshit. Me and Betty know. By the time we got here you'd finished the bottle and passed out.'

'Luce . . .'

'I know. I'm good, coming around at that hour. But all I did was respond to a friend in need. I think even a bloke like Christ would be happy with that.' Lucy paused for breath and then said, 'Although, it beats me why you weren't ringing Travis Hunter.'

'I think I tried but he wasn't home.'

'Probably for the best. You seriously look like shit.'

Tammy shut her eyes again, counted to ten. Be nice, Tammy. 'Thanks for that.'

'Hey, don't you ever wash your milking clothes?' Tammy opened her eyes and saw her friend, who was by now back near the door, wrinkling her nose. 'I think I'll go make coffee. Much easier on the olfactory senses.'

'The *what* senses?'

Lucy gave Tammy a sympathetic glance. 'Don't you worry your pretty little head over my nose. I'll go inhale caffeine. That'll fix it.'

'Fix what?' Tammy was by now completely lost. But Lucy and Betty Boop were gone.

Tammy flipped the lid of the loo closed and sat down. How the hell was she going to get through all this? As well as the headache, her face was now coming out in sympathy and throbbing too. Probably from all the crying the night before. Crying never got anyone anywhere, anyway. She'd learned that a long time ago from her grandparents.

Tammy had been told right from when she could first comprehend that her mother had died and had assumed it was when she was being born. Of her father she had no idea, didn't even put it together that there was a missing significant 'other', until she got to kinder and school and met other children with two parents.

She also worked out very early on not to ask about Natalie, otherwise her grandmother would get upset, disappear into her room for hours. For days afterwards she would walk around with a tragic and grief-stricken air that struck Tammy to the core. She was the cause of her grandmother's pain; it was her fault for being born.

And compared to Tammy's friends' mothers, Mae was a distant maternal figure, like mothering was something she did out of reluctant duty. Beautifully groomed, Mae also seemed to want a replica of herself in her granddaughter, a mirror image that could be moulded to fit Mae's idea of perfection. But all she got was a tomboy with a wild streak.

'Oh, but you're always wearing jeans!' Mae would say, in *that* tone of voice. 'Oh, but your hair is so short . . . You're so strong-minded . . . You're such a *farmer*,' like it was the worse thing in the world for a girl. Much and all as she loved her grandmother, Tammy eventually shut it all out and spent her time outside with Grandpa Tom or running wild around the property and surrounding hills. Somehow she instinctively knew she would never meet Mae's high standards and approval no matter how hard she tried.

On the day Mae let it slip that Tammy's mother had actually drowned, they'd been in the middle of a howling argument over whether fifteen-year-old Tammy could stay overnight at her boyfriend's place.

'I'll tell you why you can't,' cried a distressed Mae at the rebellious teenager after the argument had rocked back and forth. 'You'll end up just like your mother, pregnant and then dead in a river!'

Her grandmother had then clapped a hand over her mouth, sat down and broken into tears, while a shocked Tammy had yelled back, 'What do you mean, *dead in a river*?' The only answer she got was heartbreaking sobs, crying that went on and on from a woman who sat swaying back and forth.

It'd taken the sudden entry of Tom into the kitchen for a cup of tea to end the stand-off. He'd taken Tammy down the paddock, giving a distraught Mae time to collect herself, and explained the story of Natalie's death. That they really didn't know who Tammy's father was. The fact Mae couldn't deal with her daughter's death, the sense of failure of it all, so it was just easier never to mention her, to forget Natalie even existed. There was only one reminder left now and that was Tammy herself.

Tom had held his granddaughter's hand tightly while he tried to explain her grandmother's fragile state of mind on the matter, his eyes begging forgiveness for not telling her the whole story earlier. His need to protect Mae had overridden everything else.

And finally Tammy had understood why she'd felt like an outsider to her grandparents' relationship. They were supposed to be a family circle, but they weren't. She sat slightly to the left or right, never tight within. She wasn't Natalie. She didn't entirely belong. And it was all about Mae. Tom and Tammy pleasing Mae, the whole *world* pleasing Mae. It was just the way it was, whether the older woman did it consciously or not, and they were all a party to the deception.

Tammy spent hours dreaming of Natalie, and what she would have been like. It wasn't that her grandmother didn't love her, because Tammy sensed in her own way she did, it was just . . . well . . . Mae never focused solely on her granddaughter. Subsequently Tammy would have given anything to have known Natalie. What was she like? Was she a tomboy too? Would her mother have been proud of her?

She sure as heck wouldn't be proud of me now, thought Tammy as she stood up and made her way out of the bedroom, steadfastly ignoring the mirror on the dressing table as she went. She could hear Lucy in the kitchen singing along to Rod Stewart. Time to suck it up, stop thinking about the past and move forwards.

First things first though, to have breakfast or not? Tammy knew she had to get something in her stomach, otherwise she'd never make it through milking without spewing. She'd have to run the gauntlet of Lucy and Betty Boop. God help them all.

'I still don't see why you have to sell the farm!' Lucy was horrified all over again. 'The bastard can't make you do that.'

Tammy held a cup of tea in one hand, the other palm was in front of her face as if subconsciously trying to deflect Lucy's attack. 'Apparently he can,' she mumbled into the hot tea. Then she mimicked the solicitor's voice, 'It's going to be a great outcome all round.'

'I'll give her a great outcome all round. All round the bloody district. She'll never get work in this valley again!'

'Well, she's getting plenty of work at the minute. Apparently there's a run on divorces.'

'Mmm, another reason I should look into becoming a lesbian.'

'Because lesbians *never* break up. Come on, Luce. What makes you think that'd be any different? They're still your partner. Marriage certificates don't mean jack-shit any more.'

Lucy looked taken aback. 'I suppose you've got a point.'

'Too right I have. Doesn't help me with Shon though.'

'So what do you have to do now?'

'Go to town. Sign some papers. Sell the place. Give Shon his share of the proceeds. One hundred and fifty years of McCauley history – all over rover.'

When Tammy looked up from smothering jam on her toast, Lucy's eyes were welling with tears. 'Oh man, Tammy. No wonder you got drunk. What're you going to do?'

Tammy picked up the jar of plum jam she'd made with the fruit from the century-old Montmorency orchard. Screwed on the lid. Got up from the table and pushed her chair in. 'I'm going to milk my girls. Enjoy every last minute I've got with them. They'll have to be sold too, I guess.' Tammy felt tears started to prick her eyes. Damn. She wouldn't cry again. She'd done enough of that. 'And I have to try and work out how I'm going to tell Joe.'

Lucy gasped. 'Oh, my Lord. I forgot about him. He'll be shattered.'

'I know,' said Tammy. 'He mightn't have set foot on the place until recently but it's still a big part of him, whether he knows it or not.'

'How're you going to tell him?'

'I don't know. I guess I'll just have to blurt it out.'

'Wait a bit,' advised Lucy. 'Just until you've got your own head around it.'

'You reckon?'

'Yep,' said Lucy nodding. 'You'll need every bit of strength you've got for that conversation. In the meantime, go see to your girls. Me and Betty are going back to bed. We've got some serious beauty sleep to catch up on.' And Lucy formed a pose reminiscent of Ms Boop.

Tammy couldn't help but laugh. 'You do that.' She went to walk out onto the back verandah to find her boots, but then she paused and popped her head back into the kitchen. 'Luce?'

'Damn it, girl. You've gotta go milk those cows. You'll miss the tanker.'

'Thanks. Thanks for being there for me. Again.'

Lucy Granger glanced over her shoulder as she carried the plates to the dishwasher, and winked. 'No worries. Where else would I get my drama-queen fix, if it wasn't through you?'

Chapter 35

The milk tanker roared out the drive as Travis Hunter wheeled in.

'Ms McCauley.' He doffed his hat like they did in the old days. The gentleman was back again.

'Trav.' Geez, the man looked good. He'd obviously just had a shower as his hair was still damp and curling softly at the nape of his neck. It made him look vulnerable somehow.

'How'd you go this morning? Any sign of the dog?' asked Tammy. If he was taking the time to stake out her paddocks in the hopes of killing the mutt that was attacking her calves, she needed to show interest even after yesterday's news.

'Nope. Not a thing. I'll keep watch though every other day for a week or so. See if he comes back. Sometimes they take more stock right away, other times they wait awhile. No rhyme nor reason to it all.'

Tammy nodded, which in turn hurt her head something fierce.

Trav got out of the ute and changed tack. 'Me and Billy are off to town now to catch up with the audiologist. The lady comes to the hospital once a fortnight and they managed to squeeze us in.'

For the first time Tammy noticed Billy in the passenger seat, also dressed in what looked like his best clothes – a pair of clean blue jeans, a chequered shirt, sleeves folded precisely to the elbow. A miniature version of his dad except for the red hair. *He* didn't look vulnerable, just pale and anxious.

Tammy leaned into the cab, making sure she kept her dark sunglasses on. She didn't want to scare the kid. 'Hi, Billy. How's it going, mate?'

A small voice answered, 'Orright. I think.'

'Going to have your ears tested?'

'Yep.'

'You okay about that?'

'Yeah, I guess . . .'

'It'll be fine, mate. No worse than me yelling at you to open the gates when we feed out hay.'

'I'd prefer to be doing that. Feeding out the hay, I mean.' The little boy ducked his head, but not before Tammy had seen a pair of glassy eyes.

Tammy tried to lighten the mood. 'So, after your appointment, have you organised to do something special in town?'

Billy shook his head. He was biting his bottom lip now.

Tammy turned to Trav, who was listening intently but not saying a word. 'C'mon, Dad, you have to do something special after our little mate here has been so brave and got his hearing checked.'

'Like what?'

Tammy wondered if she looked as exasperated as she felt. She forced a smile for Billy's sake. 'Oh, I don't know. Something fun. Maybe go to McDonald's for lunch?'

Billy appeared eager. Trav screwed up his nose.

'A play at the park?'

Trav seemed interested. Billy frowned.

'A swim in the heated pool?'

Both father and son looked horrified.

Tammy mentally threw her hands in the air. 'Well, surely between the two of you you can think of *something*!'

Father and son glanced at each other. Something seemed to click. 'The saddle-shop?' suggested Trav.

Billy nodded and suddenly a wide smile lit up his face. Trav responded with a half-grin of his own and Tammy felt her legs melt away from beneath her. Goddamn it, the man was sex on legs. Get a grip on yourself, McCauley. She dragged her attention back to Billy. 'What's so good about the saddle-shop?'

'A stockwhip. One of my very own. I've been saving my money.'

'Of course. What every boy your age should have. But don't come cracking that thing around my girls,' said Tammy, winking at the child to take the edge off her words. 'Or I'll have to whip you back.'

'I won't. I promise. But old Joe has promised to teach me how to crack a whip. Like a real *pro*-fession-*al*, he said.'

'He'd know how to do it, too, I'll bet,' said Tammy, with wry twist to her words. 'He's a real expert at anything like that.' Along with fishing, and shooting – especially ducks. And hares. 'You have a good time then. I'd better let you head off.' She made to move away from the ute but Trav grabbed her around the waist. Tammy felt the warmth of his fingers through her shirt. Then the feel of his thumb as it caressed her skin through a hole in the cotton. Shivers thrummed through her body, right down to her very toes. She looked up at the man. 'Yes?' she breathed. It came out sounding like a wheeze. She cleared her throat. Had another go. 'Yes, Trav?'

'We wondered if you'd come with us?' Trav hesitated, then, seeming to realise he had hold of her, let her go. The loss of warmth was staggering. He stood back and formally said, 'Billy and I would be most obliged if you'd come to town with us and . . . argh . . . ummm . . . help us choose a whip . . .' The last words came out in one almighty gush, '. . . and come to the hearing test.'

Tammy pointed down to her cow-yard clothes. 'But –'

'Please Tammy? Pretty, pretty please? I'll wash down the yard tonight for free,' said Billy. 'We'd really like you to come. Wouldn't we, Dad? Please say yes.'

'We'll wait while you change. We've got time. Don't have to be there until eleven-thirty.'

Tammy considered them. Billy's face was still stuck in a comically pleading pose. Trav's face was now impassive but his fingers gave his agitation away. He'd grabbed hold of her hand and was almost unconsciously drawing her towards the ute.

She flung her free arm towards the house, where Lucy's car was evident. 'Luce is here. She stayed the night.' Some of it, anyway. 'I can't leave her; that'd be rude.'

But just then, Lucy appeared out the back door, heading towards her car, still wearing her Betty Boop PJs.

Trav gaped. Even from this far away the scarlet pyjamas were something to behold. Especially when topped with yellow and pink hair.

'She wear those all the time?' asked Trav.

'Ummm . . . yes. That's why I wear dark glasses.' Liar, McCauley.

'I can understand that,' said Trav as Lucy Granger poured herself into her little white car and moved off.

'Watch out, here she comes. You might need some sunnies yourself,' said Tammy with a wry smile. So much for Lucy's beauty sleep. She wondered what had happened.

'Hey, Hunter.' Lucy pulled up beside the ute. 'And how's my buddy-boy Billy?'

Tammy watched as Billy hid a wince. 'I'm good thank you, Mrs Granger.'

'Mizz Granger to you, kiddo. Or Lucy. Or Luce. Or maybe Betty? Have you met Betty Boop?' She pointed to her top.

Tammy thought she'd better save the child. 'What happened to sleeping in?'

'Oh that danged phone of yours rang and rang and rang. I had to get out of bed and tripped over the tissue box and then had to find the phone, which someone had managed to hide *under* the bed. It must have slipped off after you rang me in your drunken stupor –' Lucy clapped her hand over her mouth. 'Oops! I wasn't supposed to say that, was I? Did you hear me say anything, Billy?' She looked hard at the boy. 'No of course you didn't. We won't say anything about Tammy swallowing a whole bottle of wine *by herself*, and then ringing me in the middle of the night, all maudlin-like, shall we?'

Tammy could feel Trav's eyes burning holes in her skull but she wasn't going to glance at him. No, all her dirty looks were focused on her best friend. Her very nearly *ex*-best friend.

'Goodbye, Lucy.'

'Goodbye, Tammy. Oh, and by the way, your bed is *so* comfortable. Betty and I had a lovely catnap before that Alice woman from the gallery rang.'

'Alice rang again?'

'Yep, said to tell you the gallery opening starts at six o'clock on Friday. She sounds very nice and invited me too. I said I'd let you know and I'd make sure you told all your mates, who you obviously *hadn't* told.'

'She only rang yesterday morning, and I've been a bit busy since then, *as you well know*!'

'Yes, yes, yes. No worries. Anyhow, I'll tell Dean and Jacinta and anyone else I can think of.'

That meant the whole town, thought Tammy uncharitably.

'You coming, Hunter?' asked Lucy.

'I haven't been invited yet.'

Lucy sighed. 'Tammy! For goodness' sake, do I have to do *everything* for you?'

'No –'

'Travis Hunter, will you hereby take Tammy McCauley to the Narree Gallery Opening next Friday night? There. Done. So?' Lucy raised an eyebrow.

'Yes. I will.'

'That sounded like you were getting married,' said Billy.

'Thank you, Lucy. That will be all,' said Tammy. 'And you, Billy, don't go getting any weird ideas. One marriage is enough for me.'

Billy looked downcast. 'That's what Dad always says.'

Tammy glanced at Trav but he was staring at Billy, an unreadable expression on his face.

'I'll be seeing you all,' Lucy called, driving off.

'Yeah, right,' muttered Tammy. 'In another life.'

'So, are you coming?' This was from Billy. 'It'll be better fun with you, Tammy. C'mon. Plea-se?'

How could she say no to the boy? Plus the fact his father still hadn't let go of her hand.

'I did have to run into Narree today anyway. Got to do some stuff at my solicitors. Would I be able to do that while we're there?' She directed her query towards Trav.

He nodded in response. 'Yeah, while we're at the appointment maybe?'

'All right then, I'll come. But you'll have to let me grab a quick shower.'

'Sure thing!' said Billy, now jumping up and down on his seat. 'That's okay, isn't it, Dad?'

'Absolutely. We've got time for a shower,' said his father.

'Not you,' said his son. 'Tammy.'

'Oh yeah, right.'

But Trav's eyes told a different story. Her stomach started to do a weird, fluttering thing like a squadron of moths or butterflies were on the loose. Her knees went weak, and then he did that bloody half-smile thing again. Oh. Dear. God. She was in trouble.

'I'll go and um ... get started ... um ... shall I?' She waved an arm vaguely towards the house.

'You do that,' said Trav, not taking his eyes off her for a minute.

Goddamn the man.

'I'm going now,' said Tammy, not moving an inch. She'd forgotten she was wearing dark glasses, so intent was she on his gaze, which now seemed to be slowly undressing her. That was until a hand came up and removed the sunnies. She tried to snatch them back but she was too late.

'Tammy?' said Trav, concern quickly replacing lust. 'What's wrong?'

'Nothing.'

'But –'

'I had a migraine. It hurt a lot.' Oh damn it. She could have thought of something better than that. She slid the glasses back onto her nose.

'You had a migraine so you drank a whole bottle of wine?'

'Yes,' said Tammy, crossing her arms. 'I thought it might deaden the pain.'

He'd let go of her hand, stepped back and was now leaning against the bonnet of the ute, his arms folded.

'I find it helps. You get a migraine, have a glass or two or three of wine, then you pass out and hey presto, no more pain. Well, not until the next morning at least.'

'And where does ringing Lucy in the middle of the night come into all this?'

'Oh that,' said Tammy, flicking her hand as if brushing her best friend away like a bush-fly. 'Just a minor detail.'

'Yes?'

'Well,' said Tammy, purposely putting an exasperated note in her voice. 'She *is* a nurse with a well-stocked medicine cabinet.' Tammy smiled. 'Now, I'll just run up to the house and have that shower. We don't want to be late.' She walked, then jogged, then ran towards the house. As she got to the garden gate she slung one look back across her shoulder.

Trav was still leaning against the bonnet of his ute, frowning. Damn it. That whole charade hadn't worked. But she didn't want to tell him about Shon and the farm. She didn't really want to tell *anyone* besides Lucy.

And in any case, Joe had to know next.

Chapter 36

Tammy was waiting in the sun outside the hospital. She'd been to see the solicitor and it had been awful. She didn't know why she'd expected otherwise.

'Sign here,' said Hilary Stratton. 'And here. And here.'

Tammy had gone through the motions, scribbling her signature in a daze, pretending it was someone else holding that pen, someone else putting her property up for sale.

And then Tammy was out on the street again. She couldn't help but wonder if, in the near future, that's exactly where she and her belongings would be.

She was now back on the same park bench where she'd sat when old Joe had been admitted to the hospital. That seemed like years ago, but really it was only weeks. Could she find another solution? Could she keep any of the property at all? Start again with the homestead and say half the land? She swallowed. Even if it turned out to be possible, the idea of carving up her great-great-grandparents' legacy made her feel physically ill.

What about finding another investor? Did she know anyone she'd trust as a partner? The problem was Shon was so set on her losing Montmorency she knew he'd do whatever it took to stop her finding a way around selling the place. Shit, this was hard. Perhaps she should just start buying lottery tickets.

Tammy watched a young boy and his father walk through the electric doors and come towards her. She couldn't see the expressions on their faces. Couldn't work out if the news had been good or bad. Billy was almost skipping along but whether it was from sheer happiness or just to keep pace with his father, she couldn't have said.

'So, how'd it go?' she asked as soon as they were within earshot.

Trav's headshake was slight.

'I'm getting hearing aids,' shouted Billy. 'Bright yellow ones!'

'*Really*? They make them in bright yellow?' said Tammy, while she searched Trav's face.

'Yep, they come in lots of colours, don't they, Dad? Like liquorice allsorts, the lady said.'

'They sure do, kid,' said Trav. Tammy finally saw that it was pain on the man's face. 'Billy's going to get two new behind-the-ear aids and they are going to make his life so much better.'

'Yeah,' said Billy. 'I might actually be able to hear Joe when he's teaching me to ride the old motorbike.'

'He's *what*?' said the two grown-ups together.

'He's teaching me to ride his old Honda 110. It's so cool. Boots just loves riding on the back. His ears fly out like mud flaps. I reckon once I get a bit better at balancing on the bike, I might even be able to dink Joe!'

Tammy shuddered. Trav looked to the heavens. 'But, Billy.' Tammy thought she had to say something. 'Don't you think it's a bit dangerous, you being so . . . well, little . . . and the bike being a bit big?'

'My feet touch the ground.' The child's tone was indignant. Then guilty. 'Well, on tippy-toes.' Trust Billy to be honest. God love him.

'So, back to the hearing aids. What happened, Billy?' asked Tammy.

'I'm deaf,' he stated in a matter-of-fact voice. 'I've got a mild to moderate hearing loss which the lady said might get a bit worse as I get older.'

Tammy glanced at Trav, questioning.

'He's suffering nerve deafness,' said Trav. 'Even if it does get worse, things will even out. Probably genetic.'

Tammy could see he'd already taken another bucketload of blame onto himself. As if Trav needed to shoulder any more of that. Right at that moment, she felt real animosity towards the woman who'd caused all this pain.

'So, what now?'

'They stuffed this white Plasticine stuff in my ear and that took its shape. It was really cold and came out looking weird. They make a mould of it so it fits right into my earhole and then they attach it to my new hearing aids. I can pick them up the week after next, can't I, Dad?'

'Yep, that's right.'

Tammy watched as Trav's hand came out to stroke the hair on his son's head. The strong fingers then massaged the boy's scalp.

Tammy nearly groaned aloud. She could remember him doing that to her, only two mornings before. The feel of those fingers in her hair, on her breasts, across the whole of her body . . . She tore her eyes away. Then looked back, because it finally hit her what was actually happening in front of her eyes. Trav was touching Billy. He was really touching his son! And Billy was loving it. The child was leaning into his father's hand like Boots did with Old Joe.

Tammy felt tears prick at her eyes. Don't you dare, McCauley, not now. 'So, I guess a visit to the saddlers is in order, hey?'

Trav removed his fingers from his son's head. 'Yep. One stock whip coming right up.' He held out a hand to Tammy. 'You ready?'

'Too right. I wouldn't miss Billy spending my money on his very own stockwhip.'

'Your money?' said Billy, looking puzzled.

'Isn't this purchase from all the work you've been doing for me?'

'Well, yes.'

'So, I reckon I've got a vested interest. C'mon, cowboy, let's go find a good piece of leather for you.'

Billy smiled and started walking towards the ute.

As Trav pulled Tammy up from her seat he leaned down and whispered in her ear, his breath tickling and making her shiver. 'I'll give you a good piece of leather any time.'

Tammy stood stock-still in shock. 'What did you say?'

'You heard me.' And Trav winked. *Winked*! And a wink had no right to look so good on a man. It made her tummy dive to her own Ariat boots. 'If what I heard was what you actually said, I think I'll pass,' she stated.

'Since when did you become so prudish?' He went to give her a side-shove with his hip as they walked across the parkland towards the car, but she dodged away. This wasn't the normal in-public Hunter she knew. This man was being *playful*, just like he was in bed. Those hands, that hot sensual mouth, the things he did with it . . . Oh. My. Lord. Tammy could feel herself starting to blush. Time to get the conversation back on track. 'How about we have lunch? I'm hungry.'

'So am I,' said Trav, and he grabbed her by the hand, pulled her behind a bushy tea-tree and kissed her.

Tammy's mind went numb. As his fingers ran ragged through her tumbling hair, she felt her whole body slump against the hard muscles that were holding her upright. She kissed him back, urgently. Goddamn it, the man was good at this. His lips trailed across her face, down her neck. She arched her body in response, his stubble tickling and making her shiver with delight.

'Hey, Dad! Tammy? Where've you gone?' A little boy's voice called across the park. 'Dad? *Tammy?*'

'Shit,' said Trav as he reluctantly let her go. 'Here, kid. Coming!' And he stepped away from behind the tree then glanced back at her. 'Hold that thought for tonight, woman.'

In a daze she nodded. She'd forgotten how to speak. She tried to subdue the red flush she knew would be leaking all over her cheeks. Damn, the man could kiss. She straightened her shirt, fluffed her hair back around her shoulders and went to follow him.

'Ah-ha, Mrs Murphy.'

Tammy spun around. There, peering at her with black-currant eyes, was Beatrice Parker. How much did she see?

'And was that Mr Hunter I saw heading across the grass?' There was a knowing quirk to her eyebrow.

Everything, thought Tammy. 'Yes, that was Travis Hunter.

He's been at the hospital with his son, Billy. I'm just helping them . . .' She was gushing but powerless to stop herself.

'Helping them?'

'Ah, yes. Lending moral support, so to speak.'

'Mmm . . . moral support. Is that what you call it?' said Beatrice, her eyebrow lifting once again.

The woman had *definitely* seen it all.

'And just where is your husband today, Tammy?' said Beatrice with a look at the car park. 'I can't see him around.'

Surely this old gossip knew all the dirty details already. Beatrice had seen firsthand the way he'd treated her at the dance and in fact had commented on Shon being with Joanne when she talked about collecting a donation from her. 'I really wouldn't know, Mrs Parker. Probably with Joanne at the pub. He's left me and moved in there, you know. And what's more, I don't miss him one iota. He's been abusing me for years.' She really wasn't sure why she felt she had to explain all this to the woman, but for some reason she couldn't stop herself. 'Our marriage is over.'

Beatrice Parker's disapproving stare vanished in an instant, replaced by something softer. 'And so it should be, my dear,' the woman said mildly. 'My Donald was exactly the same. I tend to think mental abuse is sometimes even worse than the physical kind. The world can't see the scars. Thank the Lord in Heaven Donald left. Took off up north with some theatre woman. Life was better – much easier – all round without him.'

'What?' How on earth did this woman know Shon's abuse had been more mental than physical?

Beatrice flapped her hand in a dismissive motion. 'That's the problem with you young ones these days. You just don't seem to think we oldies know what life's all about. Well, I can assure you, my dear, we *see* things. In fact I've seen more hard times than you've had Rice Bubbles. And I know what it's like to live with a bad man.' Beatrice paused and looked towards Trav's ute where he and Billy were waiting patiently. 'And I don't mean the delicious kind of bad either.'

Tammy stood there, speechless.

'My guess is Shon Murphy will be a nasty man to deal with. If you want my advice, be rid of him as quick as you can.'

'I intend to.'

'Good.' Beatrice nodded in approval, her little head bobbing like a willy wag-tail. 'Say hello to Mr Hunter for me, won't you? Tell him I'll drop in a sponge shortly.' The woman then gave an enigmatic smile. 'One that's actually *meant* for him this time.'

Tammy wondered about that but decided it was safer not to ask. 'I will. No worries. And Mrs Parker?'

'Yes, my dear?' said Beatrice, the blackcurrants blinking a few times.

'Thanks.'

'My pleasure. But, maybe next time, avoid snogging the likes of Mr Hunter in the park. It really doesn't sit well with my blood pressure.'

Toot Toot! A horn went off behind them. She glanced towards the ute. Trav and Billy were beckoning her.

'Goodbye, Mizz McCauley,' said Beatrice, shooing her away. 'Don't forget my message to the Hunters.'

'C'mon, Tammy!' shouted Billy out the window. 'Let's go!'

Let's go indeed. Onwards and upwards, as her grandfather would have said. He had been such a strong and capable man. She guessed the estrangement with Joe had been Tom's life-long regret, but not one strong enough to temper his adoration of Mae, nor his love for his farming heritage. He'd just soldiered on. The sale of Montmorency would have devastated Grandpa Tom.

But at least she had people around her who really cared. Lucy, Trav and Billy, and even old Joe, which was a bit of a turn-up for the books. A couple of months ago even to *know* the old man seemed as unlikely a possibility as Lucy becoming a nun. Then again, Lucy would probably consider *anything*.

And now even Beatrice Parker was being nice. They'd all help her through, she was sure. She just had to get the courage to tell them what she was going to do.

Chapter 37

They were all sitting around Joe's verandah before heading off to the art show. Lucy and Cin had called by to drop off his groceries. Tammy and Hunter were checking up on him (the sooner they put a stop to this babysitting or 'old man-sitting' nonsense, the better), and by the looks of the car coming up the drive, Dean Gibson was tracking his niece. Why the hell they'd all had to congregate here rather than Montmorency, he didn't know. They were disturbing his early-evening rabbit shoot.

'I didn't pick up anyone on the night of the dance,' said Lucy Granger, swinging her legs as she sat on the new verandah rail. Joe hoped Hunter'd bolted the plank on real good. That amount of weight would test out any screw. 'Not one likely candidate! So that's it.'

'That's what?' said Tammy.

'I'm officially looking for love with a lady,' stated Lucy. 'I'm going to embrace womanhood in all its glory.'

'Oh, my sister's a lesbian,' said Cin Greenaway. 'All my male friends cry their eyes out when I tell them.'

Joe flicked his gaze towards the schoolteacher. She had on a long flowing top with a deep neckline and no sleeves and a pair of tight trousers which made her legs look like they went up to her armpits. Very nice armpits they were too, thought Joe, before he realised what he was thinking. *Armpits*? For fuck's sake!

'Well, if your sister looks anything like you, Cin, I'd be crying too,' said Dean Gibson who was walking up the steps wearing what Joe could only describe as the most God-awful shirt. And Dean Gibson was a Tucker. His pants were pulled up so high they looked ridiculous.

'Why thank you, Deano,' simpered Cin.

Joe looked around for someone to roll his eyes at, but Tammy was too busy shoving a ball around the verandah boards with her feet. To Trav, back from Trav, to Trav, back, to, back –

Boots was the only other body showing a modicum of interest in the footsies going on. Which, thought Joe, was probably just as well. He glanced across the house yard at Billy, who was trying to crack a rather long whip. Every second night while Hunter had been staking out Tammy's paddocks, trying to catch the bloody feral dog, the kid had been staying at Joe's rather than be left on his own. A turn up for the books, thought Joe. Previously Travis'd had no hesitation leaving the child by himself. Although Joe himself wasn't sure who was keeping an eye on who. Billy on Joe, Joe on Billy, or both of them on Trav?

'Lesbianism is my true calling after all. I thought for a second it might have been the nunnery. But then I remembered when I was –' said Lucy, pausing as Tammy nearly choked on her drink. The soon-to-be-a-lesbian glared at her friend. 'What?'

'Remembered what?' croaked Tammy.

'When I was at uni –'

Tammy flapped her hands. 'Lucy! Do we have to hear –?'

A snapping crack from Billy's whip came from the yard. 'Yay, buddy-boy!' yelled Lucy. 'That worked a treat!'

Billy smiled across at the grown-ups.

'Anyway, where was I?' Lucy was now holding up one finger. 'Oh yes. Never mind. But I thought about our conversation on the night of the dance and reckoned I should take this side of myself more seriously. Maybe I'll have a bit more luck with the sheilas.' Lucy leered at Cin's breasts.

'Don't do that!' said Cin crossly.

'Don't do what?'

'Look at my breasts like that!'

Now everyone was staring at Cin's chest with interest, even Billy, who'd come back onto the verandah. He pulled up a chair next to his father, which killed the ball game between Travis and Tammy.

'Because that's what *men* do. They look at them, they talk to them . . .' Cin blushed, shot a look in Dean's direction.

'And the problem with that would be?' asked Lucy, still intent on Cin.

Cin heaved a big sigh. 'I want a man to love me for my head.'

They all looked around at each other, puzzled.

Billy spoke up, hesitant in the contemplative silence. 'Do you mean intelligence, Ms Greenaway?'

Trav kicked Billy's chair. The boy mumbled something about grown-ups and glared at the ground. 'Probably time for us to travel,' said Trav to change the subject.

'Yes, it's six o'clock. We really should be going,' said Dean, looking at his watch. 'If it starts at six-thirty that'll give us five minutes to get into our cars, twenty minutes to drive there and then five minutes to organise ourselves again.'

'Ooooo, lovely,' said Cin, knocking back the rest of her drink and trying to stand up.

It was then Joe saw the bottle of vodka left on the verandah. It was stuffed with old-style Redskin lollies. No wonder the girl was high. Straight Vodka and all that sugar. Old Deano was in for a wild night. Well, wild for Dean anyway, Joe guessed.

'We're heading off now, Joe.' It was Tammy, standing beside his chair. 'I've got these two prints to get into the gallery for hanging.'

'Oh right. Well shoo, the bloody lot of ya then. Leave me and Billy in peace.'

He only just caught the edge of Billy's agonised look. 'What?'

'Billy's coming with us, Joe,' said Trav. 'He really wanted to and, well, I thought what harm is there in that? It'll be a bit of culture and we Hunters are a bit light on that sort of stuff.'

The boy was smiling now.

Joe looked from one Hunter to the other. Then at his niece, all raring to go.

'Well,' said Joe, sweeping them away with his hands, 'get the buggery out of here and leave me alone.'

Trav laughed and moved towards the ute. 'No worries. We'll be seeing you then. C'mon, Billy.'

With a last glance at Joe, Billy scampered after his father.

Harrumph. So much for loyalty then, thought Joe, uncharitable though he knew his response to be.

'So you'll be right, Joe? I've left your tea on the bench. You just have to heat it up,' said Tammy.

He hadn't realised she was still beside him. 'Yes, of course I'll be right. What, do you think I'm fucking useless?'

'Far from it,' said Tammy, her tone wry. 'We'll catch you later.'

'Yeah. Righto. Now go on, piss off, all of ya.'

Joe felt a soft pair of lips on his cheek. Then they were gone.

He put up a hand to his face to touch the spot as he watched his niece clamber into the passenger side of the ute, Billy perched up in the middle of the two adults. Watched them all drive off down Hope's Road; Lucy and Cin, then Deano, their lights in the distance, the others now hard on their tail.

He stretched back in his chair and relished the peace. The only noise to be heard was Trav's ute heading through the low-level crossing and towards the main road to Narree. Then it too was gone. Finally there was absolute silence. Well, except for the early evening gaggle of birds and creatures of the bush as they went about settling down for the night.

It was peaceful. Silent. Beautiful. The mountains out to the north were inky blue, huge dark shadows looming in the night sky. And there wasn't a bunny to be seen.

Old Joe inhaled the sweet tangs of the bush and the vibrant mountain air and revelled in the completeness of it all. He was happy.

Until a weird little feeling crept up his backbone. He looked around furtively. What the fuck was wrong with him? He loved being out here on the verandah. He loved sitting here on his own, looking out across his kingdom. Didn't he?

The shiver came again and it wasn't from cold. It was like an icy hand was tracing a feeling of dread up his vertebrae, one by one, finally coming to rest with a strong clasp around his throat.

Old Joe didn't like this feeling. He didn't like this feeling at all. If he could just work out what it was maybe he could fix it.

It was Boots who gave him the answer. The dog had woken up from his place near the fire and walked to sit at Joe's feet, right where his ears could be fondled.

Boots didn't want to be alone. And neither did his master.

He, Joe McCauley, was lonely.

Chapter 38

The gallery thrummed with people, all ooing and aahing over the paintings displayed around the walls. Tammy and Trav carried the two prints, which they'd carefully stashed in the tray of the ute amid bundles of old blankets and eiderdowns.

'Tammy! How lovely to see you,' said Alice Stringer, spotting them immediately. She must have been waiting anxiously for them to arrive. There were two places on the main feature wall ready for the pictures.

'Hi, Alice,' said Tammy. 'So sorry I couldn't get here any earlier. It's the cows, you see.'

Alice Stringer gave a gracious smile. 'Yes, I'm just starting to understand how cows are the real bosses in this district. I didn't realise milking could have such an impact on one's social life.'

'I had to start milking at two o'clock this morning to get here tonight,' Tammy explained as she bent down to help Trav unwrap the first print.

'And this would be?' asked Alice.

'Travis Hunter.' He shot her his half-smile, but to Tammy's amazement Alice barely registered it.

'How do you do, Mr Hunter? And you're a dairy farmer too?'

'I run a few head of beef cattle on the side, but no, I'm a dog trapper.'

'Right,' said Alice, who obviously had no idea at all what that meant. She directed her attention back to Tammy. 'Well, be sure to make yourself known to Reyne, Tammy. She'll be here soon. The mayor and a few councillors have just taken her for an early dinner at the hotel.'

Trav eased the first print out of its makeshift cover and lifted it up onto the wall.

'Gorgeous!' the woman gasped.

Tammy had to agree. Trav was like Adonis with modern clothes on, which just seemed to make him all the more sexy. And his bum. The way it clenched in his Wranglers while he lifted the print onto its hook. Yum-my.

'That would have to be one of the most beautiful things I have ever seen,' said Alice.

Tammy agreed again. You should see him with his clothes off, woman, she thought. It only gets better and better . . .

'*Travis?*' A shocked voice punctured Tammy's daydreams.

Trav swung round and his face turned from a healthy brown to a pale grey. '*Katrina?*'

Oh my Lord. It's not, is it? thought Tammy.

'What are *you* doing here?' said the exotic-looking woman dressed in a peacock-green cheesecloth skirt, long and brightly beaded Aztec-style top, dangly earrings and crystal necklace to match. She stood out like a bright jewel among the more sedately dressed country crowd.

'I live here.' Trav's tone was edgy, his face still a sickly grey. 'And you?'

The woman's hands fluttered in the air in agitation. To Tammy, she looked like a cornered cow. Not knowing which way to run, but escape was paramount.

'I'm the feature artist,' she said finally.

No. She couldn't be Reyne Jennings. Not the one who created her angel-sphinx prints?

'I'm touring regional Victoria, New South Wales and South Australia with my artwork,' the woman explained.

Tammy took in the beautiful creature standing in front of her. Masses of shiny, dark auburn ringlets floated across the woman's shoulders, cascading down her back, almost to her waist. Her figure was slim but voluptuous in all the right places. The eyes of most of the men in the room (not to mention Narree's newest lesbian), Tammy noticed, were drawn to her.

'Well, there's no need to introduce our feature artist to you two. Looks like you've already done it yourselves,' said Alice Stringer.

'Katrina . . . or *Reyne* . . . and I,' said Travis in quiet, yet expressionless voice 'already know each other.'

'Really?' said Alice sounding surprised. 'Gosh, it's a small world, isn't it?'

'You can say that again,' muttered Travis, glancing around. Tammy watched as his eyes landed on Billy, who was playing in the corner of the room with a set of carved wooden trucks. His gaze seemed to soften slightly, then harden as he turned back to his former partner.

'You haven't met Tammy McCauley then?' said Alice, oblivious to the tension in the small airspace between them. 'She bought the set of prints I had of yours.'

'Ah,' said the artist, slightly inclining her head. Her gaze assessed Tammy from head to toe, and Tammy found she didn't like the scrutiny one little bit. 'The original paintings of those prints mean a great deal to me.' Katrina's gaze floated back towards Trav as if she wasn't sure whether to go on. Trav wasn't looking at Katrina, but Tammy could tell he was listening hard enough.

'Reyne was telling me those paintings were what got her noticed,' interjected Alice with a big smile. 'We're so lucky to have her here in Narree.'

Yep, *real* lucky, thought Tammy.

'I suppose you'll want to meet Billy?' Trav said in a rough voice, interrupting Alice.

Katrina Jennings seemed shocked and a slim freckled hand came up to pull at the long ringlets. Her face flushed a bright pink.

'I guess so,' she said after a few moments, her eyes darting around the room until they came to rest on the little red-haired boy in the corner. The woman went perfectly still then let out a deep sigh. 'Yes, I'd better, I suppose.'

She *supposed*? thought Tammy. She was looking at her son for the first time in eight years and she *supposed* she should meet him? What a crock of shit. But then again this was a woman who'd walked out on her partner and baby boy. What did Tammy expect?

Alice Stringer, finally sensing the tension, had hurriedly moved on to greet more guests coming through the gallery door. Travis was just standing there; Katrina was still gazing at Billy with a nervous frown.

'I'll go and catch up with the others,' said Tammy. Travis barely nodded. Katrina didn't respond.

She escaped towards Dean and Cin, who were discussing a painting. Tammy, listening with only half an ear, turned back to watch Travis and Katrina.

'But, Dean, it really is a vase. I'm sure it is,' said Cin.

'No, you're wrong, Cin. It's a painted windmill. Look, see these bits here,' said Dean and he touched the painting. 'These are the blades, there's the pump rod and that's the crank shaft.'

'You're both wrong. It's a cow,' said Lucy, coming up from behind.

'It can't be a cow!' said Dean. 'A cow doesn't have green and red all over its middle bits.'

'It does if it's gone down with bloat. Stick a knife in and there you have it, green fermented grass spewing out with blood.'

'Oooo, that's disgusting,' squealed Cin.

'What's disgusting?' asked Tammy, tuning into the discussion. Travis and Katrina were finally moving. She looked at the painting. Dropped her head this way and that, trying to work out what it was. 'Yeah, that's pretty awful. It looks like a cow down with bloat.'

'It's actually a representation of a mother giving birth,' Alice Stringer explained as she passed by. 'The green is indicative of new life and the red conjures up images of passionate love amid the conflicting emotions of having children.'

'Could have fooled me,' said Lucy, rolling her eyes. 'I still think it's a cow down with bloat.'

'A vase.'

'A windmill.'

'Go ask the artist herself,' said Tammy. 'She's with Travis.'

All of her friends turned as one to look at the dog trapper, who was fighting his way through the throng of people towards Billy, closely followed by his stunning redhead of an ex-wife.

Lucy grabbed hold of Tammy's arm. 'What's wrong, Tim Tam?'

Tammy sighed. 'Nothing . . . well . . . No, nothing.'

'Don't give me that shit.'

Tammy took a deep breath and levelled her gaze at her friend. 'The feature artist is his former wife.'

Lucy and Dean looked blank. But Cin didn't.

'She's Billy's *mother*?'

All four of them turned towards the little boy, who was now sitting on a window seat in the far corner of the room. They could just hear his voice over the hum in the gallery.

'Does Billy know she's here?' asked Cin.

Tammy shook her head. 'Don't think so. But I reckon he's about to find out.'

'What the hell?' said Lucy.

'And so, my friends, can you see the representation of motherhood now?' Alice Stringer rejoined them, smiling broadly. 'It's an interesting manifestation, I do agree, but if one looks hard enough you might be able to see it, depending on your outlook on life at the moment.'

'My outlook is fundamentally flawed,' said Lucy, facing the painting again and shaking her head. 'How the hell you can get anything from a bunch of blobs and brushstrokes like that is anyone's guess.'

'And you are?' asked Alice.

'Lucy. Lucy Granger.'

'What a lovely name. My cat's called Lucy.'

'Really?'

'Oh yes,' said Alice. 'Susan – my partner – and I separated just before I moved up here. Lucy's my best friend now, really.'

'So you're a lesbian?' said Cin. 'My sister's one of those. And Lucy here's thinking of becoming one.'

301

Tammy groaned. Oh my Lord. What a night this was turning out to be. 'I'll just go over and check Billy is okay.'

But what she saw across the room stopped her in her tracks. Trav was walking up to the child with Katrina. Billy's mouth fell open, then closed and then opened again. The woman held out her hand to shake his. He looked wondering, amazed and pleased beyond words. Excitement suffused his whole face when Billy finally realised that here, at long last, was his mother.

Chapter 39

Travis wasn't quite sure if he was in the middle of a dream or a nightmare.

Katrina was here. In Narree. After eight long and heartbreaking years, his ex-wife was standing in front of him. Reuniting now with her son. And the boy was looking like all his Christmases had come at once.

How he hated Katrina for that. Hated the fact his child was gazing up at her like she was an angel from God. What had she ever done to deserve such a look? Except to waltz out of their house one sunny afternoon, leaving her toddler asleep, and never come back. Now she was leaning down towards the boy, looking at the trucks he was excitedly showing her.

But all the while her eyes were darting to the left and the right, clearly seeking a way out.

Well, stuff her. She could wear it for a little while. Screw the fact this was her evening. Every night had been *her* night, while he and his mother had had to bring up her son on their own.

'I can't believe you're really my mum,' said Billy as he piled the trucks into her arms.

Katrina gave a brittle smile. The lift at the edges of her mouth didn't quite marry with the dullness of her eyes.

'Yes,' she said. 'I am.'

'So why'd you leave us?' Ever straight to the point.

Katrina glanced at Trav in mute appeal.

He folded his arms. He sure as hell wasn't going to help her out with that one.

'Oh, Billy,' she said with a sigh. 'Some things just happen for a reason.'

'And that would be?' ground out Trav.

Katrina frowned at him. 'Now is not the time nor the place.' She glanced around. 'Oh, Alice is waving. She needs me. We'll talk about this later.' She turned to the child, who was still gazing up at her in mute appeal. 'Nice to see you, Billy,' and she walked off. The look in the boy's eyes nearly broke Trav's heart.

Billy turned to his father. 'Go after her, Dad,' he said. 'Go get her and bring her back.'

'Mate, I can't do that!'

'Why not? You were together once. You can try again.'

Hunter's turn to sigh. 'Billy. Things just don't work like that.'

'Why *not*?' he said. 'You loved her, didn't you?'

'Well, yes but –'

'So you can love her again.'

'No, Billy. And she doesn't love me either.' Trav was getting cranky now. He could hear Katrina's laughter from across the room, like tinkling ivory keys on the upper end of the piano.

'You okay?' asked a voice by his side. Tammy.

He forced himself to smile and look into her eyes. They were a warm brown, like burnt caramel.

'Trav?' queried Tammy again.

'I'm *fine*.' He inwardly cursed himself. He hadn't meant to sound so harsh.

Tammy recoiled like she'd been slapped.

'That lady over there is my mother,' interrupted Billy, jumping up and down in front of Tammy to get her attention. 'See the one with all that lovely red hair?' The boy then turned to his father. 'You didn't tell me she was so beautiful, Dad.'

No he hadn't. He hadn't told Billy a lot of things. The child didn't know his mother had walked out of the house and left him lying there in his cot. Trav had always made out the separation had been relatively civilised.

'She looks very pretty, Billy,' said Tammy.

'Yes,' said the young boy with pride. 'She's *really* pretty.' His eyes were glued to Katrina as she flitted from this group of people to that. Every now and then, she'd cast a glance in their direction, and Billy would wave. But Katrina would hurriedly turn back to concentrate on the discussion at hand.

Trav watched all this with growing concern.

'Trav?' It was Tammy again. She had a hand on his arm.

He shrugged it off, not sure why.

'Sor-*ry*,' said Tammy, offended.

Trav shook his head and sighed. '*I'm* sorry, Tammy. It's just, Katrina –'

'It's okay.' Although Trav could hear by her tone that it wasn't.

'Look,' he said. 'How about I get us all a drink?'

'You and Tammy get a drink,' said Billy. 'I'm right, thanks.' The boy's eyes remained trained on his mother. 'Really and truly right.'

'Coming, Tammy?' Trav started to move off towards the bar set up on a trestle table. 'We'll be back, Billy.'

The child just waved his hand and fled in the opposite direction. Towards Katrina, who was standing centre of attention in a knot of laughing people. Trav noticed him go, a frown on his face.

Tammy caught the look. 'Trav, is there anything I can do?'

Why in the hell did women ask such an inane question at times like this? It just made him distance himself further.

'There's nothing.' It came out as a snap. But his mind was on the little boy who was moving with intent towards his mother. How on earth could he have fallen in love with someone so self-obsessed as Katrina?

※

Billy's mother was gorgeous. Stunning.

Out of the corner of her eye, Tammy observed the boy skulking around the edges of Katrina's group. He was bobbing his head this way then that, obviously just trying to get the best view of his mum. You couldn't blame the kid. All he'd ever wanted was his mother and now she was here. It was just a crying shame the mother so obviously didn't give a rats about her son.

Hunter handed Tammy a glass of red wine. She couldn't stand the stuff. She tried to look grateful, even went so far as to take a sip. Yuck. What to do? Spying a pot plant nearby, she made her excuses to Travis. He muttered a noncommittal response, his eyes still trained on Katrina and Billy.

Tammy couldn't help but stare at Katrina Hunter a la Reyne Jennings either. She was clearly a free spirit, just like the angel-like sphinx she had painted. Tammy's beautiful prints didn't seem quite so beautiful now. The woman who created them had abandoned her whole family for the freedom they portrayed.

She wondered if she could sell the pictures.

Tammy watched as Billy stalked Katrina across the gallery. Warning bells started to sound in her mind. The child was desperate to be noticed and the woman was just as determined to ignore him. It wasn't right. Someone was going to get hurt here, and Tammy suspected it wasn't going to be Katrina. Why the hell wasn't Hunter doing something? Surely he could see the look in his son's eyes.

Tammy glanced surreptitiously across at Trav. She could see him watching it all play out, a drink to his lips, a frown on his face. In a matter of a night he'd turned back into a wild man and all it had taken was a bundle of red auburn curls and the spell they'd cast over his son.

Chapter 40

'Why didn't you ask Mum to come out to the farm?'

Billy's tone was accusing, verging on belligerent. Trav had never heard his son speak like that before. They were walking towards the ute. Tammy was back in the gallery trying to find Lucy to say goodbye.

'Didn't think of it,' he said, not entirely sure how to respond.

'You don't like her any more, do you? You don't want her to be part of our family.'

'It's difficult.'

'It's not difficult.' The child's voice was scathing. 'You just have to have a go. Old Joe's always telling me that. Give it a go, a chance.'

Trav could have cheerfully throttled the old man. 'Love's not that simple, mate. Your mum and I . . .' He paused, not sure how to put into words his feelings, especially to a child. 'Well, let's just say we're too different.'

'But, Dad, *I'm* different. Just ask the kids at school.'

'That's a different type of different, Billy.'

'But how hard can it be to love someone you've loved before?' protested Billy, his voice rising with anger.

Travis was at the ute now and feeling really pissed off. He wasn't going to explain himself to an ten year-old, even it was his son. 'Look, she'll always be your mum. You can see her as much as you both want. But I'm not getting back with her, Billy. And *that's it.*'

Billy came around the bonnet and stood in front of his father. Put his hand on the door to stop Trav from opening it. 'Is it because of Tammy?'

'What do you mean?'

'Come on, Dad. You like her, don't you?'

'Of course I like Tammy. Don't you?' Trav paused then tried for a joke. 'We don't want a woman in our lives, Billy. They're nothing but trouble.'

The boy stood up straight, his eyes flashing in the light from the gallery. 'You're wrong, Dad. Tammy's looked after me and Katrina is my mother. My *real* mum. Just like the kids at school have got. I want my mum back, Dad. Plus, you *owe* me.'

Trav took a step back at the ferocity on Billy's face. 'I owe you? How do you figure that?'

Billy ducked his head for a second then looked back up. 'You know why,' he muttered before walking around to the passenger side of the ute, leaving Trav with shameful memories of just how lonely his kid had been – because of him.

Billy fell asleep on the drive back to McCauley's Hill. Both Travis and Tammy sat out the journey in strained silence, looking anywhere but at each other. Travis was off in a world of his own, obviously thinking so hard there was a frown permanently etched into his face. The vibes coming off him were negative. *Real* negative.

As the vehicle pulled to a stop outside the Montmorency Downs homestead, the electric tension in the air ramped up till it could have rivalled a high-tensile powerline.

Tammy opened the door. Got out. Travis exited his side as well and came around the back of the vehicle. 'Tammy. Look, I'm sorry, it's just . . .' Trav ran his hands through his hair. 'Billy wants . . .' His voice stumbled to a halt.

'His mother?' Tammy was trying hard to keep her voice even. 'But what do you want, Trav? What do *you* want for you and your son?'

Trav said nothing, just leaned against the ute and folded his arms. Finally: 'I don't know what I want, Tammy.' His voice was barely audible in the still night air. 'Not Katrina. I mean, not as a partner or a wife or anything. But Billy wants to know his mother. What right have I to deny him that?'

'You've got every right, Hunter.' Tammy could hear her own voice rising. 'She walked out on you both. Has never contacted you again. She forfeited her right to be his mother years ago.'

'I *owe* my son his *mother*,' said Trav, grinding the words out. She had never seen him so angry. 'I've done little enough for the kid, I can at least . . . give . . . him . . . that.'

'But, Travis. Can't you see –?'

'Billy wants his mother.'

'He'll get hurt –'

'For fuck's sake, surely you of all people can understand what's driving the kid!'

Yes, she would have given anything to have known Natalie. Except death didn't give you a choice. 'She's not interested. The way she treated him tonight . . .' She stopped. Travis's face was like thunder. But still she felt driven to make him see he needed to protect the child, not hand him over to be toyed with and then discarded. 'Tonight, that child was desperate for his mother to pay attention to him – but she didn't. She's not interested in Billy, Travis. She's a free spirit. And they hurt people who try to tie them to the ground.'

Travis didn't respond at first, then his shoulders slumped and all the anger seemed to seep away.

'I don't know what to think, Tammy.' He ducked down to check on Billy again. 'Look, how about we take a break?' To his credit, he sounded almost apologetic. It was the gentleman in him again. 'She won't stay long.' She had never heard him sound so bitter. 'I just don't want Billy hurt. And I don't want him blaming you.'

His hand came from nowhere to lightly stroke her cheek. The strong but gentle fingers tracing patterns on her skin. What emotions other than anger were travelling through him? In the darkness she couldn't read his face.

But there was one thing she did know with certainty. He'd made up his mind to concentrate on his son and she couldn't fault him for that. Anything she said now was unlikely to move him. Damn Katrina to hell for coming back.

'I understand,' said Tammy. The words came out stiff and stilted. She tried again, 'I understand, Trav. I really do.' And she did. She didn't want to understand but she did.

'You do?' He dropped his hand from her cheek.

'Of course. Guess I'll just be seeing you around then.'

She wanted to jump into his arms and yell, *'Don't go, don't leave me, even for a minute. Tell Billy the truth and start building him a real family!'* but instead she turned towards the gate. 'Thanks for the ride in and out.'

Even though she knew he was just asking for time, she felt as rejected as she had by Shon, by Old Joe back when she was a kid . . . by Mae, for whom she could never replace the lost daughter. C'mon, McCauley, keep walking, you can do it. Goddamn it. One foot after the other. Just get the hell inside and let the man do what he has to do.

'I'll still be staking out the dog,' he called down the path. 'I'll give you a yell if I see anything.'

She threw out a hand in acknowledgement but didn't turn round. Not until she heard the car engine crank over and the set of tyres crunching on the gravel. He drove off, down the long drive, out onto Hope's Road and towards McCauley's Hill.

Only then did she finally allow herself to cry.

Chapter 41

'Billy wants me and Katrina to try again,' said Trav, cradling a mug of coffee and listening to the rain on the corrugated iron roof.

Joe gave a snort.

'I told him it doesn't work like that,' he continued, 'but he wouldn't listen. The kid is so bloody excited he's finally found his mum.'

'Yes, but for how long?'

'That's what Tammy said.'

'Mmm . . . that's interesting.'

'You reckon? You're both cut from the same cynical cloth.'

'Us? Hardly.' Joe gave another snort.

There was silence for a while as Trav blew on then slurped at his coffee. Cripes, the old man made the stuff hot. A bit like Billy's newfound temper.

No! Today, not tomorrow! Take me to see her now!

Joe cleared his throat, breaking into Trav's reverie.

'Look, I know I'm a negative old bastard . . . and you don't have to nod your head. But, Hunter, these are the facts, short and curly. She up and walked out on you. Left a toddler in its bed, for fuck's sake. She's not fit to have a pet, let alone a kid like yours.'

'She might have changed.'

'She might,' said Joe, nodding, but his tone was disbelieving.

'I don't need to try again with her, do I?' said Trav quietly. 'For Billy's sake?'

'Don't be so bloody stupid. Can't you get it through your thick skull? Marriage is hard enough when you're in love. And anyway, she did it once, she's perfectly capable of doing it again.'

'You didn't hear him, Joe.' Or see the look of utter determination in the child's eyes. *She's my mum. You owe me. I want my family back.*

'Where does Tammy fit into all this then?'

Trav's eyes snapped towards the old man. 'What do you mean?'

'Well, you've been keeping company with her a fair bit.'

Trav's sharp intake of breath must have been audible.

'C'mon, Hunter. What do you think, an old man can't see things?'

'I didn't realise it was that obvious.'

Joe gave another snort and looked away.

Trav sighed. He didn't want Katrina. He could never trust let alone love her again. He had been so hurt last time. And now there was this thing with Tammy. 'Tammy was good last night. Said she understood. I guess she meant about Billy.'

Joe nodded. 'She'd sure know all about that. Was probably wishing it was Natalie returned from the dead.'

Trav moved uncomfortably, remembering how in his anger he'd thrown Tammy's own loss at her. She didn't even know he knew Natalie was dead.

'What did you say about you and her?'

'That we'd better give it a break. See what happened.'

Joe rocked his chair a bit. His thoughts sheltered behind an impassive old face. Eventually he said, 'Women. They're a different breed,' and he reached a hand down to stroke Boots, who was leaning against his knee. 'I'm not concerned about you and Tammy, so much as the boy. You're both big and ugly enough to make your own mistakes, but that child is special.'

'Yeah, he is.' And he really meant it. He gazed out across the verandah rail. Mount Cullen and the Burdekin Gap were shrouded in grey; the whole valley was drowning in water. The bloody rain had started after they'd all got home from the disastrous opening and just wouldn't let up.

'How long's she stayin'?' asked Joe.

'Not sure. She didn't say.'

'I'll bet she didn't.'

'What do you mean by that exactly?'

'You be careful's all I'm saying. And take care with that child. Now, what are you doin' about the attacks on them calves?'

The change of subject threw Trav for a moment. 'I'll keep staking the paddocks out even in this rain. I reckon the dog might have gone for a wander around its patch. That, or it's just laying low, waiting for a chance. They're sneaky bastards and clever enough to wait it out until you're gone.'

'You be out early tomorrow? Want me to have Billy?'

Trav was surprised at how eager Joe sounded. Damn it, he was going to have to disappoint him again. Trav cleared his throat. 'Ummm . . .'

'Well, c'mon. If you got somethin' to say, say it,' said Joe.

Geez, why did it all have to be so hard? It was a lot easier when it was just him and the kid. 'Billy and me are going into town this arvie. We're picking up Katrina. Probably bring her out here, show her around, take her back and have some tea somewhere. The boy's at home now sorting out his stuff to show her. I'll be late home, and Billy'll be with me so I won't go out in the morning.' Trav stopped. Joe's face was scrunched into a frown. 'The kid wants to know his mother, Joe, and I have to run with that, regardless.'

'Since when did you develop a conscience?'

Fuck it! Joe could hardly bloody talk. How dare he be so judgemental? Trav stood up, put down his cup and turned on the old man. 'I've always had a goddamned conscience. That's why I brought the kid here, to a place where he could set down roots, have a place he could call home. And that's why I brought my mother back where she belonged. My brother was going to put her in a nursing home in Adelaide. Wanted me to send Billy to a hostel for kids whose parents lived remote. I wasn't going to do it. So I left my job on the fence and came back here.'

'You neglect your kid and then, just when you realise what a good father you can be, when your life's just getting on track, you welcome his shitty mother back? Yeah right, that's not a conscience. That's just fuckin' stupidity.'

'You *bastard*!' spat Trav. 'I'm not welcoming her back!'

Joe tried to stand up, couldn't. But that didn't stop his tirade. '*Yes, you are* – you want to be the man – to fix what you broke back then – and you *can't*. You're only thinking about yourself. You've only ever thought about yourself. That child's going to get hurt, Hunter, and it's your bloody job to make sure it doesn't happen.'

Trav didn't want to hear any more. He shot Joe a look of near hatred, turned on his heels and walked off, headed for his ute.

He could hear the old man shouting from behind him. 'That woman is trouble with a capital T. She'll just cut and run for the hills. You'll see!'

Chapter 42

Hours later and Joe McCauley was still pissed off. He'd been having trouble seeing through the rain, which had got even heavier since Hunter had left in a huff.

The bloody stuff had been coming down all morning with hardly a break in between showers. He wasn't going to be able to pick any bunnies off in this fuckin' weather. A rabbit would have to be mad to be out in it. And what's more, it looked like the rain was coming in from the east, which meant it could be here for a while. Them buggers that forecast the weather very rarely managed to predict this sort of stuff.

He spotted a flash of white, way off in the distance. It seemed to be coming towards the Hill. He grabbed his gun and brought the scope to his eye. Hunter. Comin' back from town. And there was a red-haired woman in the passenger seat. Joe snorted, wondering what the high-falutin artist would think of Hunter's shack at Belaren. It wasn't what this woman would be used to. Darn it, he was feeling a bit edgy this mornin'. Must be all the rain. At least an inch had come down since yesterday. He sat a while, looking out across the flats. They weren't their normal emerald green today, that's for sure. More grey, with wisps of white around the edges where the low clouds were skimming the tops of the foothills that rimmed the valley.

It was still beautiful. But in a different sort of way. It made his home on top of the hill seem almost cosy, especially with the fire going in the kitchen, and it wasn't often he could say that. Usually the old shack was as uncomfortable as a twisted gumboot, especially now Nellie was gone. Not as cold as Montmorency used to be though. With that thought his mind floated to places he usually preferred not to visit. Tom and Mae. More Tom than Mae, really. Lately he'd been thinking a lot about his brother. Even wished he could see him again. Maybe have a yarn, bury a hatchet or two, or three. It was funny how time and age made you see things in a different light.

He put down the gun and rubbed his hands together to get the blood running through his fingers. They were numb from sitting out here in the moist, cool air. He didn't want to go inside though. Four walls felt encroaching even on a day like today. Maybe a cup of tea would be the answer, to settle both the edginess and the cold.

Joe staggered to his feet and slowly shuffled his way into the house. Placed a worn old black cast-iron kettle on the kitchen stove. While the water boiled he took a milk coffee biscuit from an old Arnotts tin, with its Rosella parrot emblazoned on the lid. Nellie had loved that tin.

A wisp of air seemed to pass by his cheek. An angel's kiss, maybe? It was a nice thought, and he found himself strangely comforted by the idea his wife might be in the room.

Filling his mug, he grabbed another couple of biscuits to share with the dogs, and shuffled back to the verandah.

Digger was nowhere to be seen, but Boots put his shaggy head up and thumped his tail. At least someone was good company today, even if it was only a dog who'd spied a biscuit in his hand. Maybe the radio would be a help. Joe leaned over and flicked the knob on the old Bakelite radio he had sitting beside him.

'*Heavy rainfall is expected over Gippsland during the weekend. Falls of one hundred to two hundred millimetres are expected, with higher totals likely in East Gippsland and across the ranges. There is a minor flood warning current for the Narree River downstream of Narree . . .*'

Well, that was hardly surprising with all this shit bucketing down. Joe brought the mug of tea up to his lips and felt the warmth of the liquid fill his mouth, his throat and then slowly, ever so slowly, seep into his stomach. The warmth of it was comforting, soothing even. As was the dog at his feet, chewing happily on the biscuit he'd been given. Joe dunked his own into the dark brown brew and munched away. He felt the tendrils of contentment seep into his bones, his muscles relaxing. Finally his edginess seemed to melt away.

His mind drifted, flitting from one thing to the next. He fed Boots another biscuit. Thank God for Lucy Granger. She'd left him and Boots enough tucker to sink the boat that would be needed to get out of here if this wet stuff didn't ease up.

Joe chuckled as he brought his cuppa back up to his lips. Miss Granger sure was a square peg in a round hole. He wondered if she'd go through with her new idea for her ideal partner. He mentally shook himself. Why was he even pondering the wherefores of these people who'd snuck into his life?

But then he recalled the scene on his verandah the night before and that gave him another little chuckle. Poor Deano. He hadn't known which way to jump when Jacinta Greenaway had started making a play for him. Although to be honest, Joe was happy enough to see Gibson taken off the market. He didn't want him to come sniffing around Tammy again. Not while Travis Hunter was available.

But he's not available, Joseph. And there she was. Old Nellie. Infallible as always. Telling him what he didn't want to hear.

Course he's available. This woman will piss off like they always do and it'll all be right as rain. Back to the way we were.

Whatever that was.

Joseph, you are a cynical old man. This is the mother of his child!

Nellie had always been a bit touchy when it came to mothers and their kids. That's why she'd wanted him to make up with Tom and Mae, especially after they lost Natalie. But he didn't want to. Not then.

A waft of icy air came spilling across the verandah, upsetting the plastic dog bowl near the screen door. The dish went skittering across the wooden boards, rattling its way down the steps to land in the mud at the bottom. Boots jumped at the sudden noise, whimpered and then huddled into Joe's legs, coming to rest on the man's socks.

Joe grabbed at his mug, seeking the comfort of its now fading warmth.

Crikey, Nellie. You're scaring the shit out of us.

But there were no answers coming from his late wife. All the old man could hear was the rhythmic sound of raindrops falling on tin. Joe finished his cuppa and biscuit, then leaned back in his chair and closed his eyes. A nap might be in order.

Nothing much else was going on. Boots, sprawled at his master's feet, agreed.

Joe woke to the sound of a ute roaring towards the T intersection. What the hell? He must have dozed off. He glanced at his watch. Even though the sky was getting darker it was just going on a quarter past four. He grabbed his gun and took a look through the scope at the vehicle. Hunter. It was a bit early to be heading back into town for tea. Maybe they were coming to see him? Hardly. Not after this morning's little effort. Perhaps they were just going for a drive? But where to in this weather?

The ute headed steadily past the front gate of Montmorency and continued on into the gloom. In the grey smudges of misty water he could just make out an amber-coloured blinker light. They were going right, heading towards Narree. Well I'll be darned, he thought. So much for Billy showing her around.

Hang on. There was another amber light in the glass. It was coming this way though. Dang it, what a busy place Hope's Road was today. Joe settled back into his chair, scope still glued to his eyeball. This one was creeping up the tar towards the hill, stealth like. Slowly it moved along until it traversed the whole road, past Montmorency, through the low-level, up to the T intersection and then it disappeared from view. Joe hoped to hell it hadn't turned in his direction. If it headed right, the only place it could come was to his driveway. He strained to hear a motor over the rain pounding on his tin roof. Nope. He couldn't hear a darn thing. But then the vehicle reappeared. Obviously hadn't gone towards Hunter's Belaren either. It had a whole load of stuff in the back. Big yellow boards. Some star pickets. What was it doing? It had gone right back to the start of Hope's Road. Stopped on the corner. Two blokes got out, dressed in a big black Akubras and Driza-Bone coats. One pulled some pickets out of the ute tub, another a sledgehammer.

Joe pulled the sight back from his eye – things were blurring in the wet. He blinked a few times then had another go. By now both blokes had wrestled one of the big signs out. They were putting a frame of some sort together. The star pickets came next, hammered in nice and easy with the soft ground.

Joe strained his eyes to see what the sign said, but it was no good. The angle wasn't right as the words were facing the main road. Maybe it was one of those seed company signs advertising their wares on Montmorency, although he hadn't seen any paddocks worked up of recent times. Perhaps it was a fertiliser mob instead?

He continued to watch with interest as the men piled all their tools into the ute tray and drove back towards McCauley's Hill. They stopped a second time right in front of the main gate leading into Montmorency. Out came the tools again, starpickets and another big yellow sign. Joe pulled the sight back and blinked again, desperately wanting his vision to clear so he could see what the hell these men were up to.

He pulled the gun sight up to his eyeball just as the sign was being hauled into the air on its frame.

AUCTION PENDING
MONTMORENCY DOWNS
Historic Homestead
First time offered.

That was as far as he got.
No!

Joe tipped himself forwards in the chair violently and staggered to his feet. Threw the gun to the ground, not caring what damage that might do to his precious rifle. The bitch was selling up!

He snatched at the rifle again, intent on a second look, but missed in his agitation and went sprawling, his out-of-kilter body taking little time to thump onto the boards.

His hip hit the ground. Hard. Boots was on his feet, barking and yelping.

Oh holy hell, that hurt. Shit. His hip. Had he broken it again?

But that was secondary to the pain that was hammering through his heart. Please God, no, not *Montmorency*!

She couldn't do it to him. Fuck it. She couldn't do it to the *family*. Five generations of McCauley blood, sweat and tears.

First time offered.

The bitch. The lying, scheming . . . Just when he thought he could trust her, she did this.

It was Mae. Mae Rouget all over again.

Lying sprawled on his own wooden verandah, gasping with pain, Joe McCauley was shocked to find himself crying. Tears he should have shed years ago. For the pain throbbing down his leg. For the people he would never see again – not in this life. For his father, his mother, his brother. For Mae. For Nellie. All his regrets.

It was all too late. All too fucking late.

How could she sell Montmorency Downs?

He should have known.

The land-grabbing little fucker.

Chapter 43

Tammy had just climbed out of her ute into dismal weather when the bullet came skidding over her head.

Bang!

'What the hell are *you* doing here?' the old man roared.

What? They were back to this again?

Oh my Lord. He'd seen the sign. She'd only just spotted it herself coming out the gate. It'd been like a kick in the guts. She couldn't believe they'd have it up so quickly.

'I don't need you up here on my hill. Get the hell off my farm, you –'

Tammy threw her arms in the air. 'I know, I know. But if you'd just let me explain –'

'There's nothing to say!' roared Joe. 'The fuckin' auction sign says it *all*!'

Bang!

Tammy ducked. The bullet was closer this time.

'If you'd just stop shooting and let me come up there and talk –'

'Talk? *Talk!* Get off *my land*! I know you wish you could offload this place too, you little strumpet. You're just like your grandmother!'

Tammy stood in the rain, a drowned rat, water pouring off her head, her body. 'What do you mean, just like my grandmother?'

'She wanted me first. Not my brother. But he had the best of it coming to him, so she chose Tom. It should have been *me*!'

Bang!

'*Joe*, just listen to me –'

'*No*!' the old man roared. 'Get the hell off my property and never come *back*!'

Bang!

Tammy could feel herself getting angry. If he'd only just listen to her, she could explain. She would tell him about Shon forcing her hand. Tell him it was the only option she had, the only thing she could do.

Bang!

Oh *hell*.

She jumped back into the ute. He was sitting on the top step of the verandah, red with rage. She could see him reloading the magazine with bullets, which any minute now he'd slot into his rifle . . .

She'd better leave. No way was she going to be able to talk with him today. Possibly not ever. She wound down the window to have one last go, oblivious to the sheet of water now pouring through her window.

'Joe? Can we just talk?'

'Get off my property!' he yelled again. Then he leaned forwards to grab at his leg.

Christ, what had the old bugger done now? 'Uncle Joe?' she called. 'Are you all right?'

'Fuck *off*!'

'Okay, I'm going. I'm out of here, you stiff-necked old bastard.' She cranked the engine, put the ute in gear and took off, wheels spinning in the slippery mud. The last thing she heard was Joe McCauley's voice, chasing her in the rain.

'Good riddance to rubbish. And don't ever come *back*!'

The anger Tammy felt towards Joe escaped like air from a plumped-up balloon as soon as she reached the front gate of Montmorency. The big yellow sign seemed to mock her. *First time offered.*

'This title is so old, it'd be an original,' Hilary Stratton had told her. And Tammy could hear the crackling of thick paper over the phone. 'Obviously the property hasn't been sold before. That doesn't happen very often.'

She remembered the first time she'd seen that precious piece of her heritage. Her grandfather had shown it to her when she was a little girl. The paper it was on was called vellum.

They'd been in the ancient office in the old part of the house. Musty, filled with cobwebs and dust, the room exuded odours of days long past. The title had been in an antique ornate frame up on the wall. Her grandfather had taken it down, carefully removed the backing plate and taken the vellum from against the glass. He'd let her touch it, saying, 'Here, place your fingers on history, Tim Tam. And one day this will be yours to carry on the McCauley bloodline.'

'I'm just organising the vendor statement, which includes the title of course, and any other certificates that pertain to the property. The flood level certificate from the Shire has been a bit slow. Is there a history of flooding on Montmorency? Will there be any difficulty with that?' The solicitor had sensed a foreboding silence at the other end of the phone. 'Never mind. All will be in order once the Shire gets their paperwork sorted. I'll be in touch with a date for the auction.'

Tammy drove down the drive and parked the ute. The phone rang as she made it inside. She looked at it – it seemed to deliver nothing but bad news lately. Finally she willed herself to pick up the handset, just as it stopped ringing. Good. Tammy went to walk away, when the damn thing started ringing again, insistently. Someone really wanted to get hold of her. It was probably Shon ringing to gloat about the property being on the market, something which he knew would break her heart. She let it go to the answering machine.

'Tammy. Rob Sellers here. Just ringing to let you know they've put out a minor flood warning on the Narree River. The weir outflows have been upped to eight thousand megalitres per day. They're expected to keep rising –'

Tammy, by then, had dived for the handset, anxious to catch the man before he rang off. Rob lived upstream of her, just below the weir wall, and he was the flood warden. 'Rob! I'm here. What's going on?'

'Tammy. Thank God I've got you. It's not looking good, mate. The telemetry systems that measure the inflows have gone down above the weir. We're not sure of the volume of water coming but from what they're saying further up in the mountains there's a lot of it heading our way. I reckon we're dead certain to go to at least moderate flooding so thought I'd give you the heads up so you can start dropping your fences.'

Shit. This was all she needed. The cows were right where they shouldn't be. The water came out of the river into her lower paddocks whenever outflows from the weir exceeded twenty-two thousand megalitres.

'How long have we got, Rob?'

'Not sure, mate. But I'd be starting to put your flood plan in action right about now. I'll ring you back as soon as I hear from the weir-keepers. Better go. I've got a truckload of others to ring.'

'No worries. Thanks, Rob.'

'I'll be in touch. Stay safe and get Hunter to help you.'

'I will.' Not while she was supposed to be keeping her distance. Plus she was perfectly capable of managing this.

Rob rang off and Tammy wasted precious seconds trying to get Jock and Barb on the phone until she remembered they were off shopping in Melbourne, seeing it was so wet. They were staying overnight, where she didn't know. *And* they didn't have a mobile phone. Damn, damn, damn. Maybe old Joe could help her in the ute? Ha. He'd just thrown her off his property.

All that time spent mending fences and forging trust with her uncle had come to naught. He was the only family she had left, and now he too was gone. She hadn't realised just how lonely she really was until Joe had come along – and Billy and Trav.

Tammy felt her heart dip at the thought of Travis Hunter. She could feel a dark pit of anxiety deep down inside her belly. Whatever happened with his family, right now she was on her own. Again. And she didn't know if she could bear it this time.

The phone jolted her out of her reverie once more. She grabbed the receiver. 'Tammy McCauley.'

'Ha, ha, ha – got your comeuppance this time, haven't ya, bitch?' Shon Murphy's voice, slurred and full of hate, came down the line. 'That auction sign gone up yet? Bet that kicked ya in the guts. It'll teach ya for sooling your good-for-nuthin' uncle on me.'

Why had she answered it? 'I hate you, Shon Murphy, with every fibre of my being,' she said out loud.

Drunken laughter spilled from the phone. Laughter which then erupted into a fit of convulsive coughing and spluttering as her husband choked. *Die you bastard, die*, was all she could think as she slammed down the hand-set.

The phone immediately rang again. Bloody Shon. He never gave up easily. The message bank clicked in.

'Tammy, it's Rob again. They've just upped the outflows to at least thirty thousand megalitres. It looks like we're heading towards a major flood.'

Shit.

She dived for the handset. 'Rob, I'm here. A major?'

'Yep. Pretty sure she's gunna be a big one. You can't do this on your own, girl. Have you contacted Hunter yet?'

'Nope. But I will,' she lied. She'd be fine. Floods had come and gone all her life. She knew what needed to be done.

'They're expecting the water to be here by the morning.' Rob's voice broke into her thoughts. 'I'll ring both your mobile and home phones if I hear any more.'

He disconnected quickly, no doubt in a hurry to ring the next person on his list. The man must live on adrenaline, reflected Tammy, what with his community ambulance work and this flood warden business. But, she had to admit, without people like Rob to spread the word, all those in the Narree flood zone would be so much worse off.

She needed to move the cows up near the dairy. The young stock were on the run-off block with Jock and Barbara, out of the flood zone, so they would be right. The autumn calving cows and their calves were already near the house because of the wild dog attacks. They might get a bit wet but she'd had the laser grading people build up a high pad of dirt in that paddock a few years earlier for a new hay-shed. If the cattle moved onto that they'd be able to get out of the water, and if she deposited a round bale of hay in a hay-ring up there, that would see them through the duration of the flood. Then there were the fences. She needed to drop the wires so they would flow with the water rather than have the pressure and accumulated debris reef the posts from the ground.

Tammy quickly sorted in her mind the best order in which to do all the work. Then she strode onto the enclosed back verandah, donned a Driza-Bone, a broad-brimmed Akubra hat and gumboots, and stepped out into the rain to do battle with the river-borne demon that was to come.

Chapter 44

It had been a disaster right from the start. Kat had stared at the old ute in consternation from the doorway of her motel room and had looked terrified when she spotted Billy bouncing up and down on the seat. 'Hi there, Mum!'

She'd glanced towards Trav and he read the panic in her gaze as clearly as he could read the tracks of wildlife in the scrub. His heart sank towards his Ariat high-top boots.

She was going to bolt. Tammy and Joe were right. He shouldn't have thought it could be any different: he should have told Billy she just wasn't up to it and worn the boy's grief himself. Putting it off like this was only going to make it worse. He could *still* hear Katrina's quavering voice on the end of the phone that fateful day after she left.

'Look after our baby. One day . . . tell him his mummy loved him . . . but I have to go. I have to leave to save myself, Travis. Can't you see? I've lost *me*. So many hopes, so many dreams . . . all gone.'

Hope – the stuff dreams were made of. He could tell *her* a thing or two about them being gone.

'C'mon, Mum,' yelled his boy again. 'Get in. We're heading back out to Belaren. I'll show you all my stuff.'

'Lovely.' Katrina's voice was faint. Her hands fluttered around the long auburn curls hanging down off her shoulders.

Travis, still sitting at the wheel, watched it all like he was observing from above. He'd once hoped he and Kat would be together forever. Her spirit and more gregarious nature had balanced his preference for silence. She'd encouraged him to be something he'd thought he'd never be: outgoing and unreserved. She'd made him feel like the only person in the world capable of making her happy, of loving her and she, him. It was all an illusion, he could see that now. He could never be anything other than himself no matter how hard he tried, and that wasn't good enough for Katrina. She wanted more than him – and their child.

His ex-wife slid gracefully into the ute, where Billy grabbed her hand, eager to stake his claim on his mother.

'Belaren is Nanna's old place. You'll love it,' said Billy beaming, and then he shot a serious glance towards his father. It was a look of warning – be nice to her. *You owe me.*

'Katrina,' said Trav, acknowledging her with a nod. 'You okay if we go out home? Billy'd like to show you where he lives.' He was painfully aware of how stilted and polite the words sounded.

Katrina's eyes narrowed over Billy's head. 'Yes, that's fine. So long as we don't take all afternoon. I have to be back in town for dinner. Some artist friends of Alice's. They want to organise another showing. A city gallery this time.'

Yep, that was the way of it. Art before her son. He glanced down at Billy, who was frowning and shaking his head.

'But Mum! Don't you want to have tea with *us*?'

Katrina had the grace to look slightly abashed. 'I'm sorry, Billy, but this is really important to me.'

'But –'

'Billy,' interrrupted Trav, his voice laced with warning, 'your mum's made other arrangements. We'll take her out to the farm and see how it goes.'

Katrina seemed to withdraw into herself from that moment. Billy chattered on, pointing out this and that – things that were of importance or significance in his young life. 'So that's my school where Ms Greenaway teaches me. She's away today otherwise we could've taken you to meet her. She's really nice, isn't she, Dad?' Billy ran on before Trav could answer either way, continuing his litany until they turned down Hope's Road. 'And that's where Tammy lives. She employs me to do farm work. And then that's Old Joe's place up there on McCauley's Hill. You can't see it clearly from here but he sure has the best view. He taught me to drive, didn't he, Dad?' On and on the child rambled, never pausing for breath, which only served to make Katrina's disconnection more apparent.

The mention of Billy driving was the only thing to jolt her. She had darted an appalled glance at Trav and he'd responded with a shrug. 'He's good at it,' he commented in Billy's – and possibly Joe's – defence. Her big brown eyes widened slightly and then she sank back into her apathy. Trav didn't know whether to be flattered by her confidence in his judgement or horrified by her lack of interest.

The pain had ramped up a notch as they'd parked in front of the ramshackle cottage they called home. Kat's face had said it all. *This? This is what you call a house?*

They'd gone inside and Katrina had climbed the ladder up

to Billy's loft. Trav didn't know what took place up there but it seemed like only minutes before she was back down again, crowding his personal space. He didn't think any room would be big enough for him and Kat. Too much hurt, too much time and angst were lying between them.

He couldn't help but compare her to the woman who'd been in this room only nights before. Tammy had looked like she belonged here, despite her more affluent upbringing. She'd made the shabby smallness seem all the more cosy with her warmth and easy-going presence. She hadn't made him feel defensive. If anything, she'd made him feel proud of the space he shared with his son. The way she wandered around the walls, asking questions about his photos, their homemade frames, enjoying the stories of the bush that went with each one. He could hear her laughter in the air, see the caramel in her eyes, feel the silkiness of her soft yet firm skin.

Trav shook himself. *You're taking a break from her, remember?*

He moved to put on the kettle, trying not to look towards the fridge and the rum and coke he would have preferred, just to get himself through this. He glanced across at Katrina, who was trying to appear interested in a bright green grasshopper that Billy had caught and ensconced in a jar with nail holes in the lid for air. After doing some research on Tammy's computer, the kid was planning to take it to school for Show and Tell.

She was now heading for the couch like it was a refuge. She sat down for a few seconds, then was up again as if the seats were full of blackberry thorns. How on earth could he have even contemplated getting back with her? She was like a flitting moth, eyes darting here and there, not able to meet his gaze for longer than a glance.

'Would you like a cup of tea?' he asked, pulling out a couple of mugs.

'Do you have herbal?'

'Nope, sorry. Just normal stuff.'

'Then no, thanks.'

You would have thought she'd just take a mug of tea and pretend to like it. That was how you did things in the country. Just to be polite. To be mates.

But this woman didn't want to be mates. She barely wanted to be friendly. She was just biding her time until she could head back to town. Well, stuff her, he thought. She could put up with it for a few hours after what she'd done to him and Billy.

So he let Billy drag her out into the wet. Let him haul her all over the hill in the rain. Pointing out the dogs, his bike, the track to the weir, and the place he called a cubbyhouse – a massive cypress tree so old the timbers had joined and made slabs big enough to stand on.

'I really need to get back to town,' Katrina muttered to Trav while they were waiting for Billy to bring out his favourite truck.

'Why so hasty?' He watched as she squirmed like a worm trying its damnedest to snig itself off a sharp hook.

'I need to get ready for tonight. You don't seem to understand, Travis. It's really important to me.'

Trav pushed himself off the verandah pole against which he'd been leaning, shocked at the anger which was surging through him. 'No, Katrina, *you* don't seem to understand. This boy is your *son*. Your own flesh and blood. *He's* supposed to be important to you.'

Startled, wide-eyed, Katrina was like a gazelle in the sights of a .243 rifle. She swayed a moment like she didn't know which way to turn. 'I've worked hard to get myself to this point, Travis. You don't know how difficult it's been to try and prove myself.'

'Believe me, lady, I've got a pretty fair idea.' He shook his head in wonder at her self-absorption.

'Mum! Mum!' Billy broke in. 'This is my most favourite truck ever.' The boy shoved a shiny black Western Star Prime Mover into Katrina's hands. With a shy smile, he added, 'You can have it if you want. Can't she, Dad?'

Trav looked at Katrina. Saw her sudden withdrawal. An indistinct little movement but to a dog trapper trained to *observe* it was as clear as a full moon on a dark night.

And his heart went out to Billy. He wondered what he was going to do, what he was going to say to his son to alleviate the pain when his mother was gone. Again.

※

They dropped Katrina off around five o'clock. Her dinner date wasn't until seven but she was as keen to get away from them as Trav was to see her go.

Clearly in Katrina's world, she came before anything else. Had it always been like that? Even way back when they'd been together?

With startling clarity, Trav realised it had. And when he'd told her how he saw it, she'd got angry . . . just like he'd got this morning with old Joe. No wonder Joe had been so pissed off with him. In his own way, Travis was no better than Kat. All this time he'd been trying to convince himself that everything he'd done this past six years had been for his son. But in reality it had all been for himself. To hold hard to the security of the boundary fence – hold hard to what he knew – rather than wander off a well-worn track and delve into something new.

Billy didn't say much at tea. They'd gone to the pub anyway, and it wasn't a success. He stared across the table at his child. At the kid's thatch of red hair, his hazel eyes. The face, which was even now screwed up in concentration as he tried to read the wine list sitting between them. Studiously avoiding looking at his father.

Trav'd really buggered it up. But there was time to change. He just had to find a way to get off the fence.

Chapter 45

The phone rang on the bedside table beside Tammy. She slung out an arm, and answered it with a voice groggy from sleep.

'Rob Sellers here, Tammy.'

The man sounded exhausted. 'Yes, Rob?' said Tammy as she struggled to sit up. She took a look at the clock. It was five in the morning. She couldn't believe she'd finally slept. She hadn't dropped her head on the pillow until well past midnight.

'It's a big one and it's on its way,' said Rob.

'How much water?'

'About ninety thousand megalitres.'

Ninety thousand? That was *beyond* a major flood. Tammy swallowed, trying to stem the tide of panic rushing through her body.

'You ready, girl?'

'Yep. About as ready as I'll ever be.' Far out. How was the old place going to handle that much water? Maybe she should sandbag the back of the house?

'Stay safe then,' said Rob as he rang off.

Tammy struggled out of bed. Cocked her ear, thinking she'd heard a rifle shot.

She donned her milking clothes, grabbed a piece of toast and headed out into the rain, to bring in her cows to milk and face whatever the day was going to bring.

Ninety thousand megalitres? Tammy shuddered. Montmorency had never seen a flood that size in her lifetime.

※

Travis Hunter was ecstatic. He'd finally shot the damn wild dog. He'd got it right on dawn, in the pouring rain, just as the bastard came under the fence and was heading for a cow giving birth. The dog had stopped to lap up some calf shit, the look on the scraggy face blissful as it tasted all that creamy muck.

Trav got that black head in the crosshairs of his .243 rifle, propped up on a bipod, sucked in a breath to steady himself and squeezed the trigger.

Bang!

The shot rang out from his gun. The wild dog was punched in the head by the bullet, dead centre of the eyes. It was a classy piece of work. Finally, he was in the right place at the right time. Trav breathed a normal breath. Thank God that job was done. He'd grab the carcass and head back up to Belaren. He'd left Billy up there on his own. He ignored the nagging voice in his head that he was just putting off seeing Tammy. Go visit her now, you gutless bastard, it said.

Trav walked the boundary fence to his ute. Dragged the carcass over the wire. Stashed his rifle in the locker on the trayback and threw in the body of the dog. With a determined set to his jaw, he pointed the ute in the direction of Belaren.

❧

Old Joe was worried. It was seven in the morning and in the still air he could hear the klaxon sirens going off up at the weir wall to warn anyone who was downstream fishing that they were about to let a shitload of water go. Rob Sellers had rung earlier to let him know – even though up on his rocky hill he had no country that would be flood-affected, it was still good to be kept in the loop.

There was a bloody lot of water to come down the river. More than he'd ever seen before. He might get a better view of the valley below if he crossed to the edge of the hill. He reefed himself out of his chair and limped to the verandah steps but changed his mind. Thank goodness he didn't seem to have done any more damage to his hip when he fell yesterday, just bruising, but climbing down those steps might be pushing the friendship a bit. He shuffled back to his chair. Cursed – he didn't have any binoculars. He'd lent them to bloody Hunter for tracking that wild dog. He picked up his gun again. Even though the gun scope gave him a narrow view, it was better than nothing.

The rain was still falling and he'd seen lights moving around for what seemed like half the night down on Montmorency Downs. That conniving little strumpet dropping her fences, no doubt.

Travis Hunter hadn't lit his fire this morning either, causing Joe to wonder where the hell the man was. 'Probably with that ex-wife of his,' he muttered to Boots as he rocked his chair back and forth. 'I don't know why the man would want to go near that woman after all she's done to him.'

Boots whimpered in return. 'Argh, Boots, what would I do without you to talk to, mate?'

The phone rang. An old-fashioned trill, urgent in its appeal. Could he be bothered? Was there anyone he really wanted to talk with today? Hardly. They'd all shown their true colours and pissed off.

The damned thing rang and rang. As Joe didn't have an answering service there wasn't anything to stop it. Bugger. He'd better get up and answer the bloody piece of junk.

Joe staggered to his feet and shuffled into the house.

'McCauley,' he said into the receiver, annoyance apparent. He listened to the voice on the other end of the phone. 'What do *you* want?'

'Nup,' said Joe, in response to a question. He listened some more while he swung around towards the front verandah. He could hear Boots moving across the boards, like he was dragging something. Damned dog. He'd probably got hold of Joe's gumboot. He'd give that dog what-for in a minute. He refocused back on the phone conversation. What was that about Billy?

'Fuck,' he said into the phone. And then his world fell away.

༄

Trav couldn't find Billy. He'd called him. '*Billy!*'

He trailed around the kid's favourite haunts on Belaren, his panic increasing as each spot yielded no sign of him. Where the hell could he be this early in the morning? Maybe Tammy's or Joe's? But last night he'd promised to hang around while Trav went to stake out the dog.

Trav searched for some clues. The kid normally took his pushbike when he was heading to Tammy's and the old BMX was still leaning up against the shed, so that counted her out. Plus seeing he'd just been down there Trav was sure he'd have spotted him somewhere. He heard the insidious voice in the back of his mind whispering, *You should have gone and seen her.*

He shut that thought down. He'd ring Joe, even though their last words to each other hadn't been the best. As he ran towards the house, he cocked his ear at the sound of a sudden district siren.

A flood? He raced inside and there, on the bench, was the answering machine blinking. He hit the play button. 'Rob Sellers here, Hunter. A big flood's coming. Just thought you should know. Can you look out for Tammy for me? She's down at Montmorency on her own. Thanks, mate. Ring me if you need anything.'

Now he *really* needed to find Billy. He dialled Joe's number. Waited and waited until he finally answered, 'McCauley.'

The old man didn't sound happy to be disturbed. Well, bugger him. Billy was more important right now.

'Joe, it's Hunter here.'

'What do *you* want?'

'Is Billy there?'

'Nup.'

'Shit. He's not here either. He was supposed stay put until I got back. I've been down at Tammy's. Shot the wild dog this morning. Got back and Billy was gone.'

'Fuck,' said Joe. And then there was an almighty crash on the other end of the phone.

'Joe? *Joe?* Goddamn it, *Joe!*'

'I'm still here. Me hip just gave way. Tryin' to see what the damn dog's doin'.'

'Are you all right? I'll come over.'

'Fuck off,' the old man said. 'I'm all right. Get out and find that boy.'

'You sure?'

'Course I'm fuckin' sure.'

Trav hung up and took off at a run. Where the hell should he start looking?

※

Joe slowly got back up onto his feet, using the solid oak telephone table to aid him. In swinging around to check on the dog the pain in his hip had dropped him like a sinker on a fishing line. He'd hit the floor with a dull thud.

Now his thoughts were running rampant. Where was Billy? He'd better not be down on the flats; the flood would be here in no time and the kid wouldn't stand a chance. Water was insidious. It rushed into places you wouldn't have believed possible. After a lifetime of watching floods and their consequences, Joe could feel his heart starting to hammer with panic. He couldn't believe how much that boy had come to feel like his own. He'd never forgive Hunter if something happened to Billy. He'd never forgive *himself.* Maybe he would see something through the gun sight. He'd give it a whirl – anything to find the child before the water found him.

Joe carefully limped back towards the front verandah using the wall to steady himself. At the screen door he paused. No Boots. Where the hell was that damned dog? Probably lit out for the sheds knowing Joe'd be after him for chewing on his gummies.

Joe kept moving, eyes focused on the gun, until he glimpsed a scrap of black. Then some shaggy white. What the hell?

He shuffled towards the steps, peered down over the verandah and saw Boots lying in the rain, the rubber side of a gumboot propped in his mouth. 'Ya bugger of a dog. Get back up here and help me look for this boy.'

The dog was on his tummy and facing towards the valley of Narree.

'Boots! Get up here, ya mangey old bastard.'

The dog was still. Didn't even look up at the sound of Joe's voice.

Cold dread started to trickle down Joe's spine. A leaden feeling pitted his tummy. He tried calling again, hesitant and soft. 'Boots?'

The dog and boot just lay still in the rain.

He didn't even think about the steps, didn't even consider the fact he might be risking his gammy hip. He just launched himself towards his best mate lying in the slop and mud. He stumbled the last few feet, threw himself forwards so that he landed right beside the dog. He tried to lift the animal but the weight was too much and man and dog slid sideways into the muck. Joe buried his face into the wet, shaggy mane of the border collie – the friend who'd never left his side for sixteen long years.

'Boots?' whispered Joe. His chest started to convulse with sobs. 'Oh, Boots,' he said again. He let out a howl of despair that echoed across the expanse of McCauley's Hill, the place he and Boots had shared so much.

And then he just lay with the dog at the foot of the steps. Allowed the cold and wet to seep into his bones. For Joe McCauley didn't care about much of anything any more.

Chapter 46

Tammy had finished milking in record time. The cows were in the house paddock, close to the homestead, one of the highest pieces of ground. That'd have to do. The cows and calves were on the other side of the house behind some cypress pines and poplars. The wild dog hadn't come back yet after his last little effort, which was a relief. She guessed Travis would be too busy with Katrina to be worrying about staking out her paddock anyway. He had bigger fish to fry than looking out for Tammy McCauley.

She tried to push the Hunter family from her mind. The sooner she sold those paintings or used them as fertiliser pallets the better. Or maybe she could give them to Lucy for her birthday. She hadn't seen or heard from her best friend since the gallery opening.

The mobile in her pocket started to vibrate. The damned thing had been rattling all morning with farmers up and down the river trying to find out what was going on with the weir and the water. The weir keepers were flat out trying to balance water inflows and outflows in an effort to limit the damage to farms downstream. She wouldn't like to be in their shoes, that's for sure.

'Tammy McC –'

'Tammy, it's Travis . . .'

What did he want? Was he ringing to see how she was faring? Had Rob been talking to him?

'I'm just wondering if you've seen Billy?'

How stupid of her to think he might be interested in *her* welfare while facing down the biggest flood in history.

'Nope. He's not here. Why do you ask?'

There was silence then Travis's voice came back, strained and fraught. 'He's missing, Tammy. I can't find him. I went down to your place this morning to stake out the dog and he promised to stay put. But now he's gone.'

Alarm scrambled through Tammy's body. She remembered the shot she thought she'd heard earlier. Not Billy. Please not Billy.

'You didn't shoot *him* by mistake, did you? A ricochet or something?'

'No!' yelled Trav. 'What do you think I am?'

Tammy felt instant remorse as she heard the stress in the man's voice.

'I only shot the dog. I got him, Tammy. But I can't find my son.'

The hairs at the back of Tammy's neck prickled. 'Travis, you have to find him! There's a huge flood coming. Water's going to be everywhere down here shortly.' She stopped. 'What about Joe? Have you tried him?'

'He's not there either. I've looked everywhere I can think of, and I can't find him. His bike's still here – everything is still here. He's disappeared into thin air.'

Tammy thought quickly about Billy. Where would he have gone that was beyond Belaren, Joe's and Montmorency? 'What about your mother in Lake Grace? Would he be there?'

'Can't think why.'

'How about Katrina? Would he have hitched a ride into Narree?'

'Oh God, hadn't thought of that,' said Travis. There was a deathly silence. 'I hadn't thought of that at all. Might be worth a try. He was pretty pissed off with me last night . . .'

Tammy held her breath, hoping he'd continue. Why had Billy been pissed off?

'Kat came out here for a look around. We thought we'd have some tea together but Kat had other dinner arrangements. Billy thought it was all my fault. We took her back to the motel . . .'

Did they stay the night?

'. . . so she could get ready. Billy and I ate by ourselves and then came home.'

Tammy sighed with relief but then realised Trav probably heard it. Damn, did she have to be so obvious about it all? 'Your best bet might be to ring . . . Katrina.' Tammy mentally cursed as her voice quivered on saying the woman's name. 'In the meantime I'll try and think of anywhere else he would be.' Anything to get him off the phone, away from her traitorous voice, and out looking for Billy.

'Good idea. I'll get back to you shortly,' said Travis before disconnecting.

Great. So she now had a flood, a missing child, and a man

she wanted badly but couldn't have to contend with. Not to mention a deceitful, faithless husband, an irate uncle and a property that was about to be sold from beneath her.

She shuddered. Take things one step at a time, like her grandfather always told her.

First, and most important, was Billy. Where else could he have gone? Her eyes wandered across the landscape she could see from the milk-room doorway. As she scanned the paddocks her mind dismissed places one by one. She hesitated at the sight of the huge red gums that lined the river. Fishing? Maybe the child had taken it into his head to go fishing. In the rain? Knowing Billy's idiosyncrasies, it was possible.

She hated going near the river. Her mother had been lost in its murky depths. Tammy contemplated the huge trees for a few more minutes. She'd never forgive herself if Billy was down there with a wall of water about to descend. She ran for the four-wheel-drive. She might just make it there and back before the road was cut off. It was worth a try.

※

Travis scrambled in his kitchen drawers for the phone directory. It was here somewhere, he was sure. He swore and grunted and slammed one drawer after the other until he thought to look on top of the fridge. There it was, damn it, right where he'd last left it. He snatched the book up and searched for the number of the Narree Motel.

'This number has been disconnected. Please check and try again,' recited a mechanical voice.

'Fuck it!' he shouted at the walls that were covered in pictures of his life. He stopped, horrified. Not one photo on that wall had a child in it. Not one photo was of his son. Christ, he'd really fucked it all up.

Who to ring? There was a directory assistance number somewhere but he didn't know it off by heart. He thought hard. The Lake Grace *pub*. They knew everything. And he knew their number.

'Lake Grace Hotel.' A gravelly voice, loaded with what Trav guessed to be a mother of a hangover, answered the phone. It was Shon Murphy.

'Travis Hunter here. Would you have the number of the Narree Motel?'

'And if I did, why should I tell you?'

'Just give me the fucking number, Murphy.' He didn't have time for this shit.

'No.'

Trav let out a roar of frustration. 'For land's sake, give me the *fucking* number! My boy's missing and there's a flood coming. Do you want to be responsible for the death of a child?'

There was silence on the other end of the line. Then Shon said, 'Hang on.'

Trav could hear Shon bellowing, 'Hey, Joanne, what's the new number for the motel?' There was the sound of a shrill voice then Murphy was back on the line. 'You got a pen?'

Shon read out the number twice, to make sure Trav had it right.

Even though it pained him to say it, Trav squeezed out, 'Thanks.'

'Hope you find him.' Shon banged down the phone.

Trav dialled the motel. Asked if Katrina – Reyne – was there.

'No, Mr Hunter,' said the receptionist, 'I'm afraid you've just missed her. She's checked out.'

'Do you have a contact number for her?'

'Well, yes, but due to privacy measures I can't give it to you.'

The girl must have heard his groan. 'I'm really sorry. I could have rung her for you myself if it was really urgent, but our computer system's just gone down – something to do with a flood at Lake Grace – and I can't access our records right now.'

Trav tried to think how else he could discover whether Billy was with Kat.

'She and the child left about half an hour ago, Mr Hunter,' came the young woman's voice. 'They didn't say where they were headed but the little boy seemed very excited.' She giggled. 'They're like peas in a pod, those two. They look so alike!'

Trav couldn't remember if he said thank you or not as he hung up the phone. He had to get to Narree and head them off. They were probably clear of the flood zone but who knew where Katrina would leave his son this time.

※

There was water already across the road in the dip on the run-up to the bridge. Surface water from the rain, Tammy guessed. She gauged its depth from the fence posts running down each side of the road, using the theory that the posts would be lower than the middle of the tar. She should make it, she thought.

Engaging low range, she crept forwards, keeping to the middle of the road until she saw a truck coming towards her. It was a 1418 Mercedes Benz, a nine-tonne tray truck with a crate and load of cattle on it. She gingerly moved the LandCruiser to the left side of the road. The driver was making wild gestures at her as he bored past. Waves of water flung themselves at her ute. The bastard. Luckily the vehicle had a snorkel to prevent water getting into the engine. She kept driving, knowing she might as well keep going – the bridge was right in front of her and it was dry. As the tyres hit the tar on the concrete structure that spanned the Narree River, she let out a sigh of relief. From what Rob had said, they'd be opening the weir any time now. She didn't have long.

She stabbed at the clutch and rolled the ute to a stop for a moment to allow the stress that had been building inside her to melt away. She'd made it. She could see Billy's fishing spot out to her right on the far bank. She'd just drive over, check it out and then head back.

A dull noise was building in her ears. She snatched a quick look to her left and her mouth gaped open in utter terror. The flood. It was here. Coming right at her from a couple of Ks upstream. A wall of water throwing logs and trees left and right like they were twigs. She floored the accelerator, panic making her flounder with the gears. The ute jumped forwards, then coughed, spluttered and stopped. She snatched another look at the water coming at her like a freight train. Tried to fire the ignition. Nothing happened. It was dead. She tried again. And again. And again.

'C'mon, c'mon. Start, damn you!' she sobbed. Nothing. 'Goddamn it!' she yelled, staring wildly across at the water, which was bearing down on the bridge.

She bailed out of the ute and ran to the front of the vehicle. Threw open the bonnet. Saw the air inlet hose hadn't been reconnected to the snorkel after the last service. Oh dear God, the motor *had* ingested water. *Fucking Shon!* He always did the maintenance on their vehicles rather than spend money on a mechanic. His tightfistedness was going to cost her her life.

Suddenly her subconscious noted the roar of the oncoming water. Drowning out any other noise it was like nothing she'd ever heard before. The bridge shuddered slightly under her feet, making her look up. A massive raft of uprooted trees pushed ahead of the big wave had belted the side of the bridge. *Do something*, her mind screamed.

She snapped a look to the left and then to the right. Both approaches to the bridge were now under water. Way too much water, moving far too fast for her to swim through.

Her blood ran cold. She was running out of options. *Think, think, think!*

The radio.

She jumped back into the ute to try the UHF in desperation, knowing in her heart that it was too late. 'Help, *help*, somebody, anybody, help me!' she screamed into the receiver.

Silence.

Tammy dropped the handset to the floor, slumped back in the seat and closed her eyes.

And waited for the water to smash into her vehicle and carry them both away.

Chapter 47

Travis didn't know whether he'd catch the pair of them before they left town, but he had to try. He couldn't believe Katrina would do this to him – take his boy. Why hadn't she rung him to let him know she had Billy? Maybe she was making him pay for yesterday? He wouldn't put it past her.

Billy must have left the house this morning soon after Travis and, so his father didn't see him, cut through the bush to the main road. Then he'd obviously hitched a ride into town. Why was the child so desperate as to run away? Had he really been that bad a father?

Well, once he found the kid, he'd rectify all that. He'd try harder.

But he had to find him first.

He jumped into his ute, sped down the hill, past Montmorency. Realised he hadn't rung Tammy. He'd call her once he reached town and located them. If he found them. He shook his head. He couldn't even entertain that thought.

He turned right towards Narree and saw water over the winding road all the way to the bridge. Fuck it! In his mad panic to get out the door, he'd forgotten about the flood. He stared at the road in frustration. A roll of water coming across the paddocks caught his eye. He'd get flooded on all sides by a mini tsunami if he stayed where he was. He thumped the steering wheel of the ute in frustration. How could he stop Katrina now?

There was a flicker of white in the gloom. Was there something on the bridge? He stared hard through the windscreen, so hard his eyes blurred. He swiped at them. There it was, a blotch of white in the teeming rain.

He snatched another look at the oncoming water. How much longer did he have?

Long enough. Maybe.

He jumped out of the vehicle and dug into the workbox on the tray-back, ignoring the water now running down his neck. He snatched up the binoculars he'd borrowed off Joe and focused the glasses on the bridge.

It was a white ute, slammed up hard against the guard rail on the wrong side of the road by the first big wave of weir water. The flood was pouring around it halfway up the side of the vehicle, over the running boards, probably up to the door handles.

Holy shit! Was there anyone in it?

He pulled the glasses away to clear the moisture off the lenses, then peered hard again. He thought he might have seen a flicker of movement on the driver's side. Realised at the same moment the vehicle looked familiar.

Tammy.

His blood ran cold.

What could he do? There was no way he'd get through that water in his ute. It was insane to even try. And more floodwater was rolling across the paddocks towards him at a pace. If he didn't move now he'd be in the same situation.

He jumped into the ute, reversed, spun the vehicle around and sent it hurtling back towards Hope's Road and Montmorency Downs. His heart was beating so fast he thought it would explode out of his chest. He felt sick leaving her but he had to get hold of a piece of machinery that could withstand the force of that water.

He screeched sideways into Tammy's driveway, not noticing the big yellow sign at the entrance. His eyes were focused on Backwater Creek and the low-level crossing between McCauley's Hill and Tammy's place that was now flowing full and fast. Shit, shit, shit. He wouldn't be able to get home now – and what about Billy?

The whole world around him was going to hell and he had no way of stopping it. Deep breaths, he told himself. One thing at a time. Tammy was the priority at the minute. At least Billy was safe with Katrina – he hoped.

He needed to find a tractor and he knew Tammy had one. Down the drive he went, coming to a halt in front of the machinery shed. He scanned the contents. No tractor. Fuck it. He drove on, scanned the paddocks around the dairy. Where the hell had she hidden her 150-horsepower bright red Massey Ferguson tractor? Surely she didn't have it over on the run-off block? Not with a flood coming?

A glimpse of scarlet through the trees near the hayshed caught his eye. A round baler? A silage cart? He barrelled the ute in that direction – and there it was, a serious piece of machinery. Just what he needed. He prayed she'd left the keys in the damn thing.

She hadn't.

He belted across to the house and bored through the back door. Water poured from his clothes onto the kitchen lino. He didn't care, just scanned the walls for a key-holder. And there it was. A key with a cattle tag proclaiming Massey. He snatched it off its hook, took off back outside, climbed into the tractor and roared down the drive.

The water met him coming the other way. The whole landscape in front of him had changed within minutes from a dull grey-green to a sea of murky brown and silver. The tops of the fence posts were like short stumps floating on liquid. It was a frightening sight. He entered the water, the tractor making short work of driving through the tonnes of liquid coming towards him. He attempted to keep himself slap bang in the middle of the white guideposts, where the centre of Hope's Road would be, knowing he was taking a terrible risk. The water could have wrecked the tar beneath him.

Round the corner he went, towards the bridge, and then finally he was there. There was a torrent of water rushing through but it appeared the bridge was holding up. Down the dip in the road, and up onto the bridge itself, making his way towards the ute, the big motor on the tractor screaming in his ears. He saw movement as he pulled up alongside the cab. He peered down into the vehicle. What he saw made his blood run cold again. Though she was only waist-deep in water her head was back, eyes closed.

Then she looked up. Thank God she was still alive. He could see the expressions on her face. Shock, relief, chased by hope.

He opened the tractor door, and the roar of the water filled the cabin. He mimed winding the window to Tammy.

She struggled towards the passenger side, wound the glass down. Water now poured through the gap.

'Can you climb out through the window?' he yelled.

She nodded, wriggled her way up onto her haunches and hauled herself through the gap. A tree trunk came out of nowhere as she perched on the sill. It hit the ute side-on. *Whack!*

The vehicle shuddered under the impact, rocking. Tammy screamed and scrambled back inside the ute. Terror was written across her face.

His heart was in his mouth but he tried to look as reassuring as possible. 'Try again! You can do it!'

He watched her take a deep breath and launch herself out the window gap again. Man, this woman was incredible. He was so proud of her. She grabbed hold of the side of the tractor and reefed her body out of the vehicle and onto the top step of the big machine. He grabbed at her desperately with both hands and hauled her inside. Her wet and cold body landed hard on his lap. She sank into his arms and lay with her head against his chest, breathing hard, shaking so violently he thought she'd never stop. He threw his arms around her and hugged her close, muttering into her straggled hair, 'It's okay. I've got you . . . I've got you.'

She started to sob, big wracking shudders that shook them both. He gently pushed her head back and gazed into her eyes. His hand lightly brushed the wet strands of hair out of the way. So close. So close to losing something very special. He was shocked to realise just *how* special. Once again, what an idiot he'd been. 'It's okay, Tammy. I've got you, sweetheart. I'm here. But we need to get off this bridge.'

Tammy didn't want to leave the warmth of his body, but knew she had to because they weren't out of the woods yet.

She tried to get a hold on her emotions, to stop shaking and shuddering.

'What's the plan?' The words came out wobbly and shrill.

Trav gently deposited her on the jockey seat beside him. 'We reverse off the bridge. At least I know the road's still in reasonable shape behind us.' He got the tractor moving again and slowly reversed his way across the bridge. Down the road they went, backwards, until he could see the sign for the intersection to Montmorency Downs. He kept reversing up the tar to Lake Grace and then, shifting gears, headed forwards and around the corner and down Hope's Road towards McCauley's Hill.

Tammy could see her whole farm was now under water, except for a few acres around the house, which her far-seeing forefathers had placed on a rise. The cows were all huddled around a snatch of green grass between the house and the dairy. She was relieved to see the pad of built-up dirt was doing its job.

'Billy! What about Billy?' she said suddenly. She saw Trav start as he clocked the yellow auction pending sign, but he didn't say anything.

'I'm pretty sure Billy's with Katrina,' he said. 'I was on my way to find them when I saw you. I came back for your tractor.' He looked towards the low-level crossing. 'I thought I might have been able to get through there in this to get home but now I don't think I can. That's way too deep even for this thing. When the water goes down a bit, can I borrow the tractor to get home?'

'Of course,' she said, her heart sinking. He'd said it all so dispassionately. What had happened to their connection, that burning need she was sure she had just seen in him? She tried to focus back on the child. 'What are you going to do about Billy?'

'Find him,' said Trav in a bleak voice. 'I don't know what's happened, or where they are, but I intend to track them down. I need to convince him to come home.'

Chapter 48

'Joe McCauley! What are you doing stuck in that muck?'

One scarlet gumboot landed beside Joe's nose. Followed by another.

'Don't you have better things to do than wallow around in mud like some common thug?'

He'd known only one person in the district who talked like that. But he couldn't work out why the hell *she'd* be on his hill, so he figured he must be in purgatory with Boots. It was just his luck she'd be there too.

'What are you and Boots doing down here in the rain?' said another voice, male this time. A young voice.

This person he *did* want to talk to. Joe opened his eyes and swiped at them to clear mud from his vision. He didn't know how long he'd been lying there cuddling the body of his dog.

'Randal? Randal! Get out of the car this instant and help Mr McCauley,' came the woman's voice again. The boot disappeared. There was the sound of a car door being opened and shut. Joe snuck another look. This time he saw a late 1960s white Chrysler Valiant complete with chrome and bright silver trim sitting in the driveway on the side of his hill. How in the hell did that get here with all the water lying on the roads? Fly?

More footfalls came sloshing through the mud. Joe shut his eyes, then opened them as the steps stopped in front of him. A long pale face, studs poking from an eyebrow, a nose and chin, came floating into view. The youth's cheeks were stacked with white-topped mountains of adolescent acne. A bony hand with black-painted fingernails came towards him.

Who the fuck? Joe scuttled backwards.

'Settle, petal,' came the woman's voice again. 'Randal might look scary, but deep down he's a fairy.'

'Hey, Mrs P, I'm not a poofter!' Joe assumed this protest came from Randal. The kid's voice was slightly high-pitched, as if he wasn't sure whether to be a boy or a man, but it confirmed the identity of the woman. Oh hell.

Determined not to let Mr Metal Face touch him again, Joe muttered, 'I'm fine.' He tried to sit up but found he was frozen into a crouch.

'Here, Mr McCauley, I'll help you up.' The small figure of Billy Hunter made to move towards Joe and haul him off the ground.

Beatrice Parker beat him to it. 'Billy, stop. Randal, go get the man up.'

Joe scuttled backwards again. No way he was letting that gothic-looking creature near him and his dog.

'Oh, for heaven's sake,' said Beatrice, losing patience as Randal hovered unsure. She took Joe by one hand, indicating

Billy should take the other, and they heaved together. 'One, two, three – *hup*!'

Beatrice would have ended up down in the slush and mud too but for an agile Randal, who grabbed her as she overbalanced. 'Mrs P!' shouted the teenager. 'You said you'd give me a hundred bucks to get you here. You won't give over if you're in hospital.'

Beatrice made a little moue with her mouth. 'Surprisingly, Randal, there's more to life than money. I'll just get you a prop, Mr McCauley.' She stomped her walking stick across to the verandah, and tottered up the steps to retrieve an old willow cane leaning against the wall.

In the meantime, Billy was peering at the dog. 'What's wrong with Boots? He sick or something?'

The old man looked down at his beloved mate, lying so still.

'Mr McCauley? What's wrong with Boots?'

'Argh ... Billy, mate.' Joe swallowed hard. Tried to work out how to put it out there nice and soft, palatable enough for a kid to understand. He couldn't. It hurt too much.

'He's dead.'

The words hung in the air. Three sets of eyes stared at the dog, who was by now a sodden black and white lump.

'His old heart must have just stopped,' said Joe. 'He didn't want to be here any more.'

'Not him too?' said Billy, choking back the tears.

Joe was too immersed in his own grief to pick up on Billy's words. But Beatrice Parker wasn't. She hobbled back to them and handed Joe the makeshift walking stick, before turning to Billy. 'Now young man, we went through all that on the drive over. You know your mother wasn't in a position to take you with her.'

'She didn't *want* to take me with her,' spluttered Billy. 'She didn't want me at *all*.' The child burst into tears and ran up the stairs into Joe's house. The screen door banged so hard it fell off its hinges, falling to the verandah with a loud *splat*.

The noise jolted Joe out of his morbid state and he looked across at Beatrice. 'Where'd you find him? His father's beside himself with worry.'

Randal started to laugh. 'At the Lake Grace Nursing Home. Bit young to be in there.'

A hard glance from Beatrice quelled the laughter. 'Guess I'll go wait in the car,' he muttered, before slouching off.

They both watched as the teenager got back into the classic vehicle on the driver's side. For the first time Joe noticed the Learner plates clipped to the front windscreen.

'A bit desperate for a ride, were you?' he said to Beatrice. Her blackcurrant eyes pinned him to the ground with their disapproval. The woman hadn't changed. Those eyes were killers. He coughed, spluttered a bit. Decided the best form of defence was retreat. 'Yes, well, thanks for bringing the boy home. His father'll be pleased.' He paused, realising he hadn't the slightest idea where Hunter was. He'd missed an hour or so lying there in the mud. 'You haven't seen the man, by any chance, have you?'

Beatrice now peered at him like he was slightly deranged. 'If I had, Joe McCauley, I'd hardly be bringing that boy to *you*.' Her expression told him more than any words what she thought of him. 'I didn't want to leave the child on his own and his father isn't at home.'

Joe could feel his hackles rising. How dare the woman make such judgements?! Okay, he was a bit different. Okay, *a lot* different, but that didn't mean he wasn't able to be responsible. He automatically dropped a hand to his side, expecting to feel a wet muzzle nudge his fingers. The sadness he felt steal through his body when it didn't was overwhelming.

Beatrice went on, 'In fact I thought you're the last person in the valley a child would want, the way you go on. But he said to come here, even though I thought it very wrong.'

Joe felt a tiny suffusion of warmth in his heart. Billy wanted him. After not finding his father, he had wanted to come home to Joe. Now wasn't that something?

'Billy's me mate,' said Joe, feeling himself gain strength. He stood up a little straighter, using the stick as a prop. 'He's like my family.' He suddenly realised the truth in those four little words. 'Yep, he's like family, so my bloody oath he can come home to me.'

Beatrice stared at him in shock. Moments sped past. It seemed like she was trying to work out the truth of his statement. He stood and weathered her appraisal.

Then all of a sudden her face softened and she broke into laughter. A rumbling kind of sound that came from the very depths of her belly. He hadn't thought a full-throated noise could possible come from such a dainty person. But then he'd forgotten her family were bushmen. People who'd loved humour and used it to withstand the stark and rough surroundings in which they existed.

'What you laughing at, woman?' he said, scratching his head. Beatrice now had tears running down her cheeks. What the hell? What was so funny?

'I'm . . . laughing at . . . you,' she eventually spluttered. 'Joe McCauley, I think you might have found it at last.'

Found it? What was she talking about?

'You didn't want anyone after Mae Rouget. Not another girl, not your family. You buried yourself in the bush. Then along came your saint of a wife.' Beatrice paused to make the sign of the cross, then went on. 'You became *almost* normal after you married her. Then she died and away you went again, out of your tree.'

Joe clamped his lips shut. He didn't go out of his tree! He just didn't want no bastard comin' around annoyin' him, that was all. All them do-gooders and stuff, they'd do a man's head in.

'And now you have a boy who thinks the world of you and finally you've reconciled with Tammy' – Joe frowned at the mention of that bloody strumpet but Beatrice sailed on regardless. 'It might have taken you ninety-odd years, but you've worked it out, Joe McCauley. Finally you have a family.'

'Some bloody family . . .' Joe started to rant. 'That bloody Tammy –'

'Don't you that bloody Tammy me!' said Beatrice, laughter changing to anger in nanoseconds. 'That girl looked after you when you were crook. She didn't have to because, God knows, you haven't ever given her cause to want to. But she did. You mightn't be able to see it because you're a stubborn, pig-headed old mule, but that girl loves you. And what's more, just at this moment, she needs family as much as you.'

'I don't need no bloody family. She's selling my farm.'

'What, this place?'

'No. Montmorency Downs.'

'It's hardly your place, Joe. You reneged your right to it sixty years ago.'

Now it was Joe's turn to cast Beatrice a dirty look.

'You walked, Joe. You walked away and didn't look back. It broke your mum and dad's hearts the way you treated Tom. And your brother? Well, that man never did a wrong thing by anybody. I can't say the same about his wife, but that's another story.' Beatrice crossed her arms. 'Did you even think to ask Tammy why she was selling?'

'Well, argh . . .' spluttered Joe.

'I didn't think so. Too busy yelling and shooting that gun of yours at her, were you?'

Joe opened his mouth to protest and then shut it again. His hand went to drop down towards Boots, only stopping midway as he remembered. 'Don't know why I'm standing here in the rain arguing with a woman.'

'I don't know why you are either. You know I'm right. I'm always right.'

'That's usually my line.'

Beatrice smiled and again her face and cheeks relaxed into apple dumplings. The woman was almost pretty like that, thought Joe.

'We're more alike than you know, Mr McCauley.'

'You looking for a family too then?' said Joe, regretting the words even as they fired like a gunshot from his mouth. As hurt as he was, she didn't deserve that one. Donald Elliot had been a useless piece of rubbish.

He shouldn't have worried because Beatrice just smiled some more. 'Oh, but I've already got one . . .' She pointed towards the old but magnificent car. 'He's a bit morbid and has a tongue that needs curbing but he'll do. His parents didn't know what to do with him, didn't want him around. I said he could live with me so he could finish school. Nice kid, just needs a bit of fine-tuning.' And she winked, a flutter of the eye, just like her father had delivered when he took the mickey out of one of his bush crew.

Joe was speechless. The things you learned when you least expected it.

'And now we'd better get going.' Beatrice beckoned to the teenager, then turned towards the scrub and threw out a hand. 'We came through the bush on an old logging trail along the ridge.'

Joe gaped at the vague hole in the trees she was pointing to. No one had used that track in decades. What a classy broad.

'Most of the main roads here are all closed but I wanted to get the child to his father. He was very upset. The woman left him with his grandmother and she isn't in any condition to be dealing with him. I just happened to be visiting the nursing home. Found him crying in the front foyer.'

Joe stared hard towards the house. It must have been bad for Billy to cry. What had that bloody Katrina done to his boy?

'You'd better be hoping Hunter's not caught out in that,' said Beatrice, now waving her arm to encompass the Narree River Valley down below. He swung to look and let out an almighty yell.

'Holy *shit*!'

There was not a blade of grass to be seen, just a mass of shimmering water.

Chapter 49

Tammy's heart felt like a blizzard had just blown through it. Just for an instant there on the bridge she'd thought . . . Well, it didn't matter now what she'd thought.

And she'd lost Billy too. They both had. That little boy brought a brilliant spark to all their lives. Trav, old Joe and her. He was a good little mate to all of them. But obviously that hadn't been enough. The boy had needed his mother more. And she had to admit she felt a little betrayed by that. Billy had crept into her heart and helped fill the hole left by not having children of her own. Why hadn't she been enough for him? an unworthy part of her asked.

Her tummy lurched. What if Trav didn't find them? What if it was too late and they were long gone, throwing dust over their shoulders at Narree, Lake Grace and McCauley's Hill. Australia was a big place. If Katrina wanted to disappear, it could take years to find them again. How would Trav bear that? How would they *all* bear that?

And then there was Joe. Betrayed. Irate. Not letting her explain. The one person left on this earth who was actually related to her by blood had disowned her again too.

Trav swung around in his seat, cupped his hand under her chin and raised it so he could look into her eyes. Tammy didn't resist. What good was it now? He may as well know how she felt. She was too exhausted and wrung out to hide it. A near-death experience tended to put things into perspective. Who cared if he knew she had fallen in love with him?

'We need to get you into the house. A shower, some warm stuff into your belly,' he said softly. But he didn't move. He didn't even flinch from the naked message that she knew was blazing from her eyes. He simply stared at her. Drank in the love.

'Oh, Tammy,' he muttered, a hand going up to softly stroke her cheek.

She held herself back. A girl had to have some pride. It was his turn now. He either wanted her or he didn't.

But to her surprise, there was no shying away. He just stared at her, a soft look in his eyes, that gorgeous half-smile hovering around his sensual lips. The man had absolutely no idea what that whole package did to her insides. No idea at all. She closed her eyes. It was unbearable to have to look at him any longer and know that he might not even choose her in the end.

She moved aside from his hand, leaving the warmth of his caress. 'Well, I guess I'd better move. Go get warmed up.' Her voice came out like a squeaking rubber duck's. She cleared her throat. Fingers touched her lips. She stopped. Opened her eyes.

Trav was still drinking her in, smiling that little half-smile. Oh please. Why did he have to make this so *hard*?

'Tammy –' he said, breaking off like he didn't know what to say.

'Just say it. For Christ's sake, just *say* it,' she said, shutting her eyes again. Get it over with, goddamn you, and then they could all move on.

'I thought I'd lost you.'

Tammy snapped her eyes open. 'What?'

'I thought I'd lost you,' he said again, shaking his head. 'I thought you were gone too. When I realised that ute was yours . . .' He swallowed. 'I've been such an idiot.'

What was he trying to say?

'That night of the art gallery thing, all I could think of was how I felt after Katrina left me. How to keep Billy from feeling the same thing.' Trav looked up towards the roof of the tractor. She was shocked to see tears in his vivid blue eyes. Travis, the wild 'Hunter', *crying*?

'And then you on the bridge; Billy gone.' He shook his head again. 'I've had a huge fight with Joe, and that old man means a lot to me too. I've fucked up big time and lost it all.'

'You haven't lost it all,' said Tammy, not understanding where all this was leading but knowing she had to say something to reassure him. 'Billy's out there, somewhere. We just have to find him. And Joe? Well, I've had an argument with him too. It must be a fighting kind of week.'

Trav gave another half-smile and Tammy felt her tummy turn over again. The man looked out the tractor window, like he was trying to see beyond all the water, trying to work out where his son and former wife would be.

'We could try ringing the police. See if they can help track them down?'

Trav glanced back at her. 'I don't have a court order or anything preventing her from taking him. I didn't think I needed it.'

Tammy's heart contracted at the pain in his eyes. 'You know, Trav, Billy loves you. He hasn't done this because he hates you or anything. He just wants to get to know his mother, that's all. And even though I don't agree with how he's done it, I can understand that. I'd have done anything to know mine.'

Trav sighed. 'Yeah, maybe. I just wish he'd talked to me about it. Maybe we could've sorted something out.'

With someone like Katrina? Tammy sincerely doubted it. She couldn't even believe the woman had taken the child with her. She hadn't seemed too interested in being a mother up till now.

'Can I come inside?' he asked, at last. 'Use your phone. I will try the cops.'

'Let's do it.' Tammy moved to get up off the dickey seat.

'Hang on,' said Trav, pushing her back down.

Tammy glanced across at him. What now? She really needed to get out of this tractor cab *right away* before she ditched her dignity and did something stupid.

'Can you forgive me for being such a dickhead?'

'What?'

'Asking you to wait. Taking a break. It was . . .' He stopped, obviously searching for the right words. 'What we've got is *right*. I realise that now.'

Was he asking . . . ?

'Is there a chance we can start over? You and me?' he said, an almost bashful expression stealing across his rugged face.

What it must have taken for a man like Travis Hunter to ask a question like that. 'So? What do you think?' he said after a few moments, slinging her that half-smile again. A slightly nervous one this time though. Like he was worried what her answer might be.

'Well, I guess we could try. See where it goes,' said Tammy, trying with all her might not yell with joy, Yes, yes, *hell yes!* 'When would you like to start?'

Trav smiled. A full-on smile. 'How about now?' He moved quickly to gather her into his arms and slide her across his lap. Then slowly but surely his mouth came towards hers, his hand coming up to cradle her cheek.

She could feel her lips part. Watched as he lowered his head and brought his mouth down to touch hers. Gently at first, like it was a test, a question. And when she responded, his lips moved to demand more. His soft warm tongue entered her mouth, tasting, exploring.

She felt like she was going to combust with heat. Wriggling, she tried to get closer to him, but he tore his mouth away from hers, moaning with frustration. His lips trailed down her neck and into the sweet spot in the crook of her shoulder. He then returned to her face, kissing her cheeks, her mouth again, the top of her head.

'Oh Tammy,' he muttered into her hair. 'I thought I'd lost you.'

'You're not alone there,' she said. She pulled away from him a little so she could look up into his face. 'I thought I was a goner. But you know, when I was on that bridge, I realised how much my life has been ruled by the farm and all that goes with it. At the end of the day it's family and friends that count. Not holding onto betrayal and pain. Family and friends are what we need to keep close.'

Trav hugged her tight. 'You're right. And I've let mine go.'

'We'll find him, Trav,' she said. 'I love that boy too. And so does Joe. He'll help. For Billy's sake, he'll do it, I'm sure he will.'

'He told me to watch over the kid. Told me it was my job to look after him.' Trav looked at Tammy with such sadness. 'I didn't do a very good job of it, did I?'

'You did the best you could.' It was her turn now to stroke his cheek. 'You have to hold onto that, Trav. Now c'mon, let's go phone the police.'

Chapter 50

'What happened, boy?' The old man lowered himself onto the bed, the smell of dampness rising from his clothes. He was just grateful to sit and rest his weary bones.

He'd limped to the shed and got an old canvas tarpaulin, brought it back and spread it over Boots. He should've thought to ask Randal to shift the dog into the shed before he left, but he hadn't, so he covered the old fella instead until he found someone to help bury him. Boots couldn't feel anything now anyway, not where he'd gone.

But the child beside him could and he was huddled amid the grey woollen blankets. Joe cocked an ear. Not a single drop of water fell on the tin roof. Finally, it had stopped raining. Thank heavens for that. He turned his attention back to the child.

'C'mon, Billy. I can't help you if you don't tell me what's wrong. What happened with Katrina?'

'She didn't want me!' Arms and legs and blankets went flying and Joe shuffled slightly to the left. Billy appeared, his face the colour of his hair. Trackmarks of tears streaked down his cheeks, his chin. 'My mother doesn't want me, Joe!'

Joe snorted. 'Well, she'd be a bloody idiot then, wouldn't she? Can't think of a finer young man I'd like to know.'

'But I wanted *her*, Joe. I wanted the whole Big Mac, just like the other kids at school.'

Joe moved on the bed slightly, trying to ease the ache he could feel starting in his hip. 'Sometimes, Billy, we can't have everything we want,' he said, wincing. He shouldn't have lain out there in the rain.

'But, Joe –'

'No, Billy. Sometimes God or whoever's up there's got another plan for us. Oh, we mightn't like it at first, and don't I know that. But it's usually all for the better.' Personally he couldn't think how losing Boots could be for the better, but it sounded good. The sort of thing a grandfather would say.

A little hand crept up his leg and grabbed hold of his old weathered fingers. 'You're going to miss Boots, aren't you?'

Joe ran his rough thumb over the boy's soft young fingers. He stared up towards the mended ceiling, trying to compose himself, before looking back at the child. 'Yeah, boy. I'm gunna miss him. Heaps.'

'He was a good dog.'

'That he was,' said Joe, nodding.

'My mum's good too,' said Billy. 'Isn't she?'

The pleading note at the end of the question nearly broke what was left of Joe's heart. 'Yeah, mate. She is. She just isn't built for staying in one spot, that's all. A kid like you, you need to stay put. Get a good schooling, seeing you're so clever with your books. Your mum, well, she's just not programmed to do that.'

'My dad doesn't like staying put either,' said Billy. 'That's why he heads bush. Why he liked being a boundary rider too.' The boy swung his legs around parallel to Joe's, so he was sitting hard up against the old man. 'I think I'm the same. That's why I come and annoy you.' He smiled at Joe before adding, 'And Tammy. But she's not a wanderer. She's got roots, she says. Roots that are sunk deep into the dirt at Montmorency.'

Joe snorted again. 'She's got a funny way of showing it then, selling the joint.'

'But she has to,' said Billy with a furrowed brow. 'Didn't you know? That man, Shon. He's making her do it.'

Joe frowned. Shon? Making her sell up? He thought about that for a bit. It would make sense, he supposed. The bastard was pretty riled up the day they shot him off the property. Despite himself, Joe gave a small grin. That was one of the best days of his life, getting the better of bloody Shon Murphy. That and being on Montmorency again.

He looked down at the child. 'So what else do you know about this?'

'Not much,' Billy admitted. 'Just what I overheard her say on the phone the other day. She has to sell the joint to pay him a shitload –' He clapped a hand to his mouth. 'Oops! Sorry. A whole lot of cash.' He suddenly looked guilty. 'I didn't mean to listen.'

Joe continued to frown. Thinking. Murphy wanted a divorce so he could be with Joanne. Of course he would want money. And what better place to get it than out of one of the best farms in the district? Why hadn't he seen that? He hadn't given Tammy the chance to explain. What a fucking idiot. He was as bad as Travis Hunter.

Travis!

Joe lurched off the bed. 'Bloody hell, Billy. We need to find your dad and tell him I've got you! He was goin' out of his mind with worry. Was heading to town to find you.' The old man staggered to his feet, his young mate jumping up to steady him.

Joe chuckled. Cuffed the boy over the head. 'C'mon. Let's find your father.'

While Billy tried the phone, Joe picked up his rifle from the verandah and peered through the scope. There was not a single patch of grass to be seen at the bottom of his hill. Well, aside from a stretch right near Montmorency's dairy. There was a huge crowd of dairy cows huddled there looking miserable.

'Hey, Joe. The phone's not working,' called Billy.

'Water in the lines,' muttered Joe. 'Damn it all.'

He walked his scope across the paddocks towards the Montmorency homestead, swinging it around to see if he could detect movement anywhere.

Not a human soul stirred. His sight flickered past sheds and buildings. He spotted the tractor parked not far from the garden gate. Higher ground and a levy bank built years before had kept the flood from the immediate surrounds of the homestead itself. Still, he could see water lapping the concrete foundations of the back fence. It was gunna be close, that was for sure. He only hoped the flood had reached its peak.

Then another, more terrifying thought struck him. Had they been caught out by the water? Hunter had been going to Narree pretty much right when the flood would've been coming. Maybe he got caught on the bridge? Or on the flooded road? What if he had, and was drowned, and then Billy would have a mother who didn't want him and a father who was dead? Joe could feel his blood pressure rising. And those cows were waiting to be milked. Where was Tammy? Maybe she'd been washed away too? Oh my God – another one taken by the water. Mother and daughter. The gun started to shake in Joe's hands. He forced himself to get a grip, keep looking across the landscape with his gun.

There were a couple of utes parked in Montmorency's driveway. A small part of him wondered if one of them was Shon Murphy's. He pulled back his eyes, blinked a few times, took another look. Now he recognized the utes and neither of them belonged to Murphy.

'Can you see my dad?' asked a hesitant voice.

The boy was staring up at him like he was God about to deliver Judgement Day.

'I can't see him but I can see his ute.'

'Really? Can I see it too?'

Joe thought about that. How would the boy take seeing his father at Tammy's and not with his mother, considering how much having a Big Mac family had meant to him? Only one way to find out, he figured. 'Yeah, sure. Have a look. But be careful of the trigger. I don't want to have found you only to lose you again. Your father would kick my butt.'

Billy laughed, took hold of the gun and peered through the scope like a seasoned pro. 'Where am I looking?' he asked.

Joe cleared his throat. 'Ahem . . . well, just a little more to the right.'

The child moved the gun, then paused like he was sucking in a breath. 'There's my dad! He's with Tammy!'

Joe snatched the gun off Billy and thrust it up to his eye.

And there they were, the pair of them, swinging down from the tractor.

Kissing.

It was only a fleeting kiss, Joe saw as he took another look. The pair were now running across the back lawn of Montmorency, towards the house. Tammy had stopped and was throwing her arm in the air like she was directing Hunter to do something. Travis reversed and ran like the devil was after him towards his ute, grabbing something off the seat. He pelted towards the old barn and quickly disappeared into its dark depths. A few moments later he reappeared, but up high in the doorway of the loft overhead. With a pair of binoculars he looked out across the farm, out over the flooded valley. What was the man doing?

Billy.

He quickly passed the gun to the boy. 'I'll give them a ring. Let them know you're up here with me.'

'The phone's not working,' Billy reminded him.

Joe kept on moving. 'I'll give it another try anyway. Sometimes it gets through.'

He picked up the handset. It was dead. He jiggled the phone toggle. 'C'mon, c'mon. Give over, you bastard.' He toggled some more. Finally, success. A dial tone buzzed in his ear. The piece of paper Tammy had left for him after the accident with her and Hunter's phone numbers was still stuck to the wall. Quickly he dialled Montmorency, not knowing how long he'd get before it went dead again.

The phone at the other end rang and rang. 'C'mon, Tammy, answer the bloody thing!' The answering machine clicked in instead. Fuck, fuck, fuck. He hated these things.

'Tammy, Joe here. Billy –' The handset went dead.

Fuck, fuck, fuck... He tried again. Toggled the darn thing, over and over, with no success. What was he going to do now?

※

Trav belted through the back door of Montmorency. 'I can't see anything but bloody water out there.' He stopped as Tammy held up her hand. She was beside the phone.

'There's a message from Joe. I just missed it.'

'What'd he say?'

'That's the thing. Could Billy be up there with him? Joe says something about him, and he sounds stressed or upset. But he just says Billy's name, then it stops and I can't get the phone to work now. Where's your sat phone?'

Trav's face drained of colour. 'On the charger at home. Can't you get it to work at all?'

'Nope,' said Tammy frowning, 'I only just missed it so he must be up there on his hill watching us.' She thought a minute then her face lit up. 'I know! There're some tins of cattle-tail paint in the dairy. Can you go grab the brightest colour there? Bring it back here?'

Trav was out the door before she even finished the sentence.

Tammy dashed into the depths of the house and appeared minutes later with a couple of huge white sheets.

She met Trav at the garden gate. 'We'll take it all into the garage.'

'What are you going to do?'

'No time to explain. Can you go get my gun out of the cabinet?' she said. 'The .243 should do it.' Trav took off again.

She quickly laid the sheet out on the old concrete floor, took the spray can then set to work.

IS BILLY OK?

She sprayed the huge letters onto the sheet and stepped back as Trav arrived with the rifle. 'Now we hang this on the clothesline and fire the rifle. Joe'll have to check out a gunshot. He won't be able to resist.'

They headed outside again. It hadn't rained since they'd left the tractor so the air around them was quiet and still. Just the thing for a gunshot to be heard for miles.

They wrestled the sheet onto the big old Hills Hoist and swung the material towards McCauley's Hill. They looked at each other. 'This is ridiculous,' said Trav. 'Like something they'd do on that old TV show, *F-Troop*.'

Tammy shrugged. 'It's worth a try, isn't it?'

Trav nodded. Fired the gun into the air. The sound echoed around the valley, carried by the acres and acres of floodwater.

Up on McCauley's Hill, Joe was wrestling with the phone again. He was halfway through another abusive tirade when the gunshot rang out. He shuffled to the doorway. 'You hear that?' he said to Billy.

'Yep. It came from that-a-way.' The child pointed towards Montmorency.

Joe moved as fast as his hip would let him. Snatched up the gun, the scope to his eye. It really was all too much for ninety-year-old bones, this rollercoaster of a day.

He trained his eye on Montmorency. There was the tractor, the utes, the homestead. There was Tammy standing with her hands on her hips facing him. Staring right at him. And beside her was Hunter, looking for all the world like he wasn't sure what he was doing.

Then Joe noticed the sheet. It was hanging on the Hills Hoist clothes line but this washing was different. It had big cobalt blue letters on it. Joe squinted. Couldn't make out the words.

'Here, boy. Have a look through this. Tell me what's written on that sheet on the clothes line, will ya?'

Billy took the gun so he could see through the scope. 'Hey, there's Tammy. And my dad. Dad doesn't look happy. You think he might be a bit worried about me?'

''Course he's fuckin' worried about you! You run off like that and don't tell him!' Joe stopped. Going crook at the boy wasn't going to help anyone. 'Hunter loves you, Billy.'

'He doesn't ever say it,' said the boy, a sullen look on his face.

'Well, I can assure you he thinks it. And right now he's out of his mind with worry about *you*.'

'Oh.' A little smile snuck across his face.

'The sheet, Billy,' Joe reminded him.

'The sheet? Oh, yes, the sheet.' And the boy took a look through the scope again. 'It says . . . Is . . . Billy . . . okay?' The child stopped. 'That's me!' he said to Joe, a smile lighting up his features.

Joe grinned back. 'Sure is, boy.'

'What do we do now? You haven't got a clothesline they can see.'

Joe's eyes wandered across the yard. Nothing appropriate for a return message was in clear view of Montmorency. Then he spotted his gun. Maybe, just maybe . . .

'Grab the gun, boy, and follow me.' Joe shuffled across the verandah, snatched a bullet from a box near his chair and clambered down the steps, Billy hot on his heels.

He grabbed his gun, loaded it. Pointed it into the air.
Bang!
'What do we do now?' asked Billy.
'We wait,' said Joe.

⁂

Down on Montmorency Tammy was jumping up and down. 'Joe's there!'

'What now?' said Trav, scratching his head.

'Another message,' said Tammy. 'Quickly.' They ran to the shed, grabbed another sheet and the can of paint. Tammy started spraying.

ONE – NO
TWO – YES

Trav snatched up the material and ran with it to the clothes line.

Tammy arrived behind him, just as he put on the last peg. He spun and grabbed hold of her. She could feel his body shaking with tiny tremors as they waited for the answer. She pressed her own body against his, trying to lend him her warmth, her strength.

They waited for what seemed like hours.

Then finally . . . *Bang*!

No more. Just one loud gunshot.

Tammy felt like she was going to faint with the stress of it all. Behind her Trav was sprung like a high-tensile spring.

Another shot, goddamn it. Just one more is all we want, all we need. She tried to will it to be. Sent prayers up to Natalie, to her grandparents, to anyone who might be listening. Please take care of this little boy. Just one more shot, *please*.

Behind her Trav had started to slump, like he was giving up hope.

Bang!

The second shot seemed to ring out with glee.

Chapter 51

'Better now?' Trav's caring voice was directed at a clean and dry Tammy as she came through the kitchen door.

She had immersed her cold and shaking body in a hot bath, allowing the soothing fresh water to wash all the shock, stink and grime of the flood away. Now wearing faded worn jeans and a soft cotton top, her face was scrubbed and rosy cheeked, her long hair floating around her shoulders.

'Yes,' she said, suddenly feeling shy of the way Travis Hunter's blue eyes were drinking her in.

'Come here, woman.'

Tammy slowly moved into Travis's wide-open embrace, relishing the warmth and strength as he closed the circle around her. The relief of getting Joe's message about Billy and everyone finally being safe left them in a silent and contemplative hug for a while.

Finally, Trav spoke up, 'You got a bed in this huge place? Preferably one Shon Murphy hasn't slept in?'

'Come,' was all Tammy said, and she led him onto the verandah, into the old McCauley homestead to the side of the main house. Down a dark passage into a room at the back. It was a small but cosy space. A delicate writing desk on one wall, a man's wardrobe on another and an old-fashioned double bed with an iron bedstead in the centre. She pulled Trav into the room, kicking the door shut as she went. 'This is the guest bedroom.' She looked up at him through lowered lashes. 'You want to be my guest?'

'You bet I do.' He pushed her backwards onto the bed and slowly and methodically undressed her. He then unclothed himself while her eyes drank in every inch of the hard male body being revealed. When he was finally gloriously naked, she reached up and pulled him down to her, revelling in his weight and the feel of his obvious need.

His lips nipped hers before he slowly sank to pay homage to the sweet spots along her arching throat, across the curve of her shoulder, then down towards her breasts, his tongue trailing paths of fire across her skin. Exquisite shivers of desire shot through her veins to join with the adrenaline still slithering in her blood from the last few hours.

She closed her eyes and drank it all in. Felt the path of his lips draw to a halt at the rounded mounds of her breasts. A soft tongue rasped across a tender nipple. Licking, sucking, teasing.

Writhing in pleasure she reached for him, tugging him up towards her seeking mouth. He resisted, flashing her a wicked grin. Focusing back on her soft skin, his lips peppered a lazy line of kisses towards the other breast, the red rosy bud there already standing to attention. Waiting. Setting his hot mouth to her flesh, he laved, sending her rapidly disintegrating senses and mind into further disarray. She couldn't think beyond the sensations that were running across her skin, plunging through her body, rushing into her brain.

She, Tammy McCauley, was being ravished and she gloried in it.

Inch by inch, Travis slowly and methodically worshipped her nakedness, evocatively plundering until she couldn't take any more. 'Trav. Enough. Please,' she begged.

A soft laugh came from somewhere near her feet. She had had no idea her toes could be so sensually exquisite.

And then he was there. Right above her. Finally. The firm flesh of his chest meeting her sensitive swollen breasts, flattening them as he delved for her lips, rendering kisses on her mouth with a passion that, after his adoration of the rest of her, nearly drove Tammy over the edge.

Until suddenly he drew back.

Hovering, his intense and roving gaze took in her flushed cheeks, the want and need in her gaze, the feelings and passion laid bare in them for him to see. Myriad expressions flitted with the lightness of butterfly wings across his face, until finally wonder settled in.

'Oh, Tammy,' he whispered. 'I think I'm in love with you.'

Tammy smiled. A soft smile. She drank in the sight of the man above her, the love beaming from his eyes. Here was a man who'd never thought it would happen again for him. She treasured this moment. For Hunter would never carry his heart on his sleeve like she did, but she could deal with that.

With Travis Hunter by her side, she could deal with anything.

And now they had some serious loving to do . . .

Sometime later, after Tammy had fallen asleep, her hair splayed across the pillow, face soft with slumber, Travis Hunter lay and watched her. He couldn't remember his heart feeling as full as it did right now. Looking down on this beautiful, incredible woman. And he'd nearly lost her. Just like he'd nearly lost the other most important thing in his life. Billy. He still had to sort that one out, but with this woman beside him, he felt as though he could conquer the world. They'd do it together, but right now . . .

He slipped from the bed. Pulled on his jeans, padded out through the old house, onto the verandah, into the kitchen. Found the phone, picked up the handset and was rewarded with a dial tone.

He immediately rang Joe.

'McCauley.'

'Joe, it's Trav. Where's Billy?'

'I'm fine too, thanks, how are you?' said Joe, a chuckle to his voice.

'Joe!'

'Argh, can't an old man have some fun? Billy's fine, he's here with me.'

Trav sagged with relief.

'We're tryin' to set another rabbit trap. This one's a bit rusty. Been up in the shed rafters for a time; that'll do it to a fine piece of machinery.'

'So he's with you?' repeated Trav, just to make sure.

'That's what I said, isn't it?' Joe's tone was kind but gruff. 'It's a long story but he's come home and that's what counts.'

Trav couldn't speak for a few moments.

'You still there?' asked the old man.

Trav took a few deep breaths to get a hold of himself. 'Yeah, I'm still here,' he said.

'Hunter. He's *fine*. Now if you don't mind, we've got some serious things to be doin'. A man's gotta do what a man's gotta do. Might pay you to remember that.'

Trav leaned back against a nearby wall and chuckled. 'No worries, McCauley. Take care of him for me, won't you? Until I can get there, that is.'

'I'll take as good a care of him as I would me own grandson. That do ya? Now piss off. We got work to do and I'm guessing you've got a bit to be doing yourself.' The old man's laugh was wicked.

'You spying on us?'

'Me? Nooo. I'd never do that. Might take a bit of a look now and then, but I'd never *spy*. Leave all that mumbo-jumbo to young Billy.'

'Thanks, Joe.'

'For what?'

'You know,' said Trav, trying to find the words. 'Everything.'

'Piss off, Hunter.'

'I'm going.'

'Good.' And the phone clunked in his ear.

So Billy was safe, and what's more he was still up there on McCauley's Hill, right where he was supposed to be. Travis didn't have to go searching high and low for Katrina and his son. He slid to the floor and closed his eyes. Sat there for a while, just breathing and thanking God it had all turned out all right.

It took a little time but another thought struck him. Something said on a night around a fire drum. *Forever is a long time to live with regret.* Wasn't that what old Joe said?

He stood up, stared hard at the phone. Thinking. Would the bloody thing work again, and did he remember the number to dial?

He picked up the receiver and breathed a sigh of relief when he heard the dial tone. He allowed his fingers to walk across the numbers of their own accord, trusting instinct and memory wouldn't send him wrong.

At the other end of the line a phone started to ring.

He counted under his breath.

One, two, three ... He'd give it to ten and if no one answered he'd hang up.

On number eight, someone picked up the call.

Travis Hunter sucked in a breath.

'Homeview Station,' said the deep male voice.

'Danny? It's Travis ...'

Epilogue

Six months later . . .

They were all gathered on McCauley's Hill. Deano and Cin had just arrived, the new dog they'd brought creating havoc with the party decorations Billy had put up. Streamers and balloons fastened at an ten-year-old's level were bliss for a four-month-old kelpie-cross. Joe could hear Billy's screams of laughter and knew disaster had struck without even looking along the verandah. The bang of a balloon confirmed it.

    The occasion was Joe's ninetieth birthday. And they were having a barbecue to celebrate the occasion, much to the old man's feigned disgust and displeasure. But underneath it he was as happy as a pig in shit. He had them all together again. Over the last six months this group had spent time helping Tammy put Montmorency back to rights after the big flood. It was worth celebrating his birthday just to say thank you, especially since now he had a vested financial interest in the property. It was only right.

He rocked back in his chair and glanced across at Tammy, who was laughing at something Lucy had said to Alice. When had Lucy *not* had something ridiculous to say? But his niece was also sneaking glances down at Trav, who, ably assisted by Billy, was cooking the meat for lunch on a hotplate over a campfire. The girl was happy and that meant a lot to Joe. Ever since she'd accepted his offer of a financial partnership to save Montmorency, they'd been working hard to pull the old place back together. It had given him an inordinate amount of pleasure to see the old boundaries reinstated, with his place and Tammy's now rejoined as one working property.

The girl was doing a good job managing the lot. With Hunter's help of course. The former boundary rider had cut his dog trapping hours back to part-time in order to be a better father and farmer. He worked side by side with Tammy now and practically lived at Montmorency Downs. The ute was often there overnight. Billy was on his way to getting the whole Big Mac.

Funny how he'd mellowed in this last little while. Maybe it was turning nine decades old. But then, he admitted to himself, maybe it was his newfound partnership with Tammy. It'd helped him to let go of all the old hurts and feelings of betrayal and pain. He was happy to see the back of them really. They'd never done him much good anyway. And he couldn't help but quietly hope Tom was looking down approving of it all.

He gazed out across at his kingdom, his eyes lingering near the front fence on a small white cross emblazoned with the word BOOTS, before skipping across to the blue, hunched line of rugged mountains. They staggered drunkenly across the horizon, immense and solid in their intent to boundary this part of Gippsland from the rest of Australia. He took in the mid-afternoon blaze of sunlight that was spreading its rays out across Mount Cullen and the ranges beyond. It was dazzling when the sky did this. Like God was beaming down on his magnificent creation, saying, 'Gee, look at this. See what I did, isn't it beautiful?'

His eyes then drifted out across the irrigated valley of Narree. After the flood receded, the open plains had slowly returned to their patchwork quilt of brilliant emerald green and rich brown. The river, like silver thread, winding through properties, made its way down to the sea. Joe sighed. Things were as they should be. Everything was in order. He felt ... What? His thoughts fumbled for the word. He felt, well, content. He didn't think he'd ever experienced that feeling in his long life before.

His gaze then slipped back to the world that was Montmorency Downs – both the irrigated flats and McCauley's Hill now. And he could see the gate that led across the paddocks and down the hill to his old home, Tammy's place. The gate which, like many others on the hill, had for so long hung open, leaning sideways and naked. It was now standing proudly straight, closed and latched.

But hang on, someone was coming through it. Joe squinted his eyes, trying to see through what looked like a swirl of grey mist. It was a woman. He could see the outline of her dress. She undid the latch, let herself through. Closed it again. Then she turned and Joe caught his breath.

It was Nellie. A glint of white to the left and there was Boots, gambolling around at her feet just like in the old days, when she'd dig in the vegie garden beside the house.

And behind her came ... Mae.

Walking towards him, through the long grass. She was smiling. Laughing. And there . . . Oh my Lord, there was Tom, his elder brother, like Joe had never seen him before. Tall, strong and erect, walking free of the shackles of responsibility. A smile on his face, striding hand in hand with his wife.

They were all still coming towards him as he sat in his chair. Not realising what he was doing, Joe got up and left the verandah, drawn by what, he didn't know. Maybe it was their smiles? Their beckoning arms? He walked easily down the steps and across the yard, through the paddock of long spring grass flowing like a river in the wind.

Nellie was now holding hands with Mae. They'd left Tom and Boots behind, waiting near a solid old fence post. Tom was throwing a stick to the dog and Boots was loving it, running backwards and forwards, bouncing and yapping. Only thing was, Joe couldn't hear the dog. Maybe he was too far away?

The women kept coming. Closer and closer, swinging their arms in an exaggerated way, giggling, hips swinging in perfect concerto, moving towards him. Then they were right there, in front of him. Smiling. Laughing. Nodding. Beckoning him to come.

'Joe?' said Mae, in her beautiful, lyrical voice. 'Joe!'

Then, 'Travis! Luce! It's Joe, come quick!'

Joe looked around. Travis and Lucy weren't anywhere to be seen. What was Mae talking about? He looked back at the women. Gazed questioningly at Nellie. She was smiling. His wife indicated he should take Mae's offered hand while she took his other one and turned it over. Felt for his pulse.

'Oh, Joe . . .' Mae said again.

It really *was* her, Joe thought in amazement. The voice rang with the seductive and unmistakeable tones of Mae Rouget. And it really *was* Nellie. *His* Nellie.

'Oh Joe . . . Joe . . .' said Mae, repeating his name over and over. Like she couldn't believe he was really there. She smiled, held out her hand like he was a child. He looked to Nellie. She smiled too, her solid, wonderful, all-encompassing smile. She looked good. Happy. He held on to both women and the three of them turned and walked back across the grass towards Tom and Boots.

Tom grasped Joe around the shoulders and held him tight. Joe could feel his brother's weight against his chest. His brother's heartbeat strong against his body. There was no need to say a word. They stayed like that for a while and then Tom let him go. And finally the weight on his chest eased.

Joe stood back, rocked on his heels and looked around at all the people he had known and loved. He glanced down at Boots barking silently at his feet. Found his hand was still in Mae's. He studied hers for a moment. It looked a little different from the one he remembered, more tanned and firm and strong. She looked like she'd been working, wherever she'd been.

But Mae wasn't his wife, as much as, years before, he'd wished she'd been. She wasn't the woman who had shared his bed, put up with his cranky ways, made him the one true love of her life.

He glanced across at his Nellie . . . and his focus drifted back to the other hand still held in his. He gave the beautiful fingers of Mae Rouget one last gentle squeeze.

Then he let her go.

And felt something release from deep within.

Acknowledgements

The control of wild dogs is a significant issue for livestock producers across country Australia. Bodies such as the government-appointed Wild Dog Control Advisory Committee of Victoria, representing landholders and the appropriate government agencies, are currently working to advise government on improving wild dog control management practices into the future.

I would like to thank the Wild Dog Controllers (formerly Dog Trappers) in East Gippsland for sharing their time and wisdom with me, especially Peter Lee, Jim Benton and Terry Higgins. Any errors are mine. To Dan (and Harvey) Mayo, Jenny Lacey, and Peter and Mary Bevan, many thanks for insights into the world of the boundary rider and life in remote western New South Wales. Appreciation and love also to Erlina Compton.

Sincere thanks once again to my wonderful publisher, Beverley Cousins, and the rest of the team at Random House

Australia, particularly Jessica Malpass, Tobie Mann, Brandon VanOver, the fabulous reps (especially Lyndal, Di, Anthony and Jim) and the talented Kate O'Donnell for her insightful editing. Much gratitude also goes to my lovely agent, Sheila Drummond, for your wise advice and friendship.

To the people of Gippsland, I offer my sincere thanks for getting behind one of your own. The support has been incredible. To all the booksellers across Australia – those who hand-sell my novels – I am very grateful for your faith in my work. A special cheer to Liz and Trevor Watt and Di and Duncan Johnston.

All my fabulous friends – you know who you are – your support and love means so much. Particularly our wonderful Helen White, my incredible 'Lardner Park team', the Dekker and Ross families (for Dekkerby adventures), Jenny Green (for saving my butt over and over), Emma and Buck Williamson (for campfires and brainstorming), and the Nambrok tennis girls – you rock. To the people who read drafts and/or gave specific advice – Pam and Mal Beveridge, Glenda and Ross Anderson, David Wadey, Jen Scoullar, Leonne Seymour, Melinda Bentvelzen and Wayne Doull, to name a few – sincere appreciation.

To Kim Wilkins (aka Kimberley Freeman), gratitude for your lessons and counsel; the awesome Little Lonsdale Group for your support; the talented *Gippsland Country Life* team – another great year; Kath Ledson and Kate Belle, my go-to editing and critique stalwarts, thanks is never enough; and Karen Chisholm, website extraordinaire, I salute you.

Much love and appreciation to Andrea Killeen for planning assistance, the road trips, keeping me focused (and on time!); Fleur McDonald for a treasured friendship; Helene, Nicole and Fiona for the chats and all the other rural authors and readers for your enthusiasm and support.

As the theme of *Hope's Road* centres around family, I would like to acknowledge mine. To the entire Osborn, Jones, Justice and Kerby families, I am so proud to stand among you. In particular, Deborah and Joshua Westland for all things bright yellow; Graeme Osborn for, once again, the serenity of the homestead to write; Margaret Caffrey for her encouragement; the beautiful and courageous Tamara Kerby for her name; and Margot, along with the rest of the Kerby clan, for welcoming us with such open arms.

To my cherished family – my father John, Pat, Kerry, Des, Stephen, Patrick, Trish, Silas, Paul, Emma, Eliza, Tom and Will – thank you for your love, support and encouragement. You mean the world to me.

And finally to my beloved husband, Hugh, and beautiful, talented children, Brent, Callan and Katie. You make me so proud. Thank you for allowing your wife and mother to live a dream: family, farming and fables.

MARGARETA OSBORN

Bella's Run

Home is where the heart is . . .

Bella Vermaelon and her best friend Patty are two fun-loving country girls bonded in a sisterhood no blood tie could ever beat.

Now they are coming to the end of a road trip which has taken them from their family farms in the rugged Victorian high country to the red dust of the Queensland outback. For almost a year they have mustered on cattle stations, cooked for weary stockmen, played hard at rodeos and outback parties, and danced through life like a pair of wild tumbleweeds.

And with the arrival of Patty's brother Will and Bella's cousin Macca, it seems love is on the horizon too . . .

Then a devastating tragedy strikes, and Bella's world is changed for ever.

So she runs - from the only life she has ever known. But can she really turn her back on the man she loves? Or on the land that runs deep in her blood?

Margareta Osborn's bestselling debut – set in Victoria and Queensland – is brimming with the energy and vitality of life on the land

Available now

Loved the book?

Join thousands of other readers online at

AUSTRALIAN READERS:

randomhouse.com.au/talk

NEW ZEALAND READERS:

randomhouse.co.nz/talk